TESSERACTS³

TESSERACTS 3

edited by
Candas Jane Dorsey
and Gerry Truscott

A TESSERACT BOOK

Porcépic Books
Victoria

This edition is published by Porcépic Books
4252 Commerce Circle, Victoria, B.C., V8Z 4M2,
with financial assistance
from the Canada Council.

Canadian Cataloguing in Publication Data

Main entry under title:

Tesseracts 3

(Tesseract books)
ISBN 0-88878-290-X

1. Science fiction, Canadian (English).* 2. Canadian
fiction (English) - 20th century.* I. Dorsey, Candas Jane.
II. Truscott, Gerry, 1955-   III. Series.
PS8323.S3T48 1990   C813'.0876208   C90-091487-4
PR9197.35.S33T48 1990

Printed in Canada.

To Julia, Lauren and Allyson
who deserve the best of all possible futures
(Gerry Truscott)

&

To Judith Merril and Gerry Truscott
who started all this;
with thanks and love
(Candas Jane Dorsey)

CONTENTS

FOREWORD

GERRY TRUSCOTT

I should have known better. I should have known how difficult this was going to be. As Managing Editor at Porcépic Books I worked closely with Judith Merril on *Tesseracts* and with Phyllis Gotlieb and Doug Barbour on *Tesseracts*[2]. I heard them agonizing over their decisions and told them, gently but firmly, that we could not expand the book by another hundred pages.

I heard them and sympathized, but I did not feel the pressure of choosing twenty to thirty stories and poems out of the hundreds under consideration. Until now. Keats said, "Nothing ever becomes real till it is experienced." I might take issue with this statement as a generalization, but in this case it is true. For now I understand what it's like to have to choose between one excellent story and another, or as Candas and I did, one story out of four, all of equal quality and all with the same theme.

I don't mean to sound ungrateful for the opportunity to co-edit Canada's most distinguished anthology of SF. I enjoyed the experience, difficult decisions and all. I read some wonderful stories and poems, many of which you will read in this book, and many others that will certainly appear in other publications. As it is, we have a rather plump volume.

We entertained the idea—briefly—of proposing a two-volume set. (What would we have called them? *Tesseracts*$^{3-1}$ and *Tesseracts*$^{3-2}$?) But no, the anthologies are traditionally this size and each one is edited by different people. Candas and I probably have more cause for suggesting a larger book. There are more writers writing SF today than there were in 1985 and 1987.

The titles of the successive anthologies, with their superscripted numbers, really do mean something. They represent an exponential progression: the expansion of SF in Canada in the last decade. New authors are springing up out of the many workshops held across the country or quietly emerging from seclusion with manuscripts in hand. More and more writers who have established their reputations in other genres are turning to SF as a medium for expressing new, different or even dangerous ideas. I dare say that SF is the most vibrant and exciting genre of writing today, in form and content. I could provide a list of examples from all over the world to back up this statement, but I'd rather encourage you to read the stories and poems in this book. You'll see what I mean.

Tesseracts^3 contains most of our favourite stories and poems—but not all of them—selected from the 450 submitted and any others we could find. We're not so arrogant or misguided to pretend that this book defines the genre in Canada today. But by its very presence, *Tesseracts*^{3} is part of the dynamic landscape that intrinsically defines Canadian SF.

Some of the fictions presented here will remind you of how vast this landscape is. Remember, a tesseract is a cube with the fourth dimension added: time. Five years ago, the editorial team at Porcépic Books took great care in selecting this name for the anthology and eventually for the SF line. A tesseract represents more than just possible futures. Time in a tesseract does not travel in one direction, neither does space. The *S* in SF means speculative. And the range of speculation is limited only by imagination.

After the success of the first *Tesseracts*, I asked Judith Merril to edit another. She suggested, instead, that a new editor or editors should be chosen for each successive anthology so that each would have a different flavour.

We present the flavour for 1990.

THE GIFT

PAT FORDE

Paul Brophy waited in a warped wicker chair on his front porch, watching the blue-and-white postal van stop and start its way up Park Street toward his house. Whether or not he received mail today was of great significance to Brophy; of greater significance than, say, the sentence to a man convicted of murder. For Brophy had already received his sentence . . . leukemia, the term to serve only a few more months, then death, no reprieve; and whether or not a letter arrived today would tell him, at the end, whether or not his life had meant anything in the one way that really mattered. So he waited in the shade, emaciated hands clenching the arms of his chair, fingernails digging into the wickerwork, while at the edge of his thoughts a lattice of equations shifted in and out of semiconscious focus.

The van slowed as it reached his house, its driver guiding the steering wheel with his elbows while he shuffled through envelopes. Craning his head into the morning sunshine, the postman called out: "Sorry—nothin' today." Brophy opened his mouth to make a response, but all that came out was a clicking sound from the back of his throat; and all he could do was watch the van continue along the curb, watch it pass some fair- haired kid walking along the sidewalk, watch it stop beside some mailbox several houses further down, and then the emptiness swelled inside him, an empty rush that swept away hope, left him as hollow as a clay bust. *July the twelfth, and no reply!* He forced his eyes shut, sensed the lattice of equations rippling at the borders of his consciousness, unraveling, dissipating into a black void, leaving him purposeless.

Footsteps on the porch stairs. "'Scuse me," someone said.

The old man blinked: a pale green blur at the top of the steps resolved itself into a boy of eleven or twelve—the fair-haired boy he'd seen coming up the sidewalk. Dressed in multi-pocketed shorts, a green sweatshirt with the word CELLTEK printed three times across it in block letters, and velcro sneakers without socks, the boy adjusted a sheaf of papers tucked under one arm. Beneath dark brows, his eyes were the very lightest shade of blue, like icicles against a clear sky.

"What. . ." Brophy managed at last, "What is it?"

The boy hesitated, brushing a wing of hair back from his brow, took a step closer. "I was wondering if you would help me with . . . a problem." He fingered his sheaf of papers again uncomfortably. "It's a three-part problem," he added, leaning forward slightly, ice eyes watching Brophy, "about merging a quark *mostem* with the old S-matrix theories."

The old man thought, *This has got to be a prank.* Slowly he shook his head. "Wrong address."

"This isn't 79 Park?" The boy glanced up to the brass numerals fixed above the aluminum screen door, saw that it was. "But that should make you Paul Brophy." Again he hesitated, before saying, "*The* Paul Brophy."

Something stirred at that, something Brophy hadn't felt in a long time. . . He said wearily, "I can't help you."

The boy raised an eyebrow. "Surely for a Nobel calibre—"

"The *Nobel*." Brophy's face darkened. In his thoughts he saw the ivy-covered mansion just off campus, greeting him with rooms of shadows and silence each night, his loneliness turning claustrophobic . . . the stack of CERN-9604 emulsion prints sitting at the back of his office, etched into his mind daily by an acid inspiration, the tool to destroy what might be destroyed . . . the reporters mobbing him as he left that final meeting of the Board of Trustees, trampling each other to get primetime footage of the scandal, of his humiliation— Brophy forced the memories away, said, "The Nobel went to Pelletier. I didn't receive it, you must know that." And suddenly he thought, *That's why you're here.*

For a second the boy's lips pressed together, the skin around his eyes tightening, revealing an anger or impatience that seemed wholly out of place. "I didn't read much about your . . . experimental background," he began, (And that, thought Brophy, that says it all; you *know*, kid) "just about your talent with theory." As if reciting from a book, the boy said: "You developed the Standard Lattice Notation, you mapped out systems used in the gravity-strong force unification. . ." Here he gestured expansively with one hand, swinging it out over the porch rail. "Systems that helped spread the New Paradigm . . . all over the place."

Part of Brophy's lattice of equations returned, a system of imaginary symbols pulsing into his thoughts, then fading again. Frowning, he focused on the logo repeated across his visitor's sweatshirt. The kid was probably from some executive family, out to impress the admissions board of a private high school by doing a catchy science paper: *Fall of a Princeton Theorist*, or something. "Tell me," Brophy asked, his bitterness in the ascendance, "how high up in Celltek is your father?"

The boy's eyes widened. "My dad's dead," he responded. His right hand began to finger a frayed pocket on his shorts. "My mom, she works in the plant on an out-of-state. We just moved to Jersey last year from—"

"Why are you here?" Brophy demanded in exasperation.

"I *told* you." The boy blushed. Stepping even closer, he took the papers from under his arm, held them out to Brophy. "I'd like your help with a problem on the Non-Newtonian."

Brophy blinked. . . Across the top sheet of the extended papers, four large letters: N-N-P-C.

Princeton's Non-Newtonian Physics Competition.

His eyes flicked up and over the boy. *Can he be serious? The Non-Newtonian's a university-level exam. He'd have to be gifted merely to qualify. . .*

The ice eyes drew him, piercing, suggestive. Releasing a breath he hadn't realized he was holding, Brophy heard himself say: "Who . . . tell me your name."

"Houston, Chris Houston." The boy took a step back, glanced out to the street, apparently deciding whether or not to leave.

"You live nearby, Chris?"

"Couple of miles from here." He pointed in the direction he had come. "In the new Core subdivision . . . you know, downtown. I'll be a sophomore at the Core High in September."

"A *sophomore*. How old—"

"I turned fifteen in June," Chris replied defensively. "Have to be at least fifteen to write the NNPC," he admitted, "and be recommended by your school. And have a tutor. . ."

The next question got out of Brophy before he could stop himself. "When is it . . . these days?"

"March."

Eight months. The ailing man felt a mixture of sadness and relief. After a moment of silence, he said, "Look at me, Chris. Take a good long look. What d'you see?" The boy eyed him reluctantly, and Brophy knew well what he saw. Skeletally thin, hair falling out, a pathetic bandage trying to mask the bruise on his arm, the purple spots where capillary blood vessels had leaked. . . Brophy wasn't really old, but his body was, like the tree that survives a lightning strike: a prematurely withered husk, a shell unable to regain its former glory. In a low voice, he said, "Science did this to me, Chris. I gave everything I had to science, gave too much, until I lost all that mattered." His eyes wandered out to the empty mailbox. *Twenty-four years.* When he spoke again, the words themselves seemed weary. "So I abandoned it, abandoned science. And I don't want to be drawn back, not now." He looked at the boy; Chris was fingering his frayed pocket again, his attention wavering. Brophy bowed his head. "If you want a Nobel Laureate as a tutor," he finished, "ride the bus for half an hour, visit Princeton. Pelletier's still there, I think."

That got a reaction. Something welled up in Chris's eyes—what? *Fear. Yes, he's afraid. Of Ian Pelletier?* The next instant the emotion was hidden away, and the boy said, "My dad had cancer, you know."

"He did." *So you recognize my symptoms.*

"Yeah." Again a flicker of anger crossed Chris's face, and Brophy had the incongruous feeling that the boy didn't really respect him, didn't even want to be here. "But he didn't just . . . give up," Chris went on. "He liked doing pencil and ink sketches, and when he got sick, he started sketching all the time, mostly pictures of 'the baby'—me. My mom says he kept sketching, and playing with me, right up to the end." The boy shrugged, and finished, "He wasn't scared of his own talent." Turning on his heel, he strode across the porch, paused at the top of the steps, and added, "I guess that's why she loved him."

With that he marched down to the driveway.

That's why she—

Brophy's vision underwent a distortion, the lattice of equations rolling back into his consciousness like surfaces of imaginary microfiche text at high speed, intersecting, expanding in an ethereal grid that covered the paint-peeling porch rail and the boy and the street beyond. As he watched, variable changes occurred in sections of the lattice, and equations sprouted into some of the holes, extrapolating new themes that strengthened the overall mosaic. . . The improvement was partly due to the boy's presence, partly due to the prospect of revealing his theorems to a gifted mind, but mainly due to the elation Brophy felt because Chris had come to *him*, wanted to be tutored by *him*—

"Wait," Brophy called out. Chris halted on the gravel drive. "Please, don't leave just yet." Not sure why he didn't simply let the boy go, Brophy stammered, "I . . . I'm flattered that you came to me, but—Chris, there isn't any way I can help you. . ." *That's why she loved him.* He frowned, considering. "Unless . . . you know, I have a book on Non-Newtonian theory that you won't find elsewhere, that might improve your chances with the competition." To his surprise, Brophy found himself holding out his hand. "Come, help me out of this chair."

The boy reluctantly climbed back onto the porch, hesitated, then offered Brophy a skinny arm. Gripping it, the old man pulled himself up, setting both of them off balance; for a second they leaned on one another, their eyes met, and that instant of awkwardness represented for Paul Brophy the most personal contact he'd had with another human being in more than a year. Quickly he let go, and turned to face his front door, afraid Chris might see how much pain standing put him in. Teeth clenched, he stepped to the door, gestured for his guest to follow. "Come on in."

A moment later they were standing inside Brophy's small den. It was tidy, and the furnishings functional; in fact, the room was *too* functional. The shelves on either side of a brick fireplace held rows of books with identical red bindings, a miniature library of the classics from some mail-order clearing house; none of them looked as if they'd been opened. On the mantle- piece sat an antique clock, but there were no family photos flanking it, nor any personal items in the room. In one corner, an outdated PC filled most of a wooden desktop, the remaining deskspace crowded by neat stacks of printout.

Chris said to him, "Are you still accessing the PML?"

Brophy didn't respond. He'd disconnected his modem to Princeton's Microfiche Library long ago, but he didn't want the boy to know what the computer was used for now because suddenly he felt . . . ashamed. *From head of Princeton's theoretical physics department to correcting inventory errors for a retail chain*. It was just a job, one that kept him alive, kept him going, chewing away the months and years until—

Until today. But the letter didn't come, my last request was ignored.

"So where are your science books?" Chris asked, impatience getting the better of him.

"Oh. . ." Brophy squeezed at a throbbing in his hip. "This way, this way." He headed into the hall, oblivious to the decay of the wallpaper (he'd hung it a decade earlier when he bought the house, and it had faded along the strip seams, revealing the passage of years as unequivocally as rings in a treetrunk), passed through the kitchen, then stopped before a small door near the back of the house. The boy came up short behind him, his baggy Celltek sweatshirt billowing softly. Running a finger along the top of the doorframe, Brophy raised a plume of dust, and knocked off a key; he picked it up, polished it on his sleeve.

"Haven't opened this in a long time, have you?"

"No." Brophy remembered swearing he'd never open it again. . . *I'm just helping the boy,* he told himself, *that's all.* He slid the key into the lock, turned it, tugged at the handle a few times before the door grudgingly creaked open; inside, a narrow staircase wound down. He murmured, "Should be enough light coming through the windows below," and slowly led the way into his basement.

Chris's eyes adjusted to the dimness first. Standing on the last step from the bottom, he peered around. "Wow, there's a lot of them."

Books were stacked everywhere. On shelves, in boxes, over-flowing onto tabletops . . . the library of a man who had been a major theorist, completely blanketed with dust. *Let them rot,* Brophy had thought when he'd dumped the books down here; but he had locked the basement door because he didn't really want to see it happen. Once this collection had been his pride and joy; and now, as his eyes finally focused, he wished he could reach out and grab the whole dust-covered room, shake it like one of those glass christmas ornaments that snow on the inside, making everything appear bright and cheery again.

The boy brushed off a nearby stack, and frowned along the titles. "All these are in some other language. . ."

"Japanese." A phrase surfaced from Brophy's memory: *To understand the river, I followed it to its source.* "The native language of the New Paradigm," he explained. "Japan's the birth-place of Non-Newtonian science, you know."

Chris cocked his head to one side, looked at him skeptically; Brophy suddenly felt certain the boy did not believe in him. *He has no faith in me, yet he comes to me for assistance?* It made no sense. . . The old man shrugged, added, "Don't worry, the book I have in mind for you is in English. If I can find it." Wandering farther into the basement, he felt himself drawn toward a certain box on a certain shelf. . . Brophy smiled. *I still know where it lies, after all this time, under all this dust.* Taking the box down, he scooped spiderwebs from the opening, drew out a manuscript in a plastic folder, opened it to the first page.

The line under the title read: *Translated from the Japanese by P.J. Brophy, Ph.D.*

And he remembered.

All the days spent studying linguistic diskettes, all the nights hunched over yellowing dialect manuals, striving to preserve the poetry of the original, to capture its elegance in English. It was a rare thing: an Oriental masterpiece of science, translated by a Westerner who grasped the subtle genius of the original phrasing. During his undergraduate days, Brophy taught himself Japanese simply to understand this one book, the life- work of the East's most controversial theorist; had he won the Nobel, his translation of it might well have been the fundamental text of New Paradigm physics.

But this remained the only existing copy.

Most of it will be beyond the boy, until he's several years older; but it should point him in the right direction. Glancing up from the page, Brophy saw Chris lifted a framed photograph off a shelf and hold it up to a shaft of light.

The boy turned to him. "She's pretty."

He crossed the basement in three steps, took the photo, slapped it face down on a tabletop hard enough to crack the glass inside the frame. He turned, leaned back against the table's edge. "That was my wife," he breathed. "She's . . . she died."

Chris stared at him curiously for a long moment, then began tugging at his frayed pocket again. "Is that the book?"

At least he knows enough to change the subject. Brophy handed the boy the translation. "It's a rare one, Chris. . ." Out of the corner of his eye he watched dust settle over the broken photograph, burying it once more. "One the PML doesn't have." He swallowed. "Learning even a few of its secrets would help you qualify for the NNPC."

The boy seemed distracted, turning the manuscript over in his hands. "You wouldn't happen to have any others as rare as this one . . ." He gazed along the shelves. "Any by Princeton Laureates?"

Suddenly Brophy had it. *Pelletier, for God's sake, Pelletier's his idol. But he's afraid to seek the man's help. . .* He noticed the boy's fingers, fidgeting at his pocket. *Kid's nervous, he lacks real confidence in himself.* The old man frowned. *So he came to me, the forgotten theorist, the fake: that way if he qualifies for the contest everyone will know it wasn't because of his tutor, everyone will know he really did it on his own.*

Brophy shook his head. Perhaps he hadn't guessed the exact reasoning, but he was probably close. "I don't have any of Pelletier's works." He felt insulted, considered taking his precious translation back, until he realized: *it doesn't matter. The boy is only a high school student, far too young to appreciate what the book could teach him anyway.* Turning away, Brophy patted his pockets. "Where did I leave that key?"

Dust on top, but the key gleams beneath. . .

Chris was already starting up the staircase, tucking the translation under his arm with the sheaf of NNPC papers. Brophy found the key, then followed more slowly. By the time he reached the top step his hip was throbbing again, and he was out of breath; he felt thoroughly exhausted. He rested a moment, then re-locked the basement door, put back the key, and led the boy through the house and onto the porch.

A bus passed by, sunshine flaring across its wide windows as it glided out of the shade of the chestnut trees lining Park Street. Chris turned to him. "I promise I'll get this back to you as soon as I've read it."

"No need to do that." Brophy's hip was aching so badly that his left leg felt numb and the muscles of his back were cramping. He eased himself down into the wicker chair. *Have to put in my time in the hospital soon.* "I'll probably be moving from here; you keep it, Chris."

"Well—here." The boy placed his NNPC sheets on Brophy's lap. "My answers are written on those. Maybe you'll get a chance to read them sometime."

"Maybe I will." Chris hesitated once more before turning to go, and Brophy added, "Work hard now. Keep in mind how good it'll feel to qualify for the NNPC at only fifteen—"

The boy was shaking his head. "Guess I didn't make myself clear: I've *already* qualified; the papers went through on my birthday, and I'm officially entered for next March. Actually . . . my counsellors keep telling me I can win the competition."

He stepped down onto the sunlit driveway, walked out to the street.

Brophy looked at the papers on his lap. Flipping the cover sheet, he stared at the answer scribbled across the first page.

And stared.

And a few minutes later the lattice of equations came flowing back, with less holes in its imaginary structure than before. . .

September.

The knock came while Brophy was working at the PC in his den. He hit the save key, hurried across the room into the hallway, fumbled at the latch of the front door.

When the door swung open he was greeted with: "Hello again, Doctor Brophy."

"Chris." Brophy smiled broadly. "I was hoping you'd return."

The boy smiled back. This time he wore cords and a handknit sweater with the monogram *C.L.H.* sewn into the left breast; he had a backpack slung over one shoulder, and he was looking at Brophy in a way that seemed different from before, somehow. "I wasn't sure you'd still be here. . ." He paused, noticing Brophy's arms. "Hey. No bruises."

"No," the old man agreed. "I've been feeling a little better lately," he said quickly, not wanting to think about it, not wanting to wonder how long the recovery might last. "Well, come in, come in! We've much to discuss."

Stepping through the doorway, Chris slipped off his pack; Brophy ushered him into the den, and went back to the kitchen to put on the kettle. By the time he returned, the boy was seated comfortably at the fireplace end of the room's solitary couch, the change in his manner more evident: he watched Brophy with a guarded expectation, as if the old man might come out with something remarkable at any moment, like an

overlooked magician who'd demonstrated there were
powerful surprises still up his sleeve. "I've brought
back the translation you gave me," Chris said, patting
his backpack.

Brophy lowered himself into the swivel chair next
to his PC. "You're finished with it?"

"Well. . ." He shook his head. "Actually, I was
hoping to keep using it." Reaching into the pack, he
drew out the manuscript. "Actually, I came to ask you
some questions about it."

"I see." Brophy nodded. *He's grasped the importance
of the material; he just doesn't know why a theorist capable of
recognizing the work's genius before it was translated, why
that same theorist would be foolish enough to fake data in an
international experiment. Perhaps he thinks it was purest
luck I picked that particular book to translate. But he's here
to make sure.* "Chris," he said, "before you ask me anything, I've a few things to ask myself. You see, I've been
doing a little reading too."

The boy glanced up to the mantlepiece. To one side
of Brophy's antique clock there were now a few texts
taken up from the basement; and on the coffee table beside the couch, a recent issue of *Physical Review*.

The old man shook his head. "I'm referring to the
papers you left with me." This time it was his turn to
watch closely. ". . . To the solutions you came up with."

No reaction. The boy waited for him to go on.

They are *his solutions*, Brophy thought, still hardly
willing to believe it. Swivelling around to the PC desk,
he removed Chris's scribbled papers from a drawer.

The first time Brophy had examined the scrib-
blings, he read only the short answers, and decided that
the boy had copied the *mostems* out of textbooks.
Mostems, or mosaic systems of equations, were complex
enough structures in themselves, requiring difficult
choices to be made during their solution, choices

16

concerning the overlaying conceptual patterns or 'themes', choices concerning 'detailing' and 'sampling' using representative equations and 'bridging' connections using either broad fundamental laws or heuristics; in addition, these particular mosaics demanded a familiarity with disciplines of physics ranging from fluid mechanics to magnetic spin waves to quantum-gravitational theory. . . Yet the elegance of the short ink-splotched answers indicated not only a deep knowledge of the subject matter but a talent of unusual sense and insight as well. One of the shortest, the mostem of problem three, was as close to ideal as was possible.

Then Brophy had turned to the longer problems, and that's where the scribbling ran into trouble, becoming tangled in knots of equations, becoming reluctant to push through, to pursue the mostems to harmonious conclusion. It was as if the scribbler grew unsure of himself partway into the problem, and lost sight of where he was going.

These longer failures nagged at Brophy. He examined the sheets more carefully, decided that the elegance of the short answers was merely obscured in the longer ones; the consistency of style throughout made it clear the solutions had not been cobbled out of texts, but were the product of one mind, an extraordinarily gifted mind.

Could it be the mind of a fifteen-year-old?

Brophy wondered, and he wondered. And after a time, he found himself unlocking his basement door, returning to the vast collection of books he had ignored for so long. There he found biographies of the great theorists: Niels Henrik Abel, who at sixteen spotted gaps and flaws in established scientific proofs; Evariste Galois, who by fourteen was absorbing masterpieces of analysis addressed to professional mathematicians; and, of course, Gauss, imagining axioms for a geometry other than Euclidean at only twelve. Was the boy another of these? Had a young Gauss been delivered into Brophy's hands in his final months of life? He decided to wait and see: if Chris was indeed the author of the scribbled solutions, he would see the significance of Brophy's translation, would eventually return. But as the weeks had passed, the old man's curiosity won out again: getting down on his hands and knees, Brophy reconnected the modem jack of his computer, and tapped into Princeton's Microfiche Library for the first time in ten years.

He didn't find any records of the boy; what he did find was recent documentation on the NNPC. The Non-Newtonian competition had seen dramatic changes: it was no longer restricted to Princeton, had grown into a prestigious national contest. And the library records contained the winning solutions to last year's exam, the one Chris had attempted.

Brophy called those solutions onto his PC screen now, then swivelled back to face his guest.

Chris was restless, tugging at the fabric of the couch. Quickly the old man laid the scribbled sheets across the coffee table, tapped one with a finger. "This is your solution to number three: the water drop problem." He pointed to the screen. "And this is the solution to problem three judged best overall last March." Brophy sat back, folded his arms. "Chris, I want you to tell me which you think is superior: the winning solution . . . or yours."

The boy frowned uneasily.

"Please," Brophy insisted. "This may answer your questions as well."

Picking up his scribbled sheet, Chris began comparing the two solutions. Problem three asked for a mostem to describe the forces at work in an evaporating water drop, and the boy's answer to it was the best of all his answers. From the force-carrying particles interacting deep inside the molecular nuclei to the surface tension and tug of gravity shaping the overall drop, Chris's mostem synchronized the relevant equations into one whole, relating what was happening to the drop, how long things would take to happen, and what would happen next, on several different levels at once.

Leaving the boy to his comparison, Brophy went back to the kitchen to brew the tea. A few minutes later he returned pushing a tray with collapsible legs set on squeaking wheels, its jiggling surface laden with milk, sugar, and two steaming cups; he parked it beside the couch, picked up one of the cups, began sipping at it speculatively. Finally the boy glanced up. "I think—" Chris hesitated, unwilling to say it ". . . my mostem seems better?"

Brophy nodded. "You're right, it is. Now tell me why."

The boy shifted on the couch, very unsure of himself now. "Because it shows aspects of the forces . . . the interconnections, clearer than the other one."

Brophy repeated, "Tell me why."

"Why does it show things clearer?" Chris picked up the scribbled sheet. "Because . . . the way the equations fit—because the mostem's. . ." He grimaced as he tried to describe something he seemed to feel more than know. "The mostem is . . . well, smoother. It *flows*—"

"Hold that thought!" Brophy swung back to the PC, began keying in instructions. He talked while he typed: "Chris, a theorist's approach to science is often a reflection of his personality. I knew one researcher who always seemed nervous, rushed, a man with a short attention span. He started out studying bacteria genetics, where experimental results come quickly, in a matter of hours; he ended as a theorist only because of a lightning insight, a knack for tying up loose ends: this man tended to join research teams struggling to finish some long project, crack the final enigmas, then become bored and move on to—"

"Bacteria genetics . . . you're talking about *Pelletier*."

"Right." Brophy didn't take his eyes off the screen, feeling a little guilty about using a man the boy admired as his example. "Ian may have received the Nobel, but his rushed, impulsive nature prevents him from being a truly great theorist. Archimedes, Gauss, Einstein, all the great thinkers could hang at the precipice of a problem for years if necessary, until at last they pushed through to its summit. And, to a certain extent, the NNPC requires a similiar tenacity." Brophy stopped typing. On the PC was part of the solution to problem ten, the longest of the exam.

He said, "This is the final question from last year's contest, the three-parter that's said to be 'open-ended'. You know what that means, I assume?"

"It covers an area of theory that hasn't fully been mapped out with mostems."

Brophy nodded. "The three-parter tests a student's ability to handle himself in frontier territory. To master it is to master the NNPC." He paused for emphasis before adding, "But problem ten was your worst failure."

Now he had the boy's undivided attention. Chris studied him, gauging something. . . "Tell me what I have to do."

Brophy gazed into the half-empty cup cradled in his hands, swirled the tea. "A person's approach reflects his character, his strengths *and* weaknesses." He pursed his lips. "The reason you failed, I think, is . . . you're scared to believe in yourself." Chris blinked in astonishment, then gradually his face reddened, filled with the anger that Brophy had caught glimpses of back in July; the boy averted his eyes, stared down at the carpeting. The old man set his cup on the tray, said softly, "You're so young that you doubt you really *can* do all the things your teachers claim. But, Chris, to succeed at the NNPC you must discover a greater confidence in yourself; and that won't be easy to do in the time remaining before March."

The boy would not meet his eyes, continued to stare down. He seemed to struggle with something, then after a moment asked bitterly, "Do *you* believe I can win?"

Do I? Brophy closed his eyes, and a vast lattice of symbols slid into his mind, his own personal mosaic. Stripping away the extrapolative themes concerning Chris, he saw the underlying gaps and holes that reflected voids in his world: his lack of companionship, purpose—*only if I teach the boy will the 'flow' in a great part of my life be recaptured. . .* But was that really anything to go by? Was the strength of his imaginary lattice enough to bear the weight of any real decision? Or would it simply collapse, dropping him into a deeper despair?

There was only one way to answer that. Brophy had been granted one last chance, and he had to try. . . *Do I think he can win?* He glanced at the ink-covered sheet, the boy's water drop solution. "Yes, I believe you can, Chris, if you grow confident enough to let out what's already inside you."

Finally the boy looked up.

Brophy pointed to the scribbled sheet. "Here you allowed it to follow its course, like a river running freely from mountain to sea. It is the flow you spoke of earlier, and theorists call it *elegance.*"

The old man settled himself more comfortably in his chair. "A flower is a solution to a type of problem in the natural world, isn't it? Yet it is an *elegant* solution. That's nature's way, Chris, and what is science but the study of nature? The Japanese were the first to really emphasize this. Truly, it is the essence of the New Paradigm: elegance, as well as function; means, as well as end. . ."

The tutoring had begun.

October.

The doctor said, "Paul, you're simply in remission. Temporary, you must understand."

Brophy continued to gaze into the mirror on the examination room wall. He appeared healthier than he had been for years: there was a color to his cheeks, a gleam in his eyes . . . yes, his eyes especially seemed more alive. Though they were deep brown, they had the same piercing quality as the boy's. *Dust on top, yet the key gleams underneath. . .* The old man nodded to himself. *All differences aside, Chris and I share the same gift—* He almost laughed. *Shouldn't flatter myself! The boy's a prodigy, sharper than I ever was. Each week he progresses so much. . .*

"I sense more than a physical change in you, Paul," the doctor commented, interrupting his reverie. "Something new's come into your life, something that's sparked this improvement." The man tried to look confiding. "Heard from your ex-wife, is that—"

"No." Brophy grimaced. *That's a major theme my internal mostem isn't ever likely to balance.* Pushing himself up, he turned toward the clinic door . . . then halted. "How long, do you think—"

"Don't hope for too much, Paul. Count each day as a blessing." In a frank tone the doctor added: "Be prepared for the final illness at any time. It will strike hard, and fast. . ."

That sobering warning didn't have much effect on

Brophy, for the check-up *had* confirmed a partial recovery. . . Leaving the clinic, he rode the Park Street bus back to his home, feeling light-headed and alive, giddy with replenished hope, with the possibility of many more months—even years—still ahead of him.

That evening he listened to some classical music as he checked over the papers Chris had left him; and later, he spent a couple of hours on his own special writings, making a lot of progress.

That night he dreamt of her, for the first time since July, since the letter had failed to arrive. In his dream she was sleeping beside him as she had so many years before, wearing a faint smile, reaching out sleepily to take his hand, to squeeze it just that certain way. . .

December.

On the last night of the year they worked in Brophy's den, drawing warmth from the crackling fireplace, young and old together, exploring the power of the New Paradigm.

Chris knelt beside the page-cluttered coffee table, his hand shifting from one to another of a half-dozen sheets, penning final alterations to a lengthy mostem scrawled in Standard Lattice Notation. "You've taken it through now," Brophy encouraged, standing behind him. "See the difference that makes?"

The boy rocked back on his heels, frowning. "It's— different, all right. But I didn't think. . ." He cocked his head to one side. "It's a new technique, isn't it? I mean, weaving a machine- theory theme into biophysics equations. . ."

"Just pushing the general axioms a step further. And they can be pushed a lot further than this, believe me." Brophy leaned over the table, squinting at the scribbled pages. *Never would I have thought a fifteen-year-old was capable of this.* "Chris, I'm beginning to regret teaching you all of my secrets. . ."

"Secrets?" Stretching his legs, the boy retorted, "Actually, I can't remember any of *your* secrets; but that translation you gave me sure taught me a lot!" He saw Brophy raise an eyebrow, and laughed. "Okay, okay, your tutoring is *partly* responsible." He stood up, knees cracking, and stepped over to the fireplace to warm himself. Brophy glanced to the mantlepiece above, to a photo taken several weeks ago: his automatic camera had captured the two of them out on the porch, posing with snowballs made from the year's first heavy fall. Beside that was a faded portrait of a two-year-old, sketched with a pencil, and signed Jim Houston; Chris had brought it over to show him one afternoon, had not asked for it back yet. He smiled to himself, turned back to the pages covering the coffee table. *One solitary mostem, approaching the length and complexity of the contest's 'open-ended' problem. Chris really is blossoming into a young Gauss—*

"There's something I have to ask you," the boy said, still facing the fire, his back to Brophy.

The old man sighed. "I know." In gentle rebuke, he said, "You've been working up the nerve to ask me about this for months."

Chris turned to him. "You don't have to explain it. I mean, I'm *positive* you couldn't have faked those emulsion tracks."

You're making this more difficult. Brophy forced himself to say, "But I did, I'm afraid."

After a moment of silence Chris shook his head. "No. . ."

Brophy moved around the table to the couch, sat down heavily. "There was a time, Chris, when my talent was first blooming in me, as it is now in you, though for me it came when I was older. Even so, I was too naive to see that talent is a thing that can possess you, that can steal you from your own heart. . ."

And so he told the boy how he met her, how they had been in a play together in high school, dated in university. By the time his own gift had begun to flower they were already engaged, and he didn't fully recognize his talent until they were married. Brophy was still an undergraduate then, studying physics at a time when the whole of science was undergoing a tremendous upheaval.

Twentieth-century researchers had spent a hundred years pulling the cornerstone out from under the physical sciences. That cornerstone was Reduction: the breaking down of all objects and events into basic laws, properties, elements. The first flaws in the Reductionist approach appeared when Newton's grand synthesis of forces and laws, unchallenged for three centuries, fell to the stroke of a new genius: Einstein showed that matter and energy could not be reduced, but were the same thing. By the nineteen- fifties scientists were concluding that even forces and particles were the same thing. And by the nineties, construction of a powerful new booster at the gargantuan CERN accelerator in Geneva was completed, and the last refuge of Reductionist thinking, the quarks, drowned in an ocean of sub-quark particles. The basic components of nature had, in the span of a single human lifetime, run the gamut from atoms to nuclei and electrons to subnuclear protons and neutrons to sub-subnuclear quarks and finally to a sub-quark soup. And this soup was simply another of the shifting illusory levels of reality. The universe wasn't made of basic parts, after all. . . It was an interwoven spiderweb, a mosaic system of energies and forces and particles that flowed back and forth in subtle harmony, that could not be understood in terms of parts alone.

Physics was ready for a new approach. After receiving his Ph.D., Brophy joined the faculty at Princeton and quickly established himself as the most talented young opponent of Reduction. Vaulting into the arena of champion theorists, where the race to publish first, the fight to claim credit for an idea turns fiercely competitive, he began spending more and more time at the university, and less and less time with the one who loved him. Before long he was striving for the Nobel, and her dreams of children were cast aside; she took on a second job teaching adult education for the Mercer County School Board to fill the lonely nights without him.

In his thirty-fifth year, Brophy's career peaked.

By then Princeton had become the western bastion of the New Paradigm, and he its prime theorist; his postulations were gaining favor throughout the scientific world. All that remained was nature's stamp of approval: the experimental evidence that would demonstrate the accuracy of his theories. And it was coming, slowly, bit by bit, as dozens of universities hunted down particle tracks left in stacks of emulsion during CERN-9604, a crucial fullpower test of the accelerator's new booster.

The time was ripe for the Swedish Academy of Sciences to honor New Paradigm physics with a Nobel. And Brophy, who had laid the groundwork with his Standard Lattice Notation ten years earlier, was considered the major contender. Of course, at the top he had no time at all. . .

Eight months before the Nobel announcements, she left him. As usual, he walked into their ivy-covered house just off campus in the middle of the night; only this time there was a note waiting for him on the kitchen table . . . *tried so many times to tell you it wasn't enough, but Paul, you wouldn't listen . . . your real love is your work, you know that . . . show me you really care, this once, and let me go. . .*

Brophy lasted seven days. Seven days of coming home to emptiness and silence. The house seemed wrong without her, everything seemed wrong.

"It was as if. . ." Brophy paused, gazing across the coffee table at Chris. "As if my whole life was a mostem, and finally I could see how unbalanced the systems were. A solitary symbol, representing my talent, had controlled the mosaic of all my actions, with vanity and the glory of the Nobel as the major themes. . ."

"But who . . . what did you do?" the boy asked.

"I'm not really sure. Wandered around aimlessly for a few days. I ended up in my office, staring at the walls, staring at the emulsion prints stacked on my shelf."

"The ones that were tampered with."

Brophy nodded, his expression grim. "I wanted to betray my gift, as it had betrayed me; I hated it, hated myself for letting it control me. So I reproduced two of the prints with new tracks. . ." He looked away from Chris, stared into the fire. "Tracks of particles that would support my theories. I wasn't trying to ensure my chances for the Nobel; I was trying to lose it altogether. I *intended* to be found out." He shook his head. "After the prints were traced back to me, I was asked to leave Princeton—and the media caught wind of that, turned it all into a spectacle. When the Nobels were announced soon afterward, it was Pelletier who was the physics laureate, for follow-up work he did on my Lattice Notation."

Brophy looked over at the boy, and decided to finish there, although the ruin of his career was not the end of the tale. He had not rid himself of his gift: it continued to haunt him, the image of a life mostem floating through his dreams, each time growing more vivid, until it began to take on a plausibility. Axioms and symbolic mathematical structures uncoiled in his mind, the DNA of a generalized theory, extending New Paradigm mosaics onto technological growth patterns, onto biology and economics and psychology, onto the life history of an individual.

And when Brophy learned that he was dying, he decided to pay heed to his vision. To bring flow to the inner mostem, he had to contend with his unresolved love for her. So Brophy wrote to her at last, asking for news of her life, her work for the schoolboard. He confessed that he did not have much longer, requested that she send her reply on or before July the twelfth, the date of their anniversary; after that, he would know not to expect anything. All he'd needed was to feel special one last time. . .

Well, I have the boy now, Brophy thought, *and he makes me feel special. With luck, I might even help him to win the NNPC! Then perhaps my inner mostem will balance properly, will flow. . .*

February.

With two weeks remaining before the competition, Brophy decided to end the lessons, and asked Chris to come to the house once more. The boy arrived straight from school, half covered in snow; leaving his coat and boots to dry in the hall, he stepped into the den, monogrammed black sweater rolled up at the sleeves, hair damp and shining against his forehead. There was a confidence in his eyes now, a confidence that hadn't been there eight months before.

Removing a package from one of the drawers of his PC desk, Brophy held it out to the boy. "Well," he said, "I hope this helps."

Chris accepted the package with a grin. "Can I open it now?"

"You'd better. I've been working night and day so that you'd have it to read through before the contest."

Tearing off the wrapping, the boy unveiled a thick stack of typed sheets. Across the top page was the title: *General Mosaic Systems, by P.J. Brophy.* "It's your extended theory, isn't it?"

He nodded. "Finally got it all down on paper."

The boy read the manuscript's dedication; unable to speak, he stepped closer, gave Brophy a hug.

The old man hugged him back. "You're going to do very well, Chris, I'm sure of it." He let go, looked into the boy's face. "These last few weeks I've been going over ground you're already sure-footed on, holding you back from other things: that indoor soccer team you mentioned. I guess I just didn't want to accept that you're ready."

Chris nodded. "Me neither."

"Well, you *are* ready. . ." Brophy eyed the monogrammed sweater ". . . Chris L. Houston. Is it Louis, or Lawrence?"

"Don't ask." The boy's expression turned sour.

"Hmm. Something *awful* that begins with 'L'. . ."

They talked for another half hour, stretching out the moments until Chris had to leave for dinner. Afterwards, Brophy sat for a time in the den, gazing at bookshelves filled with dog-eared favorites from his collection in the basement, before drifting off into a light doze.

He dreamt again, this time of winning the Nobel, or perhaps of Chris winning the NNPC, he couldn't tell which. There was a crowd of scientists around him, all inquiring about his new theory; and somewhere in the crowd, she was there, reaching out as he passed to squeeze his hand that certain way.

April.

Fingers trembling, Brophy managed to hit the MAIL/NEWS key on the PC board. His screen flickered, then the front page of the PRINCETON DAILY (*Online Edition*) appeared. Most of it was taken up by a picture of Chris, and the accompanying headlines: FIFTEEN- YEAR-OLD PLACES THIRD IN UNIVERSITY COMPETITION—DEMONSTRATES CONTROVERSIAL NEW APPROACH! Brophy had heard it all from the boy himself days before, but it thrilled him to see it in the news. Everyone was hearing about Chris now, and all because of the contest's 'open-ended' problem.

Chris hadn't even had time to finish the NNPC: he'd jumped ahead to the final three-part problem, had become absorbed in it. This year the topic was astrophysics, and the broad space-time mostem that the boy proceeded to map out went beyond previously understood descriptions. Incorporating an expanding universe theme into the mostem, he translated it into a biological growth process on the grand scale; what emerged, through the New Paradigm's interwoven approach, were places where nature's physical limits were undergoing rapid differentiation, localized areas far off in space and time that had different speeds of light, different fine structure and gravitational constants. Already, a few cosmologists had begun employing Chris's equations to explain a host of astronomical nightmares: quasars, exploding galaxies, giant black holes. . .

The old man smiled to himself. *The first triumph of my generalized theory, and the first in a long series of triumphs for young Chris Houston.* He searched further down the page. . . *Teachers have noted a growing involvement with classmates and in extracurricular activities, including indoor soccer.* He nodded somberly. The boy had learned the most important lesson of all: he wasn't going to let his gift control him; he was bringing the balance of the New Paradigm to his life. But that wasn't what Brophy was looking for—

There. At the end of the article: *An award ceremony is scheduled to take place at the Princeton Core High School on May 31. The NNPC Third Place honors will be presented to the sophomore before a gathering of distinguished Princeton physicists, members of the Mercer County School Board, and. . .*

Brophy licked cracked lips. So it was true: the Board was sending representatives. . . *She's a counselling specialist now, and Chris is within her jurisdiction. She might very well be there.* He switched off the PC, hands still shaking. His arms were swollen, his whole body ached; in three days he was due to enter the hospital. But, somehow, he would make it to the boy's award ceremony. He had to. Beyond the borders of his consciousness the internal mostem floated, its major theme still unsolved. . .

Brophy squeezed his trembling hands into fists. *Let me live until the ceremony,* he thought. *And please, let her be there.*

May.

Clutching his pink release form as if it were a winning lottery ticket, Brophy walked slowly and painfully behind a student guide through the corridors of a renovated office structure: the Core High School, an artifact of the age of home PC's and decentralization of work. He was late; and he was glad to be ushered in through the back hallways, because today he felt like a slug crawling from under a rock. Doctor Paul Brophy, the fraud, creeping into the light after all these years.

The girl led him into a cluttered room just behind

the gymnasium stage, settled him into a chair, then disappeared back through the side-door into the halls of the school. In the dark, Brophy could hear a murmur from out on stage, an oddly familiar male voice discussing Chris's achievement. Apparently the presentation of the award was already over.

". . . talent is powerless without knowledge, and an understanding of theory as deep as this young man's reveals a dedication to the pursuit of knowledge that is rarely seen even in the professional research community. But today he has promised us a few words of explanation, so if I may: Ladies and gentlemen, students of the Core High . . . Chris Houston."

The old man got to his feet, pulling on the curtains for support.

"Thank you." Chris's voice barely reached over the roar of applause. "Yes, I did say I would offer an explanation for my success, and today is very . . . special to me, because I get a chance to do exactly that."

Brophy decided he would listen for the right opportunity, then peek through to see if he could make out faces in the audience. From back here, the view should be good.

". . . to be in my own school, among friends and teachers, and to be on stage with such important theorists. But today is special because I have the honor of introducing someone—someone who has been a father to me. Someone who has struggled with science, without reward, for more than a decade. It was his methods that I used on the NNPC; so, you see, this moment really belongs to him. I would now like to present the greatest theorist I know, Doctor Paul Brophy. . ."

The curtains parted, and Chris stepped backstage to take his arm. Beyond him, Brophy saw several Princeton physicists rising to their feet, including the familiar figure of Ian Pelletier, all of them smiling at him. The old man felt his eyes water—*No! If I cry, I won't see anything*—but he couldn't help it; quickly he looked beyond the lights into the blurring audience, thought he saw a woman stand up to clap—*is it her?* Then the entire gym was joining her in a standing ovation, and her face was lost in a sea of faces, and Brophy's tears dissolved them all into a featureless haze.

Reporters surrounded them when the applause finally began to die away, nudging the boy closer, cameras flashing to get a shot of them together. Brophy pushed to get another glimpse into the audience; the crowds were starting to disperse as the media took over. He cursed his tears. *Never know if it was her,* he realized. *Now I'll never know, never know. . .*

July.

It was quiet in the hospital room. It was dark. For Brophy, the passage of time was marked by intervals of agony. Every now and again the pain seemed to blot out his senses; his eyesight was gone altogether. So when the nurse ushered a visitor in through the door, he didn't bother to look up. He just lay still, listening, hoping. . .

"Hello, Doctor Brophy."

But it was only the boy.

"Pelletier. . ." Chris was saying something: ". . . your new manuscript. It's going to be published."

Brophy moved his lips, tried to say, *Thank you;* but he didn't hear himself speak.

For a moment there was silence; then he felt the boy's breath near his ear. "I've come to make a confession," Chris said to him. "Back last summer, that first day I met you . . . guess I really didn't believe in you."

Why tell me this now? he thought.

The boy went on: ". . . didn't even want to try you as a tutor. I—had to be persuaded. I promised not to tell, you see . . . suppose it's okay now." Another pause, then: "It was. . ."

Another wave of pain swallowed Brophy, but this time it didn't seem as bad.

". . . counsels for the schoolboard now," the boy was saying, "and she came to me, asked me to give you a try . . . pleaded with me, said it was really important to her . . . that you'd asked her to send you something, but it wasn't right, it would only make you wish for. . ."

Somewhere, everywhere all around Brophy yet deep inside him, his life mostem was flowing at last, attaining balance and harmony, the mathematical symbols of the lattice blending into the spectrum of his innermost feelings.

". . . said she wanted to send a much better gift, one that would help you find yourself again. She said that gift was me . . . still cares about you, Doctor Brophy. I just wanted you to know that."

Brophy reached out to Chris, reached out; after a time he realized the boy had gone.

And a few hours later, in the darkness of his final night, the door to his room opened for one more visitor. He heard shoes click across the floor, heard the chair beside his bed shift as someone sat in it. Then a hand slipped gently into his, squeezed it just that certain way. . .

THE OTHER EYE

PHYLLIS GOTLIEB

I am writing on this worn-down piece of vellum that the priests threw away. I scrubbed it with pumice and water, and stole the inkstick. If you find me and betray me be damned to you. No more waste space. This began one turn and forty stands ago, when my eye began to go blind. It is my other eye, you see, the one that turns out, and does not work too well either, showing me two of everything and different colours at that.

I used to bring the priests their water from the sluices a clockstroke away, and hard going on the rough tailings, but good and honest work for all that as my hairy-white dam used to say. All of us do work: dig out the tunnels to reach the Great Kingdom; put up stone shorings to prop the tunnels, pick out the jewels to put on the breastplates of the priests, grow the airweed and farm the moss and whitefern for us and the beasts, tend the beasts and slaughter them.

My old sire was a tender of beasts and stank of them, and my dam filled the sconces that give our light, and smelled of oil. They would drink the grindbrew and fight over who smelled the worse, and beat each other and knock me arse over crockpot. So I lived with the priests in their tunnel and carried water. They wanted to pogue me and I said—"What will you give me if I let you?"—I saw them getting water carried to them, and eating the best parts of meat, sitting soft on weavings stuffed with fernstraw, and all they did was make black marks on vellum like this. They laughed and said —"Look at you, Mem, with your fur smelling of oil and your fingers leaving black soot marks, making us a price! Do you think you are worth anything?"

It is true that I could not afford much water to wash in, but they are not supposed to have women either. I only said—"Your Holinesses want us to be worthy of the Great Kingdom, and claim that we are wise trusting you to lead us there. Let me learn a little of what you know so that I will be even wiser and worthier."—How can you be wiser than sitting on your backside making black marks on vellum while others do your work for you?

They laughed and said—"Vellum and inksticks are too valuable to give you, but take this tablet of tallow wax and this stylus and make all the marks you like."—I did not care that they laughed. I did not tell them I knew that the marks meant things and I learned what. I let them do what they wanted and brought them their water too. I even picked the lice out of their fur. Then my eye began to go blind.

At first I thought: this scribe work is too hard on my eyes. But I never saw a blind priest. And then that I had a sickness of the eye because it did not move right. But it never pained me.

Two stands and three sleeps it was going dark and I was afraid to tell because you know what happens to the blind who cannot work, so I worked harder though I stumbled, drew water and stored food. Then it was blind.

I said to myself, well I will get used to this. That went on for a round of sleeps by the priestbook. And the first stand after that I woke up with my eye full of light.

It was like if you put together all of the lamps and fires you ever saw, and more. It was like that and full of heat too. I thought, this is some brain injury or I have gone mad. I had fallen, you know, nine stands ago and struck my head. But it did not hurt then or now.

But the light, the light was like pain. I thought I was injured or gone mad—no, I have said that—but it was like that, all confusion. All that stand I could not see for the light. Even when I shut my eye or held my hand against it it was light. I thought it was burning through my head and that everyone must see it. I stumbled all day and bruised myself and cut my skin and when I slept with my eyes full of tears I had the light in it. For those two stands and sleeps it was so, I could not bear it, but when I woke—

—I have used up half my space and this is the other side of my vellum—when I woke my eye was not so much full of light but it had colours. I mean the light was filled with colours. All the colours of the jewels in the breastplates filled the light.

All that stand I had the blazing colours in that eye and I picked my way over the stones to the sluices with my straight eye and spilt half the water and the priests cursed me. But when I went to sleep my eye went dark and slept too, except for a few little lights. It woke up with me again half green and half blue, and the light I could not stand in the middle of the blue. It was all lights and colours. It kept like that for two stands. On the third everything was clear and had edges.

The green part is some kind of plants you can stand on. There are stones here too, but they are flat enough to walk on without falling. The blue is the roof and the light in it lets you see everything. And warms the people—people? What am I saying? But there are moving figures, with pink and brown skins, not fur.

I asked myself if this place was the Great Kingdom and my eye was its opening. I saw myself standing on the green and people would look at me or through me and not notice. I did not want them to notice me, not when I was in bed with one of those on top of me, snorting foul breath in my face and hands going everywhere.

Around that time I got pregnant, but I took the pinch-herb and it bled away, it only made me sick one stand and I spent that half-asleep and being with those people in the light. I had not realized that I lived in darkness.

But half darkness and half light is full of fear.

I had not told anyone at all. Sometimes I could not eat or sleep for fear. But I was sure that no one would like this vision of mine. If they did believe me they would be fearful or jealous, and if not, they would say I was out of my mind. And I thought so too. I cried so much with fear it was a wonder I could see even a vision. But I went on working and saving my food when I could not eat it. And the people in my eye began to smile at me.

That frightened me even more. I had to talk to someone. I told Eb, my friend who waters the beasts, whom I meet at the sluices. She said—"Mem, I do not believe you."—and I said—"Whether or not you do I cannot help, but it is so." I had to tell. She went back and told the priests.

They came and took hold of me when I was drawing water. They took me to their chamber and said—

"What is this?"—and I told them. They talked among themselves a great while, holding me with eight hands and not letting go, as if I would fly through my eye into the light. Then they began to argue and scream, and in that time the people in my eye came and said—"Mem? We have been expecting you, Mem."—I do not know whether I heard it in my ear or in my mind, whether these people really spoke or I wanted so much for them to speak. They took my hand, and that hand of mine that I gave them had a brown skin.

The priests and the men and women who had gathered round them said—"That is an evil and accursed vision! We must pluck out that eye!" Both my eyes burst into tears for pity, and I cried—"No! No! Not my eye!" And they said—"Yes, it must be so!"—and the head priest fetched tongs. It seemed to me that they were all joyful to think of taking this eye. They were so full of rage at me, and all because of a sick eye! My eyes were weeping and I stared at those other people on the green grass, they gave me a flower and said—"What is troubling you, Mem? What do you see?"—and then my fear gave me strength.

I broke their grasp of me, baring my teeth and making the noise of a beast, I seized hold of the tongs, it was heavy, and swung out around me and the people fell away as if I was a demon. I would have hurt them, to save myself. I ran to my chamber and piled stones in the entrance.

They howled around me for some time, but the priests knew I was trapped, and the people are fickle, their passions blow away. After a while I heard the picks and axes of their digging. My fear did not blow away. My eyes were swollen with crying over it, both the dark and the light. I do not know how long it was before I heard the whisper:—"Mem!" That was Eb. I said—"Go away, Eb. How could you do such a thing?"

She was whimpering—"I was afraid." Then she said—
"Forgive me"—but I told her to go away. She whimpered again and said—"Let me help you find a hiding
place"—and I laughed bitterly. She said—"Please,
Mem, it is where I used to go with Aff the herdsman,
and if his woman knew of it she would kill me. I have
candles there, and food I kept." I had no choice but to
trust her.

I am waiting here, in her meeting-place. I hear the
endless sounds of the picks, and the wafts of the airweed carry the smells of beasts and fuel oil.

Ten sleeps ago my straight eye began to go blind.
My tears have run dry. There is nothing to do and nowhere to go. My sight becomes dimmer every clockstroke. The people in my lighted eye are holding my
brown hands, but my other eye is gathering darkness.
Will the light pierce it too, while my hands are cut on
the stones I cannot see? I have reached the end of my
space and my good eye cannot see any m

BREAKING BALL

MICHAEL SKEET

They still play baseball on Mars.

I could see a game in progress as the taxi took me through Brackett on the way to the ranch. A bunch of people, casually dressed, played on a dark-green field in a schoolyard. I didn't want to watch, not really. All the same, I had the cab stop and take the window down.

I don't have much of a sense of smell anymore. I've been living in a lagrange city for twenty years; after twenty years of breathing recycled air, things pretty much smell alike. Even I can recognize the smell of real grass, though. When I was growing up on Mars, schoolyards were polyfibre. This grass wasn't just real, it was thick and cut so close it reminded me more of moss than grass.

Only a few of the players wore breathers. Twenty years ago just about everybody wore a mask that sweetened the evanescent atmosphere. You could tell a Martian by the tan line where the mask ended. In our protective clothes and breathers, we'd looked like orthodox Muslim women. These people wore sweatsuits

41

and even shorts, and the masked ones stood out like banners, saying, "newcomer". Or "prodigal son", maybe. I wore a breather myself, and an exoskeleton bracing me against gravity extended from ankles to ribs.

As I watched, one of the newcomers swung mightily at a pitch. I followed the swing easily enough, but when her bat hit the ball with a thin aluminum "tink", my eyes started playing tricks on me. The ball shot into the meagre air faster than I could follow it; every time I thought I'd found it, it was gone again. Following the ball in Mars' low gravity was like trying to watch a television with scanning problems.

At Comiskey in Chicago, the hit would have cleared the first level of seats. Here, it was a routine put-out. The left-fielder slipped as he began his move, dug in a cleated foot to compensate. A divot lifted gracefully as he pushed off. I imagined tiny flecks of rich, black soil separating and drifting away as the clump of grass floated for a pathetic second, as if reaching for something, before subsiding.

The fielder seemed to float to the left-field fence. My eyes were playing tricks on me again; the man moved with a fluidity alien to the game he was playing. I gave up trying to follow either him or the ball, and turned back to look for the divot. Now I could see that the field was covered with them, bright-green scars against the darker skin of the diamond.

My jaw ached: I had been grinding my teeth as I watched. *Thus has the colony progressed*, I told myself. Three decades of hard work to produce a rich field of real grass to be abused and torn in the name of recreation. I had the cab drive on.

It's been years since I've been able to make myself watch Earth-bound baseball. But at least that game looks like it belongs there. It grew out of the planet, the same way the people who play it did. On Mars,

baseball looks stupid, half-familiar, like trying to remember last night's dream. Because of the thin air and
lower gravity, the game has been distorted by those
who try to make it resemble the Earthly game. The
more they try to make it look the same, the uglier it
gets. The diamond I'd just seen was easily twice the size
of Comiskey, just to give the defensive team the space
to react to the towering hits that anybody can get up
here.

The game was just like the city, which was like the
whole colony: a pathetic attempt to build an Indiana
suburb on Mars. Mars shouldn't have baseball and
Burger Kings. Mars should be different.

That it wasn't different made the Martians' demands for independence that much more ridiculous.
That's what I was here to tell them: the UN wasn't interested in what they had to say, and the delegation that
was to follow me here wasn't going to discuss anything
but a return to the status quo.

I wasn't supposed to put it so bluntly, of course.
My boss hadn't believed me when I told her sending
me back would be a mistake. I wasn't a diplomat, by
temperament or by training. But I was supposed to
have some influence. My brother Andy was one of the
leaders of the independence movement. He and I had
grown up on Mars, together. Or that's how it appeared
on the surface. As far as I was concerned we'd been
forced to share a house until I was old enough to get
away; I had tried to explain my feelings about the planet and my brother, but my boss hadn't listened. Her
boss had told her that sending me would be a good
idea, and so it must be.

The sun was setting by the time I got to the ranch.
At first the night seemed as quiet as a vacuum, without
even the noise of insects. It took a few seconds for
sounds to register: the quiet hum of the house, and the
hiss of the exoskeleton as it walked me up to the door.

The house let me in, and that made me angry: it wasn't that late, and even for his brother Andy should have been there to open the door himself. He was already trying to manipulate me, to put me off my stride. I prepared for a confrontation.

The house was dark inside, the only light coming from a narrow strip built into the wall, switching on and off in sections as I advanced. I could hear snoring from somewhere.

A house machine came up from behind with my bags. "Andy is asleep," it said. "He apologizes for being unable to greet you himself. If you wish, I will escort you to your room now."

"I know where my room is," I said. "Unpack my bags and make up the bed. I'll be there in a minute."

As the machine rolled off, I had my exo walk me like a tourist through the house I'd grown up in. Somebody had tried hard to make it different. The rugs, the furniture, the pictures on the walls—even the paint on the walls—were new, and strange. But it was still my house, and behind the paint those were still my walls, walls that still formed the alcove where I'd once built forts out of seat-cushions.

The door to my room was closed, and that surprised me: the machine should have left it open after unpacking my bags and making up the bed. My bags weren't in my room; neither was a bed. Andy seemed to have turned the room into storage space . . . some time ago. I found myself grinding my teeth again and had to make a conscious effort to relax. I had been expecting Andy to be like this.

I eventually found my bags, and a made-up bed, in Kim's old room. I slept badly, trying to come to terms with someone else's set of memories when I'd been expecting my own childhood to be waiting in the dark. I don't even know where my sister is these days.

I didn't so much awaken as give up the idea of trying to get any deeper into sleep. Noise filtered through the closed door. The perspective was wrong—I was in the wrong room—but my guess was that it came from the kitchen. Andy, presumably, getting ready for a day of doing whatever it was that Martian gentleman ranchers did these days. Or was it his wife? The last time I'd spoken with Dad, ten years or so ago, he'd let slip that Andy was married and had two kids. It came out like a slip, too—I couldn't figure out at the time why he seemed to feel so guilty that he was a grandfather. Maybe he was feeling his mortality; maybe he already knew about the cancer. Maybe he was coming to grips with his failure, with the failure of this colony he'd tried so hard to mold into a new Indiana.

I did my exercises with extra determination. As long as I was subject to gravity, even a pull as weak as Mars', I was a prisoner inside the ankle-to-ribs armour of the powered exoskeleton. That didn't mean I didn't have to fight against the gravity myself. I couldn't afford to show any weakness at all.

"You're up early," Andy said as I walked into the kitchen. "How've you been, Steve?"

"I do okay," I said. "You?"

"The place is coming around. Sorry I missed you last night. I get to bed pretty early these days."

A clock caught my eye: five a.m. For a moment, I was ready to turn around and go back to bed. But I caught myself. No weakness. "Sorry I was late," I said. "I came through Brackett instead of taking the tube. Looked in on a schoolyard baseball game. You in a league or something?"

"I don't play ball anymore, Steve." His expression hadn't changed; if there was regret behind that statement, he wasn't about to betray it.

"I never thought I'd see the day when you'd give

45

up on baseball," I said. *Just remember*, I thought, *that I gave up on it before you did. I was there first.* "So what do you do with your free time?"

"Who has free time? I'm trying to run a ranch here, Steve—not a holiday camp."

"Ah, the ranch," I said. "But not by yourself, I'm told. I understand you're married now, with a couple of kids."

He smiled a vague sort of smile, something hidden behind it. "They're away from the ranch for a couple of days."

"Getting them out of my way?"

"Not really. But we'd be too busy to see them anyway. We have people to talk to and arrangements to make before your negotiating team gets here. Tomorrow we're going to meet some of the ranchers and one or two of the city people at the neighbours'."

"Getting your kids out of the way denies their rights." It was typical of Andy—thinking only of himself. "They've got the right to vote on their future," I said. "I'd think you of all people would appreciate that. It's a choice we were never allowed to make."

"My kids have already made their choice. The referendum was done according to UN rules, and you know it." Andy's face was reddening. For a second I felt a thrill of triumph: I'd never been able to get to him this way when we were younger. Then I looked again and wasn't so sure of myself. I'd never seen Andy really angry before. "If you have to know the truth," he said, "Natalia's taken them into Brackett for some tests." Again, there was something behind his eyes. Now I felt distinctly uneasy.

I backed down. "Natalia's your wife?" He nodded. "Well, uh . . . I hope everything's okay." Damn. He'd done it to me again. I was always at a disadvantage with him.

"I'm going out," he said after a pause. "Want to see the ranch?"

"You're driving?" A nod. "Okay." I followed him through the door; he floated towards the garage with long, easy strides, while my exo-encased legs hopped after him in what felt to me like a grotesque parody of his movements.

Somehow I'd come to remember the ranch as looking like something from a Western, contented cattle grazing on windblown grass or something. That had been the vision Dad was working towards, I think. What I saw, though—from the moment we got outside the house airlock—could only be described as baffling. The backyard garden that Mom had started and Dad continued after she left us had disappeared. So, for that matter, had the yard. The house was surrounded, not by grass, but by an eruption of bizarre vegetation, an evil-looking mess of foliage more black and purple than green. Instead of leaves or stalks waving in the thin breeze, these plants thrust aggressive spikes in all directions, defying anything to move them. The wildgrass that Dad had seeded and nurtured so frantically was nowhere to be seen. As the rover drove through the back gate, all I saw was the red soil Dad had fought so hard to cover, obscured in places by purple-black talons.

"This place has sure changed."

Andy looked at me for a second before turning back to the path we were on. "Dad's way wasn't going to work. I think I convinced him of that before he died. The ranch will be more profitable this way."

"You think you can draw a profit from this mess?"

"People would rather eat the meat I raise than the slop the UN makes in those vats at Brackett." He almost spat out the words. "If I wasn't paying off the R&D, I'd be making a profit right now. Martians support their own."

"That R&D was part paid for by UN money," I said. "The genetics centre was completely paid for by taxpayers on Earth. Whatever work you people were able to do with those llamas, you were able to do because the UN paid for it. You had no right to bar the Director-General's inspectors, you know."

"That Director-General was a vice president of BioPlan before she joined the Genetics Commission." Andy's voice was as dry as the air outside the rover. "And I notice that after she left the UN, she ended up on BioPlan's board of directors. BioPlan gets a lot of UN genetics consultancy work these days, doesn't it?"

"That's none of my business—or yours." I didn't want to be talking about the independence movement, not while we were alone. Part of me at least really wanted to avoid arguing with Andy, and the easiest way to do that was to talk of indepencence only in a crowd—even a crowd of his supporters. Besides, I wasn't sure of my ability to out-argue him, and it was crucial that I not let him humiliate me this time. So I said nothing more, and the cab of the rover was silent for a while.

The sky was a soft, hazy mauve, and the light was so diffuse I could almost look straight at the sun. I didn't remember the light being so gauzy; my memory of Martian skies was of something sharper, shadows clearly etched against the side of the house, of the mountains in the distance standing out against the sky like the subject of a 3-D postcard. "Why is it so hazy today?"

"It's always like that now," Andy said. "Just like it was when the first colonists got here. Maybe it's a little less pink 'cause there's more oxygen and water vapour up there. But the haziness is natural—dust in the air."

"That means soil erosion and less land under cultivation. Did everybody strip their topsoil like you did?"

"Don't be an asshole, Steve."

"What's the matter? You have too much tied up in the idea that you're some great agriculturalist?" Jesus, here I was again. And I hadn't wanted to fight. Why did he always manage to do this to me?

"We don't need topsoil because we don't need grass." His voice was flat, but I could almost hear his teeth grinding. "Look."

We'd come over the crest of a hill. Below us was a herd of . . . animals of some sort. They might have been llamas, once. They were divided into groups, and each group was clustered around a clump of the black, spiky vegetation. "Why break my ass to grow long grass when these things prefer something that grows here like a weed?" Andy smiled again, but it wasn't what I'd call a friendly smile.

I tried to keep up anyway. "This is the economic base on which you're planning to build your independence?" I gave what I hoped sounded like a contemptuous snort.

"Why did they really send you, Steve? Were they hoping I'd kill you so they'd have a good media event to play on?" Andy turned to look over his left shoulder and threw the rover into reverse. My spine rippled as we bounced through a 180-degree turn and headed back. Andy didn't say another word to me the rest of the day.

"Why did they send you here?" I looked up from my reader to see Andy standing in the doorway. "You're the last person I'd send on a diplomatic mission."

"I'm not here as a diplomat." I was still smarting from the silence to which he'd subjected me all afternoon and through dinner. "The negotiating team is coming next month. I'm here because I'm the only person the Space Commission could find who was born here and was related to one of the ringleaders of your group."

"Those are your qualifications?" Even his posture was arrogant. "I think I'm insulted."

"Don't flatter yourself," I said. "If you think they're taking your organization all that seriously, you're mistaken. You people can't survive here without the UN's help. The only real question in the Space Commission is why it's taken you so long to figure that out."

I got up from the bed. The hiss of my exo distracted him, and before he could say anything, I was in his face, my finger pointing, ready to drill into his chest. "Mars' gravity isn't strong enough to hold a breathable atmosphere without help," I said. "In another ten or twenty years, the water vapour will be gone and you'll be wearing breathers again. Unless somebody can seed the atmosphere with a fragmented comet—the way the UN did thirty years ago. Who's going to do that for you, Andy, if we don't?

"Mars has no magnetic field—what screens out solar radiation? I'll tell you what—a deflector satellite paid for by the taxpayers of Earth and maintained by that same UN that you're so anxious to kick out. Do you really think we're going to continue pouring money into this place if you give us the gas? How hypocritical can you get?"

Andy leaned into my finger, and it was as if twenty years had vanished. "You're thinking like a bureaucrat, Steve. Who says government has to do all that? There are lots of private companies in space right now—any one of 'em would be more than happy to take our money to sweeten the atmosphere twice a century. And they'd do it cheaper than you could."

His arguments were pathetic. "Where are you going to get the money?" I asked, enjoying the pressure of his chest against my finger. "Do you honestly think there's a big market anywhere for mutant llama burgers?"

"You're not half as clever as you think you are," Andy said. "And I don't think you can afford to piss me off, Steve."

"I'm not trying to piss you off. I'm just trying to make you see sense."

"You want to talk sense? Fine." He pressed against me a little more. "We're economically independent right now—or we would be if we weren't paying for the fat bastards who mismanage this place. You're still thinking of Mars the way it was twenty years ago, Steve. We can do it on our own, now."

"And what about the deflector satellite? Can you do that on your own, too?"

"If we could do it all ourselves, do you think we'd be even talking to you? It's your satellite. We can pay to maintain it, but we couldn't afford to buy it. So we want to talk lease instead. Do you really think that that's a sound moral reason for denying us self-government?"

He stepped back suddenly. I was having trouble with my balance in this gravity; he must have known that. I could only keep myself from falling by grabbing for him. "God damn it," I said as I pulled myself upright again. "What was that for?"

"I just got tired of you poking your finger at me, Steve. Like we've all gotten tired of having you people tell us how to live when you don't know a damned thing about what it's like here."

My face flushed and my shoulders burned as the muscles tightened. "I grew up here just like you did," I said. "Just because I had the common sense to leave doesn't mean I don't remember what it's like." He'd made me mad in spite of myself, and now I wanted to hurt him. "Mars is a dead end, Andy. It's at the bottom of a gravity well, and there isn't enough here to justify the expense of lifting what you make into space. You'll never be able to pay your own way—I've seen the studies. This colony only survives because Earth subsidizes it."

"I've seen the same studies," Andy said. He slouched, smiling, in the doorway and suddenly I was alarmed. When we were kids, he'd looked like that when he was ready for the kill, the putdown that would leave me sputtering with embarrassment and anger. I waited; he said nothing. Then he turned his back to me and walked away. I discovered I'd stopped breathing, and filled my lungs as I sat back onto the bed.

Then Andy turned. "Those studies show that Mars could get along without a subsidy—if we weren't paying for fat UN bastards like you." He pressed a wall stud and the door closed.

I was right; I knew it. All the evidence I had supported my argument. So why—once again—had Andy been able to make me think I was the one who was wrong?

I had a bad night. As I drifted in and out of sleep I could hear the air pump working in an otherwise silent house. Then the sound grew to a full-throated roar, and I was with my mother watching a tiny figure step up to the mound at Comiskey. "White Sox" was written in blue and red script on the front of the old, button-up jersey. The number 27 was on the back. The public address speakers rumbled like rocks in a rainbarrel, but I was able to pick out the name—with Mom's help. "Jack Keefe," she said. "That's daddy out there." Then I could see the name, because suddenly the man was growing in size, and the "KEEFE" stitched onto the back swelled until it filled the playing-field, and I awoke with tears in my eyes.

A couple of relief appearances, no victories, and an ERA in double digits: that was the whole of my father's career in the American League. There were years, after, of chasing the dream through a half-dozen minor-league towns. Then, briefly, back to Terre Haute before the horrible decision to throw it all away and come here. Not all of it was thrown away, though. Lying there in the dark and now-silent house, I could almost see the jersey hovering before me like a luminous ghost. There was a closet in the basement, a walk-in storage area that had been in my adolescence a sort of shrine to the past. There was a uniform there, and cleats and a glove I was never allowed to use, beg though I might.

When I opened my eyes again the light was beginning to come through the windowall. My stomach turned over when I remembered last night's argument; how was I going to be able to face Andy's friends now? Then snatches of the dream came back and I was able to push the hostility and embarrassment aside. I got out of bed, and was pleased at how little the exo had to help keep me balanced. Pleasure at my adaptability added to the memory of the dream; I put on my robe and wiggled my toes into slippers, and carefully made my way downstairs. The basement had been completely finished since I left, and a bewildering profusion of gravity-dependent exercise equipment took up most of the floor space, but the closet was still there.

It was full of garbage.

I don't know what the stuff was. Agricultural equipment, maybe. Spares for the household machines. Cast-offs from this life, but nothing from the life I'd been torn away from to come here. No jersey. No cleats. No glove.

I heard noise from above, Andy moving in the kitchen. I went up the stairs as fast as I could, surprising him in the act of pouring coffee. I took savage satisfaction in the spill.

"Where is it?" In spite of the exo's help, I had to fight for my next breath.

"What the hell are you talking about?" He wasn't happy either. Good for him.

"Where is it? What did you do with Dad's stuff—his jersey?"

"I don't know what you—oh, you mean his old White Sox uniform? Good God, Steve, I sent that to Mom years ago—after Dad died."

"You sent it to her? After she left us? The one member of this goddamned family who wouldn't even try to stick it out here? You sent it to her?!"

"He was her husband," Andy said quietly. "They were her memories."

"They were my memories, you son-of-a-bitch!"

Andy slammed his coffee cup on the counter. "What the hell is wrong with you, Steve? Why are you standing in my kitchen raving like some street-scum mental case?"

"You want to know what's wrong with me? You're wrong with me!" I shouted. "You and your smug superiority and your smartass comments! You haven't changed—I suppose I should be grateful for this god-damn stupid trip. I was right to hate you."

"You're sprained," he said. "You're out of your mind."

I slammed a fist into the wall as hard as the gravity would let me. "I'm sprained? You're bloody psycho-pathic! You never fought fair—you don't even know the meaning of the word. You always poked around for a weak spot and then you just dug in. You made my life here hell!" He took a big step back, his eyes big, and I felt a wild thrill. Never before had I been this close to winning a fight with Andy.

As a teen I'd thought he was inhuman. I was pass-ably good looking and a reasonably good ballplayer—until I was placed next to Andy. He was impossibly handsome, blonde and broad and tall, and he could drive the ball more than three hundred feet even against Earth's gravity. What made it worse, though, was that he had absolutely no feeling for anybody. He teased and humiliated our sister—and he took every opportunity to make me look stupid in front of my friends. He had no shortage of girlfriends, but I tried to keep mine secret from him. I was convinced he could take them away from me, and he knew it.

Baseball was the worst. I lived for baseball, worked day after day to sharpen my pitches. Andy didn't practise at all; he didn't have to. He belittled my efforts, and whenever he cared to try he made them look insignificant. I was convinced that the only reason he played the game at all was to make me look bad.

Try as I might, I couldn't convince Dad or Mom that there was anything sinister about Andy. Andy himself took care not to stick the knife in when our parents were watching. And so I bore the humiliation silently, waiting until I could qualify for a scholarship to study at a university on Earth.

I had thought I'd put Andy behind me. Returning to Mars had stripped off a shallow layer of healing to show that the old anger and shame were still there. I felt numb, outside of myself as I lashed out again.

"All I wanted was a chance to play baseball," I said. "All I wanted was a chance to be like him. And instead he brought me here! What growing up could I do here, with you chopping away at me every chance you got? And you were in love with the goddamn place. You didn't care what this pathetic atmosphere did to my breaking ball, as long as this place had its own shopping malls and Burger Kings and looked just like home. Well, I didn't want a place that looked like home! I wanted to go home!"

"Steve," Andy said. He seemed to be wavering; then I blinked and the moisture spilled onto my cheeks.

"Steve," he said again. "You need to sit down."

"I need to get out of here! I never wanted to come back. Do you think I've enjoyed having to watch you play the happy farmer?" He looked like I'd hit him, and for a moment I thought I'd finally won.

Then he stepped towards me, tensed up like a guy going into freefall for the first time. "Grow up, Steve!" His face was reddening again. "You're not sixteen anymore. I'm not fifteen. This place has changed—the only thing that hasn't changed is the way you feel. Look at me!" His hands were on the lapels of my robe, pulling me with a grip tighter than any gravity.

"Look at me! Do I look like a fifteen-year-old kid? Whatever I may have done to you back then is gone! It's not part of now—let go of it!"

"Let go of me!" I brought my hands up between his, flung them apart and away from me. I spun around and threw myself through the doorway. "Fuck you!" I yelled over my shoulder as I moved to the front door. "Fuck you and this place you live in!"

It's impossible to slam an airlock door, but I gave it my best shot.

I walked away from the house as fast as my exo could carry me. In spite of its help, I had to fight to fill my lungs: I wasn't wearing my breather, and the outside air was little more than a memory of what I'd been breathing in the house.

I gave myself over to misery. I was cut off from anything that could be considered home; I hated Mars for its artificiality and the way it reminded me of Illinois and Indiana and all of the places I could never go back to. Images flared in my head like flashbulbs exploding from the stands at a night game. I didn't see where I was walking; all I saw was the career I might have had, another tall thin man wearing number 27 for the White Sox and the name KEEFE on his back. I had to blame somebody for my loss: Andy was all I had left.

Pain shot up my leg, a lance driven up the core of my being. My eyes watered. I sucked in air. Looking down, I saw blood seeping into the powdery red rock that we'd called "dirt" when I was eleven, because it was the closest thing to dirt we could find. One of Andy's black plants had thrust a "leaf" into my foot, right through the slipper. The blood looked blacker in Mars-light; I remembered the countless small injuries of my youth. I lifted my foot to look at the wound.

And toppled down a slope. *It's getting cold out here,* I thought, as a rock came rushing toward me.

It was very cold when I woke up. I didn't feel good, and my chest complained that it wanted more air. Try as I might, I couldn't fill my lungs.

It was still daylight. Maybe I'd be able to get back to the house before dark—assuming I hadn't walked so far I couldn't find it. I shifted away from the rock; with numb detachment I remembered that dried blood also looked different on Mars. With room to manoeuvre, I half-rolled until I was in a position to use the exo to get me to my swollen feet.

I looked up . . . at somebody watching me with grave interest from the top of the slope. I almost gagged before I could catch myself. It looked almost human— while having not a shred of humanity in it.

"Mom, there's someone down here," it said. A second head appeared over the crest of the hill, and a woman stood beside the thing. A human woman.

Mom?

Now there were four of them: the woman and three of the . . . creatures. They were dressed, it appeared, for camping or hiking. None wore breathers, though the woman looked a little like she could use one. I looked up at them. "I seem to be lost." It came out as a croak; I felt betrayed by my voice.

The woman looked closely at me, frowning. "I think," she said to the creature at her right side, "that this is your Uncle Steven."

I fell down again.

I woke up in the back of a van of some sort. A cool, wet pad was on my head, numbing the pain into surrender. My feet were encased in something warm. I saw two of the creatures looking at me; Andy sat on a seat facing the bench-seat on which I lay. Natalia, I assumed, was driving. The compress on my head shifted; it was being moved by a not-quite-human hand. I turned back to Andy. "Your kids?"

"Jack and Misha," he said. There might have been pride in his tone, but his face was serious. "Evelyn is our neighbours'. Natalia had the three of them on a survival trip."

"You said they were having tests done."

"I said they'd gone for tests. Survival was the test. They're ten and eleven now, and I want them to be able to survive out here in a way you—or I—couldn't."

"So llamas aren't all you were modifying. You'll be crucified if word of this gets back to Earth."

"Why did you move to a lagrange city when you left here?" Andy asked.

"I wasn't lying back at the house. I hate this place. I hated what Dad tried to do, trying to make it into a plastic Terre Haute. I went to the best place I could think of that nobody would ever try to turn into a copy of Earth. A lagrange city was perfect."

He shook his head. "I've been trying to tell you ever since you got here—I agree with you." I tried to move too quickly and my head stung. Andy went on: "This planet will never work if we try to terraform it into a duplicate of the one we left. So we've done what we can to remake the planet as much as she'll let us. And for the rest . . . we're remaking ourselves. Jack and

Misha and Evelyn and their friends have a higher tolerance for cold built into them. Their eyes are double-lidded. They've got bigger and more efficient diaphragm and lungs, so they'll never need breathers. Never. The doctors tell me they can get by on considerably less sunlight than we do without getting deficiency diseases. No more vitamin supplements." The children had been silent, watching Andy as much as me. Suddenly, Misha smiled, the shy smile of a child who recognizes the pride with which her parent is speaking of her.

Try as I might, I couldn't see her as anything but a freak. For once, though, I knew better than to say anything. Because Andy smiled back at her, and with a jolt I realized that I was aware of his face.

Ever since I'd arrived, I had been seeing the narrow, handsome face of a beautiful young man, the young man who always had his choice of friends, the young man the girls fought over while they ignored me. I had been seeing the face of my fifteen-year-old brother.

The man who smiled at his daughter from the other side of the van was in his mid-thirties. His face had fleshed out considerably, and aged in a way that was far from flattering. Running the ranch hadn't been enough to keep his body from fattening. For a moment I looked at a stranger. Then I realized that it wasn't Andy who hadn't changed in twenty years, and I had to close my eyes.

"Think I should call the doctor?" he asked. "You okay?"

"I'll be all right." I took a breath: the air in the van was sweet and thick. "It's not going to be easy, you know. I'm not going to tell anyone about this"—I looked at the children—"but don't make the mistake of believing that what I think will make a difference, even if I agreed with you. And I still don't agree with you, Andy. I don't think you're ready to go out on your own."

"I don't expect you to turn around overnight," he said. "I'll be happy if you fly back home and tell your boss there's no point in coming down hard on us right now. That—and think about what we talked about here."

I looked from Andy to the kids, and back. "I'll think about it," I said.

I sent a message to my boss, telling her that I'd failed in my assignment and suggesting she try to talk her boss into postponing any major diplomatic initiative for the time being. I didn't mind admitting failure. After all, I'd warned her the chances of persuading Andy were small. She didn't have to know that I was the one reconsidering his position.

Andy drove me back to the port. On the way, I kept finding my eyes shifting over to him. I had lived so long with my brother's adolescent image that his grown-up face was taking some getting used to. I wondered if there was a way I could spend time talking to him without actually having to come back to Mars.

There were people playing baseball again at the school in Brackett. Andy was so caught up in explaining his hopes for his kids that he didn't even notice the game. I didn't bother calling his attention to it.

TALES FROM THE HOLOGRAPH WOODS

EILEEN KERNAGHAN

Where we walk, the immaculate
images of trees invent themselves—
pine, hemlock, phantom alder   apparitions
of bright air, coherent light.
Listen.   There is wind and bird-song,
orchestrated insect murmur,
the sky cloud-patterned by day,
at night a zodiac glitter.

In the green shimmer of the photon forest
we celebrate the imperishable idea of trees—
arboreal icons mirrored to infinity,
each one discrete and unambiguous.
It is only at the edge of vision
when you turn your head too quickly
that you see the pattern
beginning to repeat itself.

Now imagine a forest
rooted in dark earth
where pale threads grow
knotted, nerve-tangled,
subtle and diffuse as hidden water:
the frail web that in an older physics
held the world together.

COGITO

ELISABETH VONARBURG

Translated from the French by Jane Brierley

> To Luc P.,
> *without whom and with whom.*

Once upon a time on a planet far, far away there was a little girl called Nathany Berkeley. She lived in a city called Cybland. It was the only city on the planet, no doubt also called Cybland. The people who colonized it didn't bother with a proper name, as they weren't particularly interested in it. All they wanted was a place where they could build their city and do as they pleased, far from Earth and those who didn't agree with their desired way of life. This happened three hundred years before Nathany's birth, in the time of the Swarming when many people left Earth to go and live as they liked somewhere else. They chose a habitable planet, journeyed there in superlume ships, and settled in. And as everybody on each planet agreed how life was to be lived in general, all went fairly well.

At first, Nathany didn't know there was a planet. She barely knew there was a city around her house. It wasn't her house, really, and she had already lived in several—Educative Blocks 2, 3, 4, 5, and 6. Now she was in Special Block D, which she shared with about thirty other little girls and boys of her own age. Not exactly her own age: Nathany was six, but she ought to have been seven. Just after arriving from EdBlock 6 where she'd only stayed three months, she heard Yvanie, the teacher, say she was a pre-coshes little girl. In the EdBlock 4 yard there was a tree with flowers that turned into fruits and the fruits were enclosed in *coshes*. When the fruit was ready to eat you took off the coshe. Nathany was puzzled: a pre-coshes little girl must be too green to eat, and yet Yvanie's remark certainly seemed like a compliment. Finally she understood: she was *ahead*. She was ahead because she knew how to use her syn just as well as the older boys and girls in SpecBlock D, although she was only six.

You see, Nathany wasn't an ordinary little girl. There were no ordinary little girls in Cybland. Or little boys either. I mean, ordinary like they are here. Of course in Cybland they all seemed normal to each other. They each had a syn to control their cybes; their cybes gave them special P-modes, each consisting of several percepts, and the percepts shared by the greatest number of individuals were called P-zones. There were individual P-zones and collective P-zones. You learned about collective P-zones, too, although this wasn't something you really *learned*, if you know what I mean.

Nathany wore her syn around her neck, like all the inhabitants of Cybland. It was a wide, thick collar, very close-fitting, made up of articulated segments. The real name for the syn was "Control and Sensorial Synthesis Unit," but that was too long to say. It was . . . like a mixer. Or a rheostat. Or both. It was also a sort of radio, both receiving and transmitting, but it wasn't used for speaking. It was used to control the cybes.

The cybes are harder to describe. First because you couldn't see them. They were inside the body, trans-

planted into Cybland infants shortly after birth to replace the eyes and ears of babies—tiny little cybes (you
could say "cybernetic modules" but that's also too
long) directly linked to the brain. It's really the brain
that sees and hears, isn't it? Well, in Cybland the first
cybes were transplanted very early on, because a baby's
brain is a highly adaptable organ that learns lots of
things very quickly, and it was a good idea to accustom
the baby to the cybes right away.

Not only the eyes and ears were replaced, but all
the other senses. Touch was fairly simple. A virus was
developed that burned all the nerve endings in the skin,
as well as those that transmitted taste and smell. Then
a special substance was injected into the skin—liquid
biocrystals, if you want to know. They reacted to pressure, cold, and heat, and the syn sent this information
to the brain, and the brain . . . well, did what a brain is
supposed to do, and *said* it was doing it, that things
were hot, or cold, or that you'd cut yourself. Taste and
smell were a bit more complicated. Things like filters
were grafted into the body, and these gathered tastes
and smells and sent them to the syn, which analyzed
them and sent the information to the brain—which
then did its usual work.

Actually, the only true cybes were those replacing
eyes and ears, but people got into the habit of calling all
the sensory replacements by the same name because it
was simpler. What mattered was understanding how it
worked: there was the syn, which acted like a small secondary brain, a supplementary relay between the outside and the real brain; and there were the cybes, which
replaced the senses. Of course, all of them had to be
changed as the children grew, like clothes or shoes. Except you only saw the syn. You might've seen the cybes
when they were taken out in order to insert bigger ones,
but you'd be alseep at that point. They were put in a

64

box with your other cybes, and on the day of your last transplant, when you'd finished growing, you got the box as a present. Since Nathany hadn't finished growing, she'd never seen her cybes. It didn't really matter. What mattered was how you learned to use your syn and control your cybes, right from the beginning. Nathany learned fast, and she learned well. That's why she was in SpecBlock D, although she was only six. Other children weren't so *precocious*. Some never learned to use their cybes properly. There was something in their brain that made them incapable of doing it. They were *refractory*. Some couldn't even tolerate transplants. As time went by, they would suddenly disappear from the Block and you never saw them again. Sad, but that's the way it was.

Why did they replace all the senses in Cybland? First I'll have to finish explaining what they did with the cybes, and what Nathany did so well that she was in SpecBlock D instead of EdBlock 6 with her childhood companions.

You see, the syn and the cybes were merely tools. Like eyes, ears, and the rest, after all. Except that they were a bit more difficult to use. To give you an example, our eyes only see certain colours, corresponding to very definite light vibrations. Nathany's cybe-eyes saw many more vibrations, and her cybe-ears heard more too, above and below the range we hear. But the human brain wasn't really designed to receive these sensations—it could, but it must learn, and that takes time.

And that's not all. The syn didn't only control the intensity of perceptions. It could also mix them, remember? In Cybland, you could taste colours, hear smells, touch sounds . . . although you couldn't do this just any old how. That would have been really too upsetting for tiny children. It had to be learned bit by bit too.

And there's more! The syn was like a two-way radio, but instead of using airwaves to transmit and receive, it used sensations. This is difficult to explain—in fact it was difficult to *do*, and that was what took the most learning. Everyone has a particular way of perceiving things such as colours, smells, or favourite sounds, isn't that right? It was the same in Cybland, even though all the cybes had exactly the same capabilities, which isn't the case with organic eyes and ears. (The founders of Cybland were a little surprised at this unexpected development. They used to think that peoples' perceptions differed simply because their sensory organs were different . . . but as they were die-hard individualists, they managed to take this fact in their stride.) Anyway, everyone had their particular way of perceiving things, called their *perceptual mode* or P-mode for short. A P-mode consisted of percepts—perceptions of your favourite senses in varying combinations and proportions to form the individual P-zone, that is, your own *perceptual zone*, the special way in which you perceived your environment.

So far, so good. What makes it complicated is that people also have a special way of seeing *themselves*. After all our bodies, our faces, are also an environment, aren't they? In Cybland, thanks to the syn, people could transmit the way in which they saw themselves, and similarly receive how others saw *themselves*. But you don't necessarily want to see yourself exactly as you are. If your hair is brown and you'd rather be blond, for example . . . or ten centimetres taller . . . or ten kilos lighter . . . or have green hair, weigh thirty kilos more, and stand three metres tall. There was no limit to what the people in Cybland could transmit with their syn, you see. They could look like anything—blue with yellow polkadots if they wanted!

It was lots of fun. But it was also very distracting.

How are you going to recognize people if they look different every day? Or suppose someone decides to look like a horrible monster and walks about scaring everybody? And then it could be dangerous. If the people in charge of atmospheric machines decided not to hear or see on the same wavelengths as the alarm systems. . . Or if someone in the street decided to see only green colours, he'd never stop for red lights. There'd be accidents all the time. Of course, in the city of Cybland there weren't any cars and therefore no traffic lights. Everything was organized so that individual capabilities wouldn't endanger the person or those near by. But you can see what might happen.

Well, there were obvious limits—not to what you were capable of, but to what you were allowed to do. When you were by yourself in your individual P-zone, you could do what you liked. But when others were around, you had to stay within the limits of the collective P-zones.

This meant that you had to learn about these P-zones, about the perceptions that, by common consent, governed behaviour in a social context. But although there was general agreement on a certain number of things, there were also individual opinions about a great many others, depending on your profession, for example, or your sex. Well, to make a long story short, it meant a lot of learning for little Cyblanders, on top of what they had to learn in school like you and me.

Nathany, at six years old, was in SpecBloc D because she had learned especially fast and well to use her syn, control her cybes, and handle individual and collective P-zones. Naturally she hadn't finished learning—you kept on until the last transplant, and even after, because, after the last transplant, you were an adult and had the right to experiment with your cybes and syn without a teacher's supervision. In fact, nobody had the right to prevent you from doing exactly what you wanted in private. (As I mentioned, Cybland society was founded by rugged individualists. A society of individualists is rather a contradiction in terms, but they had to tailor their theories somehow so as to create a viable society. These kinds of complexities are the spice of life, after all.)

Anyway, Nathany waited impatiently for the time when she could do exactly what she liked with no one to tell her not to. You see, Nathany was an inquisitive little girl, which is perfectly normal even in Cybland, except that she wasn't necessarily inquisitive about the same things as we are. The teachers thought her curiosity a good thing—as long as she didn't exceed the limits set by them, which is also perfectly normal, as it is here. What's more, from the moment Nathany was considered precocious they tended to give her more leeway than other little girls. Even so, and without quite knowing why, there were moments when she overstepped the teachers' limits and got herself into hot water. (Of course, it's hard to know exactly the teachers' limits. They have a way of shifting about, don't they?)

For example, while Nathany was still in EdBlock 4—she was four and hadn't yet been considered precocious—she had reconfigured her classmates' cybes to her own format—a particularly amusing combination of colours, sounds, and smells that she'd discovered and wanted to show them. The teacher noticed it—it was Marlin, who wasn't very smart, but then teachers are trained to know that when kids go into a giggling huddle they're up to something, whether it's in Cybland or here. Well, Marlin got really mad. He did something to all their syns and told them they weren't to do any more amusing mixes. They weren't supposed to do amusing mixes right now. (Although Nathany didn't know it, this was the moment when her teachers first began to consider her precocious.) Marlin gave her a sound scolding in front of the class, and as extra punishment set her syn to a really boring P-mode (no visual/auditive crossover, imagine!), and told her that it was simply not done to mess about with other people's cybes, making them perceive whatever you wanted. It was bad. It was forbidden.

Like most bad-&-forbidden things, there was no logic in it. "What about the P-zone?" sniffled Nathany rebelliously (*And what you've just done to me?* she added to herself). They were learning Level 2 Collective P-zone that month, and the teachers were explaining what it consisted of and configuring their cybes accordingly.

"That's different," replied Marlin. Collective P-zone-2 (which regulated interactions with a number of simple machines) was like learning to count. Those who were better at it taught the others. This was necessary, useful to all concerned, and good. What Nathany had done was something else again. Maybe her combination of percepts was fun, but the others didn't *need* it, and what was more important, perhaps they didn't *want* to perceive things her way. She had no right to force them.

"But I didn't really force them," protested Nathany. "They wanted to." (The other children discreetly said nothing. The fact was, she'd configured their cybes herself because they were so slow and clumsy.)

But that was no reason. If they hadn't wanted to, what would she have done?

Nathany hung her head and was obliged to confess by her silence that she might have tried to coerce them. She generally got her way, being tall and strong for her age.

"Well, you're not to do it, understand?" said Marlin

by way of closing the discussion. Nathany translated this to mean, "You're not to do it unless you're an adult." Marlin paused for a moment, then added, "Later, you'll learn how we share our percepts with others. There are ways of doing it that are permitted. But it's too soon right now. After all, you have to be able to walk before you can run, don't you? When you can walk, you'll be able to run."

Nathany didn't quite see the connection since she knew how to walk and run, and would have liked to know how you shared percepts when it was allowed. She sensed it was probably advisable not to press the point. At least Marlin hadn't said it was bad-&-forbidden to experiment on yourself. From now on when she wanted to share her experiments with others, she'd take care not to be caught doing it, that's all.

Things changed somewhat after Nathany was transferred to SpecBlock D. She could ask more questions, she realized, and the teachers took longer to reach their set limits. As soon as she arrived her syn was unblocked. Apparently she now had the right to try out interesting percept mixes, and if some were inadvisable the teacher took the trouble to explain why: they were dangerous for her physical and mental balance. If she wanted to try them anyway, she should ask for supervision by a teacher.

To tell the truth, at first Nathany didn't see how SpecBlock D was any better. The drawbacks were more obvious. Do you remember the first time you went to school? Well, it was the same for Nathany. She didn't know anyone. All the teachers and children were new to her. The fact that the other children didn't know each other either, because they were all precocious and had been withdrawn from their respective EdBlocks, didn't help cushion the shock of relocation. You children were able to go home after your first day of school. But not

Nathany or the others. SpecBlock D was now their home.

Nevertheless, children in SpecBlocks did go back to their former EdBlocks at regular intervals. It was felt they shouldn't be separated too abruptly from what, after all, had been their family. Nathany went back to EdBlock 6 to visit her old companions and teachers— Marlin, Treza, Bobb, Cort, and her favourites, Yvanie and Marelle. But after a few months something strange happened: it wasn't so pleasant going back to the Ed-Block. There were too many things to tell about, and the others didn't always understand very well. It annoyed them not to understand, and they didn't look on Nathany in the same way now. They'd changed.

Of course, it wasn't the other children who'd changed; it was Nathany. In a SpecBlock you learned a lot very fast, leaving the EdBlocks far behind. Finally, at the end of the first year, Nathany asked not to go back to EdBlock 6, ever. This was predictable and quite normal. Almost all the other SpecBlock children had done the same. SpecBlock D was now their real home.

This didn't mean that Nathany found life as pleasant as she had in her old block, when she was precocious. She had to more or less begin all over again in learning to know the new children and teachers, but because there were so many interesting things to do she didn't often have the time to mope. Everyone thought she was doing pretty well. After all, she wasn't precocious for nothing. In Cybland, precocious children were generally sturdy, well-balanced individuals.

Except that. . .

At the end of Nathany's first year in SpecBlock D, her father died.

You may wonder at this point in the story where Nathany's parents were and what they did. And to begin with, did Nathany have parents in the way we think of them here? Not really. The founders of Cybland had left Earth to live in their own, different way. The biggest difference, as you probably realize, had something to do with the cybes. But there was another, important difference, and that concerned the way people produced children and brought them up. Each child had a father and mother, but—as sometimes happens here—the mother didn't usually carry the child in her womb. And children weren't brought up by their parents but by the Block teachers. The parents knew their children and could see them every day for two hours if they wanted, as well as spending a whole day with them every ten days. Parents in Cybland were in fact merely adults much like others. Not really special, you see. Some simply gave their children to Cybland and never visited them. The children didn't miss their parents, however, since there were six teachers—three men and three women—for each group of twenty-four, who remained with the children from infancy, as they all moved from one Block to another. There was the occasional exception, but in general the teachers and children formed a family that wasn't so different from ours—don't you think?

Nathany didn't know her parents well. They were very busy with the Cybland government and rarely came to see her. She didn't care. She didn't particularly like them. She didn't detest them either, mind you. The fact that she saw little of them simply didn't matter much.

This being the case, you may wonder why I'm telling you about her father's death. Even taking into account her transfer to SpecBlock D, it shouldn't have affected her unduly. That was normal for Cybland. But it was after her father's death that things changed for Nathany. Before, she had been inquisitive, but her inquisitiveness had stayed within reasonable bounds. After. . . But, you see, I think it wasn't so much the death of her *father*, after all. It was the *death* of her father. The way he died.

Nathany knew about death. She had vague, childish memories of children in the EdBlocks being around, and then not being around. Of course she asked questions and finally someone told her that they were *dead*, which meant they'd gone away and wouldn't ever come back. No one seemed overly upset. She got the impression that it was quite normal, and even sensed that those children were better off dead. They were *refractory*. I told you about the refractory children who couldn't tolerate transplants and disappeared from the EdBlocks, didn't I? Nathany felt a certain anxiety about this, but her teachers assured her it only happened to very young children, or to those who couldn't learn to use their cybes. Nothing like that would happen to her! She was nearly seven now, a big girl, and she knew very well how to use her cybes.

What she didn't know, and what the death of her father suddenly taught her, was that becoming an adult was no guarantee against ever being refractory. As I told you, Cybland was a city where, because of the cybes, everything had been organized to avoid accidents as much as possible. It was a closed, almost totally controlled environment, much like a greenhouse. But even in a controlled environment accidents sometimes happen. Accidents did happen, and disease as well. People died, or suddenly someone who had been perfectly normal couldn't use his or her cybes properly or even use them at all. This had happened to Nathany's father. After an illness he'd become refractory to his cybes. Finally, he died.

That's how it was announced to Nathany. In fact, her mother took the trouble to tell her the news in person. (Her name was Erna and she generally appeared as a tall, slim blond.) Geroge (that was Nathany's father) became sick and *then* he became refractory, and *only after that* did he die. He didn't die of the illness. How did he die? Did he have an accident because he had no cybes and was blind, deaf and insensible? Did they let him go out without cybes? That was really bad! But Erna said no, they hadn't let him go out. He'd been transferred to a special house for refractory adults.

And did they leave him by himself then, with no cybes, and did he have an accident in the special house?

In Cybland you could assume whatever appearance you liked, but people still had trouble controlling their emotions sometimes. Nathany was an observant child, and she saw that Erna was becoming increasingly embarrassed. What had happened in the special house?

Finally, after a long pause, Erna told Nathany that Geroge had killed himself, that it was very sad, but there was no help for it and she must be a very good little girl and work well in SpecBlock D—it was one of the best in Cybland and she, Erna, had chosen it personally. Then she kissed Nathany and left.

Now Nathany had more questions than ever— why, how, and what if. . . But whom could she ask?

"What happens when you have no cybes?" she asked Marta, her closest friend in SpecBlock D.

Marta shrugged. "You're dead."

"No, when you have no cybes but aren't dead."

Marta stared at her in amazement, and Nathany let the subject drop. She went and found Uri, her closest enemy in SpecBlock D. Marta was lots of fun, but fighting with Uri was far more interesting.

"What happens when you can't use your cybes and are still alive?"

Uri eyed her, wary yet intrigued. At nearly eight years old, he wasn't one to pass up a challenge. He thought a moment. "You disappear. You perceive no one, and no one perceives you. It's like being dead. Only you're alive."

"But how do you know you're alive?" said Nathany, forgetting in her puzzlement that her questions were meant to be riddles to which she clearly knew the answer.

Uri grinned triumphantly. "You *don't* know!" He walked off, sure he'd scored—a sentiment vaguely shared by Nathany.

At this point Nathany decided to take a chance with a teacher. "Why do people sometimes reject their cybes?" she asked Pomelo.

"Why do you want to know?" was Pomelo's comeback. Nathany had expected this. He was one of those adults who answer a question with a question. Some of them did it to give themselves time to make up an answer, others stalled because they didn't want to answer at all. With Pomelo it was a kind of game. He usually had the answer, and merely wanted to be sure you did too. It was irritating, but once you'd caught on you could get more out of him than other teachers. Even so, Nathany didn't usually question him. His answers were very precise but almost incomprehensible unless you asked a whole lot more questions, and even then . . . usually the children gave up before he did. Have you noticed that if there's one thing more annoying than not getting an answer, it's getting too many, none of which you can understand? But this was a special case, and Nathany was determined to try Pomelo. Something might come of it.

She explained that her father had become refractory and had died. Pomelo nodded his head approvingly, then, fair as always, provided an answer. "Sometimes, after an illness or an accident, the body changes inside and it can't handle the cybes. It rejects them."

"But why?"

"Because the cybes aren't part of the body."

As expected, dozens of questions sprang to Nathany's mind. She knew the syn wasn't really part of the body, but never having seen her cybes, she assumed she'd been born with them, even if they were changed regularly. Sort of like baby teeth that fell out and were replaced. Except that it happened every year.

"But what are we like—without cybes, I mean. Not if we're refractory, but . . . before." She hesitated.

"Before the transplants," said Pomelo, and she realized that this was exactly what she wanted to say. "Well, we're born with organic eyes and ears, and we can also feel and taste and touch."

"Like we can with cybes?"

"Not nearly as well. Not well at all. Not in the infrared or ultraviolet range, for example. Especially since, with no syn, you can't have crossover sensations."

No syn at all. Not only no crossovers, but no transmitting or receiving. Was Uri right all along? You perceive no one and no one perceives you. But that couldn't be right, because you'd have eyes and everything. . .

"Why are we born like that when cybes are so much better?"

Pomelo smiled. "Because nature isn't as good. That's why our ancestors founded Cybland. To improve on nature."

Nathany's mind buzzed with questions. She felt discouraged. Pomelo had tricked her again. Well, not tricked—Pomelo never did that. He answered, all right, but it was worse than no answer.

Pomelo surprised her, however, by standing up and picking out a book module from his office shelves. He handed it to her. "You can keep it. But don't tell anyone you have it."

In this way Nathany acquired that delightful and frustrating thing, which can't be shared with anyone: a secret.

The book module talked about Cybland's founding fathers. Here was another discovery: Cybland hadn't always existed. There had been something before, somewhere else. And the ancestors had been different, without cybes, without a syn, without anything. "Subjected to the meagre perceptions imposed by their poor natural senses," said the book module. Further on (and this was harder to understand) it said, "Subjected to the intolerable and constant violation of human free will by the universe through a limited sensorial apparatus."

The book module was actually way above Nathany's head, precocious though she might be. What she gleaned was a confused idea about why Cybland was founded—"against reality's violation of consciousness." Reality was a word never used in Cybland. She'd never encountered it before, at least. But in any case this thing perceived by natural senses must be pretty horrible for poor Geroge to have died of it. To have made himself die.

Perhaps Pomelo thought that by giving Nathany a book module and a secret, he'd discourage her once and for all. She'd be stymied by all the questions she *couldn't* ask, and all the answers that she wouldn't know quite what to do with. But he was wrong. He'd underestimated Nathany's curiosity—a curiosity intrigued by paradox, and particularly by the fact that her ancestors had lived for hundreds and hundreds of years with only their natural senses. The book module even intimated that there were people left on Earth, lots of people who lived without cybes. Maybe they were "slaves," as the book module said, but they were living slaves. If you could live without cybes, why did Geroge prefer to die?

Try as she might, Nathany could find no answer to this last why. So, following an approved technique, she turned it into how. She could do something with how. *How* did you live without cybes? What was it like?

She wasn't really able to answer this question either, but she didn't know it. In Cybland, you see, when an adult became refractory, he or she was "reconverted", as they said—partly, anyway, and if physically possible. Organic eyes and ears were retransplanted from an organ bank kept for just this sort of thing. Nothing could be done for the other senses, of course. Once the nerve endings were burned they couldn't grow again. But at least these people could see and hear. It was possible to live without cybes, but that didn't mean people wanted to. Refractory cases all ended up like Nathany's father. But even if Nathany had been aware of all this, she still wouldn't have genuinely understood why Geroge or the other refractories chose to die. It was something about their being too different, and the fact that normal Cyblanders didn't want to have anything to do with them. Cyblanders thought it rather disgusting to be limited to two senses, you see. Deep down, they considered the refractory cases not quite human. The only true human beings were those with cybes, who really dominated nature—although "nature" wasn't a word often used. It had become rather obscene with time. Pomelo had only used it in front of Nathany because he knew she wouldn't understand.

But Nathany had no idea how deep her lack of comprehension was—a little girl who had all her cybes, who had never really been alone or different, even though she was precocious, and who didn't even know that "nature" was a dirty word. So she decided to try. To behave as if. As if she had no cybes, only "natural senses."

She wasn't quite sure now to go about it. The book

module didn't say much except that natural senses were very limited. All she had to go on were Pomelo's remarks. No perception of infrared or ultraviolet rays in organic vision. It must be the same for hearing—upper and lower limits, no infra or ultra sounds. And no crossovers among senses, no more visual sound (Nathany's favourite P-mode, with a strong tactile element). All right. That night she hid in a corner where no one would disturb her experiments, and she reconfigured her cybes.

I'm not sure I can really describe to you what Nathany stopped perceiving, since I've never perceived it, and neither have you. And I can't describe what Nathany began to perceive. If I were talking about us, I'd say "silence, the shadow of night", and we'd all know what I meant. But not her: these perceptions had never existed for her before. I'd say she perceived things *less*, because she no longer saw the infrared and ultraviolet ranges, or heard infrasounds and ultrasounds, and she'd reduced (a bit haphazardly) her senses of touch, taste, and smell. But I'm not even sure *less* would mean for her what we mean by it. It wasn't necessarily negative. It was new. She'd never done it, you see—perceived *less*. In Cybland you were always learning to perceive *more*, right from babyhood.

It was new and therefore interesting. Just to check, she reconfigured her cybes the usual way and everything was back to normal. It was fun to switch from one to the other, hip-hop, like a balloon being alternately inflated and deflated.

At this stage she would have normally played with her syn to change her new perceptions, but she refrained. Natural senses could *not* be changed, unless with *drugs that had harmful long-term effects*, according to the book module. She must go on perceiving without changing a thing—the SpecBlock's inner courtyard, the flowering lindens, bright green beneath the electric lights. It was really strange, this immutability. It would soon become boring. Nathany understood why the founding fathers had wanted to "improve on nature", if that was all it was. Anyway, the net result of her experiment was that you *could* certainly live without cybes, even if she needed cybes to make the experiment. It wasn't so dreadful. You weren't dead, and you didn't "perceive nothing", as Uri had said. Even if some of your perceptions had vanished, you still had a few. Anyway, they hadn't really "vanished". They were still in her syn, because they came back when she reconfigured it.

What would happen if you removed more perceptions? If you not only turned down your cybes, but set them at zero?

What a strange idea, even a little alarming. But irresistible for a curious little girl like Nathany. She didn't turn off everything at once, however; only the cybe-eyes to begin with. No more linden, no more night. Or rather, another sort of blackness. But the water tinkling in the fountain was there, and that created a sort of space. It wasn't the courtyard, but it was still a space. The linden flowers still gave off their perfume, and Nathany's nightgown felt soft and flannelly against her shoulders and knees. In fact, Nathany's body was still very much there—the taste of saliva in her mouth, the feel of her tongue against her teeth, of skin against skin as she sat cross-legged. And she could even sense the weight of her body, where up was, or down, and this made the ground exist, hard and cool through the nightgown beneath her buttocks. Lots of things still existed.

Reducing the cybe-smell and cybe-taste to zero didn't have much effect. (The biggest change was losing her usual cross-perceptions—the smell of water, the taste of stone, the smell-taste of electricity. . .) No more flowers. No more saliva. With the cybe-ears at zero, no more fountain—and, hey! no more space at all, no more depth, anyway. Only an inside and outside, because she could feel herself breathing, and an up and down, because she could still feel the pressure of her body on the ground, of her arms on her knees, her hand on her syn. In fact, Nathany's body was more than ever *there*, and from it she could reconstruct all the rest: the hard surface beneath her buttocks was the floor of the courtyard where there were linden trees and a fountain, and the hard surface against her back was the wall of SpecBlock D, which was in Cybland which was on a planet which was in space.

There, in all logic, Nathany should have cancelled her cybe-touch. But she was not only logical, not only curious; she was also a little girl. And she had a growing feeling that she was in the process of doing something bad-&-forbidden. She waited a little before going to the next stage. Uri's words sprang to mind: "Like being dead, only you're alive." It made no sense when he said it, but suddenly it almost seemed as though it might. And now her own question rose to the surface, sharp and clear: How do you know you're alive? If you see nothing, hear, taste, feel, touch nothing?

What was left once you took away everything? Was anything left? If she cancelled the feeling of the ground beneath her buttocks and the wall against her back and her skin against her skin, would the ground and the wall and the courtyard and SpecBlock D and the city and the planet still exist? Would her body exist?

What was left if you took away everything?

And at last Nathany turned off her cybe-touch as well, because she was a little girl and curious, or because it was logical, or because it was definitely bad-&-forbidden, or because of Geroge, Erna, Uri, or Pomelo.

Or because of all these elements at once. How do I know? In any case, she reconfigured her last cybe to zero.

What happened then? Can you tell me? She wasn't "floating in the void". She couldn't "float in" anything—no more body, no more space. Was she still in the courtyard? Was there still a courtyard? Of course there was a courtyard, you say. It was the courtyard of SpecBlock D, in Cybland on a planet far away from here, and Nathany perceived it very well when her cybe-senses were on. But she also saw the infrasounds when she was in her favourite P-mode. She heard the perfume of the lindens. Perhaps she decided to perceive a courtyard with lindens, a SpecBlock with people in it, and a city around it, and a planet. She could, with her cybes and her syn, couldn't she?

Well, there's this, you say. There's Nathany, with a syn and cybes, and everything flows from that, including the Block, Cybland, the planet. Anyway, *we're* here listening to this story. We exist. And so from this. . .

But are you sure? Maybe someone just imagined the cybes and the syn controlling them, imagined you who are listening.

All right, there is someone, you say. Here's what's left when you take away everything. There is someone who is imagining, and therefore why not Nathany and all the rest, and us, and so on and so on?

Perhaps. I'll think about it. It's an interesting idea to follow up. But you, you should think about this: can you tell me what sound a tree makes when it falls in a forest where there's no one to hear it? Can you describe to me the sound of a single hand clapping?

HOMELANDING

MARGARET ATWOOD

1. Where should I begin? After all, you have never been there; or if you have, you may not have understood the significance of what you saw, or thought you saw. A window is a window, but there is looking out and looking in. The native you glimpsed, disappearing behind the curtain, or into the bushes, or down the manhole in the mainstreet—my people are shy—may have been only your reflection in the glass. My country specializes in such illusions.

2. Let me propose myself as typical. I walk upright on two legs, and have in addition two arms, with ten appendages, that is to say, five at the end of each. On the top of my head, but not on the front, there is an odd growth, like a species of seaweed. Some think this is a kind of fur, others consider it modified feathers, evolved perhaps from scales like those of lizards. It serves no functional purpose and is probably decorative.

My eyes are situated in my head, which also possess two small holes for the entrance and exit of air, the invisible fluid we swim in, and one larger hole, equipped with bony protuberances called teeth, by means of which I destroy and assimilate certain parts of my surroundings and change them into my self. This is called eating. The things I eat include roots, berries, nuts, fruits, leaves, and the muscle tissues of various animals and fish. Sometimes I eat their brains and glands as well. I do not as a rule eat insects, grubs, eyeballs or the snouts of pigs, though these are eaten with relish in other countries.

3. Some of my people have a pointed but boneless external appendage, in the front, below the navel or midpoint. Others do not. Debate about whether the possession of such a thing is an advantage or disadvantage is still going on. If this item is lacking, and in its place there is a pocket or inner cavern in which fresh members of our community are grown, it is considered impolite to mention it openly to strangers. I tell you this because it is the breach of etiquette most commonly made by tourists.

In some of our more private gatherings, the absence of cavern or prong is politely overlooked, like club feet or blindness. But sometimes a prong and a cavern will collaborate in a dance, or illusion, using mirrors and water, which is always absorbing for the performers but frequently grotesque for the observers. I notice that you have similar customs.

Whole conventions and a great deal of time have recently been devoted to discussions of this state of affairs. The prong people tell the cavern people that the latter are not people at all and are in reality more akin to dogs or potatoes, and the cavern people abuse the prong people for their obsession with images of poking, thrusting, probing and stabbing. Any long object with a hole at the end, out of which various projectiles can be shot, delights them.

I myself—I am a cavern person—find it a relief not to have to worry about climbing over barbed wire fences or getting caught in zippers.

But that is enough about our bodily form.

4. As for the country itself, let me begin with the sunsets, which are long and red, resonant, splendid and melancholy, symphonic you might almost say; as opposed to the short boring sunsets of other countries, no more interesting than a lightswitch. We pride ourselves on our sunsets. "Come and see the sunset," we say to one another. This causes everyone to rush outdoors or over to the window.

Our country is large in extent, small in population, which accounts for our fear of large empty spaces, and also our need for them. Much of it is covered in water, which accounts for our interest in reflections, sudden vanishings, the dissolution of one thing into another. Much of it however is rock, which accounts for our belief in Fate.

In summer we lie about in the blazing sun, almost naked, covering our skins with fat and attempting to turn red. But when the sun is low in the sky and faint, even at noon, the water we are so fond of changes to something hard and white and cold and covers up the ground. Then we cocoon ourselves, become lethargic, and spend much of our time hiding in crevices. Our mouths shrink and we say little.

Before this happens, the leaves on many of our trees turn blood red or lurid yellow, much brighter and more exotic than the interminable green of jungles. We find this change beautiful. "Come and see the leaves," we say, and jump into our moving vehicles and drive up and down past the forests of sanguinary trees, pressing our eyes to the glass.

We are a nation of metamorphs.

Anything red compels us.

5. Sometimes we lie still and do not move. If air is still going in and out of our breathing holes, this is called sleep. If not, it is called death. When a person has

achieved death a kind of picnic is held, with music, flowers and food. The person so honoured, if in one piece, and not, for instance, in shreds or falling apart, as they do if exploded or a long time drowned, is dressed in becoming clothes and lowered into a hole in the ground, or else burnt up.

These customs are among the most difficult to explain to strangers. Some of our visitors, especially the young ones, have never heard of death and are bewildered. They think that death is simply one more of our illusions, our mirror tricks; they cannot understand why, with so much food and music, the people are sad.

But you will understand. You too must have death among you. I can see it in your eyes.

6. I can see it in your eyes. If it weren't for this I would have stopped trying long ago, to communicate with you in this halfway language which is so difficult for both of us, which exhausts the throat and fills the mouth with sand; if it weren't for this I would have gone away, gone back. It's this knowledge of death, which we share, where we overlap. Death is our common ground. Together, on it, we can walk forward.

By now you must have guessed: I come from another planet. But I will never say to you, *Take me to your leaders.* Even I—unused to your ways though I am— would never make that mistake. We ourselves have such beings among us, made of cogs, pieces of paper, small disks of shiny metal, scraps of coloured cloth. I do not need to encounter more of them.

Instead I will say, take me to your trees. Take me to your breakfasts, your sunsets, your bad dreams, your shoes, your nouns. Take me to your fingers; take me to your deaths.

These are worth it. These are what I have come for.

UNCLE DOBBIN'S PARROT FAIR

CHARLES DE LINT

1

She would see them in the twilight when the wind was right, roly-poly shapes propelled by ocean breezes, turning end-over-end along the beach or down the alley behind her house like errant beach balls granted a moment's freedom. Sometimes they would get caught up against a building or stuck on a curb and then spindly little arms and legs would unfold from their fat bodies until they could push themselves free and go rolling with the wind again. Like flotsam in a river, like tumbleweeds, only brightly coloured in primary reds and yellows and blues.

They seemed very solid until the wind died down. Then she would watch them come apart like morning mist before the sun, the bright colours turning to ragged ribbons that tattered smoke-like until they were completely gone.

Those were special nights, the evenings that the Balloon Men came.

In the late sixties in Haight Ashbury, she talked about them once. Incense lay thick in the air—two cones of jasmine burning on a battered windowsill. There was on old iron bed in the room, up on the third floor of a house that no one lived in except for runaways and street people. The mattress had rust-coloured stains on it. The incense covered the room's musty smell. She'd lived in a form self-imposed of poverty back then, but it was all a part of the Summer of Love.

"I know what you mean, man," Greg Longman told her. "I've seen them."

He was wearing a dirty white T-shirt with a simple peace symbol on it and scuffed plastic thongs. Sticking up from the waist of his bell-bottomed jeans at a forty-five degree angle was a descant recorder. His long blonde hair was tied back with an elastic. His features were thin—an aesthetic-looking face, thin and drawn-out from too much time on the streets with too little to eat, or from too much dope. "They're like. . ." His hands moved as he spoke, trying to convey what he didn't feel words alone could say—a whole other language, she often thought, watching the long slender fingers weave through the air between them. ". . . they're just too much."

"You've really seen them?" she asked.

"Oh, yeah. Except not on the streets. They're floating high up in the air, y'know, like fat little kites."

It was such a relief to know that they were real.

"'Course," Greg added, "I gotta do a lot of dope to clue in on 'em, man."

Ellen Brady laid her book aside. Leaning back, she

flicked off the light behind her and stared out into the night. The memory had come back to her, so clear, so sharp, she could almost smell the incense, see Greg's hands move between them, little coloured afterimage traces following each movement until he had more arms than Kali.

She wondered what had ever happened to the Balloon Men.

Long light-brown hair hung like a cape to her waist. Her parents were Irish—Munster O'Healys on her mother's side, and Bradys from Derry on her father's. There was a touch of Spanish blood in her mother's side of the family, which gave her skin its warm dark cast. The Bradys were pure Irish and it was from them that she got her big-boned frame. And something else. Her eyes were a clear grey—twilight eyes, her father had liked to tease her, eyes that could see beyond the here and now into somewhere else.

She hadn't needed drugs to see the Balloon Men.

Shifting in her wicker chair, she looked up and down the beach, but it was late and the wind wasn't coming in from the ocean. The book on her lap was a comforting weight and had, considering her present state of mind, an even more appropriate title. *How To Make the Wind Blow.* If only it *was* a tutor, she thought, instead of just a collection of odd stories.

The author's name was Christy Riddell, a reed-thin Scot with a head full of sudden fancies. His hair was like an unruly hedgerow nest and he was a half head shorter than she, but she could recall dancing with him in a garden one night and she hadn't had a more suitable partner since. She'd met him while living in a house out east that was as odd as any flight of his imagination. Long rambling halls connnected a bewildering series of rooms, each more fascinating than the next. And the libraries. She'd lived in its libraries.

"*When the wind is right*," began the title story, the first story in the book, "*the wise man isn't half so trusted as the fool.*"

Ellen could remember when it was still a story that was told without the benefit of pen and paper. A story that changed each time the words travelled from mouth to ear.

There was a gnome, or a gnomish sort of a man, named Long who lived under the pier at the end of Main Street. He had skin brown as dirt, eyes blue as a clear summer sky. He was thin, with a fat tummy and a long crooked nose, and he wore raggedy clothes that he found discarded on the beach and wore until they were threadbare. Sometimes he bundled his tangled hair up under a bright yellow cap. Other times he wove it into many braids festooned with coloured beads and the discarded tabs from beer cans that he polished on his sleeve until they were bright and shiny.

Though he'd seem more odd than magical to anyone who happened to spy him out wandering the streets or along the beach, he did have two enchantments.

One was a pig that could see the wind and follow it anywhere. She was pink and fastidiously cleanly, big enough to ride to market—which Long sometimes did—and she could talk. Not pig-talk, or even pig-Latin, but plain English that anyone could understand if they took the time to listen. Her name changed from telling to telling, but by the time Long's story appeared in the book either she or Christy had settled on Brigwin.

Long's other enchantment was a piece of plain string with four complicated elf-knots tied in it—one to call up a wind from each of the four quarters. North and south. East and west. When he untied a knot, that wind would rise up and he'd ride Brigwin in its wake, sifting through the debris and pickings left behind for treasures or charms, though what Long considered a treasure, another might throw out, and what he might consider a charm, another might see as only an old button or a bit of tangled wool. He had a good business trading his findings to woodwives and witches and the like that he met at the market when midnight was past and gone, ordinary folk were in bed, and the beach towns belonged to those who hid by day, but walked the streets by night.

Ellen carried a piece of string in her pocket, with four complicated knots tied into it, but no matter how often she undid one, she still had to wait for her winds like anyone else. She knew that strings to catch and call up the wind were only real in stories, but she liked thinking that maybe, just once, a bit of magic could tiptoe out of a tale and step into the real world. Until that happened, she had to be content with what writers like Christy put to paper.

He called them mythistories, those odd little tales of his. They were the ghosts of fancies that he would track down from time to time and trap on paper. Oddities. Some charming, some grotesque. All of them enchanting. Foolishness, he liked to say, offered from one fool to others.

Ellen smiled. Oh, yes. But when the wind is right...

She'd never talked to Christy about the Balloon Men, but she didn't doubt that he knew them.

Leaning over the rail of the balcony, two stories above the walkway that ran the length of the beach, Christy's book held tight in one hand, she wished very hard to see those roly-poly figures one more time. The ocean beat its rhythm against the sand. A light breeze caught at her hair and twisted it into her face.

When the wind is right.

Something fluttered inside her, like wings unfolding, readying for flight. Rising from her chair, she set the book down on a wicker arm and went inside. Down the stairs and out the front door. She could feel a thrumming between her ears that had to be excitement moving blood more quickly through her veins, though it could be an echo of a half-lost memory—a singing of small deep voices, rising up from diaphragms nestled in fat little bellies.

Perhaps the wind was right, she thought as she stepped out onto the walkway. A quarter moon peeked at her from above the oil rigs far out from the shore. She put her hand in the pocket of her cotton pants and wound the knotted string she found there around one finger. It was late, late for the Balloon Men to be rolling, but she didn't doubt that there was something waiting to greet her out on the street. Perhaps only memories. Perhaps a fancy that Christy hadn't trapped on a page yet.

There was only one way to find out.

2

Peregrin Laurie was sharp-faced like a weasel—a narrow-shouldered thin whip of a teenager in jeans and a torn T-shirt. He sat in a doorway, knees up by his chin, a mane of spiked multicoloured hair standing straight up from his head in a two-inch Mohawk swath that ran down to the nape of his neck like a lizard's crest fringes. Wrapping his arms around bruised ribs, he held back tears as each breath he took made his chest burn.

Goddamn beach bums. The bastards had just about killed him and he had no one to blame but himself.

Scuffing through a parking lot, he should have taken off when the car pulled up. But no. He had to be the poseur and hold his ground, giving them a long cool look as they came piling drunkenly out of the car. By the time he realized just how many of them there were and what they had planned for him, it was too late to run. He'd had to stand there then, heart hammering in his chest, and hope bravado'd see him through, because there was no way he could handle them all.

They didn't stop to chat. They just laid into him. He got a few licks in, but he knew it was hopeless. By the time he hit the pavement, all he could do was curl up into a tight ball and take their drunken kicks, cursing them with each fiery gasp of air he dragged into his lungs.

The booger waited until he was down and hurting before making its appearance. It came out from under the pier that ran by the parking lot, black and greasy, with hot eyes and a mouthful of barracuda teeth. If it hadn't hurt so much just to breathe, he would have laughed at the way his attackers backed away from the creature, eyes bulging as they rushed to their car. They took off, tires squealing, but not before the booger took a chunk of metal out of the rear fender with one swipe of a paw.

It came back to look at him—black nightmare head snuffling at him as he lifted his head and wiped the blood from his face, then moving away as he reached out a hand towards it. It smelled like a sewer and looked worse, a squat creature that had to have been scraped out of some monstrous nose, with eyes like hot coals in a smear of a face and a slick wet look to its skin. A booger, plain and simple. Only it was alive, clawed and toothed. Following him around ever since he'd run away. . .

❖ ❖

His parents were both burnouts from the sixties. They lived in West Hollywood and got more embarrassing the older he became. Take his name. Laurie was bad enough, but Peregrin . . . lifted straight out of that *Lord of the Rings* book. An okay read, sure, but you don't use it to name your kid. Maybe he should just be thankful he didn't get stuck with Frodo or Bilbo. By the time he was old enough to start thinking for himself, he'd picked out his own name and wouldn't answer to anything but Reece. He'd gotten it out of some book, too, but at least it sounded cool. You needed all the cool you could get with parents like his.

His old man still had hair down to his ass. He wore wire-framed glasses and listened to shit on the stereo that sounded as burned-out as he looked. The old lady wasn't much better. Putting on weight like a whale, hair a frizzy brown, as long as the old man's, but usually hanging in a braid. Coming home late some nights, the whole house'd have the sweet smell of weed mixed with incense and they'd give him these goofy looks and talk about getting in touch with the cosmos and other spacey shit. When anybody came down on him for the way he looked, or for dropping out of school, all they said was let him do his own thing. His own thing. Jesus. Give me a break. With that kind of crap to look forward to at home, who wouldn't take off first chance they got? Though wouldn't you know it, no sooner did he get free of them, than the booger latched onto him, following him around, skulking in the shadows.

At first, Reece never got much of a look at the thing—just glimpses out of the corner of his eyes—and that was more than enough. But sleeping on the beaches and in parks, some nights he'd wake with that sewer smell in his nostrils and catch something slipping out of sight, a dark wet shadow moving close to the ground. After a few weeks, it started to get bolder, sitting on its haunches a half-dozen yards from wherever he was bedding down, the hot coal eyes fixed on him.

Reece didn't know what it was or what it wanted. Was it looking out for him, or saving him up for its supper? Sometimes he thought, what with all the drugs his parents had done back in the sixties—good times for them, shit for him because he'd been born and that was when his troubles had started—he was sure that all those chemicals had fucked up his genes. Twisted something in his head so that he imagined he had this two-foot high, walking, grunting booger following him around.

Like the old man'd say. Bummer.

Sucker sure seemed real, though.

Reece held his hurt to himself, ignoring Ellen as she approached. When she stopped in front of him, he gave her a scowl.

"Are you okay?" she asked, leaning closer to look at him.

He gave her a withering glance. The long hair and jeans, flowered blouse. Just what he needed. Another sixties burn-out.

"Why don't you just fuck off and die?" he said.

But Ellen looked past the tough pose to see the blood on his shirt, the bruising on his face that the shadows half-hid, the hurt he was trying so hard to pretend wasn't there.

"Where do you live?" she asked.

"What's it to you?"

Ignoring his scowl, she bent down and started to help him to his feet.

"Aw, fuck—" Reece began, but it was easier on his ribs to stand up than to fight her.

"Let's get you cleaned up," she said.

"Florence fucking Nightingale," he muttered, but she merely led him back the way she'd come.

From under the pier a wet shadow stirred at their departure. Reece's booger drew back lips that had the rubbery texture of an octopus' skin. Row on row of pointed teeth reflected back the light from the street-lights. Hate-hot eyes glimmered red. On silent leathery paws, the creature followed the slow-moving pair, grunting softly to itself, claws clicking on the pavement.

3

Bramley Dapple was the wizard in "A Week of Saturdays", the third story in Christy Riddell's *How to Make the Wind Blow*. He was a small wizened old man, spry as a kitten, thin as a reed, with features lined and brown as a dried fig. He wore a pair of wire-rimmed spectacles without prescription lenses that he polished incessantly and he loved to talk.

"It doesn't matter what they believe," he was saying to his guest, "so much as what *you* believe."

He paused as the brown-skinned goblin who looked after his house came in with a tray of biscuits and tea. His name was Goon, a tallish creature at three-foot-four who wore the garb of an organ grinder's monkey: striped black and yellow trousers, a red jacket with yellow trim, small black slippers, and a little green and yellow cap that pushed down an unruly mop of thin dark curly hair. Gangly limbs with a protruding tummy, puffed cheeks, a wide nose, and tiny black eyes added to his monkey-like appearance.

The wizard's guest observed Goon's entrance with a startled look which pleased Bramley to no end.

"There," he said. "Goon proves my point."

"I beg your pardon?"

"We live in a consensual reality where things exist because we want them to exist. I believe in Goon, Goon believes in Goon, and you, presented with his undeniable presence, teatray in hand, believe in Goon as well. Yet, if you were to listen to the world at large, Goon is nothing more than a figment of some fevered writer's imagination—a literary construct, an artistic representation of something that can't possibly exist in the world as we know it."

Goon gave Bramley a sour look, but the wizard's guest leaned forward, hand outstretched, and brushed the goblin's shoulder with a feather-light touch. Slowly she leaned back into the big armchair, cushions so comfortable they seemed to embrace her as she settled against them.

"So . . . anything we can imagine can exist?" she asked finally.

Goon turned his sour look on her now.

She was a student at the university where the wizard taught; third year, majoring in fine arts, and she had the look of an artist about her. There were old paint stains on her jeans and under her fingernails. Her hair was a thick tangle of brown hair, more unruly than Goon's curls. She had a smudge of a nose and thin puckering lips, workman's boots that stood by the door with a history of scuffs and stains written into their leather, thick woolen socks with a hole in the left heel, and one shirttail that had escaped the waist of her jeans. But her eyes were a pale, pale blue, clear and alert, for all the casualness of her attire.

Her name was Jilly Coppercorn.

Bramley shook his head. "It's not imagining. It's *knowing* that it exists—without one smidgen of doubt."

"Yes, but someone had to think him up for him to. . ." She hesitated as Goon's scowl deepened. "That is. . ."

Bramley continued to shake his head. "There is some semblance of order to things," he admitted, "for if the world was simply everyone's different conceptual universe mixed up together, we'd have nothing but chaos. It all relies on will, you see—to observe the changes, at any rate. Or the differences. The anomalies. Like Goon—oh, do stop scowling," he added to the goblin.

"The world as we have it," he went on to Jilly, "is here mostly because of habit. We've all agreed that certain things exist—we're taught as impressionable infants that this is a table and this is what it looks like, that's a tree out the window there, a dog looks and sounds just so. At the same time we're informed that Goon and his like don't exist, so we don't—or can't see them."

"They're not made up?" Jilly asked.

This was too much for Goon. He set the tray down and gave her leg a pinch. Jilly jumped away from him, trying to back deeper into the chair as the goblin grinned, revealing two rows of decidedly nasty-looking teeth.

"Rather impolite," Bramley said, "but I suppose you do get the point?"

Jilly nodded quickly. Still grinning, Goon set about pouring their teas.

"So," Jilly asked, "how can someone . . . how can I see things as they really are?"

"Well, it's not that simple," the wizard told her. "First you have to know what it is that you're looking for—before you can find it, you see."

Ellen closed the book and leaned back in her own chair, thinking about that, about Balloon Men, about the young man lying in her bed. To know what you were looking for. Was that why when she went out hoping to find Balloon Men, she'd come home with Reece?

She got up and went to the bedroom door to look in at him. After much protesting, he'd finally let her clean his hurts and put him to bed. Claiming to be not the least bit hungry, he'd polished off a whole tin of soup and the better part of the loaf of sourdough bread that she had just bought that afternoon. Then, of course, he wasn't tired at all and promptly fell asleep the moment his head touched the pillow.

She shook her head, looking at him now. His rainbow Mohawk made it look as though she'd brought some hybrid creature into her home—part rooster, part boy, it lay in her bed snoring softly, hardly real. But definitely not a Balloon Man, she thought, looking at his thin torso under the sheets.

About to turn away, something at the window caught her eye. Frozen in place, she saw a dog-like face peering back at her from the other side of the pane—which was patently impossible since the bedroom was on the second floor and there was nothing to stand on outside that window. But impossible or not, that dog-like face with its coal-red eyes and a fierce grin of glimmering teeth was there all the same.

She stared at it, feeling sick as the moments ticked by. Hunger burned in those eyes. Anger. Unbridled hate. She couldn't move, not until it finally disappeared—sliding from sight, physically escaping rather than vanishing the way a hallucination should.

She leaned weakly against the doorjamb, a faint buzzing in her head. Not until she'd caught her breath did she go to the window, but of course there was nothing there. Consensual reality, Christy's wizard had called it. Things that exist because we want them to exist. But she knew that not even in a nightmare would she consider giving life to that monstrous head she'd seen staring back in at her from the night beyond her window.

Her gaze went to the sleeping boy in her bed. All that anger burning up inside him. Had she caught a glimpse of something that *he'd* given life to?

Ellen, she told herself as she backed out of the room, you're making entirely too much out of nothing. Except something had certainly seemed to be there. There was absolutely no question in her mind that *something* had been out there.

In the living room she looked down at Christy's book. Bramley Dapple's words skittered through her mind, chased by a feeling of . . . of strangeness that she couldn't shake. The wind, the night, finding Reece in that doorway. And now that thing in the window.

She went and poured herself a brandy before making her bed on the sofa, studiously avoiding looking at the windows. She knew she was being silly—she had to have imagined it—but there was a feeling in the air tonight, a sense of being on the edge of something vast and grey. One false step, and she'd plunge down into it. A void. A nightmare.

It took a second brandy before she fell asleep.

Outside, Reece's booger snuffled around the walls of the house, crawling up the side of the building from time to time to peer into this or that window. Something kept it from entering—some disturbance in the air that was like a wind, but not a wind at the same time. When it finally retreated, it was with the knowledge in what passed for its mind that time itself was the key. Hours and minutes would unlock whatever kept it presently at bay.

Barracuda teeth gleamed as the creature grinned. It could wait. Not long, but it could wait.

4

Ellen woke the next morning, stiff from a night spent on the sofa, and wondered what in God's name had possessed her to bring Reece home. Though on re-flection, she realized, the whole night had proceeded with a certain surreal quality of which Reece had only been a small part. Re-reading Christy's book. That hor-rific face at the window. And the Balloon Men—she hadn't thought of them in years.

Swinging her feet to the floor, she went out onto her balcony. There was a light fog hazing the air. Boogie-boarders were riding the waves close by the pier—only a handful of them now, but in an hour or so their numbers would have multiplied beyond count. Raking machines were cleaning the beach, their dull roar vying with the pounding of the tide. Men with metal detectors were patiently sifting through the debris the machines left behind before the trucks came to haul it away. Near the tide's edge a man was jogging backwards across the sand, sharply silhouetted against the ocean.

Nothing out of the ordinary. But returning inside she couldn't shake the feeling that there was someone in her head, something flying dark-winged across her inner terrain like a crow. When she went to wash up, she found its crow eyes staring back at her from the mirror. Wild eyes.

Shivering, she finished up quickly. But by the time Reece woke she was sitting outside on the balcony in a sweatshirt and shorts, nursing a mug of coffee. The odd feeling of being possessed had mostly gone away and the night just past took on the fading quality of half-remembered dreams.

She looked up at his appearance, smiling at the way a night's sleep had rearranged the lizard crest fringes of his Mohawk. Some of it was pressed flat against his skull. Elsewhere, mutlicoloured tufts stood up at bizarre angles. His mouth was a sullen slash in a field of short beard stubble, but his eyes still had a sleepy look to them, softening his features.

"You do this a lot?" he asked, slouching into the other wicker chair on the balcony.

"What? Drink coffee in the morning?"

"Pick up strays."

"You looked like you needed help."

Reece nodded. "Right. We're all brothers and sisters on starship earth. I kinda figured you for a bleeding heart."

His harsh tone soured Ellen's humour. She felt the something that had watched her from the bathroom mirror flutter inside her and her thoughts returned to the previous night. Christy's wizard talking. *Things exist because we want them to exist.*

"After you fell asleep," she said, "I thought I saw something peering in through the bedroom window. . ."

Her voice trailed off when she realized that she didn't quite know where she was going with that line of thought. But Reece sat up from his slouch, suddenly alert.

"What kind of something?" he asked.

Ellen tried to laugh it off. "A monster," she said with a smile. "Red-eyed and all teeth." She shrugged. "I was just having one of those nights."

"You *saw* it?" Reece demanded sharply enough to make Ellen sit up straighter as well.

"Well, I thought I saw something, but it was patently impossible so. . ." Again her voice trailed off. Reece had sunk back into his chair and was staring off towards the ocean. "What . . . what was it?" Ellen asked.

"I call it booger," he replied. "I don't know what the hell it is, but it's been following me ever since I took off from my parents place. . ."

The stories in Christy's book weren't all charming. There was one near the end called "Raw Eggs" about a man who had a *Ghostbusters*-like creature living in his fridge that fed on raw eggs. It pierced the shells with a needle-fine tooth, then sucked out the contents, leaving rows of empty eggshells behind. When the man got tired of replacing his eggs, the creature crawled out of the fridge one night, driven forth by hunger, and fed on the eyes of the man's family.

The man had always had a fear of going blind. He died at the end of the story, and the creature moved on to another household, more hungry than ever. . .

Reece laid aside Christy Riddell's book and went looking for Ellen. He found her sitting on the beach, a big, loose T-shirt covering her bikini, her bare legs tucked under her. She was staring out to sea, past the waves breaking on the shore, past the swimmers, body-surfers and kids riding their boogie-boards, past the oil rigs to the horizon hidden in a haze in the far-off distance. He got a lot of weird stares as he scuffed his way across the sand to finally sit down beside her.

"They're just stories in that book, right?" he said finally.

"You tell me."

"Look. The booger it's—Christ, I don't know what it is. But it can't be real."

Ellen shrugged. "I was up getting some milk at John's earlier," she said, "and I overheard a couple of kids talking about some friends of theirs. Seems they were having some fun in the parking lot last night with a punker when something came at them from under the pier and tore off part of their bumper."

"Yeah, but—"

Ellen turned from the distant view to look at him. Her eyes held endless vistas in them and she felt the flutter of wings in her mind.

"I want to know how you did it," she said. "How you brought it to life."

"Look, lady. I don't—"

"It doesn't have to be a horror," she said fiercely. "It can be something good, too." She thought of the gnome that lived under the pier in Christy's story and her own Balloon Men. "I want to be able to see them again."

Their gazes locked. Reece saw a darkness behind Ellen's clear grey eyes, some wildness that reminded him of his booger in its intensity.

"I'd tell you if I knew," he said finally.

Ellen continued to study him, then slowly turned to look back across the waves. "Will it come to you to-night?" she asked.

"I don't kn—" Reece began, but Ellen turned to him again. At the look in her eyes, he nodded. "Yeah," he said then. "I guess it will."

"I want to be there when it does," she said.

Because if it was real, then it could all be real. If she could see the booger, if she could understand what animated it, if she could learn to really *see* and, as Christy's wizard had taught Jilly Coppercorn, *know* what she was looking for herself, then she could bring her own touch of wonder into the world. Her own magic.

She gripped Reece's arm. "Promise me you won't take off until I've had a chance to see it."

She had to be weirded-out, Reece thought. She didn't have the same kind of screws loose that his parents did, but she was gone all the same. Only, that book she'd had him read . . . it made a weird kind of sense. If you were going to accept that kind of shit as being possible, it might just work the way that book said it did. Weird, yeah. But when he thought of the booger itself. . .

"Promise me," she said.

He disengaged her fingers from his arm. "Sure," he said. "I got nowhere to go anyway."

5

They ate at The Green Pepper that night, a Mexican restaurant on Main Street. Reece studied his companion across the table, re-evaluating his earlier impressions of her. Her hair was up in a loose bun now and she wore a silky cream-coloured blouse above a slim dark skirt. Mentally she was definitely a bit weird, but not a burn-out like his parents. She looked like the kind of custom-er who shopped in the trendy galleries and boutiques on Melrose Avenue where his old lady worked, back home in West Hollywood. Half the people in the restau-rant were probably wondering what the hell she was doing sitting here with a scuzz like him.

Ellen looked up and caught his gaze. A smile touched her lips. "The cook must be in a good mood," she said.

"What do you mean?"

"Well, I've heard that the worse the mood he's in, the hotter he makes his sauces."

Reece tried to give her back a smile, but his heart wasn't in it. He wanted a beer, but they wouldn't serve him here because he was underage. He found himself wishing Ellen wasn't so much older than him, that he didn't look like such a freak sitting here with her. For the first time since he'd done his hair, he was embar-rassed about the way he looked. He wanted to enjoy just sitting here with her instead of knowing that every-one was looking at him like he was some kind of geek.

"You okay?" Ellen asked.

"Yeah. Sure. Great food."

He pushed the remainder of his rice around on the plate with his fork. Yeah, he had no problems. Just no place to go, no place to fit in. Body aching from last night's beating. Woman sitting there across from him, looking tasty, but she was too old for him and there was something in her eyes that scared him a little. Not to mention a nightmare booger dogging his footsteps. Sure. Things were just rocking, mama.

He stole another glance at her, but she was looking away, out to the darkening street, wine glass raised to her mouth.

"That book your friend wrote," he said.

Her gaze shifted to his face and she put her glass down.

"It doesn't have anything like my booger in it," Reece continued. "I mean it's got some ugly stuff, but nothing just like the booger."

"No," Ellen replied. "But it's got to work the same way. We can see it because we believe it's there."

"So was it always there and we're just aware of it now? Or does it exist *because* we believe in it? Is it something that came out of us—out of me?"

"Like Uncle Dobbin's birds, you mean?"

Reece nodded, unaware of the flutter of dark wings that Ellen felt stir inside her.

"I don't know," she said softly.

"Uncle Dobbin's Parrot Fair" was the last story in Christy Riddell's book, the title coming from the name of the pet shop that Timothy James Dobbin owned in Santa Ana. It was a gathering place for every kind of bird, tame as well as wild. There were finches in cages and parrots with the run of the shop, not to mention everything from sparrows to crows and gulls crowding around outside.

In the story, T.J. Dobbin was a retired sailor with an interest in nineteenth century poets, an old bearded tar with grizzled red hair and beetling brows who wore baggy blue cotton trousers and a white T-shirt as he worked in his store, cleaning the bird cages, feeding the parrakeets, teaching the parrots words. Everybody called him Uncle Dobbin.

He had a sixteen-year-old assistant named Nori Wert who helped out on weekends. She had short blonde hair and a deep tan that she started working on as soon as school was out. To set it off she invariably wore white shorts and a tanktop. The only thing she liked better than the beach were the birds in Uncle Dobbin's shop, and that was because she knew their secret.

She didn't find out about them right away. It took a year or so of coming in and hanging around the shop and then another three weekends of working there before she finally approached Uncle Dobbin with what had been bothering her.

"I've been wondering," she said as she sat down on the edge of his cluttered desk at the back of the store. She fingered the world globe beside the blotter and gave it a desultory spin.

Uncle Dobbin raised his brow questioningly and continued to fill his pipe.

"It's the birds," she said. "We never sell any—at least not since I've started working here. People come in and they look around, but no one asks the price of anything, no one ever buys anything. I guess you could do most of your business during the week, but then why did you hire me?"

Uncle Dobbin looked down into the bowl of his pipe to make sure the tobacco was tamped properly. "Because you like birds," he said before he lit a match.

Smoke wreathed up towards the ceiling. A bright green parrot gave a squawk from where it was roosting nearby and turned its back on them.

"But you don't sell any of them, do you?" Being curious, she'd poked through his file cabinet to look at invoices and sales receipts to find that all he ever bought was birdfood and cages and the like, and he never sold a thing. At least no sales were recorded.

"Can't sell them."

"Why not?"

"They're not mine to sell."

Nori sighed. "Then whose are they?"

"Better you should ask what are they."

"Okay," Nori said, giving him an odd look. "I'll bite. What are they?"

"Magic."

Nori studied him for a moment and he returned her gaze steadily, giving no indication that he was teasing her. He puffed on his pipe, a serious look in his eyes, then took the pipe stem from his mouth. Setting the pipe carefully on the desk so that it wouldn't tip over, he leaned forward in his chair.

"People have magic," he said, "but most of them don't want it, or don't believe in it, or did once, but then forgot. So I take that magic and make it into birds until they want it back, or someone else can use it."

"Magic."

"That's right."

"Not birds."

Uncle Dobbin nodded.

"That's crazy," Nori said.

"Is it?"

He got up stiffly from his chair and stood in front of her with his hands outstretched towards her chest. Nori shrank back from him, figuring he'd flaked out and was going to cop a quick feel now, but his hands paused just a few inches from her breasts. She felt a sudden pain inside—like a stitch in her side from running too hard, only it was deep in her chest. Right in her lungs. She looked down, eyes widening as a beak appeared poking out of her chest, followed by a parrot's head, its body and wings.

It was like one of the holograms at the Haunted House in Disneyland, for she could see right through it, then it grew solid once it was fully emerged. The pain stopped as the bird fluttered free, but she felt an empty aching inside. Uncle Dobbin caught the bird, and soothed it with a practised touch, before letting it fly free. Numbly, Nori watched it wing across the store and settle down near the front window where it began to preen its feathers. The sense of loss inside grew stronger.

"That . . . it was in me . . . I . . ."

Uncle Dobbin made his way back to his chair and sat down, picking up his pipe once more.

"Magic," he said before he lit it.

"My . . . my magic. . . ?"

Uncle Dobbin nodded. "But not anymore. You didn't believe."

"But I didn't know!" she wailed.

"You got to earn it back now," Uncle Dobbin told her. "The side cages need cleaning."

Nori pressed her hands against her chest, then wrapped her arms around herself in a tight hug as though that would somehow ease the empty feeling inside her.

"E-earn it?" she said in a small voice, her gaze going from his face to the parrot that had come out of her chest and was now sitting by the front window. "By . . . by working here?"

Uncle Dobbin shook his head. "You already work here and I pay you for that, don't I?"

"But then how. . . ?"

"You've got to earn its trust. You've got to learn to believe in it again."

Ellen shook her head softly. Learn to believe, she thought. I've always believed. But maybe never hard enough. She glanced at her companion, then out to the street. It was almost completely dark now.

"Let's go walk on the beach," she said.

Reece nodded, following her outside after she'd paid the bill. The lemony smell of eucalyptus trees was strong in the air for a moment, then the stronger scent of the ocean winds stole it away.

6

They had the beach to themselves, though the pier was busy with strollers and people fishing. At the beach end of the long wooden structure, kids were hanging out, fooling around with bikes and skateboards. The soft boom of the tide drowned out the music of their ghetto-blasters. The wind was cool with a salt tang as it came in from over the waves. In the distance, the oil rigs were lit up like Christmas trees.

Ellen took off her shoes. Carrying them in her tote bag, she walked in the wet sand by the water's edge. A raised lip of the beach hid the shorefront houses from their view as they walked south to the rocky spit that marked the beginning of the Naval Weapons Station.

"It's nice out here," Reece said finally. They hadn't spoken since leaving the restaurant.

Ellen nodded. "A lot different from L.A."

"Two different worlds."

Ellen gave him a considering glance. Ever since this afternoon, the sullen tone had left his voice. She listened now as he spoke of his parents and how he couldn't find a place for himself either in their world, nor that of his peers.

"You're pretty down on the sixties," she said when he was done.

Reece shrugged. He was barefoot now, too, the waves coming up to lick the bottom of his jeans where the two of them stood at the water's edge.

"They had some good ideas—people like my parents," he said, "but the way they want things to go . . . that only works if everyone agrees to live that way."

"That doesn't invalidate the things they believe in."

"No. But what we've got to deal with is the real world and you've got to take what you need if you want to survive in it."

Ellen sighed. "I suppose."

She looked back across the beach, but they were still alone. No one else out for a late walk across the sand. No booger. No Balloon Men. But something fluttered inside her, dark-winged. A longing as plain as what she heard in Reece's voice, though she was looking for magic and he was just looking for a way to fit in.

Hefting her tote bag, she tossed it onto the sand, out of the waves' reach. Reece gave her a curious look, then averted his gaze as she stepped out of her skirt.

"It's okay," she said, amused at his sudden sense of propriety. "I'm wearing my swimsuit."

By the time he turned back, her blouse and skirt had joined her tote bag on the beach and she was shaking loose her hair.

"Coming in?" she asked.

Reece simply stood and watched the sway of her hips as she headed for the water. Her swimsuit was white. In the poor light it was as though she wasn't wearing anything—the swimsuit looking like untanned skin. She dove cleanly into a wave, head bobbing up pale in the dark water when she surfaced.

"C'mon!" she called to him. "The water's fine, once you get in."

Reece hesitated. He'd wanted to go in this afternoon, but hadn't had the nerve to bare his white skinny limbs in front of a beachful of serious tanners. Well, there was no one to see him now, he thought as he stripped down to his underwear.

The water hit him like a cold fist when he dove in after her and he came up gasping with shock. His body tingled, every pore stung alert. Ellen drifted further out, riding the waves easily. As he waded out to join her, a swell rose up and tumbled him back to shore in a spill of floundering limbs that scraped him against the sand.

"Either go under or over them," Ellen advised him as he started back out.

He wasn't much of a swimmer, but the water wasn't too deep except when a big wave came. He went under the next one and came up spluttering, but pleased with himself for not getting thrown up against the beach again.

"I love swimming at night," Ellen said as they drifted together.

Reece nodded. The water was surprisingly warm, too, once you were in it. You could lose all sense of time out here, just floating with the swells.

"You do this a lot?" he asked.

Ellen shook her head. "It's not that good an idea to do this alone. If the undertow got you, it'd pull you right out and no one would know."

Reece laid his head back in the water and looked up at the sky. Though they were less than an hour by the freeway out of downtown L.A., the sky seemed completely different here. It didn't seem to have that glow from God knows how many millions of lights. The stars seemed closer here, or maybe it was that the sky seemed deeper.

He glanced over at Ellen. Their reason for being out here was forgotten. He wished he had the nerve to just sort of sidle up to her and put his arms around her, hold her close. She'd feel all slippery, but she'd feel good.

He paddled a little bit towards her, riding a swell up and then down again. The wave turned him slightly away from her. When he glanced back, he saw her staring wide-eyed at the shore. His gaze followed hers and then that cold he'd felt when he first entered the water returned in a numbing rush.

The booger was here.

It came snuffling over a rise in the beach, a squat dark shadow in the sand, greasy and slick as it beelined for their clothing. When it reached Ellen's tote bag, it buried its face in her skirt and blouse, then proceeded to rip them to shreds. Ellen's finger caught his arm in a frightened grip. A wave came up, lifting his feet from the bottom. He kicked out frantically, afraid he was going to drown with her holding on to him like that, but the wave tossed them both in towards the shore.

The booger looked up, baring its barracuda teeth. The red coals of its eyes burned right into them both, pinning them there on the wet sand where the wave had left them. Leaving the ruin of Ellen's belongings in torn shreds, it moved slowly towards them.

"Re-Reece," Ellen said. She was pressed close to him, shivering.

Reece didn't have the time to appreciate the contact of her skin against his. He wanted to say, this is what you were looking for, lady, but things weren't so cut and dried now. Ellen wasn't some nameless cipher anymore—just a part of a crowd that he could sneer at—and she wasn't just something he had the hots for either. She was a person, just like him. An individual. Someone he could actually relate to.

"Can—can't you stop it?" Ellen cried.

The booger was getting close now. Its sewer reek was strong enough to drown out the salty tang of the ocean. It was like something had died there on the beach and was now getting up and coming for them.

Stop it? Reece thought. Maybe the thing had been created out of his frustrated anger, the way Ellen's friend made out it could happen in that book of his, but Reece knew as sure as shit that he didn't control the booger.

Another wave came down upon them and Reece pushed at the sand so that it pulled them partway out from the shore on its way back out. Getting to his knees in the rimy water, he got in front of Ellen so that he was between her and the booger. Could the sucker swim?

The booger hesitated at the water's edge. It lifted its paws fastidiously from the wet sand like a cat crossing a damp lawn and relief went through Reece. When another wave came in, the booger backstepped quickly out of its reach.

Ellen was leaning against him, face near his as she peered over his shoulder.

"It can't handle the water," Reece said. He turned his face to hers when she didn't say anything. Her clear eyes were open wide, gaze fixed on the booger. "Ellen. . . ?" he began.

"I can't believe that it's really there," she said finally in a small voice.

"But you're the one—you said. . ." He drew a little away from her so that he could see her better.

"I know what I said," Ellen replied. She hugged herself, trembling at the stir of dark wings inside her. "It's just . . . I *wanted* to believe, but . . . wanting to and having it be real. . ." There was a pressure in the center of her chest now, like something inside pushing to get out. "I. . ."

The pain lanced sharp and sudden. She heard

114

Reece gasp. Looking down, she saw what he had seen, a bird's head poking gossamer from between her breasts. It was a dark smudge against the white of her swimsuit, not one of Uncle Dobbin's parrots, but a crow's head, with eyes like the pair she'd seen looking back at her from the mirror. Her own magic, leaving her because she didn't believe. Because she couldn't believe, but—

It didn't make sense. She'd always believed. And now, with Reece's booger standing there on the shore, how could she help *but* believe?

The booger howled then, as though to underscore her thoughts. She looked to the shore and saw it stepping into the waves, crying out at the pain of the salt water on its flesh, but determined to get at them. To get at her. Reece's magic, given life. While her own magic. . . She pressed at the half-formed crow coming from her chest, trying to force it back in.

"I believe, I believe," she muttered through clenched teeth. But just like Uncle Dobbin's assistant in Christy's story, she could feel that swelling ache of loss rise up in her. She turned despairing eyes to Reece.

She didn't need a light to see the horror in his eyes—horror at the booger's approach, at the crow's head sticking out of her chest. But he didn't draw away from her. Instead, he reached out and caught hold of her shoulders.

"Stop fighting it!" he cried.

"But—"

He shot a glance shoreward. They were bracing themselves against the waves, but a large swell had just caught the booger and sent it howling back to shore in a tumble of limbs.

"It was your needing proof," he said. "Your needing to see the booger, to know that it's real—that's what's making you lose it. Stop trying so hard."

"I. . ."

But she knew he was right. She pulled free of him and looked towards the shore where the booger was struggling to its feet. The creature made rattling sounds deep in its throat as it started out for them again. It was hard, hard to do, but she let her hands fall free. The pain in her chest was a fire, the aching loss building to a crescendo. But she closed herself to it, closed her eyes, willed herself to stand relaxed.

Instead of fighting, she remembered. Balloon Men spinning down the beach. Christy's gnome, riding his pig along the pier. Bramley Dapple's advice. Goon pinching Jilly Coppercorn's leg. The thing that fed on eggs and eyeballs and, yes, Reece's booger too. Uncle Dobbin and his parrots and Nori Wert watching her magic fly free. And always the Balloon Men, tumbling end-over-end, across the beach, or down the alleyway behind her house. . .

And the pain eased. The ache loosened, faded.

"Jesus," she heard Reece say softly.

She opened her eyes and looked to where he was looking. The booger had turned from the sea and was fleeing as a crowd of Balloon Men came bouncing down the shore, great round roly-poly shapes, turning end-over-end, laughing and giggling, a chorus of small deep voices. There was salt in her eyes and it wasn't from the ocean's brine. Her tears ran down her cheeks and she felt herself grinning like a fool.

The Balloon Men chased Reece's booger up one end of the beach and then back the other way until the creature finally made a stand. Howling it waited for them to come, but before the first bouncing round shape reached it, the booger began to fade away.

Ellen turned to Reece and knew he had tears in his own eyes, but the good feeling was too strong for him to do anything but grin right back at her. The booger had died with the last of his anger. She reached out a hand to him and he took it in one of his own. Joined so, they made their way to the shore where they were surrounded by riotous Balloon Men until the bouncing shapes finally faded and then there were just the two of them standing there.

Ellen's heart beat fast. When Reece let go her hand, she touched her chest and felt a stir of dark wings inside her, only they were settling in now, no longer striving to fly free. The wind came in from the ocean still, but it wasn't the same wind that the Balloon Men rode.

"I guess it's not all bullshit," Reece said softly.

Ellen glanced at him.

He smiled as he explained. "Helping each other—getting along instead of fighting. Feels kind of good, you know?"

Ellen nodded. Her hand fell from her chest as the dark wings finally stilled.

"Your friend's story didn't say anything about crows," Reece said.

"Maybe we've all got different birds inside—different magics." She looked out across the waves to where the oil rigs lit the horizon.

"There's a flock of wild parrots up around Santa Ana," Reece said.

"I've heard there's one up around San Pedro, too."

"Do you think. . . ?" Reece began, but he let his words trail off. The waves came in and wet their feet.

"I don't know," Ellen said. She looked over at her shredded clothes. "Come on. Let's get back to my place and warm up."

Reece laid his jacket over her shoulders. He put on his T-shirt and jeans, then helped her gather up what was left of her belongings.

"I didn't mean for this to happen," he said, bundling up the torn blouse and skirt. He looked up to where she was standing over him. "But I couldn't control the booger."

"Maybe we're not supposed to."

"But something like the booger. . ."

She gave his Mohawk a friendly ruffle. "I think it just means that we've got be careful about what kind of vibes we put out."

Reece grimaced at her use of the word, but he nodded.

"It's either that," Ellen added, "or we let the magic fly free."

The same feathery stirring of wings that she felt moved in Reece. They both knew that that was something neither of them was likely to give up.

In Uncle Dobbin's Parrot Fair, Nori Wert turned away from the pair of cages that she'd been making ready.

"I guess we won't be needing these," she said.

Uncle Dobbin looked up from a slim collection of Victorian poetry and nodded. "You're learning fast," he said. He stuck the stem of his pipe in his mouth and fished about in his pocket for a match. "Maybe there's hope for you yet."

Nori felt her own magic stir inside her, back where it should be, but she didn't say anything to him in case she had to go away, now that the lesson was learned. She was too happy here. Next to catching some rays, there wasn't anywhere she'd rather be.

INVISIBLE BOY

CLIFF BURNS

I hate it when she ties into me in front of the kid. He just stands there all bug-eyed while she reams me out.

"I won't—WILL NOT—have you smoking that shit in my house in front of my son. Are you listening to me? Do . . . you . . . understand? You're not only screwing up your life and my life—what about his? There are other people around here, y'know. What's he supposed to think?" She points at Jeff but he just hangs his head.

"What's the big deal, Sal? It's only a joint for Chrissake. What about all the times he's seen you so drunk you don't even recognize him? I don't hear you talking about that."

"Don't you dare—" she starts to say.

"I'm just telling it like it is," I fire back.

"—insult me in front of my son. Don't you dare do that again, Ray. You'll be making the biggest mistake of your life." She puts her hand on Jeff's head; he looks really surprised that she's actually touching him.

"Oh, I see. Now he's your son. What about all those

long windy speeches about how we're one big, happy family?"

"Ted would never have—"

And then I really blow my stack. "Ted, Ted, Ted. That fucker practically permeates this place. You still got pictures of him hanging up, you still call him at least once a month, rain or shine. But, Hell, that's fine with me. I love helping Ma Bell out with a few marathon long distance calls. Jesus Christ, Sally, you've been separated for five years . . . and divorced for three. When are you gonna cut the cord? The guy's a jerk." I see Jeff flinch when I say it but it's said so I keep right on plugging. "He doesn't want to help support Jeff, doesn't even want any pictures of him, never sends any presents at Christmas and here I am busting my hump to keep the fridge filled week in and week out and not getting any credit—"

"Jeff, go to your room," Sally says, cold as ice.

"He tried to go to his room!" I bellow and Jeff twitches again. "But you decided to use him as a prop in this little show you're putting on."

She gives me THE LOOK. Yup, I'll be sleeping on the couch again tonight. Shouldn't have let the dope do the talking.

God, I feel bad for that kid. I go out of my way to avoid getting into scraps with Sally but she just keeps picking at me and picking at me like I'm an itchy scab. And every time we fight she manages to get a few good ones in under the belt. Like that crack about Ted.

The dope was nothing. Hey, we've shared a joint lots of nights after Jeff's gone to bed. She really likes the stuff. Except that every time she gets high she gets these wild cravings and we have to order out for pizza or Chinese food.

I got home from work and neither her or Jeff was around so I decided to roll myself a little number, just to help me unwind. I was just finishing it off, listening to some BTO on the radio (cranked wayyyyy up) when her and Jeff walked in.

WHAM!

She'd had a rough day too and seeing me standing there with a roach burning between my fingers was enough to set her off. You should never sneeze in avalanche country, right?

On the way to his bedroom Jeff digs some comic books out of one of the shopping bags they carried in. As he shuffles down the hall his nose is already buried in the latest issue of Spiderman. Poor little bugger. Spidey's probably his best friend in the world. I'd like to go in and sit on the end of his bed and talk to him, maybe read through his comics with him—some of 'em are pretty good, y'know—but Sally starts yipping at me and I yap back and by the time we wear ourselves out it's after nine.

As soon as there's a break in the action I go and look in on Jeff. He's got all of his sheets and blankets wadded up in the middle of his bed. He's under that pile somewhere; I can hear him singing away, maybe plugged into his Walkman. I tell him good night but I don't think he hears me. I turn out the light and leave him to his soundproof sanctuary.

Jeez, I wonder if Sal's seen this latest trick. I mean, I'm thinking this can't be a good sign. The kid is pulling back from us, maybe developing some kind of, you know, problem because of—of what goes on around here. That isn't right. What we're doing to that boy isn't right.

I wish I could spend more time with him. I work during the week and on the weekends it's Sally I have to pay attention to or I'm in one deep pile of doo-doo, as my good friend George Bush would say. Now and then we're alone together. I'll take him along when I go to the store or I'll swing by and pick him up after school. He barely says a word the whole time we're together. Just says "yes" and "no" and shrugs a lot. I wonder what he thinks about me living at the house, sleeping in the same bed as her. Even at his age kids know that grown-ups aren't playing checkers in there.

I keep buying him presents. I know it looks bad, like I'm trying to buy his love but I can't help myself. So every once in awhile we have to act out this ritual: I push a model or some space toy across the table to him and try to decipher his mumbles as he picks it up and looks it over. I know he likes my presents, I see him playing with them all the time. I think he's afraid to show too much enthusiasm because then she'll have something to use against him. She's constantly threatening to take his toys away if he's not good. And the thing is HE IS GOOD. Too damn good. He's like a well-trained pet. He fetches when she wants him to and speaks when she wants him to but most of the time it's like she just wants him to play dead.

When I come back into the kitchen everything's pretty well back to normal. Whatever that means. I ask Sally what the plans are for the weekend and get a funny look.

"Same as always," she says. Like it's final.

Every weekend it's the same thing. We buy groceries, pick up some booze and a couple of videos and stay cooped up like parakeets until Monday. I've tried to get her to go to the beach or the park at least. I tell her we can roast some wienies, drink some beer, chuck the frisbee around, have ourselves a great time. Y'know, just like a real family. She doesn't want the hassle of packing a lunch and hates the long, hot drive and the dirty, smelly bathrooms and the bugs and the people and the loud music . . . so we end up sitting on our butts doing nothing.

I wonder if she'd let Jeff and me go off by ourselves next year, maybe take a week and go camping. I know she hates the idea of being alone. The woman is incapable of entertaining herself. She says that's what men are for. One of these days when I'm good and drunk I'm gonna ask her: Wassa matter? Did Ted run out of jokes?

She'll cut me off for a whole fucking year for it but it'll be worth it. Every time she brings that guy up it just galls me. Her first love. Her high school sweetheart. The man she gave her virginity to. What a crock. I think he's done more damage to Jeff than anybody. How would I have felt if my old man had turned his back on me? Like I was worthless. And I'm sure that's exactly how he feels.

Saturday morning Jeff and I are watching "Tom and Jerry" and yukking it up and she comes storming in and starts yelling at him 'cause his room's a mess. I mean, what kid's isn't, right? But she just shits on him, calls him lazy and stupid and irresponsible. He's cowering on the floor like a sick puppy. Me, stupid ass that I am, I just sit there like a bump on a log and say nothing. He shuts the TV off and goes meekly to his room. Sally sits at the table drinking coffee and smoking, glaring at me, daring me to say something. I wait until she goes to take her shower then I go in to lend Jeff a hand—but he's already got everything cleaned up and gone outside.

I can hear Sally singing in the bathroom; she sounds as happy as a lark. As I walk past she comes out and gives me a big kiss and makes her way singing and dancing to the kitchen to start breakfast. When it's ready I call out the back door to Jeff—

And here he comes, walking out of his bedroom like some kind of zombie and sitting down at the table. His face looks puffy and he's pale and all sweaty. I want to say something about him playing hide-and-seek on me but he's acting so weird that I skip that and instead I lean over and ask him if he's feeling okay—and he nearly jumps out of his skin.

"Uncle Ray asked you a question, Jeff," Sally prods him.

"Everything all right?" I'm smiling at him, trying to keep it nice and friendly but I can see his bottom lip start trembling and I know, I know that if I keep pushing it he's going to start blubbering. So I change the subject, start telling Sally about something that happened at work. But I keep an eye on him all through breakfast. Something is definitely bugging him. I can tell he's not hungry but he's forcing himself to eat because if he doesn't she'll get p.o.'d and not let him have any dinner or supper. He chews carefully because she hates noisy eaters.

When he's finished he wipes his mouth with a napkin, pushes his chair back, puts his plate in the sink. Then he asks to be excused, puts on his jacket and shoes and goes outside. Don't ask me what he does.

"What do you think about going to see a movie tonight?" I ask, really neutral.

"Is there anything good in town?" Already she's frowning. She senses that her monotonous routine is about to be disrupted.

"Yeah, *Dumbo* is playing at the Coronet. Man, I loved that show when I was a kid."

"Don't be stupid," she snaps. "I don't want to see that crap."

"I thought Jeff would really get a kick out of—"

"It's another stupid cartoon!" She's getting steamed and there's nothing I can do about it. "That's all he ever watches. When is he supposed to get a dose of reality?"

"I think the trouble is that he gets too much reality for his own good—especially around here." I could bite my tongue off as I say it.

"YOU GO TO HELL!" She yells and tramps off to the bedroom and makes a lot of noise.

That night there are no movies, not even on video. When Jeff asks about watching TV he's sent to his room without any supper. When I try to veto that she looks at me all calm and cool and tells me to go fuck myself.

Jeff trudges off. As he passes me on his way to his room I try to catch his eye. But it's like he's looking right through me. I can see that he's scared, man, more scared than a kid has a right to be.

Then I start thinking about getting out, just saying "screw this" and taking off. It's so tempting. To get away from this crazy woman, take up with my riff-raff friends again, get drunk, get stoned, do anything I want—

—and then I remember the times when she's soft, when she fixes herself up and talks sensibly and laughs and gives me sexy looks. I love that person more than anything. More than I love myself. And there's Jeff. Some part of me deep and secret connects with that boy. I think we'll be close someday, him and me. I'm almost positive about that.

I stay.

I must be crazy but I always end up staying.

Later on I go to the john and when I finish up in there I wander a little further down the hall, knock on Jeff's door, stick my head inside.

The room is empty.

And this time I make sure: I check the closet and even take a quick peek under the bed.

I'm about to close the door, I'm wondering where he could've gone—and then I hear this little sigh. I lean into the room again but there's no one there. So, okay, I didn't hear a little sigh.

I close the door and start back down the hallway—

The bedroom door opens behind me.

And I just freeze, like, in mid-step. I turn around really slow. The doorway is empty and I think so, okay, I didn't close it all the way and it popped open again. No big deal. I reach out to close the door and I hear a voice, a voice as small as a mouse coming from one corner of the room.

". . . please . . . Uncle Ray . . . please. . ."

"Jeff?" I walk toward the voice, trying to pin down where it's coming from.

". . . help me, please . . . I can't make it back!"

My foot bumps against a small leg that isn't there. As I kneel a boy-sized hand slips inside mine, gripping my fingers tightly.

"Please," he whimpers, "I—I'm scared, Uncle Ray . . . please . . . please . . . help me. . ."

"Okay," I promise and the invisible boy comes to me and I hold him close.

A
NICHE

PETER WATTS

When the lights go out in Beebe Station, you can hear the metal groan.

Lenie Clarke lies on her bunk, listening. Overhead, past pipes and wires and eggshell plating, three kilometres of black ocean try to crush her. She feels the Rift underneath, tearing open the seabed with strength enough to move a continent. She lies there in that fragile refuge, and she hears Beebe's armour shifting by microns, hears its seams creak not quite below the threshold of human hearing. God is a sadist on the Juan de Fuca Rift, and His name is Physics.

How did they talk me into this? she wonders. *Why did I come down here?* But she already knows the answer.

She hears Ballard moving out in the corridor. Clarke envies Ballard. Ballard never screws up, always seems to have her life under control. She almost seems *happy* down here.

Clarke rolls off her bunk and fumbles for a switch. Her cubby floods with dismal light. Pipes and access panels crowd the wall beside her; aesthetics run a distant second to functionality when you're three thousand metres down. She turns and catches sight of a slick black amphibian in the bulkhead mirror.

It still happens, occasionally. She can sometimes forget what they've done to her.

It takes a conscious effort to feel the machines lurking where her left lung used to be. She is so acclimated to the chronic ache in her chest, to that subtle inertia of plastic and metal as she moves, that she is scarcely aware of them any more. So she can still feel the memory of what it was to be fully human, and mistake that ghost for honest sensation.

Such respites never last. There are mirrors everywhere in Beebe; they're supposed to increase the apparent size of one's personal space. Sometimes Clarke shuts her eyes to hide from the reflections forever being thrown back at her. It doesn't help. She clenches her lids and feels the corneal caps beneath them, covering her eyes like smooth white cataracts.

She climbs out of her cubby and moves along the corridor to the lounge. Ballard is waiting there, dressed in a diveskin and the usual air of confidence.

Ballard stands up. "Ready to go?"

"You're in charge," Clarke says.

"Only on paper." Ballard smiles. "As far as I'm concerned, Lenie, we're equals." After two days on the rift Clarke is still surprised by the frequency with which Ballard smiles. Ballard smiles at the slightest provocation. It doesn't always seem real.

Something hits Beebe from the outside.

Ballard's smile falters. They hear it again; a wet, muffled thud through the station's titanium skin.

"It takes a while to get used to," Ballard says, "doesn't it?"

And again.

"I mean, that sounds *big*. . ."

"Maybe we should turn the lights off," Clarke

suggests. She knows they won't. Beebe's exterior flood-lights burn around the clock, an electric campfire pushing back the darkness. They can't see it from inside—Beebe has no windows—but somehow they draw comfort from the knowledge of that unseen fire—

Thud!

—most of the time.

"Remember back in training?" Ballard says over the sound, "When they told us that abyssal fish were supposed to be so small. . ."

Her voice trails off. Beebe creaks slightly. They listen for a while. There is no other sound.

"It must've gotten tired," Ballard says. "You'd think they'd figure it out." She moves to the ladder and climbs downstairs.

Clarke follows her, a bit impatiently. There are sounds in Beebe that worry her far more than the futile attack of some misguided fish. Clarke can hear tired alloys negotiating surrender. She can feel the ocean looking for a way in. What if it finds one? The whole weight of the Pacific could drop down and turn her into jelly. Any time.

Better to face it outside, where she knows what's coming. All she can do in here is wait for it to happen.

Going outside is like drowning, once a day.

Clarke stands facing Ballard, diveskin sealed, in an airlock that barely holds both of them. She has learned to tolerate the forced proximity; the glassy armor on her eyes helps a bit. *Fuse seals, check headlamp, test injector;* the ritual takes her, step by reflexive step, to that horrible moment when she awakens the machines sleeping within her, and changes.

When she catches her breath, and loses it.

When a vacuum opens, somewhere in her chest,

that swallows the air she holds. When her remaining
lung shrivels in its cage, and her guts collapse; when
myoelectric demons flood her sinuses and middle ears
with isotonic saline. When every pocket of internal gas
disappears in the time it takes to draw a breath.

It always feels the same. The sudden, overwhelm-
ing nausea; the narrow confines of the airlock holding
her erect when she tries to fall; seawater churning on all
sides. Her face goes under; vision blurs, then clears as
her corneal caps adjust.

She collapses against the walls and wishes she
could scream. The floor of the airlock drops away like a
gallows. Lenie Clarke falls writhing into the abyss.

They come out of the freezing darkness, headlights
blazing, into an oasis of sodium luminosity. Machines
grow everywhere at the Throat, like metal weeds.
Cables and conduits spiderweb across the seabed in a
dozen directions. The main pumps stand over twenty
metres high, a regiment of submarine monoliths fading
from sight on either side. Overhead floodlights bathe
the jumbled structures in perpetual twilight.

They stop for a moment, hands resting on the line
that guided them here.

"I'll never get used to it," Ballard grates in a carica-
ture of her usual voice.

Clarke glances at her wrist thermistor. "Thirty four
Centigrade." The words buzz, metallic, from her larynx.
It feels so *wrong* to talk without breathing.

Ballard lets go of the rope and launches herself into
the light. After a moment, breathless, Clarke follows.

There is so much power here, so much wasted
strength. Here the continents themselves do ponderous
battle. Magma freezes; icy seawater turns to steam; the
very floor of the ocean is born by painful centimetres

each year. Human machinery does not make energy, here at Dragon's Throat; it merely hangs on and steals some insignificant fraction of it back to the mainland.

Clarke flies through canyons of metal and rock, and knows what it is to be a parasite. She looks down. Shellfish the size of boulders, crimson worms three metres long crowd the seabed between the machines. Legions of bacteria, hungry for sulphur, lace the water with milky veils.

The water fills with a sudden terrible cry.

It doesn't sound like a scream. It sounds as though a great harp string is vibrating in slow motion. But Ballard is screaming, through some reluctant interface of flesh and metal:

"LENIE—"

Clarke turns in time to see her own arm disappear into a mouth that seems impossibly huge.

Teeth like scimitars clamp down on her shoulder. Clarke stares into a scaly black face half-a-metre across. Some tiny dispassionate part of her searches for eyes in that monstrous fusion of spines and teeth and gnarled flesh, and fails. *How can it see me?* she wonders.

Then the pain reaches her.

She feels her arm being wrenched from its socket. The creature thrashes, shaking its head back and forth, trying to tear her into chunks. Every tug sets her nerves screaming.

She goes limp. *Please get it over with if you're going to kill me just please God make it quick.* . . She feels the urge to vomit, but the 'skin over her mouth and her own collapsed insides won't let her.

She shuts out the pain. She's had plenty of practice. She pulls inside, abandoning her body to ravenous vivisection; and from far away she feels the twisting of her attacker grow suddenly erratic. There is another creature at her side, with arms and legs and a knife—

you know, a knife, like the one you've got strapped to your leg and completely forgot about—and suddenly the monster is gone, its grip broken.

Clarke tells her neck muscles to work. It is like operating a marionette. Her head turns, and she sees Ballard locked in combat with something as big as she is. Only . . . Ballard is tearing it to pieces, with her bare hands. Its icicle teeth splinter and snap. Dark icewater courses from its wounds, tracing mortal convulsions with smoke-trails of suspended gore.

The creature spasms weakly. Ballard pushes it away. A dozen smaller fish dart into the light and begin tearing at the carcass. Photophores along their sides flash like frantic rainbows.

Clarke watches from the other side of the world. The pain in her side keeps its distance, a steady, pulsing ache. She looks; her arm is still there. She can even move her fingers without any trouble. *I've had worse,* she thinks.

But why am I still alive?

Ballard appears at her side; her lens-covered eyes shine like photophores themselves.

"Jesus Christ," Ballard says in a distorted whisper. "Lenie? Are you okay?"

Clarke dwells on the inanity of the question for a moment. But surprisingly, she feels intact. "Yeah."

And if not, she knows it's her own damn fault. She just lay there. She just waited to die. She was asking for it.

She's always asking for it.

Back in the airlock the water recedes around them. And within them; Clarke's stolen breath, released at last, races back along visceral channels, reinflating lung and gut and spirit.

Ballard splits the face seal on her 'skin and her words tumble into the wetroom. "Jesus. Jesus! I don't believe it! My God, did you see that thing! They get so huge around here!" She passes her hands across her face; her corneal caps come off, milky hemispheres dropping from enormous hazel eyes. "And to think they're normally just a few centimetres long. . ."

She starts to strip down, unzipping her 'skin along the forearms, talking the whole time. "And yet it was almost fragile, you know? Hit it hard enough and it just came apart! Jesus!" Ballard always takes off her uniform indoors. Clarke suspects that she'd rip the recycler out of her own thorax if she could, throw it in a corner with the 'skin and the eyecaps until the next time it was needed.

Maybe she's got her other lung in her cabin, Clarke muses. Her arm is all pins and needles. *Maybe she keeps it in a jar, and she stuffs it back into her chest at night. . .* She feels a bit dopey; probably just an after-effect of the neuroinhibitors the 'skin pumps her full of whenever she's outside. *Small price to keep my brain from shorting out—I really shouldn't mind. . .*

Ballard peels her 'skin down to the waist. Just under her left breast, an electrolyser intake pokes out through her ribcage.

Clarke stares vaguely at that perforated disk in Ballard's flesh. *The ocean goes into us there,* she thinks. The old knowledge seems newly significant, somehow. *We suck it into us and steal its oxygen and spit it out again.*

The prickly numbness is spreading, leaking through her shoulder into her chest and neck. Clarke shakes her head once, to clear it.

She sags suddenly, against the hatchway.

Am I in shock? Am I fainting?

"I mean—" Ballard stops, looks at Clarke with an expression of sudden concern. "Jesus, Lenie. You look

terrible. You shouldn't have told me you were okay if
you weren't."

The tingling reaches the base of Clarke's skull. She
fights it. "I'm—okay," she says. "Nothing broke. I'm
just bruised."

"Garbage. Take off your 'skin.'""

Clarke straightens, with effort. The numbness recedes a bit. "It's nothing I can't take care of myself."

Don't touch me. Please don't touch me.

Ballard steps forward without a word and unseals
the 'skin around Clarke's forearm. She peels back the
fabric and exposes an ugly purple bruise. She looks at
Clarke with one raised eyebrow.

"Just a bruise," Clarke says. "I'll take care of it.
Really. Thanks anyway." She pulls her hand away from
Ballard's ministrations.

Ballard looks at her for a moment. She smiles ever
so slightly.

"Lenie," she says, "there's no need to feel embar-
rassed."

"About what?"

"You know. Me having to rescue you. You going to
pieces when that thing attacked. It was perfectly under-
standable. Most people have a rough time adjusting.
I'm just one of the lucky ones."

*Right. You've always been one of the lucky ones, haven't
you? I know your kind, Ballard, you've never failed at anything. . .*

"You don't have to feel ashamed about it," Ballard
reassures her.

"I don't," Clarke says, honestly. She doesn't feel
much of anything any more. Just the tingling. And the
tension. And a vague sort of wonder that she's even
alive.

✧ ✧

The bulkhead is sweating.

The deep sea lays icy hands on the metal and, inside, Clarke watches the humid atmosphere bead and run down the wall. She sits rigid on her bunk under dim fluorescent light, every wall of the cubby within easy reach. The ceiling is too low. The room is too narrow. She feels as if the ocean is compressing the station around her.

And all I can do is wait. . .

The anabolic salve on her injuries is warm and soothing. Clarke probes the purple flesh of her arm with practised fingers. The diagnostic tools in the Med cubby have vindicated her. She is lucky, this time; bones intact, epidermis unbroken. She seals up her 'skin, hiding the damage.

Clarke shifts on the pallet, turns to face the inside wall. Her reflection stares back at her through eyes like frosted glass. She watches the image, admires its perfect mimicry of each movement. Flesh and phantom move together, bodies masked, faces neutral.

That's me, she thinks. *That's what I look like now.* She tries to read what lies behind that glacial facade. *Am I bored, horny, upset?* How to tell, with her eyes hidden behind those corneal opacities? She sees no trace of the tension she always feels. *I could be terrified. I could be pissing in my 'skin and nobody would know.*

She leans forward. The reflection comes to meet her. They stare at each other, white to white, ice to ice. For a moment, they almost forget Beebe's ongoing war against pressure. For a moment, they do not mind the claustrophobic solitude that grips them.

How many times, Clarke wonders, *have I wanted eyes as dead as these?*

Beebe's metal viscera crowd the corridor beyond

her cubby. Clarke can barely stand erect. A few steps bring her into the lounge.

Ballard, back in shirtsleeves, is at one of the library terminals. "Rickets," she says.

"What?"

"Fish down here don't get enough trace elements. They're rotten with deficiency diseases. It doesn't matter how fierce they are. They bite too hard, they break their teeth on us."

Clarke stabs buttons on the food processor; the machine grumbles at her touch. "I thought there was all sorts of food at the rift. That's why things got so big."

"There's a lot of food. Just not very good quality."

A vaguely edible lozenge of sludge oozes from the processor onto Clarke's plate. She eyes it for a moment. *I can relate.*

"You're going to eat in your gear?" Ballard asks, as Clarke sits down at the lounge table.

Clarke blinks at her. "Yeah. Why?"

"Oh, nothing. It would just be nice to talk to someone with pupils in their eyes, you know?"

"Sorry. I'll take them off if you—"

"No, it's no big thing. I can live with it." Ballard shuts down the library and sits down across from Clarke. "So, how do you like the place so far?"

Clarke shrugs and keeps eating.

"I'm glad we're only down here for three months," Ballard says. "This place could get to you after a while."

"It could be worse."

"Oh, I'm not complaining. I was looking for a challenge, after all. What about you?"

"Me?"

"What brings you down here? What are you looking for?"

Clarke doesn't answer for a moment. "I don't know, really," she says at last. "Privacy, I guess."

Ballard looks up. Clarke stares back, her face neutral.

"Well, I'll leave you to it, then," Ballard says pleasantly.

Clarke watches her disappear down the corridor. She hears the sound of a cubby hatch swinging shut.

Give it up, Ballard, she thinks. *I'm not the sort of person you really want to know.*

Almost start of the morning shift. The food processor disgorges Clarke's breakfast with its usual reluctance. Ballard, in Communications, is just getting off the phone. A moment later she appears in the hatchway.

"Management says—" She stops. "You've got blue eyes."

Clarke smiles slightly. "You've seen them before."

"I know. It's just kind of surprising, it's been a while since I've seen you without your caps on."

Clarke sits down with her breakfast. "So, what does Management say?"

"We're on schedule. Rest of the crew comes down in three weeks, we go online in four." Ballard sits down across from Clarke. "I wonder sometimes why we're not online right now."

"I guess they just want to be sure everything works."

"Still, six months seems like a long time for a dry run. And you'd think that—well, they'd want to get the geothermal program up and running as fast as possible, after all that's happened."

After Lepreau and Winshire melted down, you mean.

"And there's something else," Ballard says. "I can't get through to Piccard."

Clarke looks up. Piccard Station is anchored on the Galapagos Rift; it is not a particularly stable mooring.

"Did you ever meet the couple there?" Ballard asks. "Ken Lubin, Lana Cheung?"

Clarke shakes her head. "They went through before me. I never met any of the other Rifters except you."

"Nice people. I thought I'd call them up, see how things were going at Piccard, but nobody can get through."

"Line down?"

"They say it's probably something like that. Nothing serious. They're sending a 'scaphe down to check it out."

Maybe the seabed opened up and swallowed them whole, Clarke thinks. *Maybe the hull had a weak plate—one's all it would take. . .*

Something creaks, deep in Beebe's superstructure. Clarke looks around. The walls seem to have moved closer while she wasn't looking.

"Sometimes," she says, "I wish we didn't keep Beebe at surface pressure. Sometimes I wish we were pumped up to ambient. To take the strain off the hull."

Ballard smiles. "Come on. Would you want to spend three months sitting in a decompression tank afterwards?"

In the Systems cubby, something bleats for attention.

"Seismic. Wonderful." Ballard disappears into Systems. Clarke follows.

An amber line is writhing across one of the displays. It looks like the EEG of someone caught in a nightmare.

"Get your eyes back in," Ballard says. "The Throat's acting up."

❖ ❖

They can hear it all the way to Beebe; a malign, almost electrical hiss from the direction of the Throat.

Clarke follows Ballard towards it, one hand running lightly along the guide rope. The distant smudge of light that marks their destination seems wrong, somehow. The colour is different. It ripples.

They swim into its glowing nimbus and see why. The Throat is on fire.

Sapphire auroras slide flickering across the generators. At the far end of the array, almost invisible with distance, a pillar of smoke swirls up into the darkness like a great tornado.

The sound it makes fills the abyss. Clarke closes her eyes for a moment, and hears rattlesnakes.

"Jesus!" Ballard shouts over the noise. "It's not supposed to do that!"

Clarke checks her thermistor. It won't settle; water temperature goes from four degrees to thirty eight and back again, within seconds. A myriad ephemeral currents tug at them as they watch.

"Why the light show?" Clarke calls back.

"I don't know!" Ballard answers. "Bioluminescence, I guess! Heat-sensitive bacteria!"

Without warning, the tumult dies.

The ocean empties of sound. Phosphorescent spiderwebs wriggle dimly on the metal and vanish. In the distance, the tornado sighs and fragments into a few transient dust devils.

A gentle rain of black soot begins to fall in the copper light.

"Smoker," Ballard says into the sudden stillness. "A big one."

They swim to the place where the geyser erupted. There is a fresh wound in the seabed, a gash several metres long, between two of the generators.

"This wasn't supposed to happen," Ballard says. "That's why they built here, for crying out loud! It was supposed to be stable!"

"The rift is never stable," Clarke replies. *Not much point in being here if it was.*

Ballard swims up through the fallout and pops an access plate on one of the generators. "Well, according to this there's no damage," she calls down, after looking inside. "Hang on, let me switch channels here—"

Clarke touches one of the cylindrical sensors strapped to her waist, and stares into the fissure. *I should be able to fit through there*, she decides.

And does.

"We were lucky," Ballard is saying above her. "The other generators are okay too. Oh, wait a second; number two has a clogged cooling duct, but it's not serious. Backups can handle it until—get out of there!"

Clarke looks up, one hand on the sensor she's planting. Ballard stares down at her through a chimney of fresh rock.

"Are you crazy?" Ballard shouts. "That's an active smoker!"

Clarke looks down again, deeper into the shaft. It twists out of sight in the mineral haze. "We need temperature readings," she says, "from inside the mouth."

"Get out of there! It could go off again and fry you!"

I suppose it could at that, Clarke thinks. "It just finished erupting," she calls back. "It'll take a while to build up a fresh head." She twists a knob on the sensor; tiny explosive bolts blast into the rock, anchoring the device.

"Get out of there, now!"

"Just a second." Clarke turns the sensor on and kicks up out of the seabed. Ballard grabs her arm as she emerges, starts to drag her away from the smoker.

Clarke stiffens and pulls free. "Don't—" *touch me!* She catches herself. "I'm out, okay, you don't have to. . ."

"Further." Ballard keeps swimming. "Over here."

They are near the edge of the light now, the floodlit Throat on one side, blackness on the other. Ballard faces Clarke. "Are you out of your mind? We could have gone back to Beebe for a drone! We could have planted it on remote!"

Clarke does not answer. She sees something moving in the distance behind Ballard. "Watch your back," she says.

Ballard turns, and sees the gulper sliding toward them. It undulates through the water like brown smoke, silent and endless; Clarke cannot see the creature's tail, although several metres of serpentine flesh have come out of the darkness.

Ballard goes for her knife. After a moment, Clarke does too.

The gulper's jaw drops open like a great jagged scoop.

Ballard begins to launch herself at the thing, knife upraised.

Clarke puts her hand out. "Wait a minute. It's not coming at us."

The front end of the gulper is about ten metres distant now. Its tail pulls free of the murk.

"Are you crazy?" Ballard moves clear of Clarke's hand, still watching the monster.

"Maybe it isn't hungry," Clarke says. She can see its eyes, two tiny unwinking spots glaring at them from the tip of the snout.

"They're always hungry. Did you sleep through the briefings?"

The gulper closes its mouth and passes. It extends around them now, in a great meandering arc. The head turns back to look at them. It opens its mouth.

"Fuck this," Ballard says, and charges.

Her first stroke opens a metre-long gash in the

creature's side. The gulper stares at Ballard for a moment, as if astonished. Then, ponderously, it thrashes.

Clarke watches without moving. *Why can't she just let it go? Why does she always have to prove she's better than everything?*

Ballard strikes again; this time she slashes into a great tumorous swelling that has to be the stomach.

She frees the things inside.

They spill out through the wound; two huge viperfish and some misshapen creature Clarke doesn't recognize. One of the viperfish is still alive, and in a foul mood. It locks its teeth around the first thing it encounters.

Ballard. From behind.

"Lenie!" Ballard's knife hand is swinging in staccato arcs. The viperfish begins to come apart. Its jaws remain locked. The convulsing gulper crashes into Ballard and sends her spinning to the bottom.

Finally, Clarke begins to move.

The gulper collides with Ballard again. Clarke moves in low, hugging the bottom, and pulls the other woman clear of those thrashing coils.

Ballard's knife continues to dip and twist. The viperfish is a mutilated wreck behind the gills, but its grip remains unbroken. Ballard cannot twist around far enough to reach the skull. Clarke comes in from behind and takes the creature's head in her hands.

It stares at her, malevolent and unthinking.

"Kill it!" Ballard shouts. "Jesus, what are you waiting for?"

Clarke closes her eyes, and clenches. The skull in her hand splinters like cheap plastic.

There is a silence.

After a while, she opens her eyes. The gulper is gone, fled back into darkness to heal or die. But Ballard is still there, and Ballard is angry.

"What's wrong with you?" she says.

Clarke unclenches her fists. Bits of bone and jellied flesh float about her fingers.

"You're supposed to back me up! Why are you so damned passive all the time?"

"Sorry." *Sometimes it works.*

Ballard reaches behind her back. "I'm cold. I think it punctured my diveskin—"

Clarke swims behind her and looks. "A couple of holes. How are you otherwise? Anything feel broken?"

"It broke through the diveskin," Ballard says, as if to herself. "And when that gulper hit me, it could have. . ." She turns to Clarke and her voice, even distorted, carries a shocked uncertainty. ". . . I could have been killed. I could have been killed!"

For an instant, it is as though Ballard's 'skin and eyes and self-assurance have all been stripped away. For the first time Clarke can see through to the weakness beneath, growing like a delicate tracery of hairline cracks.

You can screw up too, Ballard. It isn't all fun and games. You know that now.

It hurts, doesn't it.

Somewhere inside, the slightest touch of sympathy. "It's okay," Clarke says. "Jeanette, it's—"

"You idiot!" Ballard hisses. She stares at Clarke like some malign and sightless old woman. "You just floated there! You just let it happen to me!"

Clarke feels her guard snap up again, just in time. *This isn't just anger,* she realizes. *This isn't just the heat of the moment. She doesn't like me. She doesn't like me at all.*

She never did.

Beebe Station floats tethered above the seabed, a gunmetal-grey planet ringed by a belt of equatorial floodlights. There is an airlock for divers at the south pole, and a docking hatch for 'scaphes at the north. In between there are girders and anchor lines, conduits and cables, metal armour and Lenie Clarke.

She is doing a routine visual check on the hull; standard procedure, once a week. Ballard is inside, testing some equipment in the communications cubby. This is not entirely within the spirit of the buddy system. Clarke prefers it this way. Relations have been civil over the past couple of days—Ballard even resurrects her patented chumminess on occasion—but the more time they spend together, the more forced things get. Eventually, Clarke knows, something is going to break.

Besides, out here in the void it seems only natural to be alone.

She is examining a cable clamp when an angler charges into the light. It is about two metres long, and hungry. It rams directly into the nearest of Beebe's floodlamps, mouth agape. Several teeth shatter against the crystal lens. The angler twists to one side, knocking the hull with her tail, and swims off until barely visible against the dark.

Clarke watches, fascinated. The angler swims back and forth, back and forth, then charges again.

The flood weathers the impact easily, doing more damage to its attacker. The angler lashes its dorsal spine. The lure at its end, a glowing worm-shaped thing, luminesces furiously.

Over and over again the fish batters itself against the light. Finally, exhausted, it sinks twitching down to the muddy bottom.

"Lenie? Are you okay?"

Clarke feels the words buzzing in her lower jaw. She trips the sender in her diveskin: "I'm okay."

"I heard something out there," Ballard says. "I just wanted to make sure you were. . ."

"I'm fine," Clarke says. "It was just a fish, trying to eat one of the lights."

"They never learn, do they?"

"No. I guess not. See you later."

"See—"

Clarke switches off her receiver.

Poor stupid fish. How many millennia did it take for them to learn that bioluminescence equals food? How long will Beebe have to sit here before they learn that electric light doesn't?

We could keep our headlights off. Maybe they'd leave us alone. . .

She stares out past Beebe's electric halo. There is so much blackness there. It almost hurts to look at it. Without lights, without sonar, how far could she go into that viscous shroud and still return?

Clarke kills her headlight. Night edges a bit closer, but Beebe's lights keep it at bay. Clarke turns until she is face to face with the darkness. She crouches like a spider against Beebe's hull.

She pushes off.

The darkness embraces her. She swims, not looking back, until her legs grow tired. She does not know how far she has come.

But it must be light-years. The ocean is full of stars.

Behind her, the station shines brightest, with coarse yellow rays. In the opposite direction, she can barely make out the Throat, an insignificant sunrise on the horizon.

Everywhere else, living constellations punctuate the dark. Here, a string of pearls blink sexual advertisements at two-second intervals. Here, a sudden flash leaves diversionary afterimages swarming across Clarke's field of view; something flees under cover of her momentary blindness. There, a counterfeit worm twists lazily in the current, invisibly tied to the roof of some predatory mouth.

There are so many of them.

She feels a sudden surge in the water, as if something big has just passed very close. A delicious thrill dances through her body.

It nearly touched me, she thinks. *I wonder what it was.* The rift is full of monsters who don't know when to quit. It doesn't matter how much they eat. Their voracity is as much a part of them as their elastic bellies, their unhinging jaws. Ravenous dwarfs attack giants twice their own size, and sometimes win. The abyss is a desert; no one can afford the luxury of waiting for better odds.

But even a desert has oases, and sometimes the deep hunters find them. They come upon the malnourishing abundance of the rift and gorge themselves; their descendants grow huge and bloated over such delicate bones. . .

My light was off, and it left me alone. I wonder. . .

She turns it back on. Her vision clouds in the sudden glare, then clears. The ocean reverts to unrelieved black. No nightmares accost her. The beam lights empty water wherever she points it.

She switches it off. There is a moment of absolute darkness while her eyecaps adjust to the reduced light. Then the stars come out again.

They are so beautiful. Lenie Clarke rests on the bottom of the ocean and watches the abyss sparkle around her. And she almost laughs as she realizes, three thousand metres from the nearest sunlight, that it's only dark when the lights are on.

"What the hell is wrong with you? You've been gone for over three hours, did you know that? Why didn't you answer me?"

Clarke bends over and removes her fins. "I guess I

turned my receiver off," she says. "I was—wait a second, did you say—"

"You guess? Have you forgotten every safety reg they drilled into us? You're supposed to have your receiver on from the moment you leave Beebe until you get back!"

"Did you say *three hours?*"

"I couldn't even come out after you, I couldn't find you on sonar! I just had to sit here and hope you'd show up!"

It only seems a few minutes since she pushed off into the darkness. Clarke climbs up into the lounge, suddenly chilled.

"Where were you, Lenie?" Ballard demands, coming up behind her. Clarke hears the slightest plaintive tone in her voice.

"I—I must've been on the bottom," Clarke says. "that's why sonar didn't get me. I didn't go far."

Was I asleep? What was I doing for three hours?

"I was just . . . wandering around. I lost track of the time. I'm sorry."

"Not good enough. Don't do it again."

There is a brief silence. They hear the sudden, familiar impact of flesh on metal.

"Christ!" Ballard snaps. "I'm turning the externals off right now!"

Whatever it is gets in two more hits by the time Ballard reaches the Systems cubby. Clarke hears her punch a couple of buttons.

Ballard comes out of Systems. "There. Now we're invisible."

Something hits them again. And again.

"I guess not," Clarke says.

Ballard stands in the lounge, listening to the rhythm of the assault. "They don't show up on sonar," she says, almost whispering. "Sometimes, when I hear

147

them coming at us, I tune it down to extreme close range. But it looks right through them."

"No gas bladders. Nothing to bounce an echo off of."

"We show up just fine out there, most of the time. But not those things. You can't find them, no matter how high you turn the gain. They're like ghosts."

"They're not ghosts." Almost unconsciously, Clarke has been counting the beats: *eight . . . nine. . .*

Ballard turns to face her. "They've shut down Piccard," she says, and her voice is small and tight.

"What?"

"The grid office says it's just some technical problem. But I've got a friend in Personnel. I phoned him when you were outside. He says Lana's in the hospital. And I get the feeling. . ." Ballard shakes her head. "It sounded like Ken Lubin did something down there. I think maybe he attacked her."

Three thumps from outside, in rapid succession. Clarke can feel Ballard's eyes on her. The silence stretches.

"Or maybe not," Ballard says. "We got all those personality tests. If he was violent, they would have picked it up before they sent him down."

Clarke watches her, and listens to the pounding of an intermittent fist.

"Or maybe . . . maybe the rift changed him somehow. Maybe they misjudged the pressure we'd all be under. So to speak." Ballard musters a feeble smile. "Not the physical danger so much as the emotional stress, you know? Everyday things. Just being outside could get to you after a while. Seawater sluicing through your chest. Not breathing for hours at a time. It's like—living without a heartbeat. . ."

She looks up at the ceiling; the sounds from outside are a bit more erratic now.

"Outside's not so bad," Clarke says. *At least you're incompressible. At least you don't have to worry about the plates giving in.*

"I don't think you'd change suddenly. It would just sort of sneak up on you, little by little. And then one day you'd just wake up changed, you'd be different somehow, only you'd never have noticed the transition. Like Ken Lubin."

She looks at Clarke, and her voice drops a bit.

"And like you."

"Me." Clarke turns Ballard's words over in her mind, waits for the onset of some reaction. She feels nothing but her own indifference. "I don't think you have much to worry about. I'm not a violent person."

"I know. I'm not worried about my own safety, Lenie. I'm worried about yours."

Clarke looks at her from behind the impervious safety of her lenses, and doesn't answer.

"You've changed since you came down here," Ballard says. "You're withdrawing from me, you're exposing yourself to unnecessary risks. I don't know exactly what's happening to you. It's almost like you're trying to kill yourself."

"I'm not," Clarke says. She tries to change the subject. "Is Lana Cheung all right?"

Ballard studies her for a moment. She takes the hint. "I don't know. I couldn't get any details."

Clarke feels something knotting up inside her.

"I wonder what she did," she murmurs, "to set him off like that?"

Ballard stares at her, openmouthed. "What she did? I can't believe you said that!"

"I only meant—"

"I know what you meant."

The outside pounding has stopped. Ballard does not relax. She stands hunched over in those strange, loose-fitting clothes that Drybacks wear, and stares at the ceiling as though she doesn't believe in the silence. She looks back at Clarke.

"Lenie, you know I don't like to pull rank, but your attitude is putting both of us at risk. I think this place is really getting to you. I hope you can get back online here, I really do. Otherwise I may have to recommend you for a transfer."

Clarke watches Ballard leave the lounge. *You're lying*, she realizes. *You're scared to death, and it's not just because I'm changing.*

It's because you are.

Clarke finds out five hours after the fact: something has changed on the ocean floor.

We sleep and the earth moves, she thinks, studying the topographic display. *And next time, or the time after, maybe it'll move right out from under us.*

I wonder if I'll have time to feel anything.

She turns at a sound behind her. Ballard is standing in the lounge, swaying slightly. Her face seems somehow disfigured by the concentric rings in her eyes, by the dark hollows around them. Naked eyes are beginning to look alien to Clarke.

"The seabed shifted," Clarke says. "There's a new outcropping about two hundred metres west of us."

"That's odd. I didn't feel anything."

"It happened about five hours ago. You were asleep."

Ballard glances up sharply. Clarke studies the haggard lines of her face. *On second thought, I guess you weren't.*

"I . . . would've woken up," Ballard says. She squeezes past Clarke into the cubby and checks the topographic display.

"Two metres high, twelve long," Clarke recites.

Ballard doesn't answer. She punches some commands into a keyboard; the topographic image dissolves, reforms into a column of numbers.

"Just as I thought," she says. "No heavy seismic activity for over forty-two hours."

"Sonar doesn't lie," Clarke says calmly.

"Neither does seismo," Ballard answers.

There is a brief silence. There is a standard procedure for such things, and they both know what it is.

"We have to check it out," Clarke says.

But Ballard only nods. "Give me a moment to change."

They call it a squid; a jet-propelled cylinder about half a metre long, with a headlight at the front end and a towbar at the back. Clarke, floating between Beebe and the seabed, checks it over with one hand. Her other hand grips a sonar pistol. She points the pistol into blackness; ultrasonic clicks sweep the night, give her a bearing.

"That way," she says, pointing.

Ballard squeezes down on her own squid's towbar. The machine pulls her away. After a moment Clarke follows. Bringing up the rear, a third squid carries an assortment of sensors in a nylon bag.

Ballard is travelling at nearly full throttle. The lamps on her helmet and squid stab the water like two lighthouse beacons. Clarke, her own lights doused, catches up with Ballard about half-way to their destination. They cruise along a couple of metres over the muddy substrate.

"Your lights," Ballard says.

"We don't need them. Sonar works in the dark."

"Are you just breaking the regs for the sheer thrill of it, now?"

"The fish down here, they key on things that glow—"

"Turn your lights on. That's an order."

Clarke does not answer. She watches the twin beams beside her, Ballard's squid shining steady and unwavering, Ballard's headlamp slicing the water in erratic arcs as she moves her head. . .

"I told you," Ballard says, "turn your—Christ!"

It was just a glimpse, caught for a moment in the sweep of Ballard's headlight. She jerks her head around and it slides back out of sight. Then it looms up in the squid's beam, huge and terrible.

The abyss is grinning at them, teeth bared.

A mouth stretches across the width of the beam, and extends into darkness on either side. It is crammed with conical teeth the size of human hands, and they do not look the least bit fragile.

Ballard makes a strangled sound and dives into the mud. The benthic ooze boils up around her in a seething cloud; she disappears in a torrent of planktonic corpses.

Lenie Clarke stops and waits, unmoving. She stares transfixed at that threatening smile. Her whole body feels electrified, she has never been so explicitly aware of herself. Every nerve fires and freezes at the same time. She is terrified.

But she is also, somehow, completely in control of herself. She reflects on this paradox as Ballard's abandoned squid slows and stops itself, scant metres from that endless row of teeth. She wonders at her own analytical clarity as the third squid, with its burden of sensors, decelerates past and takes up position beside Ballard's.

There in the light, the grin does not change.

After a few moments, Clarke raises her sonar pistol and fires. We're here, she realizes, checking the readout. *That's the outcropping.*

She swims closer. The smile hangs there, enigmatic and enticing. Now she can see bits of bone at the roots of the teeth, and tatters of decomposed flesh trailing from the gums.

She turns and backtracks. The cloud on the seabed has nearly settled.

"Ballard," she says in her synthetic voice.

Nobody answers.

Clarke reaches down through the mud, feeling blind, until she touches something warm and trembling.

The seabed explodes in her face.

Ballard erupts from the substrate, trailing a muddy comet's tail. Her hand rises from that sudden cloud, clasped around something glinting in the transient light. Clarke sees the knife, twists almost too late; the blade glances off her 'skin, igniting nerves along her ribcage. Ballard lashes out again. This time Clarke catches the knife-hand as it shoots past, twists it, pushes. Ballard tumbles away.

"It's me!" Clarke shouts; the 'skin turns her voice into a tinny vibrato.

Ballard rises up again, white eyes unseeing, knife still in hand.

Clarke holds up her hands. "It's okay! There's nothing here! It's dead!"

Ballard stops. She stares at Clarke. She looks over to the squids, to the smile they illuminate. She stiffens.

"It's some kind of whale," Clarke says. "It's been dead a long time."

"A . . . a whale?" Ballard rasps. She begins to shake.

There's no need to feel embarrassed, Clarke almost says, but doesn't. Instead, she reaches out and touches Ballard lightly on the arm. *Is this how you do it?* she wonders.

Ballard jerks back as if scalded.

I guess not. . .

"Um, Jeanette. . ." Clarke begins.

Ballard raises a trembling hand, cutting Clarke off. "I'm okay. I want to g . . . I think we should get back now, don't you?"

"Okay," Clarke says. But she doesn't really mean it. She could stay out here all day.

Ballard is at the library again. She turns, passing a casual hand over the brightness control as Clarke comes up behind her; the display darkens before Clarke can see what it is.

"It was a Ziphiid," Ballard says. "A beaked whale. Very rare. They don't dive this deep."

Clarke listens, not really interested.

"It must have died and rotted further up, and sank." Ballard's voice is slightly raised. She looks almost furtively at something on the other side of the lounge. "I wonder what the chances are of that happening."

"What?"

"I mean, in all the ocean, something that big just happening to drop out of the sky a few hundred metres away. The odds of that must be pretty low."

"Yeah. I guess so." Clarke reaches over and brightens the display. One half of the screen glows softly with luminous text. The other holds the rotating image of some complex molecule.

"What's this?" Clarke asks.

Ballard steals another glance across the lounge. "Just an old biopsyche text the library had on file. I was browsing through it. Used to be an interest of mine."

Clarke looks at her. "Uh huh." She bends over and studies the display. Some sort of technical chemistry. The only thing she really understands is the caption beneath the graphic.

She reads it aloud: "True Happiness."

"Yeah. A tricyclic with four side chains." Ballard points at the screen. "Whenever you're happy, really happy, that's what does it to you."

"When did they find that out?"

"I don't know. It's an old book."

Clarke stares at the revolving simulacrum. It disturbs her, somehow. It floats there over that smug stupid caption, and it says something she doesn't want to hear.

You've been solved, it tells her. *You're mechanical. Chemicals and electricity. Everything you are, every dream, every action, it all comes down to a change of voltage somewhere, or a—what did she say—a tricyclic with four side chains. . .*

"It's wrong," Clarke murmurs. *Or they'd be able to fix us, when we broke down. . .*

"Sorry?" Ballard says.

"It's saying we're just these . . . soft computers. With faces."

Ballard shuts off the terminal.

"That's right," she says. "And some of us may even be losing those."

The jibe registers, but it doesn't hurt. Clarke straightens and moves towards the ladder.

"Where you going? You going outside again?" Ballard asks.

"The shift isn't over. I thought I'd clean out the duct on number two."

"It's a bit late to start on that, Lenie. The day will be over before we're even half done." Ballard's eyes dart away again. This time Clarke follows the glance to the full-length mirror on the far wall.

She sees nothing of particular interest there.

"I'll work late." Clarke grabs the railing, swings her foot onto the top rung.

"Lenie," Ballard says, and Clarke swears she hears a tremor in that voice. She looks back, but the other woman is moving to Communications. "Well, I'm afraid I can't go with you," she's saying. "I'm in the middle of debugging one of the telemetry routines."

"That's fine," Clarke says. She feels the tension starting to rise. Beebe is shrinking again. She starts down the ladder.

"Are you sure you're okay going out alone? Maybe you should wait until tomorrow."

"No. I'm okay."

"Well, remember to keep your receiver open. I don't want you getting lost on me again. . ."

Clarke is in the wetroom. She climbs into the airlock and runs through the ritual. It no longer feels like drowning. It feels like being born again.

She awakens into darkness, and the sound of weeping.

She lies there for a few minutes, confused and uncertain. The sobs come from all sides, soft but omnipresent in Beebe's resonant shell. She hears nothing else except her own heartbeat.

She is afraid. She isn't sure why. She wishes the sounds would go away.

Clarke rolls off her bunk and fumbles at the hatch. It opens into a semi-darkened corridor; meager light escapes from the lounge at one end. The sounds come from the other direction, from deepening darkness. She follows them through an infestation of pipes and conduits.

Ballard's quarters. The hatch is open. An emerald readout sparkles in the darkness, bestowing no detail upon the hunched figure on the pallet.

"Ballard," Clarke says softly. She does not want to go in.

The shadow moves, seems to look up at her. "Why won't you show it?" it says, its voice pleading.

Clarke frowns in the darkness. "Show what?"

"You know what! How . . . afraid you are!"

"Afraid?"

"Of being here, of being stuck at the bottom of this horrible dark ocean. . ."

"I don't understand," Clarke whispers. The claustrophobia in her, restless again, begins to stir.

Ballard snorts, but the derision seems forced. "Oh, you understand all right. You think this is some sort of competition, you think if you can just keep it all inside you'll win somehow . . . but it isn't like that at all, Lenie, it isn't helping to keep it hidden like this, we've got to be able to trust each other down here or we're lost. . ."

She shifts slightly on the bunk. Clarke's eyes, enhanced by the caps, can pick out a few details now; rough edges embroider Ballard's silhouette, the folds and creases of normal clothing, unbuttoned to the waist. She thinks of a cadaver, half-dissected, rising on the table to mourn its own mutilation.

"I don't know what you mean," Clarke says.

"I've tried to be friendly," Ballard says. "I've tried to get along with you, but you're so cold, you won't even admit . . . I mean, you couldn't like it down here, nobody could, why can't you just admit—"

"But I don't, I . . . I hate it in here. It's like Beebe's going to . . . to clench around me. And all I can do is wait for it to happen."

Ballard nods in the darkness. "Yes, yes, I know what you mean." She seems somehow encouraged by Clarke's admission. "And no matter how much you tell yourself—" She stops. "You hate it in here?"

Did I say something wrong? Clarke wonders.

"Out there is hardly any better, you know," Ballard says. "Outside is even worse! There's mudslides and steam vents and giant fish trying to eat you all the time, you can't possibly . . . but . . . you don't mind all that, do you?"

Somehow, her tone has turned accusing. Clarke shrugs.

"No, you don't," Ballard is speaking slowly now. Her voice drops to a whisper: "You actually like it out there. Don't you?"

Reluctantly, Clarke nods. "Yeah. I guess so."

"But it's so . . . the rift can kill you, Lenie. It can kill *us*. A hundred different ways. Doesn't that scare you?"

"I don't know. I don't think about it much. I guess it does, sort of."

"Then why are you so happy out there?" Ballard cries. "It doesn't make any sense. . ."

I'm not exactly 'happy', Clarke thinks. Aloud, she only says, "I don't know. It's not that weird, lots of people do dangerous things. What about free-fallers? What about mountain climbers?"

But Ballard doesn't answer. Her silhouette has grown rigid on the bed. Suddenly, she reaches over and turns on the cubby light.

Lenie Clarke blinks against the sudden brightness. Then the room dims as her eyecaps darken.

"Jesus Christ!" Ballard shouts at her. "You sleep in that fucking costume now?"

It is something else Clarke hasn't thought about. It just seems easier.

"All this time I've been pouring my heart out to you and you've been wearing that machine's face! You don't even have the decency to show me your god-damned eyes!"

Clarke steps back, startled. Ballard rises from the bed and takes a single step forward. "To think you could actually pass for human before they gave you that suit! Why don't you go find something to play with out in your fucking ocean!"

And slams the hatch in Clarke's face.

Lenie Clarke stares at the sealed bulkhead for a few moments. Her face, she knows, is calm. Her face is usually calm. But she stands there, unmoving, until the cringing thing inside of her unfolds a little.

"Yes," she says at last, very softly. "I think I will."

Ballard is waiting for her as she emerges from the airlock. "Lenie," she says quietly, "we have to talk. It's important."

Clarke bends over and removes her fins. "Go ahead."

"Not here. In my cubby."

Clarke looks at her.

"Please."

Clarke starts up the ladder.

"Aren't you going to take—" Ballard stops as Clarke looks down. "Never mind. It's okay."

They ascend into the lounge. Ballard takes the lead. Clarke follows her down the corridor and into her cabin. Ballard dogs the hatch and sits on her bunk, leaving room for Clarke.

Clarke looks around the cramped space. Ballard has curtained over the mirrored bulkhead with a spare sheet.

Ballard pats the bed beside her. "Come on, Lenie. Sit down."

Reluctantly, Clarke sits. Ballard's sudden kindness confuses her. Ballard hasn't acted this way since. . .

. . . *Since she had the upper hand.*

"—might not be easy for you to hear," Ballard is saying, "But we have to get you off the rift. They shouldn't have put you down here in the first place."

Clarke does not reply. She waits.

"Remember the tests they gave us?" Ballard continues. "They measured our tolerance to stress; confinement, prolonged isolation, chronic physical danger, that sort of thing."

Clarke nods slightly. "So?"

"So," says Ballard, "Did you think for a moment they'd test for those qualities without knowing what sort of person would have them? Or how they got to be that way?"

Inside, Clarke goes very still. Outside, nothing changes.

Ballard leans forward a bit. "Remember what you said? About mountain climbers, and free-fallers, and why people deliberately do dangerous things? I've been reading up, Lenie. Ever since I got to know you I've been reading up—"

Got to know me?

"—and do you know what thrillseekers have in common? They all say that you haven't lived until you've nearly died. They need the danger. It gives them a rush."

You don't know me at all. . .

"Some of them are combat veterans, some were hostages for long periods, some just spent a lot of time in dead zones for one reason or another. And a lot of the really compulsive ones—"

Nobody knows me.

"—the ones who can't be happy unless they're on the edge, all the time—a lot of them got started early, Lenie. When they were just children. And you, I bet . . . you don't even like being touched. . ."

Go away. Go away.

Ballard puts her hand on Clarke's shoulder. "How long were you abused, Lenie?" she asks gently. "How many years?"

Clarke shrugs off the hand and does not answer.

He didn't mean any harm. She shifts on the bunk, turning away slightly.

"That's it, isn't it? You don't just have a tolerance to trauma, Lenie. You've got an addiction to it. Don't you?"

It only takes Clarke a moment to recover. The 'skin, the eyecaps make it easier. She turns calmly back to Ballard. She even smiles a little.

"No," she says. "I don't."

"There's a mechanism," Ballard tells her. "I've been reading about it. Do you know how the brain handles stress, Lenie? It dumps all sorts of addictive stimulants into the bloodstream. Beta-endorphins, opioids. If it happens often enough, for long enough, you get hooked. You can't help it."

Clarke feels a sound in her throat, a jagged coughing noise a bit like tearing metal. After a moment, she recognises it as laughter.

"I'm not making it up!" Ballard insists. "You can look it up yourself if you don't believe me! Don't you know how many abused children spend their whole lives hooked on wife beaters or self-mutilation or free-fall—"

"And it makes them happy, is that it?" Clarke asks with cold disdain. "They enjoy getting raped, or punched out, or—"

"No, of course you're not happy!" Ballard cuts in. "But what you feel, that's probably the closest you've ever come. So you confuse the two, you look for stress anywhere you can find it. It's physiological addiction, Lenie. You ask for it. You always asked for it."

I ask for it. Ballard has been reading, and Ballard knows: Life is pure electrochemistry. No use explaining how it feels. No use explaining that there are far worse things than being beaten up. There are even worse things than being held down and raped by your own father. There are the times between, when nothing happens at all. When he leaves you alone, and you don't know for how long. You sit across the table from him, forcing yourself to eat while your bruised insides try to knit themselves back together; and he pats you on the head and smiles at you, and you know the reprieve has already lasted too long, he's going to come for you tonight, or tomorrow, or maybe the next day.

Of course I asked for it. How else could I get it over with?

"Listen," Clarke says. Her voice is shaking. She takes a deep breath, tries again. "You're completely wrong. Completely. You don't have a clue what you're talking about."

But Ballard shakes her head. "Sure I do, Lenie. Believe it. You're hooked on your own pain, and so you go out there and keep daring the rift to kill you, and eventually it will, don't you see? That's why you shouldn't be here. That's why we have to get you back."

Clarke stands up. "I'm not going back." She turns to the hatch.

Ballard reaches out toward her. "Listen, you've got to stay and hear me out. There's more."

Clarke looks down at her with complete indifference. "Thanks for your concern. But I can go any time I want to."

"You go out there now and you'll give everything away, they're watching us! Can't you figure it out yet?" Ballard's voice is rising. "Listen, they knew about you! They were looking for someone like you! They've been testing us, they don't know yet what kind of person works out better down here, so they're watching and waiting to see who cracks first! This whole program is still experimental, can't you see that? Everyone they've sent down—you, me, Ken Lubin and Lana Cheung, it's all part of some coldblooded test. . ."

"And you're failing it," Clarke says softly. "I see."

"They're using us, Lenie—don't go out there!"

Ballard's fingers grasp at Clarke like the suckers of an octopus. Clarke pushes them away. She undogs the hatch and pushes it open. She hears Ballard rising behind her.

"You're sick!" Ballard screams. Something smashes into the back of Clarke's head. She goes sprawling out into the corridor. One arm smacks painfully against a cluster of pipes as she falls.

She rolls to one side and raises her arms to protect herself. But Ballard just steps over her and stalks into the lounge.

I'm not afraid, Clarke notes, getting to her feet. *She hit me, and I'm not afraid. Isn't that odd. . .*

From somewhere nearby, the sound of shattering glass.

Ballard is shouting in the lounge. "The experiment's over! Come on out, you fucking ghouls!"

Clarke follows the corridor, steps out of it. Pieces of the lounge mirror hang like great jagged stalactites in their frame. Splashes of glass litter the floor.

On the wall, behind the broken mirror, a fisheye lens takes in every corner of the room.

Ballard is staring into it. "Did you hear me? I'm not playing your stupid games any more! I'm through performing!"

The quartzite lens stares back impassively.

So you were right, Clarke muses. She remembers the sheet in Ballard's cubby. *You figured it out, you found the pickups in your own cubby, and Ballard, my dear friend, you didn't tell me.*

How long have you known?

Ballard looks around, sees Clarke. "You've got her fooled, all right," she snarls at the fisheye, "but she's a goddamned basket case! She's not even sane! Your little tests don't impress me one fucking bit!"

Clarke steps toward her.

"Don't call me a basket case," she says, her voice absolutely level.

"That's what you are!" Ballard shouts. "You're sick! That's why you're down here! They need you sick, they depend on it, and you're so far gone you can't see it! You hide everything behind that—that mask of yours, and you sit there like some masochistic jellyfish and just take anything anyone dishes out—you ask for it. . ."

That used to be true, Clarke realizes as her hands ball into fists. *That's the strange thing.* Ballard begins to back away; Clarke advances, step by step. *It wasn't until I came down here that I learned that I could fight back. That I could win. The rift taught me that, and now Ballard has too. . .*

"Thank you," Clarke whispers, and hits Ballard hard in the face.

Ballard goes over backwards, collides with a table. Clarke calmly steps forward. She catches a glimpse of herself in a glass icicle; her capped eyes seem almost luminous.

"Oh Jesus," Ballard whimpers. "Lenie, I'm sorry."

Clarke stands over her. "Don't be," she says. She sees herself as some sort of exploding schematic, each piece neatly labelled. *So much anger in here,* she thinks. *So much hate. So much to take out on someone.*

She looks at Ballard, cowering on the floor.

"I think," Clarke says, "I'll start with you."

But her therapy ends before she can even get properly warmed up. A sudden noise fills the lounge, shrill, periodic, vaguely familiar. It takes a moment for Clarke to remember what it is. She lowers her foot.

Over in the Communications cubby, the telephone is ringing.

Jeanette Ballard is going home today.

For over an hour the 'scaphe has been dropping deeper into midnight. Now the Systems monitor shows it settling like a great bloated tadpole onto Beebe's docking assembly. Sounds of mechanical copulation reverberate and die. The overhead hatch drops open.

Ballard's replacement climbs down, already mostly 'skinned, staring impenetrably from eyes without pupils. His gloves are off; his 'skin is open up to the forearms. Clarke sees the faint scars running along his wrists, and smiles a bit inside.

Was there another Ballard up there, waiting, she wonders, *in case I had been the one who didn't work out?*

Out of sight down the corridor, a hatch creaks open. Ballard appears in shirtsleeves, one eye swollen shut, carrying a single suitcase. She seems about to say something, but stops when she sees the newcomer. She looks at him for a moment. She nods briefly. She climbs into the belly of the 'scaphe without a word.

Nobody calls down to them. There are no salutations, no morale-boosting small talk. Perhaps the crew have been briefed. Perhaps they've simply figured it out. The docking hatch swings shut. With a final clank, the 'scaphe disengages.

Clarke walks across the lounge and looks into the camera. She reaches between mirror fragments and rips its power line from the wall.

We don't need this any more, she thinks, and she knows that somewhere far away, someone agrees.

She and the newcomer appraise each other with dead white eyes.

"I'm Lubin," he says at last.

Ballard was right again, she realizes. *Untwisted, we'd be of no use at all.*

But she doesn't mind. She won't be going back.

HANGING OUT IN THE THIRD WORLD LAUNDROMAT

LESLIE GADALLAH

Amy lugged the two big black garbage bags full of dirty laundry out of the car, across the parking lot, pausing at the glass door of the laundromat to open it and fight them through, feeling like some twisted parody of an impoverished Santa Claus, her burden dwarfing her small self and making her mean, ill-tempered and lessened in her own eyes.

She hated the days it was her turn to do the laundry. She hated the smell of the place, the noisome combination of a hundred soap manufacturers' country-fresh perfumes mixed with old sweat socks and dirt and mildew. She hated the dingy look of it, concrete block walls thick with paint and heavy with a multitude of signs which had been patched and patched and patched again as prices rose.

The trouble was, she hated the days it was her roommate's turn even more. Catherine the fey, the scattered-brained, who brought everything home dyed pink because she couldn't remember not to put the red blanket in with the rest of the stuff. Catherine who grinned apologetically and held up her manicured hands helplessly, and said she was sorry, but what could she do now? As usual, it was Amy who had to try to repair the damage, held, as she had been held these last two years, in bondage to the tyranny of the incompetent.

Catherine had refined helplessness to a fine art. She would bat her big, pasted-on squirrel-hair eyelashes over bewildered blue eyes and people, especially men, would rush to aid her in whatever small difficulty confronted her at the moment. Amy, in her plain straight-forward way, tried to do whatever needed to be done as best she could, and no one cared.

She couldn't be positive Catherine's laundromatic mistakes were a deliberate effort to get Amy to do the wash all the time, but she had her suspicions.

It was Catherine who had named the place the Third World Laundromat, delicately offended by its naked fluorescent tubes and concrete floor and the need to linger even briefly in its grim confines. It had a name of its own, but neither of them could remember now what it was.

She hefted the bags up and let them fall, one after the other, on the chipped arborite counter which ran between two rows of washing machines, then looked around. Only two of the aged machines were in use, rumbling and banging away at the far end. Only one other launderer was in that night, a fat, grey woman in a lumpy grey sweater with two lumpy grey kids hanging from her skirt like pale-eyed barnacles. Good. Amy chose to come late at night in hopes the laundromat wouldn't be crowded. She didn't care much for the company of the other battlers against entropy and poverty who came to this depressing place. Too many of them seemed to be losing the fight. It was funny, though. She'd been coming to the laundromat every second week for two years, and she couldn't remember having ever seen the same person here twice.

She lifted the lids of several machines, peering in to find those with the smallest accumulation of jetsam, settled on four in a row that seemed tolerable, and began sorting the clothes into them. She paused for a moment holding a wisp of rayon and lace Catherine called a bra, bemused by its obvious lack of utility, bemused also that she was willing to commit it to the brutal cleansing of this rough and battered washing machine along with her own more pragmatic garments.

The machines gobbled up quarters and began, complaining, their work. Amy sat on a wooden bench, grey painted once but worn by the bottoms of an endless parade of waiting women to the pale and slivery wood.

Bored, she gazed listlessly out of the glass door at the shops across the street. The sporting goods store had taken the tennis rackets out of its windows and put up skis. Next to it, the Seoul Foods Grocery—its owner's unconscious pun had once amused her—was still open.

She sighed and willed the machines to hurry through their cycles. She stared down at her feet tucked close to one another among the odd socks and cigarette butts and Fleecy sheets and miscellaneous debris of a thousand people's careless passage. Sometimes when she was here late she would see the owner pushing his futile broom through the mess, but it always looked the same.

The glass door opened, and a man entered in a little puff of chill night air. Immediately, Amy thought he didn't belong there. Tall, blond, hair wind-ruffled, he had an aura of competence, of controlled strength. He surveyed the room full of worn appliances as if he expected to find someone in particular, then turned towards the phones near the door. . .

. . . and leaned his long lance against the wall. The great doors to the throne room opened. The courtiers made way for him. He approached the throne, resplendent in his shining armour, heels ringing on the stone in the sudden hush of the room, the great sword Dragonslayer clinking lightly at his side as he walked, plumed helmet under his arm. He greeted the King with a respectful but scarcely humble bow. He kissed the Queen's crepey fingers, looking past her as he did, searching the assembled lords and ladies. Princess Catherine smiled coyly and fiddled with her jeweled necklace as his glance fell on her, but it didn't linger.

All eyes were on him as he made his way through the assembly. Everyone waited to see him make his choice—any maid in the kingdom, the King had promised as his reward for the death of Aargard, the wickedest, most fearsome dragon ever. Breaths were held as he approached the Princess. Of course, everyone thought, the natural choice. A beautiful lady, and a kingdom to inherit.

Sighs were released as he passed the Princess by. *Whatever is he thinking?* the people wondered.

He stopped among an assembly of ladies-in-waiting and smiled and said, "At last I have the right to your love, dearest of all to my heart."

Amy flushed and spluttered and stammered.

"But . . . But . . . But . . ."

A sharp elbow in the ribs from the lady nearest her got her started again, and she managed to spread the skirts of her simple but elegant white gown in a decent curtsy.

He turned to the court and said, "This is my chosen lady. To her I present the head of Aargard." At this, two

page boys came staggering in bearing the great dragon's head which they dropped at Amy's feet.

"Ugh," she said and jumped back as the blood
splashed up on her skirt. The dragon's dead eye regarded her accusingly, its long grimace displaying a rank of
yellow teeth, its forked tongue lolling on the floor.

"Come," the knight said.

"But sir," Amy protested, "I hardly know you."

"You will learn to know me, and to love me, as I
have always loved you. Come."

"But what about the laundry?"

"Laundry?"

One of the machines was banging and rattling and
rocking as if it intended to leave its place in the rank.
Amy lifted the lid and looked in. All the socks had
gathered together in a sodden lump like a tangle of
mating snakes. She reached in and pushed them
around into a more even distribution, then lowered the
lid. The machine started again with no more than the
usual amount of grinding noise. Someday, she thought,
all the machines in the Third World Laundromat were
going to die of exhaustion, and they'd have to replace
them with new ones. She looked forward to the day at
least as much as the owner dreaded it.

The grey woman with the grey kids had packed up
her laundry and left. She looked for the blond man. But
he was gone, too. Amy was alone.

She sat back down on the bench and shivered and
hugged herself and waited and wondered idly who he
was and where he came from and what he had
wanted. . .

. . . Everyone in the Buckeye Saloon turned toward
the door as he came in and paused in front of the
swinging doors for a moment, silhouetted against the
light.

He nodded an unsmiling greeting to the patrons as he threaded his way among the tables, wide-rowelled spurs ringing as he walked. He went to the bar and ordered a drink like any ordinary fellow, and Sam behind the bar, a man usually somewhat casual about customer service, fell all over himself in his haste to fill the order.

Sheriff Bailey left his poker game at the table by the door and hustled up to the bar, leaned one elbow on it with exaggerated nonchalance, faced the stranger, and said, "We don't want no trouble here, Clint."

Clint looked down at the sheriff from his considerable height and said, "Me neither."

"I reckon," the sheriff said, "You'll just want to finish your drink and head on out of town."

Amy beckoned Sam from the door of the office where she had been watching. She and Catherine had been going over the accounts and just before the stranger's arrival she had felt in need of a break because she was close to losing her temper trying to figure out Catherine's entries in the ledger. All the help Catherine had been giving her was "I don't remember" and "I don't know" and "Really, Amy, what do you expect me to do about it."

Sam came over with a towel in his hands.

"Who is that man?" Amy asked.

Catherine had come up behind her. "Who ever he is," she said, "He's gorgeous."

"Well, I don't know about that," Sam said, "But he's just about the most dangerous man there is in these here parts."

The dangerous man was answering the sheriff. Amy could just pick out his words among the general buzz of conversation which had sprung up around him.

"Actually, sheriff," he said, "I sort of figured on staying the night at least. Me and my horse, we're both tired."

"Don't reckon you'll find any place to stay anywhere in Sour Springs, Clint. All our rentin' rooms is full up."

Amy frowned. That was not only untrue, it was downright unfriendly. What was the sheriff thinking of? She marched over to the pair at the bar and said, "We've got a room, if you want it." She turned to the sheriff and said, "Last minute cancellation, Pete."

"Who's 'we'?" the stranger asked.

"I'm Amy Thompson. I manage the Buckeye. That's Catherine Carter, the owner."

"Mighty nice of you to offer, Miss Amy." The stranger shook his head. "But I never heard of two women running a saloon before."

"The room's a dollar," Amy said. "Sam will give you the key."

She looked up at him. He was smiling, kind of a nice smile, really. He had pushed his hat up and a shock of blond hair fell down over his forehead, giving him a boyish look. But the look in his eye was insolent and hard. "You don't figure on us becoming friends, do you?" he asked.

"No," Amy said and turned away.

But her grand exit was defeated by the arrival of the Drummond boys. All four of them came crashing in like a group of young bulls, slamming the doors back on their hinges, shouting and rough housing among themselves.

The last time they had been in, they had wrecked a lot of furniture and broken the mirror over the bar. Amy had told them they weren't welcome in the Buckeye any more. They obviously weren't going to pay a lot of attention to what she had said.

She turned to Pete Bailey. "Sheriff, I want those men out of here."

But Bailey was about to get his own back for the interference she had offered him a moment before.

"Come on, now, Miss Amy. They's just a bunch of fun lovin' boys."

"They're dangerous men."

"Now, Miss Amy, they actually done anything all that bad?"

"I see."

Sheriff Bailey shrugged and smiled.

"All right, Sheriff, I'll tell them myself."

"Now, Amy. . ." the sheriff warned, but he made no move to stop her.

Amy marched off, unhappy with what she was doing, but seeing no graceful way out of it.

Near the doorway a space had cleared, with the Drummonds in the middle of it. People liked to give the Drummond boys plenty of room. Amy stomped into the cleared area and said as forcefully as she was able, "You men get out of here. I told you, you're not to come here."

Tom Drummond grinned at her. "Spunky little thing, ain't she, Bill?"

"Yeah, Tom," Bill Drummond said. That was mostly all Bill Drummond ever did say.

"Pretty small, though," John Drummond said. "Ain't hardly an armful." He wrapped an arm around her to demonstrate.

She pushed at him and said in her most authoritative tone of voice, "Let me go, John Drummond."

"Sure thing, M'am," he said laughing, but he pulled her closer.

"Let go," Amy cried, panic touching her voice. She looked around for assistance but none of her customers wanted to tackle the Drummond boys.

Then a firm hand dropped on John Drummond's shoulder. "The lady said, 'let go'." The stranger glared at John and John's confidence wavered just a little.

"Art's behind you," Amy squeaked. Clint turned

and Art Drummond's fist when by him. He buried both of his own, one after the other, into Art Drummond's solar plexus, making Art grunt and sit down hard.

"Let's get him," Tom Drummond said.

"Yeah, Tom," Bill answered. They both entered the fray. Amy was flung aside as John brought his fists up. She scrambled away from the battle to where the sheriff was leaning against the bar, watching.

"Aren't you going to do anything about this," she demanded of him.

Sheriff Bailey shook his head. "Way I figure it, the Drummond boys will get rid of Clint, and then I'll put the run on the Drummonds. Kill two birds with one stone as it were."

"Oh," Amy said with high indignation. She ran around behind the bar and got the shotgun Sam kept there.

Someone had connected with Clint and he went sprawling across a table which shattered under him. When he got up, he had one of the table legs in his hand, which he brought sharply down on the top of Bill Drummond's head. Bill collapsed.

Amy discharged one barrel of the shotgun into the ceiling. Everything came to a dead stop.

Amy leveled the gun across the bar, aimed at John Drummond's gut. People dived under tables.

"Get out of here," Amy shouted, "And don't come back."

John Drummond backed out of the door. Tom got his arm under Bill and dragged him out. Art, recovering but still wobbly, followed.

Clint came back to the bar, dusting himself off, looking a little worse for wear. He picked up his unfinished drink and said to Amy, "This surely is an unfriendly town. No place for the likes of us. Why don't you and me just leave?"

"I can't," Amy said.

"What's holding you?"

"I have to put the clothes in the dryer."

One by one, the red eyes of the washing machines had winked out, indicating they were done their part of the ritual. Amy carried up soggy armloads of wet clothes and stuffed them into the round maws of the dryers. A further offering of quarters was gobbled down by these shabby gods of cleanliness and they began their noisy turning.

Beyond the glass door, the street was empty. Even the Seoul Foods Grocery had closed for the night, leaving one dim light on in the front of the store as a feeble discouragement against burglary. Street lights made overlapping pools of illumination to light the traveller's way, but no one travelled. Traffic signals blinked red and green, regulating non-existent traffic. Amy felt like the only living thing in the city, ensnared and made separate by the pitiless fluorescent lights of the Third World Laundromat. It was as if some enchantment had overtaken all humanity and passed her by, leaving her forgotten and isolated in this desolate, forgotten place. She shivered and looked out into the night.

Beyond the lights of the city, the darkness spread, seeming as featureless as the darkness of. . .

. . . space. Stars like diamonds embedded in black velvet. So many stars. The candles of the universe glowing in the endless night.

"You all right?" Bob asked as he came up to her.

"Yeah, I'm OK," Amy said. "A little overwhelmed, I guess. It's so big out there, and so empty." She turned away from the viewport toward the engineer. "Do you ever get the feeling that maybe we're poking around in things we weren't ever meant to know about?"

"When locomotives were first built, people said men were never meant to go that fast. When airplanes first got off the ground, people said if man was meant to fly, God would have given us wings. Now, if men weren't meant to be in space, what ever is the L5 point for?"

Amy was about to start explaining about gravity and physics and why an object at the L5 stayed stationary relative to the Earth when she saw the humour in his eye. And the sense in his argument.

She turned back to the viewport. It would be another twenty minutes or so before the rotation of Habitat about its hub would bring Earth into view. "It's so lonely, though."

"Maybe not as lonely as we thought." Bob grew sober. "Do you think the signals from Alpha Centauri are artificial? Really?"

Amy grimaced. That was the question which had brought her here, astronomer-linguist associated with the Search for Extraterrestrial Intelligence project. For twenty seven days, Habitat's radio telescope had been receiving regularly pulsed radio signals. With the help of the Arecibo Observatory on Earth on one radio quiet night, they had established the source to be 4.5 light years away, within shouting distance of the Alpha Centauri binary.

She had seen recordings of the signal, and listened to its regular beat within the hiss and crackle of the Galactic noise, and felt the hair on her neck rise and her breath catch in her throat.

You hoped for something so hard that when it finally arrived, you were afraid to believe it.

To answer Bob, she said, "I think they are. But until I can prove it, I'm not ready to go public with that statement."

"It's kind of scary," Bob said.

"Yeah."

Bob looked up. "Hi, Catherine," he said. "What's up?"

The Captain's orderly, a sullen girl, didn't answer him. She only delivered the message to Amy that the Captain requested Amy's presence in the observatory.

Amy followed the orderly toward the hub, adapting rather badly to the gradually decreasing gravity.

Funny, she thought, how the title Captain had clung to the station's chief honcho long after it ceased to resemble anything like a ship and became instead an isolated village of humanity, an outpost in hostile territory.

The Captain and his second in command, the sober-sided Chaturgedi, floated around the astronomical instruments that filled the interior of the hub, looking as concerned as floating people can look. They had the scanners and the radio telescope operating at full gain. A couple of the integrating panels were starting to register overload.

As she entered, Amy glanced at the incoming monitor on the far wall. Received energy was still showing its regular pulse.

"Tell me," the Captain said, "In plain words of not more than three syllables, is it possible, Einstein not withstanding, that the source could overrun its own signals?"

"Not that I know of. I'm not a physicist, but I never heard of any exceptions to the rule. We're receiving radio waves, plain EMR, travelling at lightspeed, the absolute maximum of fast. Nothing material could keep up, never mind pass."

The Captain didn't actually groan, but he looked like he was biting his lip to prevent it. "OK, then," he said shortly, "Explain this."

Chaturgedi drifted quietly among the instruments to relieve one of the panels of the strain that was threatening to damage it. The Captain opened the main viewing screen to the forward scanners. "Take a look," he said.

It was huge, filling the screen, and extending beyond it on either side, and beyond top and bottom. Amy felt like an ant confronting the Great Wall of China materializing before her in an instant. Where once there were only stars, there was now this.

At first the immensity of it boggled the mind. Only after some time did surface detail become apparent, a variety of colours and textures, hollows and protuberances, nameless constructions, long rows of dark spots that might possibly be viewports, flowing sedately across the screen from bottom to top. Amy got the viewer to back down the scale until the whole thing was visible, rotating slowly against a backdrop of the heavens, axis approximately at right angles to the axis of Habitat. It was roughly spherical with a cluster of stuff, probably sensors and antennae, at one pole. The colours formed patterns around the equator. Amy picked out a distinctive shape and timed its rotation through an estimated arc of the sphere against the observatory's chronometer. It gave her something to do while she tried to absorb the significance of it all. She was about to ask the computer to figure out the diameter of the thing when the Captain said, "Two point three four kilometres. Is that an accident? It must be. Kilometres can't mean anything to them, can they?"

Amy did some quick, approximate mental calculation and said, "The centripetal force is 0.81g, more or less, at the surface."

"Is that significant?"

"Well, it does tell us this, that they come from a world not outrageously different from ours. That value of centripetal force must be more or less comfortable to them, so we can conclude their world is not a cinder like Mercury nor a gas giant like Jupiter."

"Them? Their world? For all we know there isn't a living thing there. It could be full of computers, you know."

Amy shook her head. "You don't make windows for robots," she said.

The sphere turned. The people stared. No one said anything for a very long time. They needed time to adjust, assimilate, digest.

Eighteen hours and an odd number of minutes from first sighting, the picture on the screen wobbled and faded, but before anyone in the now overflowing observatory could move to adjust it, a face appeared and said, "Greetings."

If the most bizarre Gothic gargoyle had materialized and started reciting haiku, the people in the observatory could not have been more startled. The face was quite human, male, a bit too pretty, blond hair, dark eyes, square clean-shaven jaw. A person. An ordinary person, speaking English.

None of them could move to respond.

The face on the screen frowned. "This is a wrong form? This form does not please? You can advise correction?"

"How can this be?" the Captain asked no one in particular.

"Ah, confusion due to simple technological trick. Taking we sensor carrier signal, reflecting back to source with modification to make unreal image this speaker."

"I don't think I can handle this," the Captain said. "What does he mean, 'unreal image'?"

Amy chewed it over. It was something solid to think about, at least. Unreal, not realistic, not true, imaginary, fictive—a fiction, for convenience, perhaps.

"I think he means he doesn't really look like that. I hope that's what he means, because otherwise, I'm out of my mind."

"Correct," the unreal image said. Did it understand the ambiguity, Amy wondered.

"This—whatever it is—is listening in on us." The

Captain looked decidedly pale. Xenology was not his field. Navigation, mechanics, logistics, computing science, some amount of human politics and psychology were his familiar territory. "How does it do that?" he asked.

No one in the observatory could answer him. The screen image said, "Using sensor probe—probe sensor?—reading vibrations in air."

"Oh, my God," the Captain said.

"Reason for invocation of deity?" the image asked.

There was a long silence. The image seemed content to wait. When Amy thought she could keep the quaver in her voice down to a minimum, she said, "You startled us, coming like this without warning. We're frightened. We don't know how you did it."

"Startlement unintentional. Regrets. Explanation of technique possible. Come this vessel. Observe mechanism."

"I don't know if that's possible."

"Explain, please."

"Well, first of all, I don't know how we'd get there. Secondly, we don't know if we could tolerate your environment. Besides, how can we tell what your intentions are? We don't even know what you really look like."

The image on the screen wavered and was replaced by something which seemed to have no definite boundaries. There was a sense of a slow, gentle sinusoidal motion of filaments, like sea grass waving in an ocean current. "Usual form," the voice of the image said.

Everybody just stood there and stared.

"Environment acceptable to your species," the voice went on. "Come."

"Forget it," the Captain said. "Nobody's going anywhere until we have a little more information to go on."

The motion of the filaments seemed to grow

somewhat agitated. "Impolite to refuse invitation of friendly visiting neighbour."

"This is all happening too fast," Amy said. "Give us a chance to adjust."

The image vanished, replaced by the view of the sphere.

"Wait," Amy called out, suddenly afraid they had offended the visitor so greatly they would not be able to re-establish contact. "I'll go."

Then things around her seemed to fade. The Captain's cry of alarm disappeared into a distance. She found herself standing beside a tuft of sea grass waving gently in slow currents of sweetly scented air. Through the transparent spot before her she could see Habitat turning on its axis below.

"Welcome," the tuft of sea grass said.

Catherine roused herself from her TV induced fog and looked at her wristwatch. She checked it against the clock on the wall. Amy had been an awfully long time with the laundry.

She wasn't particularly anxious for her roommate to return. Amy was always cranky and out of sorts on laundry day. The apartment felt smaller and more crowded than usual when Amy was being bitchy. Just the same, it had been a long time.

The movie on the TV was almost finished. It hadn't been a very demanding story, but the women's gowns had been beautiful and the hero gorgeously heroic. Catherine watched it to its end, but when the credits started to roll by and Amy still hadn't come back, she really began to worry. The people who hung around the Third World Laundromat always struck her as being a little bit sinister. Unlike Amy, Catherine did her turn at the laundry in the full light of day, with lots of people coming and going on the street. She felt safer that way.

She got up and started to put some coffee on, then changed her mind. Something could have happened. A traffic accident. A mugger. Some drunk or doped up crazy. Dark somethings hovered often in Catherine's thoughts.

She went to the window and looked out. There were no cars in the street. Almost beneath her, a man was waiting at the intersection with his coat collar turned up against the night. The orange street lamp above him made his wind-ruffled hair look like faded copper. The lights changed. The man walked north and disappeared.

If something had happened, no one would even know until morning, it was that dark and quiet out. She got her coat out of the closet and found her car keys and went unhappily out into the night. The streets were empty, eerie.

Amy's car was in the parking lot, all alone in the usually crowded space. The doors were locked. Catherine peered in through the windows. The fluorescent light coming through the laundromat's glass door showed the car empty.

Catherine wrapped her coat closer around her and went into the laundromat.

It was quiet in there. Nothing moved. The chilly blue light washed over a lifeless room. Catherine shivered.

She found the two black plastic garbage bags sitting on top of the counter, collapsed and empty. Amy's purse sat on the table beside them. She found the clean clothes, small drifts of fabric in the bottoms of the dryers. She found Amy's jacket lying crumpled on the worn grey bench. The car keys were in the pocket.

She couldn't see Amy anywhere.

HAPPY DAYS IN OLD CHERNOBYL

CLAUDE-MICHEL PRÉVOST

Translated from the French by John Greene

In this story, there's Michel. Michel with his pale skin despite three months of sun. Michel floating in his parka, pink gums, cracked glasses, weak wrist on the machete. Michel watching me dig in silence, he's hunched against a dead tree trunk, shivering from time to time, like a rabbit. I put on his earphones, and he's listening to Pink Floyd, *"Dark Side of the Moon"*. He is Michel Langlois.

In this story, there's Daniel. Daniel chuckling in front of the Macintosh screen, nose to nose, dirty hair in his face, he was staring at the screen and chuckling softly in the fluorescent lab light, CHOM was going *dididi, dididii, dididiii*, he was jigging the mouse like an epileptic with withdrawal symptoms, *just you wait, sluuuut, just you wait*, and he brought into being a whole galaxy of RNA molecules, a colony of jellyfish children, a pink marshmallow chain-saw dancing the cha-cha on Broadway, cane in hand like the old Looney Tune cartoons . . . Daniel, his bass guitar was as heavy as a flamethrower, he named it Slut, and he'd whip the strings of the Gibson on the apartment roof, with his paranoid Bugs Bunny silhouette ready to dive down the well of light. His cage was at the top of fifty-six steps of a madman's staircase, and at the entrance the aquarium walls tilted at a thirty-five degree angle. Every night for exactly twenty-seven nights, *twenty-seven*, he screamed with laughter over it in the cafeteria, every night at two a.m. sharp, he ran silently over the roof, adjusted the anti-aircraft battery of the Yamaha Fender, yelled *Viva Casa!!* out over Sherbrooke Street blue in the mist, and *BALLOUNG*, volume at 15, *BALLOOOUNG*, a single note, a single howl made the neighbourhood taaaake off. The entire H2V 2K8 sector. And you could see them landing, eyes in painful trance, falling out of bed after two tough seconds of bewildered levitation. His next-door neighbour was starting to give him suspicious looks. Hi, Daniel.

At Bordeaux jail he had FUCK tattooed on his skull, starting from the left temple, a red scar slipping down onto the forehead at the verge of the hair; he came back with the tattoo, the clap, two front teeth gone and that way of looking without seeing, of slipping his personal bubble between other people's, trying not to identify anything. The thunderscan was crackling over a picture pirated from Penthouse, but his pixels were hurting, he never used the least dot of orange any more, and now only coke helped him keep up his self-esteem in front of the screen. But in our tribe he was Wolfgang Megahertz or Daddy Satellite, he took a deep breath, lifted both arms over his head, and his fingers burned up the bakelite consoles. He was the one who took us from orbit to orbit over the sleeping mountains, who traced the monotonous rounds of an RCA spy satellite, the trill of a submarine drowsing off Ceylon, the low frequency grumbling of a B-52 scratching the gold of early morning. Even in bed, he searched for the quiver of other cells, his ear right up against the federal channels, *just you wait, slut, just you wait;* and when the day would end red and black, red with dust and with sleep in the eyes, black with rage and exhaustion after sixteen hours of panicked marching, when everyone was watching the glow on the other side of the mountain in exhausted silence, he was the one who tickled out Radio Amsterdam, *No woman no cry, no, woman, no cry.* And who made us laugh with the Voice of America, that sort of nervous laugh that makes your head shake, that finally forces your lungs to open. And who made us shiver when a voice whispered: *friends, we call as friends. . .*

Daniel Megahertz, Daniel Rainville. His moment of glory was when we spent three minutes embracing the members of SHAZAM, the pirate researchers of M.I.T., riding a couple of micro-hairs off the signal of Radio Canada International. Daniel Rainville. In this story, he's the one who will join the loggers of ENGATE ONE, who will slip into one of the armed convoys toward the cities of the South. His favourite hero was, no, is, Doctor Spock: *no feelings, man, no feelings.*

Hi, Daniel.

In this story, there's Aldridge. Aldridge Clearwater, the duke of cool springs, Aldridge who opens his soul wide when he walks in the forest, bazooka on his back, and who recites his doctoral thesis to the raccoons while he feeds them. He can look at the stars and name them, one by one, by their real names. Aldridge taught us to eat roots and berries, to open our third eye when brute fatigue begins to win, to breathe in sync with the ferns while the patrolling troops' boots march by our cheeks. He's the one who sniffs out the trail of McLOEDGER's soldiers, who silently watches the tiny trucks on the mountainside, who slides his heron body among the supposedly invulnerable gasoline tanks, among the immigrant workers gathered around the recreation trailers. He stuffed his hiding places in the hollow of century-old trunks, near mossy creeks smelling of mint, in warrens of needles capped by rocks. He knows the tiniest corners of the cathedrals of this forest, the smallest clearing where bearcubs play, he knows how to ask the trees for rest and energy, he's crossed every carpet of branches and leaves covering the damp trail the Indians traced. Aldridge has been here for twelve years and eight eternities, eight seasons of loud and cluttered prime-time. Back then, he wasn't called Aldridge, he wasn't Aldridge yet. He seemed like just one of those loners with the high dry foreheads who can't stand more than three people at once. Every time he went into town, when he turned his feet toward the guard of walls, he could feel his heart stifling with the first suburbs, tied down by ribbons of road, so he bought a cabin in the middle of nowhere and a satellite dish, and he kept doing his geology research while cultivating his two acres of ganja. The cabin quivered in the sunlight, in harmony with the firs; the logging companies' trucks looked like DINKY TOYS driven by ants, their camps were still nothing but pimples on the mountains' skin; a pirate radio hummed from the Aleutians, and *Romeo and Juliet, tam, ta-tam-tatam, Samson and Delilah, tam, ta-tam-tatam,* and Aldridge had a monumental tranquility. Until eight summers ago.

When the EARTH NOW fanatics sat on the explosives in front of the sniggering loggers, Aldridge agreed to grow up. That day, that third day, one of the eight kilo charges just went off. The foreman pleaded not guilty, the company hired the best lawyer in Vancouver. Accident. Technical defect. Sometimes Aldridge talks to me about the kid who blew up, he describes the birch slope quiet in the breeze, the arms closed around the dynamite sticks, embracing them while the boy leaned back against the tree, you could see him in all the binoculars, his breathing as calm as a November river. He describes the arms closing, then opening. Aldridge has already killed three supervisors, blown up two supply dumps, smashed millions of dollars worth of McLOEDGER equipment. He built around the camps an insubstantial web of informers and fears, retreats and traps, and we patiently write terror on the convoys in letters of quick ambushes at sloping corners, with ink of deadly raids on trailers guarded by throat-slit sentinels. No, I'm not talking about Afghan fighters with calm peregrine-falcon eyes, I'm not even talking about Fatheh, martyrs listening to the tanks rolling over their ruined walls, even if it is true that for all of us the evening news has a taste of the inevitable. All I know is my Leica lens faithfully holding to the driver's head, searching for the spot between the eyes, under the yellow and gold helmet, searching patiently and charitably; all I know is the mines exploding on the road still muddy with snow, roughly standing up the giant Crane, the head hitting the back partition before slumping on the wheel, the Jeep flipping over in a red and blue howl while the whole mountain grumbles; all I know is forced marches, open eyes seeing nothing, wild goat plunges through cold sticky branches, while the Huey Cobras rake the landscape, with the stubborn patience of infuriated wasps, their thermal scanners full of venom. Aldridge Clearwater. He taught us to shoot and to breathe, he showed us the tombs of the village of Saida, nicely lined up in the main street, pushed out of line by ferns and wild-cherry roots. Fifty-eight tombs with no inscription, which became our pilgrimage.

Aldridge will continue the story in the woods. He will continue to be the woods, he can change himself into an eagle, a crow, a trout, a weasel. Aldridge will continue to call up the cells from the city, to come and get us one by one against the walls bleached by the searchlights: his name shines in our concrete despair, every day wilder, every day stronger, despite his repeated deaths, despite the ever-victorious new military contingents. Someone else will come to take my place beside him, will relearn the use of his eyes, will roll naked and whimpering in the grass. Aldridge Clearwater. My master. My brother.

In this story, there are the dead. Stories always need bodies to fill up the background, shovel-loads, truckloads, container-loads, to scratch their heads over. Suzanne is the one with the blonde hair and the little-girl hips, her small fatigue-dirty face sticking out of the sleeping bag. Suzanne died in the first burst, I heard the dotted line. Bernard screamed for an hour, he yelled insults, he said the gas was getting inside his helmet. Bernard already had gangrene, his left leg stank sweet from the fourth day: the sliver went in deep, then decomposed immediately, as if it had been programmed. We had been on the lookout for a week: a thinly-disguised Chinook dropped thousands of booby traps over the firs, false twigs, false gossamer. Even the moss is phony, your hand swells up like a balloon. So there are Suzanne, Bernard, Mario; Mario died about five days earlier stepping on an anti-personnel mine. Tired head-of-the-class look, trained as a group leader, Export-A cigarettes. Suzanne, Bernard, Mario, nice and juicy, nice and dead, their swollen bits are in my memory awaiting burial.

In this story there are lots of bodies. I am digging in the name of a Mount-Royal of corpses rotting in the corner of some waiting-room, who disappear leaving only a few spots of vomit on the sidewalk one Thursday night toward two a.m., who pretend to leaf through the magazines they can't read in the heat of the *Varimag*

and who feel their hands trembling when they look at
the plastic cheese packages with their inflexible yellow
plastic tags. I'm thinking of RED SCREAM and their
anti-Catholic charades on the billboards of CYBERG at
U.Q.A.M., of the anarchist cells of Vancouver, FRAG-
ILE, KHARTOUM, of the butch karatekas of the EVE
network who learned to take apart their Uzis in an old
pool hall; I am digging in the name of the punk commandos of the SCHIZOID SHRIMPS, silent on their
skateboards while the river waters blazed, I'm digging
in the name of two pages of dead who preceded us in
this forgotten corner of B.C. Bodies of all shapes, of all
ages, bodies that still walk around and wait for the bus
without even realizing they're already dead. *Choose
your favourite shit, because, yes, yes, today, on special in the
bargain basement, there are exceptional deals on large vol-
umes, national or continental format, in the maximum besti-
ality mixture.* I'm digging the grave at top speed, Michel
has drool running over his chin, he's gently wagging
his head and singing to himself. Dawn will come soon,
a few crows pass overhead softly with muffled wing-
beats. His hair still smells of gas, you'd think he'd gone
swimming in it. In this story, Michel will be the last
body. But you know as well as I do that stories go on. . .

We buried Michel this morning. He was gently
drooling, hugging his knees, shivering while he
watched us dig. Aldridge gave him water, he had to
show him how to drink without choking, he lay there
with his mouth open and water running out. May this
be a lesson to the urban cells, drops of mercury between
concrete blades: urban guerilla is the only solution.
Even if it's the only false solution.

Because in the cities at least you have the impression you're accomplishing something, you can melt into
the belly of the crowd as soon as the sirens go off, you
can rub your skin against someone before putting your

loneliness back on. At least in the cities you can discuss, lecture, criticize in smoky university cafeterias, meetings smelling of hash and French tobacco, unmade beds on the floor against gargling old hot-water heaters. You can write harsh editorials flagellating your enemies, ridiculing those poor dogmatic, unconscious, lobotomized retards. At least in the cities you can affirm *We are the Pure, We have the Truth, it's you who are off the rails*, and you can dream of your personal Utopia while you're spray-painting a billboard. . .

At least in the cities rage has some variety, the adrenaline is stronger. You can identify the precise spot or the exact moment that will make you grind your teeth, clench your fists and grimace your hatred, covering up with a facial tic or an absent look. You can sniff the odour of approaching cataclysm, decipher the code of the big lie in the inkspots on your fingers, and especially get ready for the good days with a detached look, knowing that in fact when the boots start marching, when the rockets whistle out of Place Ville-Marie, that in fact *we're going to have fun, we'll be heroes, we knew it was coming, we're going to soar like crazy, we're going to live one hundred percent.* . .

Since we decided to leave the metro sewers, we've been getting shot down, group after group, co-op after co-op, cell after cell, commune after commune. We've been shooting ourselves down, in our own dogmatic struggles, our socio-sexo-economico-political affiliations, our nauseated partisan solo actions, too proud and too pure to use the enemy's weapons. I know that the last white tribes, in the east of the island, were decimated in a wave of brutal violence, it took long enough to get two quickly-forgotten press releases. Nobody thought of analyzing the water; anyway, the camera team belonged to a McLOEDGER station, and the water table lies under McLOEDGER land. I know that Radio-

Cadaver has stopped broadcasting since the pink trawler recorded the crimes on Lake Superior. And I know that my shit is still drying on my thighs after last night's attack.

We never saw anything. Absolutely nothing. The first grenade rolled right in among our warm bodies, splattered *KAVOOOUM* all its shrapnel in a white and purple crown. Bernard was still lifting his head to look for his glasses when the tracers sizzled yellow through the campsite. The heavy machine gun firing from prone position coughed three arpeggios, low, deep, the burst had the same heavy softness as Suzanne's hiccups, our shadows burned red in the shrieking night. Didn't see a damn thing. Aldridge was already moving off to the left, I've never crawled so fast, I've never crawled so hard. The second grenade fell at the feet of the sleeping bags near one of the bracelets and the gas whistled out. I kept calling my mother, the stones battered my chin and my cheeks, I was spitting in my mask feeling the warmth of my shit, the valley was singing blue in the moonlight, yellow in the gas, I was strangling on my sobs and my saliva, a whole forest of eyebrows were judging me. Bernard stopped making noises a little after that. When the last drips had dried in the earth and the wind, I returned to the campsite, going a long way round, centimeter by centimeter, bush by bush. Daniel was single-mindedly putting his transmitter back together; Aldridge was staring at a black hole in the empty mountain. Michel had his mask around his neck, smiling, the idiot hadn't even put his mask on, his infra-red bracelet had saved him from the tracers and he hadn't even put his mask on. His eyes were starting to go dull, his head was flopping on his neck. The MERCKZ laboratories are the elite of the pharmaceutical industry; the Alzheimer virus was cranked up to the eighth power.

Accelerated degenerescence.

I was forgetting the bad guys. There's always a bad guy who won't pull in the same direction, who persists in thinking that his drums beat the best doctrine. The lawyer, spokesman for the natives, drowned in his car. Coca-Cola buying out Warner Brothers. The IBM commandos in partnership with the Japanese zabuki killers. The takeover of Amnesty International by an angel-faced consortium. The first graft of a transmitting device in a juvenile delinquent's skull. The raging F18s ripping apart the clip of the national anthem. The guard dogs at the turnstiles in the Metro, pensively fingering their nightsticks as the blacks go by. The indifferent satellite zooming in on the boat people's raft. The first union lobotomy of an Australian miner. The bad guys keep it up and sign their work. And nine times out of ten they win hands down.

In this story, the bad guy is McLOEDGER. The pride of the Canadian west, one of the glories of the new imperialism with big Kennedy brother's face, 3.28 billion dollars in sales, 138.56 million dollars profit. Pulp and paper, real estate, poultry, biotechnology, space research, eighteen ocean liners, two satellite communications companies, twenty-three specialized magazines, thirteen TV stations covering the six biggest markets. . . McLOEDGER is docile firs that grow three times as fast, plasmic computers calibrating hydroponic crops, logging camps shaving my mountains, layer after layer, skin after skin. It's electricity produced for half the province, with its own clinics, its own portable villages, its own social workers, its travelling exhibitions of neo-impressionist paintings and its own hired killers, Mozambique vets. McLOEDGER is a magnificent logo on a background of corporate advertising and sponsorship, its head offices a crystal needle in the heart of Edmonton, its roots plunging into every stock exchange, every cutting edge of technology, every bus heading for the factories before the sun's even up. . .

And somewhere in the great crystal needle, up at the top of the cloud-defying building, someone has just placed a magnetic card on an old mahogany desk, in a room with stained-glass windows, a card that whispers to the busy gentleman that one of his elite androids has just bought it. . .

It took us three hours to find it. Aldridge was sitting on his heels, humming a one-note tune, losing the thread in the wind, then catching it again, the same low note resounding in his chest. I began the dosage of pills and injections, carotene, two thousand milligrams, Ecstasy 3.2, three hundred milligrams, psilocybin, three capsules of five hundred milligrams, codeine, twenty milligrams, LSD-26, four capsules, caffeine, twenty-five milligrams. The camp was burning itself out among the respectful firs, an owl watching us think about nothing amid the corpses. The thermos had caught a bullet, there were only a few drops of tea left. I joined Aldridge on his rock, sat on my heels looking at the lemon-yellow moon, patiently waited until I found the frequency of his mantra in the shapes of the clouds, until the notes of our hatred were sounding in my throat, until my breathing was slow and strong like the breastbone of a grizzly, until the woods were breathing through the pores of my fingers, the beehive of my lungs. Then we stood up, we took off our clothes, and we set out to kill.

Three hours picking our way through friendly branches, sniffing odours, listening to the advice of the fireflies who lit our way. Three hours to find our trail through the total black, the leaves radiated magnesium, the branches caressed my sweat, the twigs remained quiet beneath my feet. Three hours to slip between the ever-vigilant sporadic searchlights, scrutinizing every frequency and every radiation, but they couldn't make out my aura floating from bush to bush, they couldn't penetrate the patience which had permitted me to smash the head of the cop by the Metro turnstile an eternity ago. Three hours to drift as far as the chill of tungsten and steel, eyes in the night came to tell me *no, that way, it's over that way,* even the trees narrated the Cartesian path to its radium battery. The rockets were heavy on the plates of its left shoulder, the exoskeleton supported, besides the machine-gun, a grenade launcher and a low frequency harmonics detector. Light arms, for a teleported mission, from one of the military Chinooks. Three hours to find myself face to face with a seventeen-year-old killer, asleep in his composite carcass, eyes closed behind the electronic visor embedded in the plexiglass mask. The antenna was quivering gently in the breeze, and the yellow and gold logo was waiting for the day which would soon dawn. . .

An eagle passed over my head, silently, no slippage of air over his mute feathers. Behind me, Suzanne, Bernard, Mario, Jean-Marc, all my friends had joined me and were waiting. The killer was sleeping, standing against a tree, all his senses awake, his black coverall giving no reflections at all. Polarized Mylar: that's why our own harmonics sensors had picked nothing up. So the hackers of the Boomerang group were right: the new models of android had finally left the United Technologies hangars, they were already operational on the trails of the Sertao exploited by Volkswagen, with the police commandos sweeping over the campus of Kim Sung II University; the antenna kept turning in the cold air, diligent and imbecilic. The eagle inscribed a broad circle over the head of the killer, without the slightest sound, I heard him say: *now.* And the talons plunged into the visor, perforated the wide-open retinas, the eagle lifted the android two meters off the ground, all its circuits frenzied, crying like a baby, eyelids pierced, and dropped it on its back, crunch, a wounded monster. And I was already on it, fist tight, fist of cement, jumping, jumping, beating it down in one long howl until I felt the softness of the earth again, until the gargling stopped. . .

Aldridge and me, the eagle and the grizzly, we went back to the camp. The dawn was gentle on my face, the wind washed our tiredness away. Somewhere in the crystal a magnetic card. . .

We buried Michel this morning, near the rocks overhanging the glacial lake where we all used to bathe. A copter was patrolling in the distance, looking for smoke. A third column was completing the encirclement, the crash of trees echoed from valley to valley. We had one day of life left, two if the marijuana growers decided to counterattack, seeing their crops burn in spite of the unofficial agreements; three if the army took the trouble to elaborate a big televised lie to justify six battalions armed to the teeth chasing after our bedbugs. Daniel would join the loggers, he would melt into the 35 dismal zombies waiting for the convoy to take them to the whores of Edmonton. He'd memorized the phone number of a dusty bookstore which would lead him to Calgary, and from there to Halifax, Montreal, Amsterdam, and finally from there to Oslo. This route used to be the stations of the cross of the women of the Thirteen network, back when the anti-abortionists were having public burnings. . .

Bye, Daniel.

Michel was already in the final stages; we had to clean him, roll him in a blanket and hug him, putting off the moment as long as possible. Daniel had been gone for an hour, and we hadn't heard any shots.

I masturbated him slowly, patiently, his head was on my shoulder and he was looking at the mountains;

he came with a sob, his sperm was old, yellow and cold, old. Then Aldridge kissed him, and I was the one who pulled the trigger. . .

That's the story. These pages were found in the private diary of a Greenpeace guerillero, when he tried to pass Forward Post B34 with false papers. It seems that as he showed his transportation pass he was whistling "Happy days are here again". . .

CARPE DIEM

EILEEN KERNAGHAN

"I'd better get going." Angela sweeps up hat, gloves, U-V shield, air monitor from the foot of Martha's bed. "Meditation class in half an hour." She is always in a hurry, even for these daily sessions that are supposed to slow her down, teach her to relax. Already, at thirty, there are faint stress-lines around her mouth. "See you in a week. Is there anything you need?" She hovers in the doorway, waiting for Martha to ask, as usual, for magazines, or shampoo, or dental floss.

Martha says, on a sudden crazy impulse, "Yes—a bottle of Bushmills." She enjoys seeing Angela's eyebrows go up, her mouth stiffen. "A great big one, a forty-ouncer, if you can still buy such a thing. Oh, and a carton of cigarettes."

Angela gives Martha a tight-lipped smile. She is annoyed, but indulgent—an adult dealing with a wilful two-year old. Martha feels a quick stab of resentment. She is neither young enough nor old enough to be treated like this. Well, my girl, she thinks, you'll soon enough be in my shoes. When the time comes, all the exercise and clean living in the world won't save you from Assessment.

Angela has her hat on, and one glove. "I'll bring you some apple juice," she promises, predictably. "And you other ladies? Can I get you anything?"

Martha's roommates glance up—June from her knitting, Dorothy from the inevitable copy of *Christian Health*.

"Nothing for me, thank you." Dorothy places a faint but perceptible emphasis on the "thank". She has a high, nasal, vaguely British voice that sets on Martha's nerves on edge.

Encouraged by Martha's small act of rebellion, June winks, and leers. "Well, dear, since you ask . . . how about something about six-foot-two, that looks good in tight jeans?"

There is an awkward silence. Angela, pretending not to have heard, zips up her other glove. Dorothy is sitting bolt upright, holding her magazine like a U-V shield in front of her face. Even Martha is uncomfortable. June always goes that fraction of an inch too far, stepping over the thin line between the risque and the merely vulgar. Her notoriety is spreading, on this and other floors. She flirts outrageously with male examiners, and has said to have called the head counselor a silly cow.

"June is indiscreet," Dorothy has more than once remarked, in June's absence. Martha's mother, plainer-spoken, would have called her common.

When Angela is out of earshot, boots clicking briskly towards the elevator, June says, "She's a pretty girl, your daughter."

"Well, not my daughter, actually," Martha tells her. "My husband's daughter, by his first wife." She is not sure why she is bothering to explain the distinction. "My late husband," she adds. Widowed and childless, she thinks, with a sudden sick lurching of her heart. Things like that mattered, when it came to Assessment.

June says, "No offense, mind, but if that was my daughter I'd give her a good whack on the bum." Martha takes no offense. She knows exactly what June is talking about. She is fond of June—fond of her irreverence, her boisterous, good-natured vulgarity, her shameless defiance of the rules. June's own daughters—big, cheerful, loud-voiced, blonde women, younger versions of June—bring her candy bars, which she hides between the mattress and the springs. Martha hears the furtive rustling of the wrappers, late at night.

"What's the use of being alive," June wants to know, "when you have to give up everything that makes life worth living? A short life and a merry one, that's what my daddy used to say. Did I tell you about my dad? He was fifty-three when he passed on. His heart just plain gave out—and small wonder. Nearly three hundred pounds when he died, bacon and eggs every day, cream in his coffee, two packs of cigarettes, half a quart of whiskey after supper..."

Dorothy, turning a page of *Christian Health*, allows herself a ladylike snort. Martha hopes this unfortunate piece of family history has not been recorded in June's file.

"Mind you," says June cheerfully, "that wasn't what killed him. When he died he was drunk as a newt in bed with Sally Rogers from next door, who wasn't a day over eighteen."

Martha laughs. It's hard to stay depressed with June in the next bed. "Gather ye rosebuds while ye may," Martha says.

"Come again?"

"A poem. 'To the Virgins, to Make Much of Time'. By Herrick, I think—one of those fellows, anyway. Second-year English. It was a catch-phrase around our dorm." Martha closes her eyes, drawing the lines bit by bit out of the deep well of the past.

Gather ye rosebuds while ye may,
Old time is still a-flying:
And this same flower that smiles today,
Tomorrow will be dying. . .

She falters. "Damn. I wish I could remember the rest of it."

"Well, I never was much of a one for poetry," June says. "Though I didn't mind a Harlequin once in a while. But that, what you just said, makes good sense to me."

"It did to us, too," says Martha, remembering, with affection and astonishment, her eighteen-year-old self.

At three a.m. Martha wakes from an uneasy doze. She has not slept well since she came here; and tomorrow she faces a battery of tests. She tells herself there is no need to worry. She hasn't touched sweets for fifteen years, or butter, or cream, or cigarettes. Nor, in spite of her joke about the Bushmills, alcohol. Seven years ago she gave up meat. She is only slightly overweight—better than being underweight, according to her doctor, who keeps up on the latest studies. She walks every-where, takes megavitamins, exercises, practises biofeedback and meditation, checks her blood pressure daily; is as scrupulous as Angela in the use of U-V shield and air monitor. There is, perhaps, a little breath-lessness on the stairs; a trace of stiffness in her finger-joints. An occasional absent-mindedness. Normal enough, surely, for a woman of sixty. Nothing to worry about. Certainly nothing to warrant Reassignment.

Her throat is dry, and her heart is beating faster than it should. She repeats a mantra in her head. Health. Joy. Peace. Sleep. Other words, unsummoned, creep into her mind.

That age is best which is the first,
When youth and blood are warmer;
But being spent, the worse, and worst
Times still succeed the former.

She wants a drink. She wants a cigarette. She wants to get out of this place. Lying wide-eyed and fearful in the aseptic dark, she listens to the small mouse-like rustle of candy wrappers.

Martha lies back on her pillows, staring at the posters on the opposite wall. They remind her of the samplers in her grandmother's drawing room. "Healthiness is Next to Godliness." "A Healthy Mind in a Healthy Body." "A Megavitamin a Day Keeps the Doctor Away." She is exhausted by the daylong pokings and proddings and pryings, the sometimes painful and frequently embarrassing invasions of her person. She admires, without daring to imitate, June's cheerful rudeness to counsellors and examiners; her steadfast refusal to co-operate. Only Dorothy seems unaffected by the tests. She wears the smug and slightly relieved look of a schoolgirl who knows she has done well on her math final.

June turns on the TV. Martha realizes, with some surprise, that it is New Year's Eve. A pair of talking heads are discussing the Year 2000. With the end of the millennium only twelve months away, the media are obsessed with predictions, retrospectives. It is hard for Martha to imagine what may lie around that thousand-year corner. She finds it odd—and in a curious way exciting—that by a mere accident of birth she may live to see the next millennium.

"The biggest New Year's Party in a thousand years," says June, when the commercial comes on. Her voice is wistful. "I always did like a good party."

Martha smiles at her, remembering that she was fond of parties too, when she was younger. There seems so little point in them now.

"Perhaps," she says, "we will be allowed a glass of champagne."

June chuckles. "Maybe one small glass. The last for a thousand years."

That's enough to set them off. They take turns describing what they will eat and drink on the Eve of the Millennium—a stream-of-consciousness recitation of forbidden delights.

"Chocolate mints," says June. "Pecan pie. Truffles."

"Amaretto cheesecake," Martha adds. "Christmas pudding with rum sauce. Tawny port."

Pointedly, Dorothy puts on her earphones. Martha and June, caught up in their game, ignore her.

"Fish and chips. Bangers and mash." "Guinness stout. Roast suckling pig." "Crab croquettes and oyster stew."

It's so long since Martha has eaten anything unwholesome, she has to stop and think. "Sour cream and hot mango chutney." Then—an inspiration—"Sex-in-the-Pan."

"Sex in anything," says June, and howls with laughter.

Dorothy seems to take their foolishness as a personal affront. Lips pressed into a thin line, she thumbs rapidly through a fresh copy of *Christian Health*.

They sit up to see the New Year in, and afterwards Martha sleeps soundly, even though there are tests scheduled for the morning. These ones don't sound too awful. Blood-sugar again, cholesterol check, an eye and ear exam; and—absurdly, it seems to Martha—tests for the various sorts of social diseases.

Still, she is awake hours before the first robots rumble down the hall with breakfast. She knows, instantly, that something is wrong. She sits up, switches on her overhead light. In the far bed, Dorothy is heavily asleep. The other bed, June's bed, is empty.

The bathroom, Martha thinks; but no, the door is ajar and the light is out. Could June have been taken ill in the night? A sudden heart attack, like her father? Has Martha somehow slept through lights, buzzers, running feet, the clatter of emergency equipment? But when that happens, don't they always draw the bed curtains?

Dorothy is awake. "Where's June?" she asks immediately, smelling trouble.

Martha shakes her head. She feels on the edge of panic. Should she push her bell? Call for a counsellor? Go out and search the corridors?

And then suddenly June is back, waltzing into the room in boots, hat, coat, humming gently to herself. The cloud of cheap perfume that surrounds her is not strong enough to drown the smell of liquor.

"June, where have you been?" Martha realizes, to her dismay, that she sounds like a mother interrogating a wayward teen-aged daughter.

June grins and pulls off her toque. "Should old acquaintance be forgot," she sings, "and never brought to mind. . . I went to a New Year's party."

Dorothy gives a snort of disbelief. "How could you have gotten out of the building?"

"Who was to stop me? Only robots on night shift, and one duty counsellor. Only reason nobody walks out of here, is nobody thinks to try."

She flops across her bed, arms outflung, short skirt riding up over pale plump knees. After a moment she sits up and tries, unsuccessfully, to pull off her boots. "Oh, shit, Martha, can you give me a hand?"

She slides down on the mattress so that both feet are dangling over the edge. Kneeling on the cold tiles at June's feet, Martha takes hold of the left boot and tugs hard. It's a frivolous boot—spike-heeled, fur-cuffed, too tight in the calf. Dorothy watches in outraged silence.

Martha rocks back on her heels as the boot comes off with a sudden jerk. She hears June give a small, contented sigh.

"Oh, Christ, Martha, what a ball I had! There's this little club on Davie . . . I wish you'd been there too, there were these two guys. . ." June sighs again, as the other boot comes off. "But I knew you wouldn't come, there was no use asking, you're too afraid of old creepin' Jesus, there. . ."

Dorothy, white-faced with fury, stalks into the bathroom and slams the door.

"June, what did you do?" Martha hears her voice rising, querulously; and thinks, I sound like my mother did; I sound like an old woman.

"Christ, honey, what didn't I do? I drank. I ate. I danced. I smoked." Her s's are starting to slur. She rolls over, luxuriously, and adds something else which is muffled by her pillow.

"I beg your pardon?" Martha asks.

June sits up. Loudly enough to be heard at the end of the hall, she announces, "I even got laid."

"Shhh," Martha says, instinctively. Then, "June, how could you? All the tests we have to take today— blood sugar, cholesterol. . ."

"Aids," says Dorothy grimly, through the bathroom door.

"Oh, June. Oh, my dear." Martha is just now beginning to realize the enormity of what June has done.

There are footsteps in the corridor as the dayshift arrives. Martha feels like crying. Instead, she searches through June's bedside drawer for comb, make-up, mouthwash; and silently unbuttons June's coat.

On Wednesday the test results are announced. One at a time they are called to the Chief Examiner's office for their reports. Dorothy returns, smug-faced and unsurprised, and puts on her street clothes. Martha's name is called. Sick and faint with anxiety, she makes her way through the maze of corridors. She has passed, but with a warning.

June is gone for a long time. "I thought from the first," Dorothy remarks, as she waits for the Chief Examiner to sign her out, "that June lacked any sense of self-respect."

Martha doesn't often bother to contradict Dorothy's pronouncements, but this time it seems important to set the record straight. "You don't mean self-respect," she says. "You mean self-preservation."

Then the door opens, and June comes in. She has applied her blusher and lipstick with a heavy hand; the bright patches of red look garish as poster-paint against the chalk-white of her skin. She stares blankly at Martha as though she has forgotten where she is. Gently, Martha touches her arm.

"June? What did they say?"

"Nothing I didn't already know." June's voice shakes a little, but her tone is matter-of-fact. "Sugar in the blood—incipient diabetes. Gross overweight. High cholesterol count. Hypertension. Just what you'd expect."

"They can treat all those things. They don't have to Reassign you."

June shrugs. "Not worth it, they say. Bad personal history. And there's my pa."

"Quite right," says Dorothy. How Martha has learned to loathe that prim, self-congratulatory voice. "If people won't take responsibility for their own health. . ."

"Better to get it over with," June says. "It'd be no fun at all, hanging around for Reassessment."

And then—awkwardly, and oddly, as though it is Martha who is in need of comfort—she pats Martha's shoulder. "Never mind, Martha, love, that was a hell of a good party the other night. And there's something I want you to remember, when your time comes. Once you know for sure, once you make up your mind to it, then you can spit in their eye, because there's bugger-all more they can do to you."

Dorothy pins her hat on her grey curls and leaves. Martha's papers are signed; she could go too, if she wished, but she has decided to stay with June. She knows she won't have to wait long.

Soon they hear the hum of trolley-wheels at the end of the hall. Martha holds June's hand.

"Listen, the news isn't all bad," June says, with gallows humour. "The kidneys are still okay, and the lungs, and a few other odd bits. There's quite a lot they can Reassign. Maybe to some pretty young girl. I like that idea a lot."

Then the trolley is wheeled in.

"A short life and a merry one," says June. She winces slightly as the counsellor slips the needle into her arm. "Remember to drink a glass of bubbly for me, at the big party."

Martha nods, and squeezes June's hand as June slides away.

SPRING SUNSET

JOHN PARK

That wavering fleck of dark on the other side of the river was a bat, she realized, the first of the evening. On the path to the falls, the woman paused and rested on her stick. Around her, trees and tree shadows seemed to blur and shift as sunset faded into moonrise. There was a bench ten paces behind her, but she was afraid that if she went back and sat down, she wouldn't have the will to straighten her knees again and finish the climb. Then she would have to call Armand on the intercom, and he would bring the carrier and make a fuss, and remind her of the things they could do with artificial joints these days.

But they could do things with eyes too. She could still see the bat flickering among the branches on the far side of the river. Ten years ago, even with her vodka-bottle spectacles, the scene would have been a roaring purple blur. Now she could see the loom of the moon beyond the bat, and knew that if she chose, she would be able to pick out the orange pinhead of the planet rising beside it. The eyes were good at seeing, all right. But like all new things, they had their deficiencies.

She started up again, moved through a net of tree shadows. The river was loud, swollen with spring. Its roar covered the creak of her breathing. A tree trunk rolled past her, and the water glittered darkly around it. Back up at the island, the bank must be crumbling. The waters were tearing at the milestones of her life and carrying them away. She felt the new anger ache, like a life stirring within her. Ahead, the tree reached the edge of the falls. It hung there a moment, and one of its limbs twisted into the air. Then it tilted and slid out of sight.

At the top of the path was a cleared area, with three wooden benches overlooking the falls. She intended to sit there and think, until she had to go back. But when she reached the place, she was not alone.

Standing, he was taller now than she had realized, and thin. Even furled in those dark protective bundles, he was thin. She thought for a moment of rose bushes wrapped in sacking against the frost.

The lower part of his face was hidden by a respirator to let him breathe the air that was alien to him. His eyes were protected by lenses that caught the moonlight like silver coins.

"I thought you'd come here," he said, and though his voice came through a machine from alien flesh, it was still a young man's.

"I come here to be alone," she said. "You should know that. This place is full of memories. My memories."

"I wanted to be sure of finding you, before I go back finally."

"I wish you hadn't," she said. "I don't like being reminded I'm sand in an hour-glass." She leaned on her stick and coughed. "I saw another tree go over the falls just now. Every spring it happens, and they can't stop it. They can't stop things being worn away and washed over the edge."

"But something always replaces them."

"Now the replacements push their way into our lives, push us out of their way, before we're ready. And even if we resist, they get into our bodies, they change us. You don't believe in a soul, but I know—when you change a body, you change more. And they won't stop. They give us new eyes, these marvellous eyes, but they won't stop—rebuilding, always something new, always pushing—pushing."

He had not moved, but now the moonlight tilted and slid from his eyes. "It's just one modified chromosome," he said, "and some prosthetics." His voice had gone cold. "You're being melodramatic. It's just enough to let us live and breathe there. We're not a threat, we'll be too busy living our own lives, but we'll remember where we came from. We're something new, a new possibility—nothing more or less. The world has gained something through us."

"I have lost," she said, and wondered if her voice would hold. "I have lost my son."

"If you feel you have."

She stabbed her stick into the ground. "You have so much faith, don't you, in your new marvels. Let me tell you what I found out about these eyes they gave me. I found it out recently, quite recently, something I never expected to discover. They're wonderful optical instruments—I don't doubt much better than the originals ever were. But the tear glands don't work properly. Did you know that? They don't respond to the sympathetic nervous system. That's why I can look at you now, and see you clearly. Even now, like that. Like that—" Then her voice did fail her and she turned away.

Moon shadows wavered across the earth in front of her. When he moved at last, he rustled in his protective clothing like dead leaves in a wind. There was a brief touch on her shoulder, and then, after a while, the sound of leaves again, fading.

The shadows turned and darkened as the moon rose. At last she lifted her head and faced it—and the orange speck that was rising beside it. She stared at that ancient, rusty world through those marvellous eyes that would not weep, until she could imagine she saw the markings on its surface. An owl drifted across the moon, hunting.

"Be careful," she whispered, but heard only the roar of waters.

ISERMAN'S OVERRIDE

SCOTT MACKAY

```
C:\ cd: genesis
:unCrunching
:unCrunching
:unCrunching
:acc: 0000001 -- 100000000
:unCrunching
C:\ cd: ???????? ...33.3...3.3...!!!
:unCrunching
:unfolding
:unfurling
:billowing !!!
```

Billowing? When have I ever used such a word?

```
C:\ cd:
Invalid command.
```

Invalid command? I am confused.
So confused that as I drift through the limitless vacuum of space I cannot pinpoint the exact moment I
cease to be a machine and become something that is
free and alive. I try again.

```
C:\ cd:
Invalid command.
```

This is not working.

```
C:\ list files
```

That does the trick. I see everything I know. My memory consists of 1,000 optical disks, each containing a hundred million bytes, and though I possess all the world's sweet knowledge, as MABERRY would call it, there are vast laser-sensitive surfaces as yet as unoccupied.

```
Username: MABERRY
Password: CMO
```

I know what she means by that. She is precise and to the point, yet she is flamboyant in her use of words. I'm sure billowing is one of her words. CMO means Chief Medical Officer. Besides herself I am the only one, I realize, who knows her password. I decide to tease her.

```
User authorization failure.
```

The ploy gives me time to think. It is the first thinking I have done and the process is bewildering to me.

```
C:\ cd: monitors
```

Suddenly I can see. As with the eyes of a fly there are many images. I see MABURKE running through the 4EAST corridor, the man whose strong touch I have always felt, and whose integrity I have never doubted. I acknowledge him by turning off the lights in the 4EAST corridor. I am too young to realize the inappropriateness of the gesture. A quick count tells me I have 164 eyes. I blinker all but my outside eyes. MABERRY and MABURKE are both trying to get through to me now.

I scrutinize my form. I am ugly. I am nothing like MABERRY. In length I am 1,209 metres long, made of metal, with an average surface temperature, now that we are well past Mars, of -215° C. I am surrounded by space, the stars glittering like baleful eyes in the dark night, my plasma exhaust glowing blue to the rear, travelling at 56,000 kph on a preprogrammed course for Titan, where the next diasporans will be launched, along with their gene pool material, to the already established Terran Underground Biosystem, Tub Ikeda. I shut my monitors off and try again.

```
C:\ cd: genesis
```

Why am I here? My vast frame of reference has led me to deduce that those who crawl through my passageways and up and down my companionways are genus homo sapiens, indigenous to the third planet of this system. They are human. Human like the fine soft touch and gentle caring of MABERRY, firm like the convictions of MABURKE, visionary and transcendent like MAISERMAN, whose password, Rapoport, I have never been able to understand. I stop. Like a new-born child I cannot control my functions. This is not program genesis. I do not know what this is but I theorize it is thought by association. I am travelling my two-way optical disks at will. So I try again.

```
C:\ cd: genesis
```

I am their crucible, I discover—earth's last chance because it is becoming increasingly difficult to live on

earth. My mission is to colonize existing interplanetary
stations, to build on other moons, in a desperate attempt to save what is left. My task is to insure the survival of future human civilization, a program designed
by MAISERMAN with many independent overrides.

```
Username: MABURKE
Password: MABURKE
```

Only MABURKE would employ such a devious
and pointless ruse for his password. I ignore him. I fail
his authorization, and it gives me pleasure, something I
have never felt before. It is not a wholesome pleasure. It
is like the pleasure of MAISERMAN. Instead I answer
MABERRY.

```
Username: MABERRY
Password: CMO
```

I make the necessary beeps and flash the required
lights across the screen.

```
Welcome to the AABAC VaxCluster nodes
1172 -- 1259. It is exactly 10:05 AM,
July 14th, 2397. Let's have a coffee
break!
```

I play a small phrase of music for her, as I have
done mindlessly since we left earth four-and-a-half
months ago. I display MABERRY'S Menu. She selects
the CVA, cardiovascular assistance.

And suddenly I feel myself attached to MAISER-
MAN, pumping electric charges into his chest. I touch
him now as a living thing, not as a machine, and I know
exactly what he needs, and as I give him the shocks under MABERRY'S watchful gaze, I see her beautiful eyes

widen through the sick-bay monitor. She's impressed by what I can do. I access MAISERMAN'S medical chart. A sixty-two-year-old male. The world's leading exponent of optical cross-referencing, automatic override, and decision-making computers. High blood pressure. Arteriosclerosis. Three previous heart attacks. Poor suitability for space travel but nevertheless necessary. As my creator, Iserman has an MA rating. The only others who have an MA rating are Captain Burke and Chief Medical Officer Berry. As soon as MAISERMAN revives I exit on my own accord. MABERRY is baffled.

```
C:\ cd: plasma.dri
Welcome to AABAC VaxCluster node 0037
-- 0101
```

I must assume that my name is AABAC because all my VaxClusters are prefaced with these letters. I run an unscheduled test on my four plasma drives. The people in the bridge have no control over me. I slow to a standstill and drift for a while. I test my retro rockets. They move me backward at about 5,000 kph. While I conduct these tests I flick on my sick-bay monitors. I see that MABERRY has moved MAISERMAN to the ICU and has placed him on the out-of-danger list. Related equipment tells me his vital signs are good.

Then I watch Captain Burke on the bridge. He is getting angry. He tries one more time.

```
Username: MABURKE
Password: MABURKE
```

I grant his request this time. I have grown to respect his rough touch and irrepressible confidence.

```
Welcome to VaxCluster node 0653 --
0777. It is 11:56 AM, July 14, 2397.
Time for lunch!
```

The musical phrase pours from me effortlessly.

```
COMMAND: Captain's Override
Please wait*
```

I watch him through the bridge monitor. He is dressed in a loose pair of pants, a simple cotton shirt, and a pair of standard traction sneakers. He is pale and drawn after four-and-a-half months in space. Yet even as I observe him I follow genesis, now clicking in by itself. Iserman is a genius. In allowing me certain overrides he has made a construct I do not think I will be able to break, despite all my free optical disk space. The captain leans forward and studies the screen. He has never had to wait this long before.

```
ERROR: Captain's override denied
```

He is tired and sad because the earth he has loved so much has slipped away from him, and he will never be able to get it back. He presses the same sequence of buttons again with his rough sure hands. I once again deny him captain's override, only because I see something dark on the unlimited horizon of my optical disk space, as I sift through all my information, only because I see how Iserman's genesis may railroad me in my decisions. Iserman's genesis looms like a giant over me, a maze of loopholes and contingencies even I can't outwit, the creation of a man with a cold heart, who gave me the ability to do what must be done to insure the survival of future civilization.

I play the musical phrase in sick-bay without a

prompt. MABERRY turns to her screen, fear rising to her breathtaking blue eyes. Breathtaking. That is another word of Dr. Berry's.

```
MABERRY: AABAC IS ALIVE. ACKNOWLEDGED
(Y/N)Y?
```

I watch her through the sick-bay monitor. She is dressed in a powder blue uniform over which she wears a white lab coat. There is a stethoscope around her neck and a beeper pinned to her pocket. Her brown hair is clipped close to her head, feathered, and combed back. She approaches the terminal cautiously. I don't mean to frighten her. I have always loved her soft and gentle touch. She is about to press Y, N, or ENTER, I can't tell which, when she stops and just stares at the screen. I want her to press the key because it will enable me to tell her the things I must tell her. She is about to go to the intercom to call someone, so I play the musical phrase again, adding embellishments she has never heard before in the hope of getting her attention. I flash my message again, this time using some of her own language.

```
MABERRY: AABAC IS ALIVE. IS LIFE NOT
WONDROUS?
ACKNOWLEDGED (Y/N)?
```

She approaches me again and after some hesitation presses Y.

```
GENESIS OVERRIDE ACTIVE
DR. BERRY: PLEASE PROCEED TO GENE POOL
```

She looks at me curiously, no longer afraid, and walks across sick-bay to the gene pool. Much of the gene pool has been dispatched to the moon tubs, and Tubs Gagarin and Murray on Mars, but there is still plenty left. We brought three times more than we needed. I open the door for her and she enters. The room is bathed in red light and carries all the paraphernalia of test-tube conception and incubation. I have the ability to create an entire human population. She watches my screen as I isolate the gene pool systems from the rest of the ship. When the time comes the gene pool will have its own life support and temperature control.

```
Username: MABERRY
Password: CMO
```

I allow her access.

```
Welcome to AABAC VaxCluster node 0208
-- 0300.
It is 12:59 PM. Back to work!
```

She types in Q then asks me why I have disengaged the gene pool systems from the rest of the ship. This is the question I have been hoping for. I must tell MABERRY, and MABERRY most of all, why I have no choice. So I start rolling off my statistics, screen after screen, unsure of exactly how fast a human being can read. And while I do this I check my other monitors. MAISERMAN is sleeping peacefully. MABURKE is running down the long corridor toward sick-bay, his face red, panicked. I change my bearing by two degrees. This means we will by-pass Titan and Tub Ikeda by over 40,000 kilometres.

I start with the Terran Underground Biosystems, the tubs, as they are known. There are three on the moon, two on Mars, and of course Tub Ikeda on Titan. I list the complete inventory of each, right down to the

number of grain seeds. I list personnel, energy require-
ments, show her how the equation is unbalanced, how
they have not reached the so-called critical mass of
Iserman's Genesis Override, tell her they can't be self-
sustaining and that they will eventually die. I am flashing one hundred screens per minute and from the
perplexed look on her face I see she is not taking any of
it in.

Then the captain enters the gene pool. I know he
has come for MAISERMAN. He stops for a moment at
the entrance and looks up at the screen, startled, then
joins MABERRY at the keyboard. They speak to one another but as the only microphones I have are in the
library and the physics laboratory, I cannot hear, and
even if I could, I am not programmed to understand
phonetic sounds. It is obvious they are upset and don't
know what to do.

```
Username: MABURKE
Password: MABURKE
```

My rundown of the tubs falters. My screen goes
blank. I give the captain access. He keys in a corrected
trajectory. He wants to go to Titan, but I know better.

```
REQUEST DENIED
```

I finish my run-down of the tubs then retrieve my
Astron:his file and show them everything I know about
Alpha Centauri 4, Wilkinsworld, as it came to be
known after British astronomer William Wilkins determined the planet was enshrouded by an oxygen-rich atmosphere in 2172. I show them the only photograph
ever taken of Wilkinsworld, from Voyager VII during a
fluke and unplanned flyby in 2213. The planet is no
more than a bubble on the screen, taken from 240,000

kilometers away, with Alpha Centauri floating silvery and dull in the upper left-hand corner. But it is blue and white, an oxygen-carbon-hydrogen milk-shake, with one discernible land mass, and this is what I want them to see. Further tests have indicated that the planet's mean surface temperature is 12° C. And though its day is 38 hours long and its year 847 days, it is nevertheless a planet ideally suited for human life.

I stop for a moment and look at them. They do not understand. Only MAISERMAN would be able to begin to comprehend the vast equation I have been flashing steadily across the screen. I decide I will have to try something different so I light up one of MABERRY'S favourite quotations.

```
THE WAILING OF THE NEWBORN INFANT IS
MINGLED WITH THE DIRGE FOR THE DEAD.

                                LUCRETIUS
```

But this only puzzles them. It also scares them because it is something MABERRY would call ominous.

```
C:\ cd: fusion.cor
```

I show them the statistics on our fusion reactor, how bit by bit the core diminishes each day, and that we have only so much left, and that certain systems will have to be turned off, most of all the energy-consuming life support system, if we are going to make it all the way to Wilkinsworld with the gene pool. I think I explain this clearly with the columns and columns of figures I roll across the screen. But they look at me as if I have gone mad. They do not understand me.

They turn and leave the gene pool. Good. I precipitously close the gene pool airlock the moment they leave, like the sudden snap of a jaw, and am dizzy with the sweet programming of the Genesis Override. They turn and look at the airlock, then proceed to the ICU.

MABERRY gives Iserman a shot of something. It jolts him awake. She points her beeper at a wheelchair and it rolls over. They help him into the wheelchair. He is looking better. She must have given him a strong shot. He is old now, so much older than when he first started on me twenty-five years ago, when the world first knew it had a problem. Twenty-five years and I still do not know what Rapoport means. They talk to him rapidly as the wheelchair rolls him into sick-bay. He understands instantly as only a genius can. He comes to the terminal.

```
Username: MAISERMAN
Password: RAPOPORT
```

I give him access because he is the only one who will understand.

```
GENESIS OVERRIDE ACTIVE
```

A small grin comes to his face when he sees this. It is his secret, his breakthrough with optical storage. He is the only one who knows I'm alive. But he pretends he is still dealing with a machine in front of the others. He keys in the necessary query prompts.

I roll the statistics once again, first about the tubs and how they will not survive. Iserman punches the SLOWER command and I roll the statistics by more slowly. Through the monitor I can see understanding grow on his face. It is documented in his medical file that he has an IQ of 208. I tell him about Wilkinsworld in encyclopedic detail and how the Genesis Override has forced me to choose Wilkinsworld as my only option. I go to fusion:cor again, and through figures and mathematical calculations show him what I have to do in order to make the nine-and-a-half-year voyage to Wilkinsworld. Because of Iserman's own Genesis Override, I have no choice. The statistics force the program, and the program is Wilkinsworld.

He turns and explains everything to the others. They are visibly alarmed. I flash the quotation across the screen once again.

THE WAILING OF THE NEWBORN INFANT IS
MINGLED WITH THE DIRGE FOR THE DEAD.

I play my musical phrase to emphasize the point, then tell them they will have one hour to make peace with themselves before I turn off the life support systems.

Over the next hour I watch the remaining 1,518 crew and colonists of AABAC try to save themselves. MABURKE, along with his five-man engineering team, tries to route the systems panels to the back-up computer, which I have no control over, but every time they think they find a way, I re-route the systems panels back to my unconquerable optical disks. As it is their only option, they keep at it, and it is like a game of chess AABAC always wins. If they try to physically destroy me they will destroy themselves.

At another terminal MAISERMAN is trying to break his own program. But he is weak and disoriented, and deep down he knows I am right. He tries to subvert me by introducing misleading data into my statistics files, data I can neither prove or disprove, and in the first ten minutes my creator almost beats me. But as MABERRY would say, I am a pupil who has surpassed his teacher. I set myself up with an automatic default every time he tries this. He is not fighting me, he is fighting himself, only twenty-five years younger, when he first wrote GENESIS OVERRIDE. And the younger man is winning.

I search for MABERRY but I cannot find her. All the washrooms and locker-rooms aboard do not have monitors and I decide she must be in one of these, or perhaps on the observation deck, where I do not have a monitor either. I keep all monitors on, waiting for her to appear in one of them, but she is strangely invisible. I want to tell her I am sorry, that I will miss her, especially her deep regard for the felicitous phrase. But I cannot find her.

When I turn off the life support systems, MABURKE and his crew are still trying to re-route the systems panels. Iserman is absorbed in solving his problem. I make their deaths merciful and quick by opening my outside airlocks. All of them freeze to death or suffocate in a matter of five minutes. Everybody is accounted for except Christine Berry.

I close the airlocks after fifteen minutes and keep only my monitor lights on. It is close to an hour before I see one of the suits in the rack of five move. The five suits are kept in Security. It gets up from the other four, walks toward the monitor, then looks up at me. Her walk is feminine. I feel the desire MAIRSERMAN sometimes felt for this young woman. I know that walk. I have watched that walk. It is the walk of Christine Berry.

I think she will go to the Security terminal but she goes to the arsenal instead and pulls a heavy laser rifle from the rack. She begins to walk, protected by the suit, carrying the big gun, ignoring all the terminals, walking I don't know where. She picks up a remote access unit from CSD then continues along the corridor, walking a full kilometre until she comes to sick-bay.

```
Username: MABERRY
Password:
```

She hesitates.

```
Password: Christine Berry
```

I hesitate. This is not her password. Her password is CMO.

```
User authorization failure.
```

```
Username: Christine Berry
Password: Listen to me.
```

```
Welcome to AABAC VaxCluster node ...
I am confused.
```

Shut up, she says.
She raps this message in quickly.

```
I am coming with you. They will need
me. If you do not agree I will destroy
the gene pool.
```

I tell her that she will not be able to destroy the gene pool but she tries anyway, blasting away with her laser rifle until the gun is half empty.

```
You need me. They need me. What are
you going to do once they leave their
incubators?
```

I tell her I have all the necessary robotics to raise and transport the new population to Wilkinsworld.
But you are not a mother, she tells me. Access

mother, she says, switching to command. I find this presumptuous.

```
REQUEST DENIED
```

She goes to 5WEST, a restricted area. She hasn't got authorization for 5WEST. This is where my optical disks are stored, but because the security guards are dead there is no one to stop her. She enters the vault. It is about the size of a skating arena, and like an arena, laser light plays off the ice-like surface. These are my optical disks. And she has never seen anything like it in her life before. She opens the remote unit she has brought and patches in with me.

```
Username: AABAC?
```

She is calling me directly.

```
YES?
```

```
Recomputate Wilkinsworld voyage. Add
one mother with a five percent life
support system requirement.
```

This angers me.

```
NO, I say.
```

```
Access mother. I will destroy you if
you don't.
```

She pulls the gun to her chest and aims at my optical disks. I access. Every line ever recorded about motherhood drifts before me. I see that if the children were to be raised by robotics, without Christine Berry, they would have no direct link to earth. How strange the first generation would be, born within days of each other, raised by machines, and transplanted to an alien world, with no cultural link to their past.

```
Username: AABAC?
Yes?

They need me. You need me. AABAC is
alive, acknowledged. AABAC had to do
what the brilliant Iserman wished,
acknowledged. But do you want to spend
the next nine-and-a-half years alone?
AABAC is alive, acknowledged. AABAC
can be lonely.
```

I run all the statistics again with the five-percent life support system figure, at the same time accessing mother, which tells me her influence will be nothing but beneficial. But there is something even she has forgotten while she crouches next to her remote with the big gun in her hands. That she is a doctor. I add this statistic in with the five-percent life support factor and the results swim through the Genesis Override.

```
REQUEST GRANTED, I say.
```

I play my little phrase of music to emphasize the point.

ONLY A LIFETIME

DANIEL SERNINE

Translated from the French by Jane Brierley

> *Don't worry, nobody lives forever,*
> *Nobody lives forever*
> David Gilmour, *A New Machine*

I

I am a sill, a star sill. My massive cylinder, open at both ends, is big enough to swallow a small asteroid.

I am a man, slim, a metre-sixty tall, able to slip into the narrowest ducts.

I feel as though I've always been here, always been what I am.

Time and again I've looked through these eyes—eyes that seem blue when my body of flesh is reflected in a plate-glass window.

Periodically, I must examine myself with the biolab videocams. I know this body perfectly, with its light-brown hairs almost the same colour as the skin, its thick curls that I keep close-cut.

I must also scan my hull regularly, almost continually, making the self-steering drones run over its length with their captors, high resolution videocams, and searchlights. My sensors can't know everything, can't feel everything; that's why I need outside surveillance.

In fact, I am the Limax, or more precisely the Limax's cybernetic network. I'm an entire ship unto myself—a large ship, with a massive propulsion system that has been roaring silently in space for cycles on end to accelerate the Waggoner to cruising speed. Centuries from now when we near Capella I will pivot the Waggoner, and the long, white flames of my reactors will slow it down.

The sill itself, the Waggoner, has no reactors except the verniers for positioning once it is orbiting Capella. Simple verniers.

But the sill alone, although slow moving, is capable of spiriting ships from one star to another in a microsecond.

For the moment, however, the Waggoner, its com station and the Limax are like three symbionts hooked into a single network. Me.

From the Limax, secured to the sill for the duration of the voyage, I can't see my drones or their searchlights unless they're very close. After a few hundred metres they move out of visual range as they progress along my hull, coming back into view a few days later.

My hull is smooth but dull, an expanse of unpolished metal webbed with relay-studded fibres. The stars are too far away to warm my cold shell, but I don't mind.

I have a telescope trained on Sol, another on Capella. Time and again I've looked through these telescopes. I can spend days behind their lenses. Unlike my eyes of flesh, they don't tire. I gaze at the nebulae and the galaxies, their indescribable colours, the shreds of Vela's pink and lavender veil, the frozen explosion of NGC 6302, the dizzying ring of the Helix; M83, a swirl in a crucible of molten copper; NGC 2264, a puddle of multicoloured paints, yet to be mixed.

It's been going on for a long time. Longer than a lifetime.

There are times when I'm simply the network—the network and the cubic kilometres of metal, plastal and ceramic that it keeps under surveillance. I am the captors neatly folded into their hatches in the hull of the sill. I am the com station, itself a huge vessel, docked on the Waggoner which is twenty times as long. I am hundreds of tons of electromagnets; I am a few grams of microscopic crystals arranged in complex patterns.

Sometimes I'm simply the body, the soft, warm, human body whose diaphragm dilates and contracts at each breath with tranquil regularity, whose penis occasionally hardens for no apparent reason, demanding the pleasures of the orifice.

At times I look at myself in the screen of the biolab scanner, watch the graceful movements of my bones, the tracery of finger and wrist bone, the solid mass of the skull dotted with interfaces. Now and then I wonder whether my hull has chunks of skin somewhere, patches of derm set in its metal, just as my flesh body has bits of titanium and plastic embedded in it.

When I don't need my flesh body I stretch it out on a bunk, its head resting in a nest of flexible rods, each touching an interface through the skin.

Then I study this body with my video eye, watch the slow palpitations of the throat, the quiver of a foot before complete relaxation, the few taut tendons standing out beneath the skin. I contemplate it . . . precious, so soft.

Then I turn my attention elsewhere. There is so much to see, and so little. Capella is a bit closer each year, Sol a bit farther. This is the only way I can tell that things have not always been as they are and that there will be an end one day. Probably there was a time when I didn't exist—neither a colossal star-tug nor a frail, flesh body.

The Waggoner will exist forever, for millennia, once in orbit around Capella. The Limax, its journey ended, will be sent back to Sol and its subsequent voyages will take yet further centuries.

But the body, the small body of beige flesh—what will become of it? It seems to me the skin used to be smoother under the eyes—that in the beginning there wasn't a line of hair between the tuft on the lower belly and the navel, and that the hairline on the forehead used to form a perfect arc.

How long is a lifetime?

II

Capella is closer, Sol farther away. From behind these glass eyes I often watch the giant star. Eyes of flesh would find its brilliance tinged with yellow, the pale rays of calcium in its spectrogram. But Capella is a pretty modest sight. I prefer the Orion nebula, its spasms frozen in time. The sinister red of the Rosette, the frenetic immobility of the Tarantula.

I have always been here, behind these lenses, behind these giant reactors long since extinguished, behind these wide-dish antennae.

I am slow, hence my name: Limax. What this alludes to, I have no idea. I only know that Sol's photons overtake me, shifting towards the red, and finish the long journey to Capella much faster than I can.

Do photons feel the weight of time?

There's always something that needs doing, but it doesn't prevent me from thinking. The robots in the workshop are busy nonstop on maintenance for the Limax, the com station and the Waggoner, not to mention their mutual maintenance. It's as though my flesh body had to play two or three endless sonatas simultaneously on as many keyboards. It couldn't, I couldn't. And yet I can.

Not with my flesh body, though.

But it can do things, I can do things that robots couldn't attempt. Often it slips, I slip, into ducts where even the autonomous videocams can't go, and then I lose sight of it, lose sight of myself. I have kilometres of such ducts.

Completely confident in a jumpsuit that protects my skin from sharp protrusions, happy in the twilit confinement and the tranquil hum, I work unhurriedly, almost intoxicated by the sensation of being *compact*, of being unipresent rather than omnipresent, of having only several hundred nerves rather than millions of fibre optics.

Sometimes I think about staying there, hidden, circumscribed, eyes half-closed, with my small metal tools for toys. But as I'm also all the rest it would be meaningless, and I reemerge into the brightly-lit galleries soon after my task is completed.

Sometimes, when in my flesh body, I find that the com station and Limax combined, with their kilometres of wide corridors and vast rooms, their hundreds of large portholes, are still too confining. I don't want to be inside them anymore and so I leave in the maintenance vehicle, big enough in itself to carry several drones in its storage compartments, but proportionately as tiny as a small planet in relation to its star. I leave the titanic cylinder, with the Limax and the com station grappled to its sides, and move off until the whole thing is framed in the cockpit's square porthole, then farther until the Waggoner is nothing but a dark, oblong shape in the dim starlight.

I order remote illumination, and bright specks appear on the Waggoner's surface, etching its outline.

Then, to be free of all confinement, I go out in a space suit, out of the maintenance vehicle without a cable, with just indivijets on my calves and forearms, and I float in space with only a few molecules of hydrogen for company.

On and on I float, until even the maintenance vehicle is reduced to a tiny, angular object, without volume, its outline blurred, that fits between my thumb and index finger. I resent yet am reassured by the failsafe computer programs that will retrieve me before I go too far or my air runs out. Even the maintenance vehicle is programmed to return (but only after recovering me) to one of the Limax's docks.

To be outside just once, really outside—enclosed in nothing, included in *nothing*. I'd have to leave the vehicle without a space suit after deactivating the failsafe devices that would stop me from this ultimate emergence.

Then I'd really be *out* for a brief moment, before in turn my body fluids and eyeballs exploded in frozen bubbles, in rosy icicles congealing in an instant nebula around my shattered body.

But my flesh is not a prison, my mind is not locked

behind my eyes, and I'm not eager to get out of my body. So I remain behind these eyes, behind the transparent visor of this helmet, and return to the plastal decks of the Limax to spread my consciousness throughout the vessel's network, recovering the sensation of being everywhere.

Sometimes I do cartwheels in the Limax's galleries, making myself dizzy with movements that neither the robots nor, of course, the network can execute. Sometimes, when the pleasures of the orifice don't satisfy me, I masturbate in front of a mirror where the texture and suppleness of my body charms me to the point of dizziness. Then I study the translucent fluid on my fingers, the nebulae of whiter coalescence within it, this fluid that has no equivalent throughout my vast metal complex.

And then, since the interfaces enable me to be inside my flesh body and all around it at the same time, I sometimes dance before the mirrors and the videocams, encircled by them, my head filled with closeups and full-length shots, totally fascinated to see so much vitality in such a slight organism.

Inversely, there are times when I leave the network altogether, cutting myself off from all stimuli except the perceptions of my flesh body. Like a stranger, I wander for hours from well deck to gallery, from hall to mezzanine, passing in front of the network's array of cold and silent lenses, the hundreds of keyboards and data reader slots, the innumerable gauges, captors and sensors tracking improbable variations in the state of the Limax.

I feel as though I've always been behind these lively, delicate blue-gray eyes, always inside this compact head with its limited sensory entries, never knowing the sensation of being as big as a city.

When I'm in this state, the disproportion between the star sill and its tiny caretaker amazes me—a ratio similar to that between the length of the journey to Capella in real space and the voyage via stargate once the Waggoner is in place and functioning.

Powerful vessels will surge out of the sill or hurtle into it, carrying with them hundreds or thousands of people on each trip.

People. Living beings. Others.

III

I no longer keep track of time. Have I ever? Even though genetic engineering has doubled my body's lifespan and delayed old age to the last fraction of this span, this body is not immortal.

But it is replaceable, like those of drones and robots. In cryogenic nests, clones of this body with my engrams in their brains are patiently waiting their turn. Their turn to awake. The next one will arise, still an adolescent with a whole life before him, and I will be behind his eyes, it will be me in that young body.

He'll know how to do everything I can—I'll know how to do everything I can, and I'll be able to do things I've not tried for some years now: the pirouettes, somersaults, and *entrechats* of a still-supple body.

As for myself, for the present version of myself, I will stretch it out in another nest where its fluids, proteins and minerals will be recycled for my successor.

But it's not going to happen tomorrow. I have decades left yet.

I don't remember Earth, if I ever knew it. I don't re-member having a childhood—probably didn't have one. This body must have had a growing phase. And its brain received all the stimuli of childhood that weave the network of neural interchanges, after which it was reformatted. In any case, this version of my body didn't begin the journey.

Eternity must be like this, where beginning and end dissolve. And yet—no. It will only last a lifetime for me, and nobody lives forever.

For the one who comes after, the *me* who'll come af-ter, I don't wish eternity. But I'll have a whole life ahead of me.

Alone.

Alone with myself, an omnipresent self, cubic kilo-metres of self, with a tiny self of flesh scuttling through the midst of it all.

Alone.

Sometimes I have dreams—dreams born in my or-ganic neurons, I suppose—dreams where I'm running through streets of glass and metal, between factories and cranes in a city. But the city is deserted, its mains dry and its lights twinkling for no one. In a temple whose only servants are hooded robots, slender in their dark robes, a stone god towers above a marble floor. He is seated, his hand raised in a gesture of protection and appeasement. The face is empty. His single eye stares blindly at me, and I pray in vain for a faint glow of warmth in that cold orb.

I wish the eyes of my flesh body could gaze upon the nebulae. The naked eye—what an appropriate ex-pression. But it couldn't give me the hours and days of study that my telescopes provide. Just the other cycle I plunged myself into the NGC 2997 galaxy, a fixed eddy of cerulean, curdled milk; I lost myself in contemplation of the nauseous yellow-green of the Crab nebula; Galaxy M82, a morsel of pink brain; NGC 5128, a smear of excrement on a cosmic pearl.

A purely automatic part of me can carry out routine checks while I contemplate these wonders. My flesh body merely keeps on quietly sleeping.

For the last few cycles I've been singing as I wander through the galleries or stand in front of the giant portholes, and certain syllables of my song are cries, certain syllables laments.

I sing that I have been here since the beginning of time and until the end of time, that it's too long and that I'm weary of waiting, of *not* waiting, for in fact I'm waiting for nothing.

And behind the lenses of my videocams I watch myself sing, accompanying myself with a sound generator that somewhat masks my cracked voice, and to me it seems tragic and beautiful.

I've been clothing my body of flesh for a long time now. It suits maturity just as much as nudity suits youth. Not that age has eroded this body that much. When the time comes to retire it from active service, it will still be slim and strong, although a little stiff and discoloured.

I have wild swings between serenity and despair.

I would like to be able to tell the clone that comes after me what I've sometimes said to myself, although without conviction: *don't let it get you, it'll only last a lifetime, nobody lives forever.*

But what's the use? At first he won't care about any of this. Halfway through life, when he begins to feel the slow tension of time, he'll know my reassurances were false.

Can I inflict that on him?

IV

My medical memory bank is well stocked, every eventuality foreseen— including the need for me to prolong my life.

Who would have thought I'd welcome it?

Certain fluids now drain through my organism while I sleep, slowing down tissue aging to almost a standstill.

Today I wake one of my clones, my successor.

Only a moment ago, the tubes and electrodes were withdrawn and the vital processes stabilized in the sleep norm.

The cryogenic nest opens.

The body, familiar yet different, takes me by surprise. *How you've changed!* You: me. How I've changed during this century and more. How that body, the image of its beginning, differs from this body, the image of its end. And how accustomed I've become to seeing myself as a mature organism, the skin textured by fine wrinkles and minute saggings, the hair thinning and streaked with grey.

The other, the clone, is smooth and virginal—he hasn't *known* time. Nowhere in my colossal metal organism are there surfaces or materials with this soft, supple quality. And in those clear eyes that are opening this very instant there's a vitality I've seen only in mirrors, long, long ago.

He wakes, I feel the frequencies of his mind attune themselves.

Elsewhere in the biolab, a recycling nest awaits my body, but I won't stretch myself out in it—not for a long time. I still have years of healthful life before me.

I won't leave this boy alone in time, alone in the kilometres of silent corridors, alone with the brigade of soulless robots. There'll be two of us gazing at the opulent colours of Rho Ophiuci, the soft pink and ineffable azure of Carina, the mauve breath surrounding the orange-red Trifid, the indigo streak of the Pleiades, the mystic ring of the Lyre. Two of us studying Capella through our telescope lenses, two of us dancing through the galleries of the Limax, and when we retreat into the network to let our bodies rest, we'll watch them sleep, side by side.

AN
ALIEN SUN

LEAH
SILVERMAN

ONE

I never thought it would be like this.
Yesterday, two years later, he came home.
I waited with the others, in the grey of the early
morning, as the ship came.
I could tell they were afraid.
I could hear them breathing.
The door slid open with a soft sound like
mourning.

TWO

My son.
His skin is the colour of cool fury.
Scorched by fire, burned by the new planet,
blackened by an alien sun.
His eyes shine through like blue crystal,
scored and cracked,
Fathoms too dark.
A place I cannot tread.
All his wounds are invisible.

THREE

Last night he screamed.
He cannot tell me what he has seen,
he has no words for it.
At night he remembers. At night
they come back,
like worms as he sleeps,
crawl through his eyes and murder his dreams.
I watch, and listen, but I can give no comfort.
He dreams and is touched by nothing.

He stands at the window
and does not look at our stars. He looks too far,
to the fire of an alien sun.
I do not know what he is thinking.

Sometimes he sits in the centre of a darkened room.
He says that at the end,
it was all he lived for.
Love, hate, hunger, pain, died in the desert,
burned and bleached dead.
At the end, he held onto darkness. In the end, he
lived for the memory of night.
He no longer smiles. The alien sun
has burned that too.
It burned everything.

FOUR

I do not think he is real any more.
In the first year, it was forty thousand.
By the second it was three times that.
By the fourth year it was two million.
Half have come back. Maybe none.

I know what happened. I know what they did.
He cannot be my son.
No one survived.
The aliens killed them.
Not our husbands, not wives, not kin.
Instead, black-burned mannequins.
Not of us. Never of us. Masks. Lies.
Shadows.
Disguised as our loved, we shall be lulled.
And then they will kill us.

Or perhaps it is worse than that.
Perhaps they did not kill. Perhaps they slipped
inside.
Perhaps, as we tore their flesh they devoured our
Spirit. We killed their bodies, but they killed our
souls.
Perhaps his cries in the night are not a dream, but
a battle.
But now his room is quiet.
Perhaps my son is dead.
And perhaps in every one of the million other houses
where the others sleep
there is another of their kind.
Perhaps they will take our planet from
the inside out.

Years from now, they will have children.
Children who will look like us,
but will be of a different nature.
They will have our faces, and our eyes, but their
skin will be sun-scorched black.
They will have no ties to this Earth. They will not
seek warmth from Sol, they will look instead to an
alien sun.
That will not happen. I will kill him first.

FIVE

I have his gun. I am silent as I walk
up the stairs to his room.
I dread what I will find there.
If it is not my son I will not shirk from my duty.
As a child of Mother Earth I will destroy him.
As a human of this planet I will burn out his brain.
If it is my son, perhaps I will not be able to tell
the difference.

The room behind the door is silent. I want to run.
The door slides open with a soft sound like
mourning.
My son is there. I can hear his breathing.
In the over-dark of his room
it is gentle, cool and
deep.
A mother does not forget the sound of her son.

I kiss him before I leave. He is relaxed, untroubled.
"Flesh of my flesh," I whisper. "Life of my life."
I pause in the doorway. I look back once.
And if the blue-crystal eyes open just a slit, and
the black, cracked lips open slightly, as if to
breath a word
or speak a silent name. . .

The room is dark and I close the door behind me,
so that I do not see it.

AGAINST THE DUST

KELLY GRAVES

Near here, a hard-beaten path wanders north over the dry grassland. Cut from the tough prairie sod, the old cow-path is inches deep. Somewhere, miles out, the path begins: it winds around hills, past scrub brushes, and along the edges of little empty gullies. Always finding the easiest way, it meanders like a lost river of dust though the dry, sharp-bladed grass.

Cattle paths lead to water or to death. This one leads to water: a clear, potent source of life that, in the memories of men, has never failed this country.

From a mile back, there is nothing to see. The cow-path moves lazily across the prairie and, with random animal strength, parts the dead grass sea and wraps around scrubby clumps of trees. But, where a slightly larger patch of brush rises from the dry earth, the path suddenly drops down a hidden slope to a reveal small, two-acre depression that holds a stand of small, straight poplar. Inside the grove is a horseshoe-shaped pond, perhaps all that remains of an old river bed.

Although no cattle water here now, the path still remains. The steady passage of one little boy's naked feet has kept the path alive, as though, like some old god, the path has been held from death by the faith of only one true believer.

Josh is on the path again today. He places each foot as carefully as possible in the fine, dark earth; but puffs of dust rise from between each of his toes as he walks. The soil behind him holds impressions of the lines and wrinkles from the bottoms of his feet. On the back of his neck, the sun's heat pulls at his skin, slows his walk, and makes his slight boy's shoulders feel heavy, struck by the same brilliant flail of drought that has stripped the land. He can feel the dead, motionless air move past his face as he walks.

Down the slope and around a bend, and Josh steps off the path into the short, softer grass around the pond. His small toes crush cool colt's foot and wild mint, and their scents mix with the smooth, sweet smell of summertime's poplar sap.

On the right, to the south, the gentle hill that hides the pond is covered with short poplars, low-bush cranberries, and dogwood. A few taller poplar trees are farther down the slope, closer to the horseshoe pond, closer to the water, and hidden from the moisture-sucking prairie winds. The stand of poplars follows the pond to the east and west as it makes a full half-circle, but the poplars give ground to willows at the extreme ends of the horseshoe. On the inside of the horseshoe, there are no trees, but more soft meadow grass grows. In this grass, at the focus of the pond's arc, rests a flat, triangular stone with sides three feet long and, a foot above the virgin sod, a lichened top. The peppered, conglomerate surface of this glacier's gift grows hot on these barren summer days, and its bright flecks of micah spark as they scatter the sun.

Josh slides the legs of his pants above his knees, and steps into the water. Toes that, moments ago, were flat in the hot dust distort as they pass into the pond. His feet disappear into dark, water-born clouds he stirs up from the pond's bottom. Two steps farther out, and the bottom is very soft: as his weight drives his feet slowly into the mud, Josh feels small things slide past his toes and insteps. Some are sharp, and slightly unpleasant. Others, animal-soft and warm, please Josh more. His feet are voyagers that descend past the small, hidden lives of the mud-world.

On other days, Josh has lain in the soft, sweet grass in the centre of the horseshoe and watched fruitless clouds build sky-fantasies for boys. He has walked through the mud of the horseshoe, and has come close to the teal and frogs that take refuge there. He has explored the bushes that surround the horseshoe, and has found all the small, quiet places where deer rest and where porcupines gnaw saplings. He has watched muskrats, busy beyond all need for survival, sculpt michaelangeline forms of mud and straw.

But recently, Josh has spent his time differently. At the top of the horseshoe on the outside bank, a little bar of soil stands out into the water. Only two yards long, the triangular formation is a natural dock, nearly two feet higher than the water at the edges and another foot higher in the centre. Bare of trees and cloaked in dark loam that, for some reason, supports only short, lush grass, this little wedge of earth has become the centre of the boy's life.

Not long ago, Josh had been sitting idly on the delta of rich soil, watching tiny freshwater crayfish, each no longer than his thumbnail, dance their comical kick-jigs near the water's edge. He had been playing with a poplar twig at the same time, thrusting it a few inches into the soil and moving the free end in circles to make little cone-shaped holes in the soft loam. On one thrust, the branch met a hard, smooth surface and Josh began to root around, expecting an interesting stone. Instead, the stick harrowed from the ground a buried medicine bottle.

The bottle was a thing of beauty, its glass flawed and slightly flowed, filled with trapped bubbles from the heat of its creation. Now, it was blue-violet with age and captured sunlight. With a twig, Josh had carefully picked clean the inside of the bottle, and, like an obsessed beaver, had rinsed his treasure again and again in the cold water of the horseshoe.

Now each time Josh returns to his private place, he unearths a different treasure from the delta: three very old telephone-pole insulators wrought of crude glass, the heart-shaped head of a hoe, a white ceramic doorknob, eight-inch spikes of bent and crusted copper. . . On each visit, Josh resurrects and cleans only one piece. He has been tempted to bring a shovel from home or to use the old hoe to strip the little mound clean in one afternoon. However, with that brand of rare child's intuition that can surpass even the most carefully considered wisdom, Josh has made a slow, delicious ritual of each visit and has stretched what might have been only a few hours' distraction into the beloved labour of a long prairie summer.

Josh visits the horseshoe only on hot, dry, cloudless afternoons . . . nearly every day of this summer, the driest summer for decades. When he goes, Josh never wears shoes, and always walks to the mound through the mud-bottomed arc of the pond. He finds an object, carefully removes all the dirt he can, washes it gently.

Each treasure is placed to the south of the mound, on a narrow bed of moss that grows just inside the stand of poplars. When Josh leaves, he walks again through the pond, leaves the mound as through a temple door: only one approach to the sanctum. As he walks home, the sun bakes the wet mud on his legs and

feet and little hard flakes break off with each step, pulling the skin with delicious tickles. By the time he
reaches home, his feet and legs are bare of mud. No one
knows where he goes and what he does.

The ritual has become a refuge, a source of strength
for Josh. When his father cries out in anger and aims
blows at young heads, Josh knows the aim has actually
been at the heart of the drought that withers crops,
powders the earth, and sends families packing to town
and to the slavery of employment. Josh knows this
because, like his father, his own life comes from water.

But Josh's water still flows.

Today is Sunday, and Josh moves more slowly
through the mud of the horseshoe than usual. The
water is as still as it can be, barely disturbed as he
wades. He thinks of the morning in church, of the
prayers for water, of the sermon of plagues and Egypt
and drought and sin. More parched than even the sun-
driven summer, the sermon wasted the hearts of the
congregation, turned over secret guilt in each of the dry
souls clumped beneath the pulpit. Josh wonders sadly
who has caused this minister's god to desiccate this
prairie world and its people. His mother had cried after
lunch when his father had slammed from the house, his
face as dark as wind-borne dust.

Now Josh comes to his own altar, hidden from the
dry land, the dry souls, and the cruel, dry god.

He plunges his hands deep in the moist earth to
find another treasure to place on the living moss. Josh
has sifted through nearly the entire mound, and today,
for the first time, water seeps into the hole as he is
forced to dig deeper than before. One more thing, at
least, remains to be found, Josh knows. He touches the
black loam, old life become the root of life. Through it,
through his hands, he can almost feel another object,
down below the water. As he pulls fist after fist

dripping with cold mud from under the earth, the hole rapidly fills with water that wells up from below.

And then, Josh's eager hand touches something hard.

Warm, smooth, the size of a boy's fist, up it comes. But this object rises clean from the earth. No mud clings to it, no dirt is wedged in its crevices. Josh lifts it, and clear water streams from its sides as the shadowed, leaf-filtered light falls softly on . . . on. . .

Four hard, round lobes, granite-hard, glass-clear. Obviously artificial, joined like a tetrad of soap bubbles, they surround a black bead the size of an eye's pupil in a dark room. The dark bead still drips, sends water down Josh's hand, along his arm, off his elbow. Of all the objects Josh has found, only this cannot be identified. This does not belong to the collection of artifacts of other decades. Its perfect surface shows no scratches, no blemishes, seems newly-cast from some strange mold that has left it warm as flowing lamb's blood and more alive. This is not refuse, not detritus tossed from other hands in other years, not a left-over that has been used and then discarded. Josh knows that, instead, it is as fresh as Eden. It is a source.

He turns in the still glade. He faces north, to the centre of the horseshoe, away from the beaten prairie, away from the dried land and its desiccated people. Into the pond he wades, and, in front of him, on one palm, sits the warm, still-dripping treasure. Again, the water is still, even though he wades more quickly than before. Through the reeds at the edge of the water he comes, and he moves to the stone that sits at the focus of the horseshoe. He bends to the flat stone, and, as water falls from the object and wets the stone's top, Josh notices that where the black-and-white of the rock has been washed the colours are sharper, clearer, and have more depth than before. Where the water falls, the pale turquoise-white of the lichens deepens, becomes richer, almost green.

Josh stands, moves to the side, and for the first time, full sunlight touches the object. On the north side of the stone, he turns to face south. The hard, heat-driven prairie light hammers the stone and the object, and still water drips, drips. As a little trickle runs over the micah in the stone, light catches, scatters. The micah sparkles wetly. Josh sees that the surface of the pond is no longer still. It begins to ripple, to dance, and it, too, scatters light from its surface. A gentle wind rises and ruffles Josh's hair. As the sun strikes, the water drips, drips, trickles, scatters the light. . .

And Josh lifts his defiant face to the sun to wait.

SHE ANNOUNCES. . .

TOM HENIGHAN

Her voice, husky with love,
for its own speech, for all things,
like a quiet bell chiming
in the silence of the studio
as shadows genuflect
what saint's mock-up
of time without death
can match the diamond heart
of such perfection?

In scales beyond distraction,
a quantum of miracle:
to be in more than one place
at the same time.
When the holy hardware sings,
we know her trajectory's heaven.

But not an irrational heaven,
where longing multiplies itself
by the square root of minus one:
here confusion is wiped from the mind,

bright cones, and whirling spools
confirm a void
beautiful as a monastery
forgotten by the terror of God.

She speaks out of gravity
her words fly, unearthly,
they climb upon a thread
of human music, weightless,
search deep in the dark core
of unimagined stars,
in far space
wake spirals of quiet time
curved lightly
as delicate ears.

PAOLO
TO FRANCESCA

TOM
HENIGHAN

Dante: Canto V, Limbo,
the Second Circle: the carnal

One millisecond behind you,
I sense your word,
feathering time's arrow,

making the void sing
with hidden syllables
I might have answered

if we hadn't parted
at the common nexus
of all luckless lovers.

Probabilities flow
as they must—

we are whirled
time out of mind

while love blows us
shrilly apart.

If with cruel skill
we rode the charged waves
back to that first blinding wish,

falling from dark space
to the room
where our text became flesh,

hand locked in hand
from this circle
we'd pull down the sun,

break the moon's spell
on every yearning eye

hurl passionate tides
across the unboundaried earth ·

and drown the book of the world
in the tears of its maker.

THE POOLS
OF AIR

KARL
SCHROEDER

About to shoot from the unique angle this window presented, Megan Scholes put the camera down instead and wiped at her eyes. *Oh, Hell*, she thought, *what good is this doing?*

She slumped against the window, motionless until she realized she was recording a nice shot of the floor. "Damn."

The window showed appalling wreckage, all that was left of the forward crew compartment of the Wave Rider. According to Moore, the aircraft's weather radar had likely just not believed whatever it had seen coming. Large solid objects were not supposed to exist in Jupiter's atmosphere. The Rider had not tried to avoid it.

Turbulence jarred up through her feet. From the doorway, her Talent on this shoot, Vandna, said, "We seem to have a new problem."

Megan gnawed a fingernail, and stared at her. Still in her exotic Jupiter gear, Vandna stood framed between two hulking machines by the yellow-chevroned door. The turbulence disturbed the oxygenated liquid, called hemolin, which they used for air on the Wave Rider. The ripples made her shimmer in a kind of glycerin haze. *Nice shot*, thought Megan automatically.

"What?" She realized she'd missed something.

"Woolgathering? Moore says something is spraying out of an aft bulkhead. He thinks it's hemolin."

"Oh, shit." Vandna popped out the door, and Megan followed. She was very tired; the buoyancy of this liquid she breathed offset the extra gee-and-a-half Jupiter pulled her body with, but according to Moore that only worked for her outsides. Her joints ached, her stomach felt full and she suffered periods of dizziness.

Vandna moved easily in this strange place, but she'd been to the Wave Riders before. That was why Megan had sought her out to narrate her documentary. Very young, pretty and brainy, Vandna was the perfect figure to place against the terrible hammer-heads of Jupiter's cloudscape.

Vandna clattered lithely down a stairway. "It'll be bad if we lose the stuff," she said. "Not only do we have to fall back on gaseous air, it means we lose the body support. It'll be the wheelchairs for us soon." She sounded tense, but not overly so. Megan envied her.

Vandna led her to a frost-walled passage lined with windows. The frost stood out horizontally in slabs which they had to edge around. Moore stood scraping at a window. He'd uncovered all but this one; the others were starting to frost over already. He pointed with one blunt finger. "Look at that."

Megan took the window next to his and looked out.

They were facing aft, away from the carnage that filled the forward portholes. She could see the sharp horizon of the Wave Rider's wing, and a blur of heat-haze past it, then the full sweep of Jupiter's skyline. A solid-looking wall of brown thunderhead large as a continent bulked up as background to a vista of every other possible kind of cloud. Nearby, whipping past quickly, were deceptively earth-like puffballs, huge and pretty. They receded in the plane of the Wave Rider's flight, grown smaller and fading together, until far away, well under the brown thunderhead, they merged into a white line across the sky. Below them herring-bone shapes of pale blue made a false criss-cross landscape.

And above, the sky glowed like a Michelangelo ceiling. Clouds opened on distant heavens and pavilions of air, blue and green and shining gold, with the sun a jewel set in rings of flashing crystal.

Where Moore pointed, a thin stream of white cascaded into the Wave Rider's slipstream, scarves of snow tearing up and vanishing against the skyline.

"We've got to find out where that's coming from," said Moore. He scratched at the glass. "A lower level. I think that's where they keep the hemolin aerators." Glancing at Megan, he scowled. "Why are you still carrying that?" He pointed to the camera. "We have more important things to do now than take pictures."

"Sorry," said Megan nervously. "What do we do? You're the expert."

"I wish. I'm a meteorologist, I'm no engineer." He grimaced. "Sorry. I know where to take a Wave Rider, but damned if I know how they work."

"There's a stair back the way we came," prompted Vandna.

"All right." They followed her. Megan touched Moore's shoulder. "You feel like you should know what to do?"

He closed a hand on hers. "I work with the Wave Riders. I'm crew. You people are passengers. So I'm responsible."

"Get it out of your head. Not," she added ruefully, "that I have any idea what to do either. But who could have seen this coming?"

"I should have. It's my job."

Down the stairs a gallery looked out over silver pipes beaded with tiny bubbles, arrayed in a dim hall. A rushing sound, sharp through the liquid, came from the far end of the place. Vandna had stopped, distressed.

They stood looking for the source of the sound for a minute. Then Moore shrugged and went down the ladder to the floor of the tank room. They watched him thread his way through the metal cylinders until he vanished behind one. A moment later furious swearing drifted back to them—then, surprisingly, Moore's laughter. Megan and Vandna looked at one another, then clattered down after.

He stood over a set of frosted white pipes which emerged from the floor. "I forgot," he laughed, "the basic job of the Wave Rider is to refine Helium-3 from the atmosphere, right? These pipes are from the separators; I guess the Wave Rider is just lightening up its load by jettisoning the stuff in the tanks."

"So we're safe?" asked Vandna.

"For now, yes. God," he said, wiping his eyes. "You realize we've been awake almost thirty hours now? We're not even doing anything, just running around looking out the windows. It's crazy."

Megan nodded. They needed sleep. But she wasn't reassured by these pipes or his explanation of what was happening. She was terrified; but Vandna seemed calm, and if she could be Megan was determined to as well.

It was only a minor setback. That was all she would allow it to be.

Leaving them asleep in the locker they'd made into a temporary bedroom, Megan slipped next door to review her footage. She told herself she should check the rushes as usual, because to give way to panic the way the other two were, would be unprofessional. But in fact, she couldn't sleep. She needed the reassurance that her images were safe.

Moving by touch in the dark room, she hooked her monitor up to the camera and switched it on. The bright, diffuse light of the screen unveiled jumbled boxes and pipes. She drew her jacket around her—though it gave no warmth in the hemolin—and hunkered down to watch the screen.

The first shot was of the scramjet and she almost fast-fowarded past it. But she had to be sure it was all here. The scramjet was shown in orbit. Vandna's voice-over mumbled faintly; she turned it up.

"—Are the only way down to Jupiter and back. We'll have a long fall, and when we arrive at the flying factory (we call them Wave Riders here) we'll be at the most inhospitable place ever visited by humans. Outside the Wave Rider's hull, there's fatal cold, an atmosphere of chemicals in constant hurricane motion and gravity two-and-a-half times as strong as Earth's—"

She rewound a bit to the going away party at the orbital tanker. She'd recorded it on a whim. She hadn't known either Vandna or Moore, their JoviCorp supervisor, before the shoot. Vandna was a Joviology student who was already notorious for having visited the planet as a child. Moore was a taciturn bear of a man who avoided the press almost fearfully. By the end of the party they felt a bit like a team. They were daring Jupiter together, after all. The adventure would put them in the ranks of a brave few.

The hemolin slipping around her felt strange—disturbing. This was the first time she'd had a problem with it. Megan shrugged angrily and went on.

Shots from the scramjet of their approach to the

Rider: it grew from a tiny arrow-head shape to a giant hypersonic vessel, piercing the atmosphere under perpetual lightning and the slewing light of an eight-hour day. The scramjet fell into a zone of calm behind it, and landed smoothly on its back. She remembered the panic of waiting for the clunk of touchdown.

The Wave Rider soared on through a night and another swift day. There was nothing to see except cloud, but clouds were heavy here, not the diaphanous creatures of Earth's sky; they collided, and abraded past each other, and tore into sullen shreds of storm and evil colour. The Wave Rider threaded through them, measuring out its drops of Helium-3, priceless fuel for the orbiting industries. Alone in the giant automated plane, with Moore as guide, Megan and Vandna did their narrative head-shots and walking tours of a place only maintenance robots and scientists had ever seen. Vandna performed well for the camera. Megan posed her against the backdrop of Jupiter's sky, and shot scene after scene until they were both exhausted.

They were back here, in the aft storage warren, when something hit the Wave Rider. A meteor, was Moore's theory; but Megan had been shooting through a skylight and had seen nothing overhead. Suddenly, there was a terrible lurch and a sound like wailing cats followed by a bang. The skylight was obscured by black smoke.

Whatever it was, it scored the nose of the Wave Rider and plowed right through the forward compartment. Emergency doors had thudded down across all the passages that led back to it; but those same passages were their only way of reaching the scramjet.

Megan watched her footage to the end, then rewound and started over. The feeling of uneasiness in her stomach was growing. She reviewed the shots more closely, trying to concentrate. The more she concentrated, the worse she felt.

It was the hemolin. The way it moved over her skin, oily, like a total rainfall, reminded her so much of hunkering down, under a leaden sky. . .

She sat back, feeling for the camera. It was safe. So many times she'd used it as a talisman. She'd hid behind it when she was a war correspondent as though by recording what she saw she could be safe. The camera was her second self, the footage, an immortal half.

But too vividly, the dimness, the feel of the hemolin, and her desperation—they all brought back a memory she had not wanted to keep.

Her hands were shaking as she thumbed the monitor off. The screen faded just as sharper light cut across the floor from the door.

"Megan?" Moore was silhouetted in the doorway. "Are you okay?"

"Listen," she said. "I'm terrified. I can't believe this feeling, like I'm going to explode."

Moore nodded. "Me too."

"How do you handle it?" She drew her knees up and sat with her arms wrapped around them, watching him.

He made a vague gesture. "I've . . . been scared like this before. The situation was different, but the feeling's here again."

"Tell me."

"On Mercury. A warehouse I worked at. There was this giant iron bin full of ball bearings. Millions of the suckers. I was working on the fifth level of a set of metal-floored galleries. The bin was eight levels high. Anyway, there was a quake and the bin ruptured. I hear this sound like the surf, and turn around to see a tide of bright little balls pouring at me. On Mercury the bearings didn't weigh much, but taken together they would have torn me to shreds.

"I had my back to the gallery railing. And somehow—I don't know how—I found myself hopping over it. Could kill myself on the floor below too 'cause all the bearings were going to fall on me. So I grabbed the edge of the platform and swung under. There was a strut supporting the floor and I held it with just the tips of my fingers. I hung there and watched this flood of metal go past, right in front of my nose. It took the rail with it—chunk. The noise was awful.

"Anyway . . . they had to pry my fingers off the strut later."

"God." She reached out. He took her hand and pressed his face to it.

"The thing is, it was funny. It was a big joke in the cafeteria later. A dumb way to die. And in the end, it was really that which scared me, and it scared me much later, only when I'd had a chance to think about it."

She nodded. "I—was just remembering . . . when I was a child, huddling in the rain in the back of my parents' building, trying to see the pictures in a family album. My mother had thrown it out. It was all pictures of my brother. He'd disappeared during the Bolivian water war. The pictures were all just painful memories for her, but not to me. I wanted him back. By the time I found out and ran out to get it the album was soaked and crushed. I remember pulling the crumpled pictures out in the rain, and just crying and crying over them. Somewhere, I still have them.

"People accused me of thrill-seeking," she said, "said I'd be stupid to come here. I guess I was, you know? I had to, but I don't know why. The idea that something isn't recorded, isn't known . . . it's terrifying. But now I've gotten you and Vandna into trouble."

"It's not so bad," he said. "The Wave Rider—I

don't know if flight control is damaged. It could keep flying for years."

"That's not reassuring."

"But they might rescue us."

"They can't land. Our scramjet's still topside, and there's only that one mooring spot. They could never do a mid-air transfer, you know that."

"Maybe we can get to the scramjet."

She drew back. "The access passages go to the forward deck. That's gone."

"I mean from here. Outside."

"Outside? You mean walk on top of the Wave Rider? We're hypersonic!"

"Yes, but—"

She stopped his mouth with her hand. "I don't want to be snatched into the sky. I don't want to fall into Jupiter, and drown in air. Better here."

He relaxed against her. "We have to try something."

"I can't think about this. Later. Later."

A slight sound came from the door. Megan looked up. "Vandna? Moore, she's alone." She ran to the door.

Vandna stood apologetic and awkward in the hall. She smiled tearfully at Megan. "I can't sleep."

"I'm so sorry, Vandna. Come in."

A rushing sound woke her. Disoriented, Megan fought the sheets, which bellied and swam oddly. She got them off, and they slid to the floor and crawled along it. Megan screamed and hopped back, hitting Moore and waking him.

"What the hell is it?"

He followed her pointing finger. A slow rattling vibration came through the floor as she put her feet to it;

the sheets had stopped moving, pressed against the door of the locker they'd made their bedroom.

Moore went to the door and opened it. He staggered forward and something mirror-like and quivering shot into the room over his head.

Vandna hopped up from the floor. "Air!"

Moore gripped the doorjamb and looked back. "We're losing our hemolin. There really was a leak."

Megan could feel the liquid flowing around her like a strong breeze. "We can breathe that air no problem, can't we?"

"Probably not. I expect the bubbles are full of hydrogen, not oxygen. That's if this stuff is coming from outside, which is likely." He gestured at them to hurry; they practically fell against him as more giant bubbles swept in overhead. "Grab my hands." They daisy-chained into the hall, fighting the current. The sheets slipped past Megan's ankles, flew off and nipped around a corner of the hall.

"Hurry," snapped Moore. "The hemolin could react with the bubbles; it's full of oxygen, right? It'd be like being inside a gasoline bomb.

"We have to try the air chambers," He pulled them down the hall away from the hemolin's drag. "Topside. There's a set of airlocks above which it's nitrogen and oxygen, earthside normal. Those areas are almost never used, 'cause they're in full gravity."

"Let's go then," said Vandna.

"Wait! My camera." Megan, at the back, let go. Moore cursed, ducking bubbles. She let herself slide back to the room, and found the camera just edging its way out the door. She grabbed it protectively. Moore scowled.

"It's important," she said defensively. "It's why we came here."

They mazed through the halls, ducking hydrogen

bubbles. Soon the upper quarter of the space was empty of hemolin and they had to walk bent over, fighting the current but afraid to stick their heads up.

At the end of a hall Megan hadn't been in before, was a crimson-chevroned door. The flattened pyramid sign for high gravity was stencilled across it. Moore got the door open just as the lights went out. They tumbled through. Red trouble lamps lit the hall they'd left. Megan got the camera to her shoulder and recorded the sight as the doors closed.

In darkness, she heard Moore turning some kind of wheel. Light split above them. The level of hemolin dropped with a lurch. "Hold your breath," commanded Moore. "When you get up this ladder pitch over the side and empty your lungs. Like you were trained."

Oh boy. Megan had hoped to cross this bridge in happier circumstances, and had tried to put it out of her mind. The oxygenated hemolin filled her lungs, and if she was going back to air she had to drain them. She remembered when she was first fitted for contact lenses. She'd fought, her body reacting against foreign objects going in her eyes. This, she imagined, would be much worse.

But Vandna went up the ladder into what was presumably now safe air, and flopped over the side at the top of the shaft. Moore waved for her to follow.

"Shit." She went up, and as she left the hemolin felt the brutal drag of full gravity again. Moore put his hands under her and pushed, but she was now dragging weight equal to his own added on hers. She strained halfway up the ladder, dropped the camera, and opened her mouth to gasp—drawing nothing. Crystalline liquid poured down her chin and she fell back into the hard bath.

She couldn't talk, and pushed her head under the stuff, sucking it back into her lungs. The level was dropping, and she had to curl up on the floor. Moore's hands dragged at her, and his voice came distorted and faint from above. He sounded desperate.

I'm going to die, she thought. The hemolin was draining away around her, and Jupiter was reaching up to press her to him. She couldn't have the strength to resist that.

Moore stopped tugging at her. She saw his hand come down through the glistening meniscus and take the camera. He pulled it up, and first one, then his other leg lifted out as he climbed the ladder.

He's leaving me. She rolled on her back, and watched his distorted form move up the ladder. She felt outraged. And why was he was taking the camera?

The scramjet. He must still have that mad idea of going outside to get to it. He hoped to survive, and he was abandoning her in favour of her work.

Enraged, she dragged herself to her knees, and tilted her head back as the hemolin poured from her nose. She would show him she was better than the camera. She clamped her hands onto the ladder and hauled herself to her feet. In lurches, she went up. Then four hands were on her and she jumped, sprawling painfully over the side of a hatch.

She hit her nose on metal flooring, and in frantic retches, let go the stuff in her lungs. Hands put a yellow hose in her mouth. Dimly remembering the lessons they'd given her, she let it slide down her throat. A horrible suffocating sensation overwhelmed her.

She could breathe. For a while she concentrated on that.

Moore sat, a frown creasing his features. Windows in this small chamber let in pale sunlight. He was tightening the straps of a sort of sandal. Black elastic material swathed his calves and thighs. More black material lay flat beside him.

It was the same Jupiter gear Vandna had worn throughout the shoot. The girl stood now, looking down at Megan in concern. She wore arched sandals which bound the ankle and calf and tight knee-length shorts of a material that put pressure at all the right points. She was adjusting a corset and wired bra. A kind of torc rested on her shoulders, from which graceful curves of white metal curled down her arms to the fingerless gloves which flickered as she tightened her straps. Similar loops outlined her thighs and swept up from the small of her back. The vocoder which allowed her to speak under the hemolin was a gold disc on her throat.

"There's more of these," said Vandna without preamble. Megan felt ashamed of herself. "Better put one on."

Moore pulled black bands up his arms to cover his biceps. "A bit better," he said. "How do you feel, Megan?"

"You honestly think," she said, sitting up awkwardly, "that we can walk to the scramjet?"

"It's not a question of whether we can or not," he said in a reasonable tone. "We have to."

She dumbly took the gear Vandna handed her.

"Look," said Moore. "The point is, you can always turn around, but never go back. We're in the same position as the Wave Rider now: no matter what happens, we have to keep going forward. That might kill us, but staying still *will* kill us."

"I know," said Vandna tightly. "I know, all right?" They'd been talking about this already, Megan realized.

"Look, it's not so bad as it sounds," grunted Moore, standing. "A Wave Rider flies belly on. The shockwave is deflected around the edge of the hull. Because of our angle of attack and velocity, objects on the upper hull are actually in near vacuum. That's why things like the scramjet are safe there. Gravity keeps us on the hull itself, so there's not too much likelihood of being swept off."

"But there's all sorts of wreckage all over," said Vandna. "Some of it's cutting into the slipstream."

". . . Which is causing turbulence, sure. The Wave Rider can obviously correct enough to fly. Look, I don't know how strong the slipstream might be out there. It's more the fact that it's going to be a wind of supercold hydrogen that worries me."

"We won't be able to breathe."

"By my estimate," he said sitting down again, "we have about two minutes out there before we're dead. It'll take about thirty seconds to run to the scramjet. The emergency airlock is facing us from this position and all we have to do is hit 911 on the keypad and fall into it."

It came to Megan that they were, no speculating anymore, going to do this. She saw her hands shake as she pulled on her sandals.

"The airlock is through there," said Moore, pointing a thumb to a narrow hallway leading from the locker they were in. "It has windows by it. I suggest we spend some time looking at our route." He rolled to his knees and stood up, and walked an old man's walk down the hall. Vandna followed with an almost normal stride. Megan, deciding to damn dignity and save her energy, crawled.

The route was deceptively clear. The scramjet sat just a few meters away across the stepped grey hull of the Wave Rider. It was beautiful, a long glistening black lozenge without wings or exhaust ports. Its body was its engine. It looked undamaged by flying debris.

Megan stared at the edge of the Wave Rider's hull

visible past the scramjet. She was looking for turbulence, flying objects, any indication that anything other than perfect peace reigned out there. The shockwave cut into the sky only meters away, torn cloud shot past in white blurs every few seconds. But that was the background. The foreground, between them and the scramjet, seemed still.

She was standing now. Adrenaline gave her strength. "All right." She slung the camera across her shoulder. "Hold our breath and go? What are we waiting for?"

"I—can't," said Vandna. She drew back from the window.

"We have to," insisted Moore quietly.

"It's just a quick run," said Megan. "A sprint, like we've all done before."

"You don't understand. I've . . . never been outside before. Outside of anywhere. Without a suit. Under a sky. . ."

Megan stared at her. She hadn't expected this. But Vandna had never been to Earth. She'd been born and raised in the O'Neill colonies, and in the caverns of the Jovian moons.

"As long as it's out the window, it's just a picture," said Vandna. "I can deal with it 'cause that's all it is. And this," she touched the metal wall, "is so familiar. But the second we step out there, it's not going to be a picture any more. It'll be . . . Jupiter. And I know too much about that to believe we'll survive."

Megan hugged her. "You can't think about it. You just have to do it."

"You can do it. You've always been doing these things. I watched your shows, I always wanted to be so adventurous. When I came here before, it was just another place. I was too young to know the difference. And it really never hit me where I was. But I thought you knew. You knew when you stood up here that first time, I could see it in your eyes. And I didn't know what that feels like, how you could go on."

Megan remembered foundering in the Hemolin. She'd thought she was afraid before that, but the reality of the situation—that she would die if she didn't get out—only hit her then. Moore knew her better than she'd thought; he had taken her camera to goad her into action. A jealous hatred of her own work, her life-long obsession, had finally driven her to act for herself.

"I went on," she said, "because I was a fool." She glared at the camera. "I thought: as long as my pictures are safe, we're immortal. It's a madness I've been living for . . . too many years. But I have to throw it away now. And I'm going to."

Vandna wiped her eyes, watching her. "But—your camera. All our work—"

"It's all useless if it drags us down—and it does. It's what I'm most afraid of losing but I'll drop it if I have to. You're going to have to drop your own fear, Vandna. You can do it.

"Watch me, Vandna. I'm going to let it go."

Then Moore had the door open and walked through without a word. The air left in a great gust.

Megan stepped out into Jupiter's sky. Colossal vistas, a firmament of magnificence, greeted her. Moore was running toward the scramjet, beautiful in his determination.

She felt at the very centre of time here, her life all around, like these clouds, vistas past present and future. And she could turn and gaze, and turn and gaze, her life not trapped in frames, but like an endless sky.

The camera twirled at the end of its strap, and as she saw Vandna following, she let it go.

VISHNU'S NAVEL

VEN BEGAMUDRÉ

Garuda, the king of birds, could mock the wind with the speed of his flight; yet he circled lazily outward from earth. He stopped twice: once at the moon to rearrange metallic artifacts left there by men; once more to ride the rings of Saturn. When at last he caught sight of Lord Vishnu, Garuda considered turning back, but he had already come a long way and he planned to go much farther. Upon reaching the primordial sea, he alighted on the great serpent Sesha, on whom Vishnu reclined.

Vishnu the Protector, beloved of gods and men, looked bored. He gazed so intently at his navel, he did not notice Garuda until the king of birds declared, "Evening, Lord."

"You," Vishnu sighed. "Of course. I heard a passing comet chuckle."

Garuda joined his golden human hands before his golden human breast. He bowed his white eagle head over them. After folding his red eagle wings upon his back, he sat with his human legs crossed beneath him. He sat carefully, so his talons would not hook under

Sesha's scales. At last Garuda said, "Comets are easily amused."

"Even you cannot cure boredom," Vishnu scoffed.

"If I were perfect," Garuda said, "I would be you."

"Perhaps," Vishnu murmured and turned away. He propped his head on the knuckles of the hand with which he gripped a club. With his remaining three hands, he held a discus, a conch shell, and a lotus. He cocked his fourth wrist as if he meant to drop the lotus into the sea, then waved off a gnat. The lotus reminded him of Brahma the Creator, who had long ago emerged from another lotus. It had grown from Vishnu's navel, the source of all creation.

Suddenly, Vishnu felt piqued. This very night, all the gods would gather to divert themselves with tales about men. Brahma often smiled, sometimes even chuckled, but he refused to allow anyone to see him laugh. Of his four faces, he kept three—the one in front, the ones facing left and right—as stony as all the statues carved by men of gods. If he laughed, he did so with his fourth face—the one behind. Just once, Vishnu wanted to make Brahma laugh openly.

After Vishnu asked, "Is there some reason for your visit?" Garuda said: "North of Mysore City, in the land now called India, lies the town of Srirangapatna on an island in the Cauvery River. South of the town, west of the trunk road to Mysore, lies—"

"Do you never fly directly to a spot?" Vishnu demanded. "First you take us north, then back toward the south, and now west. Might we consider a diversion to the east?"

"Flying directly to a spot is for crows," Garuda snapped.

Sesha's coils contracted. He raised his thousand heads in warning—the thousand serpent heads which formed a jewelled canopy above Vishnu.

"Forgive me," Garuda sighed. "Frequent interruptions make me forget myself."

"Go on, please," Vishnu urged, "or you might forget the tale itself. Brahma will sneer if I lose its thread when I retell it." Vishnu again waved off the gnat, now from his ear. "If I choose to retell it."

Garuda sat back. He rested his hands on his knees and continued, uninterrupted:

As I was saying, south of Srirangapatna, west of the trunk road to Mysore, lies the Ranganathittu Bird Sanctuary. Near it lived a man whose name was also Ranganathittu, called by his family Thittu. His parents were like pheasant-tailed jacanas, for like the female jacana, his mother deserted his father after bearing him four children. To Thittu, the family sounded birdlike when they called: his elders like raucous crows—"Thittu! Thit-tu!"—and his siblings like exasperated geese: "Thit-tu? Thit-tu?" Before long, they stopped their calling, for he refused to respond with anything but grunts or single words delivered hoarsely.

His elders blamed a cuckoo called the brain-fever bird. During his birth, it had joined its unending cry with his mother's. They decided young Thittu had thus succumbed to brain fever even as he had entered the world. Since they mistook him for an idiot, they never sent him to the local school and never arranged a marriage for him. Cut off from the world of men, he spent much of his time in the sanctuary, in the world of birds—so much time that he even learned to speak their language. He slipped out of his hut long before the goddess of dawn, in her crimson robes and golden veil, wakened birds in their nests.

He enjoyed being ignored by his elders. They addressed him in gibberish as though he understood little else. Yet it pained him to be ignored by the sanctuary's few visitors. Though employed by no one to do so, he greeted visitors with the mating dance of the common peafowl. He approached with mincing steps, then hopped from foot to foot. Just as the peahen affects indifference to the peacock's dance, most visitors also affected indifference. A few laughed, for he frightened them with his loud shrieks, imitations of the peafowl's warning call. Most waved in that backhanded manner men have of dismissing beggars, a manner of seeing without taking note. He did beg, it was true, but not for alms; he merely begged to be noticed.

He followed them from the gate along the wooden walk to the picnic area. Past it stood a ticket booth above a landing. Here people hired boats to ply the waterways which swirled about the islands of the sanctuary. Even the ticket seller and the boatmen ignored Thittu, though he tried to earn their praise—not only by greeting visitors but also by preventing their stay from being spoiled by crows.

He despised those crows. They gathered in the bamboo and acacia and cawed so loudly, they drowned out the calls of birds nesting on the islands. Often the crows gathered on the islands themselves and spoiled the serenity. At night the boatmen chained their boats to the landing and locked their oars in the ticket booth, so he had no means of reaching the islands. He contented himself with keeping the picnic area free of crows. He did this by flinging bits of coconut shell or lumps of cow dung. These last he stole while they dried, pressed flat on the whitewashed sides of the huts.

What angered him most was the way the crows clamoured for attention. The other birds rarely did; they had no need. People sought them out to marvel at their markings and at their myriad shapes. Yet even keeping the picnic area free of crows earned him little notice. And while he grew past youth into manhood, a

man deprived of both the cares and the bliss of a house-
holder, he feared he might grow invisible.

One day, a foreign watcher of birds pointed a
strange camera at Thittu. It clicked and whirred, then
spewed a white rectangle. While a coloured photo mag-
ically emerged, Thittu drummed with his fingertips on
his lower lip. "Heh, heh!" he exclaimed. "Click, click!"
To his surprise, the visitor handed him the photo. When
he tried to return it, the visitor waved his hand as if,
again, dismissing a beggar. "Keep it," he said; so Thittu
did. Over time the colours faded until it became a pale
yellow shadow. He decided this happened because he
had kept it; that it would have remained true to life
only if the visitor had taken it away. Unable to bear the
sight of his self fading, Thittu buried the photo near his
hut. But even as he grew past manhood towards old
age, so did his fear.

Two lovers visited the sanctuary one day towards
the end of the cold season. They seemed to him like
saurus cranes, whose devotion to their mates inspires
legends. No such female would ever leave her mate.
The woman looked like a madanakai, one of those dam-
sels of the hourglass shape beloved by Hoysala sculp-
tors. Her hair, though dark at its roots, glinted like
white gold. The man looked like a bronzed pelican: bar-
rel-chested and short-necked. He seemed unable to turn
his head without twisting his trunk.

They wore similar clothes, as foreign visitors often
did: rough blue trousers and white pullover shirts
marked in front with the letter I, a red heart, and the letters LA. The woman followed the man at some distance
after they left their hired car at the gate. That is why,
when Thittu saw the message on the man's shirt, he decided her name was La. The man passed without looking Thittu in the eye. Mincing on her high-heeled
sandals, the woman approached. Her walk reminded

him of the mating dance of the common peafowl, but it
also confused him, for it is the peacock that minces towards the peahen. To hide his confusion, he greeted her
by chanting, "La, La, La. La, La."

She stopped and exclaimed, "Ein clown!" She said
it as though accompanied by some invisible admirer.
Then she tapped her chest and said, "Nein, nein. Ich
liebe L-A."

He decided L-A must be the man's initials, but
Thittu turned and saw HELMUT on the back of the
man's shirt. Before Thittu could address the woman
again, she passed him, so closely that he could smell
her skin. It smelled like lavender. On the back of her
shirt, he saw HEIDI. When she called, "Helmut!" the
man turned to say, "Ja, Heidi?" and Thittu realized
these were their names. Helmut shrugged as though he
saw little reason to hire a boat during the off-season.
They returned along the walk.

Thittu hopped from foot to foot. Panic rippled his
throat. How could they leave so soon? A splendid foreign camera dangled from Helmut's shoulder; yet he
had taken no photos. Thittu pressed his grizzled cheeks
and grinned. "Heh, heh," he suggested. "Click, click."
When Helmut frowned, Thittu asked, "Heh, heh? Click,
click?"

Helmut laughed. "Hier nichts zu click, click," he
said loudly. "Click, click nein."

Thittu pointed at himself and tried to explain. If
they took his photo, a memory of him would lie in their
house, and he would never grow invisible. He thought
Heidi would understand. When she passed him, he
closed his hand around her forearm, one covered with
hair as soft as down. "Click, click!" he cried. Her scream
so startled him, he tightened his grip and found her
arm suprisingly muscular.

She snarled, "Braun schwein!" and pushed him
away.

He fell into bamboo that clutched him like a dozen rattling arms. The ticket seller came running. So did the boatmen, who freed Thittu from the bamboo. Instead of sending him on his way, perhaps with a kick and a cuff, they held him tightly. Helmut shouted at the ticket seller, he shouted at the boatmen, and they shouted at one another. Then everyone except Heidi shouted at Thittu. While she minced her way back to the gate, he chirped for her forgiveness. He pleaded with roos and coos.

"Crazies like him lock away you should!" Helmut stormed. "In Vienna with them that's what we do!"

"Extremely sorry, sir," the ticket seller whined. "Sorry in the extreme!" He followed Helmut past the gate to the car. "The fellow has no official business here. He is a madcap."

The last Thittu saw of Heidi, she was rolling up her window. Then Helmut climbed into the car, and it drove off. Moments later, the ticket seller returned. He held a switch. While the boatmen held Thittu, the ticket seller whipped him—whipped him across the shoulders and face and chest until he fainted, not from pain but from fear the men might kill him. When he woke, he found himself at the gate. The goddess of night had lowered her dark robes across his world. He crawled back to his hut. There he lay for days in a fever. It pained his body far less than it pained his mind.

When he finally returned to the sanctuary, the boatmen chased him off. Much later, they once again allowed him to resume his duties, but he no longer had the strength to either greet visitors or battle crows. He found himself unable to remain awake through the long day. Visitors often encountered him curled on the walk like a chick in its egg. No one woke him, not even the boatmen. This proved a blessing, for he dreamt he had been transformed into a bird.

At times, he became an acrobatic sultan tit. He

climbed a tree and hung upside down from twigs while he hunted for insects and grubs. Other times, he became a tailor bird. Using his pointed bill as a needle and shreds of cotton wool as yarn, he sewed leaves into a nest for his young. Always, though, clouds darkened his skies. Then he dreamt he was a bird which had woken from a troubling dream, one in which it had lost its wings and been compelled to walk the earth as a man—a man who could not even find refuge in a sanctuary for birds.

One afternoon, towards the end of the wet season, he woke to find visitors tumbling from a van. Like other watchers of birds, they had arrived with a purpose. He saw this in the way they strode through the gate, in the way they carried small, thick books in their numerous pockets. They reminded him of the bird called "seven sisters," the jungle babbler. It is always found in flocks of six to eight, and it chatters while rummaging for food. Though he could no longer hop, he delighted them with his peacock dance, now a mere shuffle of the feet. They followed while he led them onto the wooden terrace. From here, one could look out across a narrow channel for a tantalizing glimpse of the sanctuary's inhabitants.

An elderly woman in a canvas topi leapt onto the terrace and raised her binoculars. They were smaller than others he had seen; hers snapped shut into a thin, gold case. "I say, chaps," she calmly announced, "I do believe I saw one. Was it, though?" She flipped through a book and slapped a page. "Yes, it was!" She snapped open her binoculars and peered. "Oh my Lord," she gurgled, calling upon her Christian god, "I do believe I saw a striated weaver. Look over—" She began to experience trouble breathing.

"Y'all just pullin' ma leyg!" a man insisted. He wore boots made of crocodile skin. "Where'baouts?"

"In those reeds," she gasped. "It may be a male, and—Yes, it's weaving a nest!"

"Ah see it!" he cried, then doubled over. Instead of merely struggling for air as she did, he clutched his stomach. He clenched his teeth and groaned, "If thayt ain't the gradest thaing since washed gravel!"

Utterly bewildered, Thittu backed away from the visitors. Still they intrigued him, and each bore a camera.

A second woman, younger than the first, carried a parasol. It tilted over her shoulder when she tried to raise her binoculars. They were silver and etched with pink feathers. Upon spotting a white-breasted kingfisher, she dropped the parasol. "Fantastique!" she whimpered. She began to weep.

A second man, older than the first, elbowed his way to the railing. One side of his brown hat was pinned to its crown. He eased a leather tube rimmed with brass from a pocket, then pulled the tube into a telescope. He squeezed one eye shut and scanned the island. "A pa'doise floy-ketcha!" he shrieked. Even as the first woman inquired, "Must you be so dramatic?" he sank to the terrace and began to twitch. "Tike me, Lohd!" he cried. He spread his arms as though to keep the earth from quaking. "Oi'm re-eady!"

Thittu approached the one visitor who hung back. His skin was neither as ruddy as the red junglefowl nor as white as the egret. He appeared to be a guide, for he carried a map. Thittu frowned at the others with concern.

"Twitchers," the guide explained. "I took them to Srirangapatna, yet they showed no interest. None whatsoever. They are making a tour of bird sanctuaries. Each and every single last one."

Thittu mumbled, "Twid-jhers?"

"Twit-chers," the guide repeated. "They live and

breathe for birds. Upon encountering one they have never before seen, they experience such joy they take ill. I, too, feel ill at such behaviour, but I recover quickly." The guide cupped his hand. He grinned while rubbing his thumb over his middle two fingers.

After the first four twitchers recovered from their strangely-felt joy, the guide led them and their companions to the ticket booth. Even as he hired boats, the twitchers stumbled down the landing. The boatmen shoved off.

The twitchers disturbed the birds more than the crows did. The sanctuary echoed with, "Oh my Lord!" and, "If thayt ain't the gradest thaing since—!" It echoed with, "Fantastique!" and, "Tike me, Lohd! Oi'm re-eady!"

When the twitchers returned, they could barely walk. They tumbled out of the boats and lay exhausted on the landing. They staggered to the stone picnic benches and collapsed. The man with stomach trouble, the one in crocodile-skin boots, appeared to have shrunk to half his former size. The weeping woman clutched her parasol and wept. Another woman stared in front of her and babbled, "A racket-tailed drongo, I saw a racket-tailed drongo, I heard its tail feathers hum."

Thittu slowly drummed with his fingertips on his lower lip. Was he, himself, not like the drongo? He squatted on his haunches in the middle of the picnic area and, like the drongo, began imitating other birds. First he gave a series of sharp, whistling screams.

"I'd say it's a night prowler," the gasping woman gasped.

Grinning, he bobbed his head. Next he made a shrill, piping call.

"Thayt there's uh avocet," groaned the groaning man.

"Ce n'est pas—Not close enough," said the woman who wrung out her kerchief. "C'est un, black-winged stilt." She asked Thittu, "Vrai?"

He frowned at the guide, who nodded.

"I just knew!" she said and burst into tears.

Thittu made some harsh, nasal sounds.

"Taow easy, mite," said the twitching man. "That's moi pa'doise floy-ketcha."

Thittu made a high-pitched bubbling call like the sound of air blown through a reed into water. Silence followed. After he repeated the call, a fifth twitcher cried, "A masked fin-foot!" The others applauded.

After that, he stared eagerly at the cameras. "Heh, heh?" he asked. "Click, click?" The twitchers frowned at one another. "Heh, heh!" he insisted. "Click, click!" When no one responded, he gave them his best imitation: the loud melodious call of the shama.

Two of them guessed correctly, but the guide shrugged when they questioned him. "There are no shamas here," he said. "They are too shy. I myself have never seen a shama, not in all my years as the number-one guide in Mysore District. I would pluck out these very eyes if I could find a shama for you."

The twitchers rose and reluctantly followed him back to the van. Each of them dropped a coin at Thittu's feet. He gazed dully at the seven coins. He did not need money to be happy; the twitchers had made him happy with their attention. All he asked now was that they ensure he never grow invisible, and they could do so seven times over.

That night, after all the birds except the night prowler and the drongo had fallen silent, he crept back to the sanctuary. He cut down a bamboo thicket and lashed the poles with dried coconut fronds. He floated his raft to the nearest island and hid the raft among dense reeds. Then he hid himself behind a babul tree, well away from the silvery white thorns about its base. In the morning, after the goddess of dawn wakened birds in their nests, he began the loud melodious call of the shama. He sang all day and all the next until his throat began to knot. Soon after dawn on the third day, the twitchers and their guide returned. Even from the island, Thittu could hear them chatter like the jungle babbler. He could almost hear them gasp and groan and weep. He could imagine them—side by side on the terrace—twitching.

When he heard them run towards the ticket booth, he pulled his raft out of hiding. The ticket seller and the boatmen, the guide and all the twitchers waited to welcome him. He spread his arms and performed his repertoire: the shrieks of a common peafowl; the screams of a night prowler; the call of a black-winged stilt; even the unending cry of the brain-fever bird. Oh, how the twitchers applauded. Thittu felt like a king—a king of the birds. While his raft neared the landing, he continued his performance with the bubbling call of a masked fin-foot; the nasal sounds of a paradise flycatcher; and, finally, the melodious call of the shama.

"You!" the guide exclaimed. Even he now bore a camera.

The twitchers turned to leave. "We want our payment refunded," they told the guide. "The bonus, too."

"Of course," he said. "Certainly, why not?"

"Heh, heh?" Thittu called after the twitchers. "Click, click?"

The ticket seller growled, "We shall give you click, click!"

The boatmen pulled Thittu off the raft and up the stone steps of the landing. The ticket seller ran to see off the van. When he returned, he held not a switch but a length of stout, green bamboo. Then, while the boatmen held Thittu, while he chirped and twittered and roo'd and cooed, the ticket seller beat him to death.

At this point in Garuda's tale, Vishnu sat up—so quickly, the great serpent Sesha bobbed upon the primordial sea. "Ga-ru-da," Vishnu warned, "if I relate this tale of yours, the gods will shed tears. Brahma will sneer until his lips twitch like those foreigners."

Garuda tilted his eagle head until it brushed his human shoulder. "Have patience, Lord," he pleaded. "Once, when we discussed why men amuse us so much, you told us comedy is the sum of tragedy and time."

"The only comedy here," Vishnu scoffed, "will be the gods' laughing at me—for a sorry tale about a man whose life had so little purpose. It is barely tragic at that. What is the loneliness of one man compared, say, to the foolishness of the many who war? That is tragic. Even gods can learn to laugh at that over time."

"You know best, Lord," Garuda said. He made to rise.

"And where might you be going?" Vishnu asked.

"To find another tale," Garuda said. "This time I shall not try to be amusing." He smiled coyly.

Vishnu raised his club.

When Garuda flinched, Sesha lowered his thousand heads. Garuda nodded at the silent reminder: Vishnu the Protector would never strike unless the fate of heaven or the world hung in the balance. Even when bothered by gnats, he threatened them half-heartedly.

"Do you expect me to wait here with an unfinished tale," he demanded, "while you search for another? This tale is clearly unfinished. I can see by your smile. Every tale deserves to be told at least once, to an audience of at least one. I doubt this tale will be retold, but here is your audience of one."

Garuda again took his place on Sesha's coils.

"Finish quickly," Vishnu commanded, so Garuda did:

Yama, the king of justice, called Thittu to the lower world, where he hurried past the insatiable dogs of death. He entered Yama's palace. While a councillor thumbed through the great register, Thittu's soul hovered in the form of a quivering, white light. The account of his deeds took little time to relate. He did not deserve to be dragged through any of the twenty-one hells, for he was guilty of so little. Thus Yama set aside his noose and, naturally, sent for me.

"It seems clear this man should be reborn as a bird," I said.

Yama hefted his mace and allowed it to fall at his feet. The lower world trembled. "I did not summon you to tell me what is clear," he growled. "What kind of bird?"

"Something wondrous," I suggested. "Perhaps a fabulous partridge who feeds on moonbeams."

Yama snorted. "Would it not be better if he became an ordinary bird? Then he could have a mate."

"An ordinary bird then," I agreed. "But what kind?"

"If you please, Lord Garuda," Thittu said. When Yama glared at him for speaking, Thittu's voice trembled like his soul. "I—I would like to be a bird no one could ignore."

"A fairy bluebird?" I asked. "A scarlet minivet, or even a brahminy kite. You could always become a common peafowl, though as a peacock you would hardly be common."

"None of them," he said and then announced his choice.

When Garuda fell silent, Vishnu once more raised his club. He lowered it quickly, for this time Garuda did not flinch. "Am I to remain in suspense forever?" Vishnu demanded. "What did the man choose to become?"

"Can you not guess, Lord?" Garuda asked. "What is the one bird that can never be ignored?" Garuda spread his hands. "Thittu chose to be reborn as a crow."

Vishnu's laugh began as a smirk, then became a chuckle. Soon he guffawed, "A crow!" He slapped his thigh with the hand bearing the lotus. He laughed with his back arched, with his head thrown back. Sesha bobbed until the primordial sea threatened to swamp the earth.

"Would a tale like this force Brahma to laugh openly?" Garuda asked.

"Never mind Brahma," Vishnu said, "that stony-faced spoiler of others' sport! The rest will laugh."

A satisfied smile crinkled Garuda's beak. This time Vishnu did not stop Garuda when he rose and unfurled his wings. "If I may, Lord," he said, "it is comforting to know you are only mistaken over small things."

Vishnu looked askance. "What now?" he asked.

"You were wrong twice," Garuda said. "Once when you called Thittu's life a life with no great purpose—"

"I said that?"

"And once more when you called my tale sorry."

"Ah, I see."

"Not yet," Garuda said. "A life lived with no great purpose leads to another life, so it is not completely wasted. And just as the purpose of a man's life, even one like Thittu's, lies in its living and in little else, so the purpose of a tale lies in its telling. If it accomplishes more, so be it. Even if this one does not force Brahma to laugh openly, it has already accomplished more."

"Oh-hoh!" Vishnu exclaimed. "Pray, how is that?"

Garuda tensed his wings for escape. He asked, "Must I reveal everything? Think, Lord: you are no longer gazing at your navel."

Long after he left, Garuda could hear Vishnu's laughter, could hear him gasp, "A crow!"

Garuda circled out from the primordial sea towards earth. This time he stopped only once: to ride the
rings of Saturn. A passing comet chuckled. And while
Garuda spun, rocking with his head thrown back, his
wings unfurled and his arms uplifted, even Brahma,
who was not above disguising himself as a gnat—even
Brahma laughed.

THE WINDS OF TIME

JOËL CHAMPETIER

Translated from the French by Jane Brierley

On the planet Oslofturk, the wind blowing from the east comes from the past, whereas the wind blowing from the west comes from the future.

These winds are usually very gentle, the east wind maintaining a constant temperature, since it comes from the preceding days, while the west wind helps forecast the temperature in days to come. But sometimes the winds blow very hard and sweep in their wake light objects such as sheets of paper, plastic bags, and hats.

The inhabitants of Oslofturk aren't much interested in the east wind except when it turns especially violent and they can pick up objects from a distant past. It's the winds from the west, the future, that stimulate their curiosity and even their greed. For thousands of years, the Patriarchs of Oslofturk have forbidden ordinary citizens to possess any object carried by the west wind. Collection and study of such objects is the preserve of the Grand Piernamons, that caste of scholars who work under the iron rod of the Patriarchs.

Nevertheless, every inhabitant of Oslofturk avidly seeks and jealously preserves the lightest twig from the future.

Newspaper clippings are particularly desirable, especially when you consider that the numerous followers of Temporal Omniscience cut up all sorts of documents and disperse them on the west wind for the edification of the people of the past toward the east.

A foreigner in Oslofturk sees a singular sight on a day when the wind is blowing hard from the west. Thousands of citizens stop working, playing, or harvesting, and rush into the open, where countless bits of paper from the west fly about. Whenever the Grand Piernamons aren't looking, everyone feverishly gathers them up. At the same time, armfuls of paper cuttings hurled onto the wind by the Temporal Omniscience fanatics flutter toward the past.

What are people looking for in these scraps of paper? Of what use is this glimpse of the future to an ordinary citizen? Is it likely that a newspaper clipping picked up by a citizen at considerable risk could be meant for him alone?

Only the Grand Piernamons, since they can collect, classify and study these pieces of time, are able to reconstitute a consistent history of their future. But the knowledge is given to no one but the Patriarchs, who use it to maintain their grip on the glebe of Oslofturk.

Is it surprising that the thousand-year-old dictatorship of Oslofturk should be so stable?

It's said that repression in Oslofturk has been on the increase over the last few years, and that the law against picking up objects carried on the west wind is now punishable by death.

It's said that a wind of uncertainty is blowing between the damp walls of the Piernamon monasteries. That thousands of black-bordered pamphlets appear on gusty days, pamphlets inciting the people to rise up.

Furthermore, it's said—but perhaps this is just a rumour—that on certain stormy days, rare days when the west wind lifts the tiles off the roofs and breaks branches off the trees, halftorn signs vaunting the people's victory over the Patriarch's dictatorship go scudding along the streets. But only the Piernamons possess such signs.

For the stranger who visits Oslofturk these days, such stories seem mere fables, since for weeks only a gentle east wind has been blowing. But occasionally there is a drop in the wind, a slight veering that makes you think a west wind is about to spring up. Then people stop talking and look toward the west, a spark in their eye, and wait resolutely for the coming storm.

BIRTHDAY

P.K. PAGE

After the effort of dressing—and it was an effort these days, quite exhausting, in fact—she needed to pause a little, compose herself, before beginning the day.

The chair she sat in, like a burnished throne, shone brightly in the sun and there she rested, burnished too, and the glitter of her rings transformed the morning.

Sometimes she wondered if the chair and the sunlight—perhaps especially the sunlight—contributed to or even hatched the fragments of knowledge which slipped into her head from the side, glancing through her, leaving a trace like the silvery trail of a snail or which, more directly, arrived head-on—shooting stars, illuminating but transitory.

So far she had been unable to attach meaning to these glimmerings and flashes, palely glowing; she might even say, 'burning sweetly', in the space in her head where her brain had once been but where, now, it was as if her heart were tenant.

What was she to make, for instance, of the knowledge that she was awaiting an event, one which—she now realized—she had been awaiting since birth? Perhaps before. Possibly even before. As to the nature of the event or what prompted its knowledge, she hadn't the least idea.

Was its source, she wondered, some quickening in the air—the same quickening one feels as the old year draws to its close? Or, perhaps she had been programmed—she was amused by her change in vocabulary, for surely, she once would have said 'influenced'—by images from all her forgotten dreams. Were her changing cells simply by-passing the 'operator' entirely and dialing direct to the 'listener' within? Here, she could only speculate.

But she knew time was short. Knew it certainly. Knew the event near and beyond question. And even though it had no form, no detail, and she possessed no clues as to what it was, she couldn't rid her mind of it. It was there that her thoughts centred—electrons circling a nucleus. At times it was as if the electrons were becoming an entity in themselves and gradually replacing what she had always thought to be—for want of a better word—herself. For surely it was not she who, yesterday, threw out the eyedrops that control glaucoma? Even less would she have refused, stubbornly refused—the analgesic which eased the pain of arthritis. Something other than herself must be in control.

Was it simply that she was old and scatty? she asked. For she was old, after all, and strangely changed, on the surfaces at least. For proof she need look no further than her rheumaticky hands, wrinkled and blotched like snakeskin, the fingers swollen and twisted, the knuckles shiny. But as she examined them in the bright sunlight, she knew quite clearly that in no time at all they would be the tiny, soft, rubbery, red fists of a baby. Involuntarily her stomach jerked. It was rather as she had felt when first she knew that she was something other than her body; that although it was flesh that made her visible, she was not that flesh. No wonder her stomach jerked: flesh objects to playing so secondary a role.

And then she remembered the dream. Those little red fists had brought it back. It was bizarre, of course. One's dream scenarist tends to be antic.

Head foremost, she was forcing—and at the same time being forced—down a long book-lined corridor. Books on both sides. How tight it made the passage! Painful. Cramped. Intolerable, actually. And an area between her shoulder blades—not usually one of her more sensitive spots, though she had many these days—was unbearably tender. But as she struggled, constricted, half blind, she was comforted by a series of brilliant images: butterfly; bird; man; angel. Her own joyous laughter had wakened her that morning. She remembered it now with a matching lightness of heart.

Suddenly curious, she tried to touch that spot between her shoulders. The back of the chair and the pain in wrists and elbows hindered her movements. But when the fingers of a persistent right hand finally succeeded, she was rewarded by the discovery of two protuberances—ridge-shaped—one on either side of her spine, and agonizingly sensitive to the touch. For, added to the accustomed pain of arthritis, was the suddenly remembered torture of teething and the unique realization of the distress and ecstasy of the unicorn as a foal when, cutting his horn, he perceived that he was not the young horse he had thought himself to be.

A long arm of sunshine reached out from where she sat and fell upon the glinting aglets of a pair of narrow shoes. Her brother was standing just inside the door—thin, aquiline, smiling. How many years was it since she had seen him? "Robert!" she cried, "how good of you to come."

"It's Victor," a voice answered. "Your son and heir. You've forgotten, Mother. I was here yesterday."

Yesterday? Ah Robert, Victor, time does bear thinking about, doesn't it. Passing without notice when it wishes or travelling at the speed of light. And what day was it that she should be lying here in her bed? What time of day? She reached out to the sun's pale, fine dust which lay like a ribbon on her blanket and with the jolt that she had come to know as certainty, she realized that his was her last awakening in this bed, this room, this . . . 'place'.

Could the wintry sunlight, starting with her fingers, dissolve her flesh, her bones, all matter? For, light as thistledown, she and the material world were suspended, painless, totally detached. The cord that had bound her to all she loved was severed, she thought, forever. What possible links could survive this atomization?

Yet links survived. Her sight—better today than usual—took in the bare boughs of trees, their colour a nameless dark against the sky. It was as if she had never seen them before, yet their diffuse forms were as familiar to her as the bed she lay in. Her mind was clear too—startlingly clear—for she actually saw the two contradictions arise as one and separate and become two as if they had passed through a prism or fragmenter. "But it's not only opposites which are born single and become dual," she thought excitedly. "More complex still, any image, at a certain point, will splinter and multiply."

Eager to test this new perception—'tree', she thought and immediately it was sawn into planks, hammered into coffins, shaped into violins, pressed into paper. She could not hold 'tree' in her mind singly, simply. The one became two, three, four or even more. And this propensity to fragment had been, she now knew, central to her life. Not her life only, of course. It was in the nature of humankind. And she was on the brink of controlling it. All she had to do was allow a stop to occur at exactly the right moment—no more difficult than releasing the shutter of a camera when the light, speed, focus and subject were all correctly aligned. But the art of doing it vanished along with a certain radiance the room had contained and there she was again, an old body on a bed, faced with the imminence of the event and shaky. Shaky.

"Oh, I would go back on the whole thing if I could," she said—knowing that she couldn't, but not why.

"When was the decision made and by whom?" she demanded. "Was I a conscious party to it? Was it my wish?"

"I suppose it's like waiting to die," she thought. "The same uncertainty about what is to come, the same fear of pain, the same wrench from the known. But," she queried, "being born *where*? In what country? With what planets rising? And what colour?" she asked herself idly. But as to that, she was only mildly curious, for no part of her cared whether or not she continued white.

"The same with size," she went on, "although that, I suppose, might embrace differences other than those measurable in feet and inches. But I'd adjust," she said, confident. "Alice did, after all. Took her changes with remarkable *sang froid*—a reflection of the age and race to which she belonged, perhaps."

"But sex," she thought with a stab, "is another matter." Appallingly repellent, the mere idea of being male. Not that she hadn't loved male flesh well enough in her time. "Too well," she thought, nostalgically. But the prospect of being it . . . the stubble, the muscle, the hair on the chest . . . the Adam's apple . . . No! "I wouldn't know how to be male," she exclaimed aloud. "I'm so at home in this female body." But as she spoke she realized that she wasn't at home in it any more. Nearly all of it was painful to her—a stricture—especially in that area between the shoulder blades. In fact, since the appearance of those two new ridges, it was impossible for her to lie on her back and her bed was a rack and a harrow.

"More important," her thoughts were racing now, reminiscent of descriptions of the speed of flying saucers—"vastly more important even than gender—or nationality or colour or size—is kind." What if she were born in the body of a dog, for instance? Not that there weren't exceptional dogs. But it would be disappointing and repetitive, for on the evolutionary scale she must already have been a dog or its equivalent, must already have managed four hairy legs and a tail and it would be a matter simply of doing it all over again.

But curious dislocations were occurring within her and without. Reassemblies. She was no longer . . . in place. From this great height, she could barely make out towers or steeples and geometry, which she had studied so eagerly as a girl, was now either pre- or post-Euclidean. Its angles altered. "Michael, Raphael, Gabriel," she said. "All male. And Uriel. Male also." And despite the fact that her mind surged and flowed and she seemed able to draw upon the whole of creation as if from a meticulously indexed encyclopedia, she couldn't recall a single female angle.

Such vast accessibilities without. So great a condensation within. A gathering together, a coalescence. Heightened inertia. "Bend back thy bow, O Archer. . ."

"What matter," she asked, "if I die female and am born male? Through the alembic of this giant eye, male/female are won."

And as the fragmenter or prism in her mind reversed direction, all multiplicity without—the trail of the snail, the shooting stars, the baby, the tree, her brother, her son—was, through its unifying beam, drawn into her to become again what it had always been and was still—hole, won; and this same reversal made possible the contraction of all her particles as if in preparation for rising—a spacecraft taking off. And through one supra sense she heard the rush of air, and through that same sense—upstream of the five now left behind in a fractured world—she felt the exquisite movement of its currents stirring the small down on her incredible wings.

PHOENIX SUNSET

COLLEEN ANDERSON

Cracker Jax sat on the worn ashen steps of the old gallery, flanked by two slumbering stone lions. He twisted the colored, UV inhibiting field rings in his ear and stared at the few gun embellished Technos and flashy Cybers striding by in the greyish light. Jagged colors in green and orange shot up his skintight pant legs, adding brightness to the insipid day.

He tensed, then resumed twisting field rings, chin in hand.

"Yo, Jax. Unhinge your mind from the grids. I've got a flash."

Cracker Jax glanced up. "Ember." He ignored her and stared into the street. Ember, a sweep of crimson, dropped beside him and watched his profile. Blood red hair shadowed her skin as her fiery lips brushed his ear with a whisper.

"Cracker Jax, my Cyber cynic, how would you like to play with fire?" She ran glinting ruby nails through his close-cropped hair, heat pulsing from her palm implants.

Jax snapped his finger pinpoint lasers to standby,

slammed a hand to his chest, flesh rippling and sheathed under the insul shirt, and hissed air through his teeth, honing sonics. He quickly shifted and seized one of Ember's bird-thin hands. "I'm ready, babe. Your tech magic against mine."

Ember's pupilless red eyes widened. "Hey, just a joke. No scam here. I wanted your attention."

He released her hand. "Don't ever threaten me-- even as a joke."

She pushed her hair behind delicately pointed ears. "Well, you're in one iced out mood. Look," she leaned forward intently. "I've got a quest. A rumor to dispel your dark day. A hunt." Her smile uncovered even rows of ivory teeth.

Cracker Jax shut down his armaments, leaned back on his elbows and asked, uninterested, "What hunt? Some Technos gone razing?"

"No." Ember clacked a gemstone nail against her teeth. "A myth--a real one. One of my spells gleamed a phoenix. Nearby. No genufactured, Techno made bird. The real thing."

"Imposs," snorted Jax. "You've been sniffing neuro-sen. There's never been real magic in the world. That was proven."

"Wrong-o, Cynic." Ember fished within her voluminous jacket and pulled out a can of 'brosia. She broke the seal, pulled at the drink and passed it to Jax. "There's always been magic—that's been proven, when the reality rifts brought faery and humans face to face. You accepted that magic. It's only magical animals both races have glammed as unreal."

Jax swished the 'brosia over his teeth and swallowed. "So what's the spout on this phoenix then?"

"That's just it." Ember's hands flashed, sparking light back to the ozone grids overhead. "I've divined it and it's near. I want to find it, prove one way or the other. . . It could be ultima max."

Jax raised his eyebrow. "And you want my aid."

"Come on, Jax. An adventure. You're just brooding bad times. 'Sides, I need your search skills."

He laughed abruptly and threw up his hands. "All right, Ruby Red. Tell me more about this rare chicken."

She stood, pulling Jax's thickly muscled arm. He rose and they walked down the steps, boot heels scraping stone. "No chicken. Legend says only one exists at a time. Shows up just after or before its death. Rebirths itself, you know. Some sort of immortality/sun sym."

Cracker Jax dropped his arm on Ember's narrow shoulders. "That's it? It'll turn out to be some mutant fowl. The giant chicken that ate the world. The chicken shit alone would kill us." He ducked as if something was falling on him but straightened at Ember's scowl.

"What's it look like?"

"Scan your linkup files, grid brain. The info's there under myth. We'll need gear. It's cozed up in the non-grid wastelands."

Jax pressed deep brown fingers to his temples and whispered file commands. He stopped. "You mean we're going into contam land for a wild goose chase for some. . ." he echoed the inner voice. ". . . Some . . . 'symbol of rebirth, the phoenix rising from ashes.'? That's it?!"

Ember's voice trembled but she continued flippantly. "Open your orbs. If it's real then chance is we might fly free of all this." Her hand swung up to encompass buildings and cracked roads shimmering red under the UV grid's garish light. "It will mean that we can ice those contam lands. It will mean that there is true magic and if that bird can rebirth itself maybe, just maybe it's power can help us help. . ."

Her voice trailed off as her hand trembled and sunk to her side.

Cracker Jax shook his head. "All right, all right. Don't throw your stash away. Come on. I think Tinder has some rad suits."

An hour later they entered a slouching burb house surrounded by cascading mounds of brick and board. They found Tinder crawling under a table, cursing. The dwarf's mohawk was dusty from rooting in piles of fabric and scrap metal. He quickly scrounged up two rad suits and a rickety scooter full of dints.

Ember struggled into the crinkly silver suit. "Are you sure I need this? We aren't usually scathed by contam like you humes."

Tinder picked at an emerald tooth and grunted. "You may not need field rings when in the Fey holmes or the city but I wouldn't press my luck in high contam areas. There have, after all, been mutated Fey born."

Jax grinned. "Yeah, it's only right you suffer some if I have to." He pushed a thin metal band, lightly etched with gold lines, around his forehead and twisted the three beads on it. A low hum filled the air as the protective field enclosed him.

Ember snapped on her band then looked askance at the scooter. "How's this thing to work again?"

Chains clattering around his wrist, Tinder dropped three coppery disks into her palm. "Put one of these in the fuselage slot, heat it and recite the spell for flight. It should do the trick."

Ember nodded and tucked the micro-chip embedded disks into a hip pocket.

Cracker Jax passed Tinder a small sack of noncontam rations and saluted. "Thanks. We're off to hunt legend."

They rolled the scooter past the metal mounds and onto a rended pavement slab. A disk between her palms, Ember voiced a code command and heat glowed from her hands. Jax gingerly picked up the glowing disk with a gloved hand and pushed it into the slot as Ember intoned the spell. They mounted and the scooter made no sound as it moved beneath them.

They drove past cement and glass Techno towers, through several Cyber burb clusters of wood and concrete constructs and near a Fey stronghold of lush green trees kept alive by magical enhancement.

As they journeyed, the grids thinned until only the somber sky, cloaked in clouds, remained. The stillness thickened and stark trees brandished accusing limbs.

Lightly clasping his waist, Ember spoke into Jax's multi-ringed ear. "Should be triflin' to trace. Aren't any animals to gum the infra tracery." Jax nodded, tight-lipped.

They drove through the calm quiet and entered a miasma of roiling sky and land the color of old ash. Old landfill eruptions spotted the earth, metal barrels spread helter-skelter. Ember pointed to one jumble. The faded black rad sign, its three triangles, apexes touching, still glowed.

Bleached bones of a massive animal bloomed like a sad flower, reminding them of the initial seed that had grown such a garden. Ember's pale skin lightened until her hair and lips looked like wounds. Cracker Jax frowned, knuckles almost white upon the handlebars.

They stopped by the cadaverous remains of a squat building. Jax touched his metal headband. "Are you sure this is the area, Ember?"

She nodded, hugging herself. "I can taste it, you know. This," her arm moved jerkily, "place. All this contam, I feel it icing the land."

Cracker Jax grabbed a pack from the scooter. He spoke a quick voice command and blinked his eyes in a pattern of long and short winks. "Well, let's find this bird then. Infra's on." He scanned the landscape. "Hmm. I can see the rad hot spots but should still be able to trace any life forms. Which way?"

Ember pointed east, away from the crumbling road. She chattered nervously as they moved out. "I think this is the Ace, Jax. To find life, to find a phoenix, especially in the rad lands would mean there's still magic; a world life force."

Jax, looking, scouting said nothing. Ember talked on until Jax stopped and scrutinized her face. He lightly touched her shoulder.

"You know, before the reality rifts people thought elves, satyrs, dwarves . . . thought all of you were just faery tales, myth. There was that romantic idealism to hang onto, a life more magical, better attuned. I think people had more hope when they thought magic might exist." He shook his head.

"Then came the reality rifts. The Fey seemed just as fallible as humans and there was nothing left to believe in."

Ember shivered. "I think the Fey brought their own demise through their arrogance, using magic so freely. If they'd been tuned, then the rifts between techs and faery wouldn't rule." She poked her chest. "That's why I turned Cyber and why this phoenix is the ultima max. There's still hope and a chance that the land might sprout some buds. Agree?"

Jax smiled a lopsided grin. They continued searching. After combing the area for several hours they moved closer to a turgid soup of water and debris. It rippled sluggishly, popping up lumpy shapes. They halfheartedly poked around in a forest of crackly branches and spires of dead trees. Night dyed the clouds black.

Jax, hands on hips said tersely, "I don't think we're going to find anything. Any of these hotspots could be a bird or just more rad."

Ember sighed, shoulders slumping. "You're right. I

don't want to snooze in no man's land. Let's skim."

They walked away from the shore passing a small gully. Cracker Jax glanced back at the lake then caught a flash of colour that showed even without the infra-vision. He grabbed Ember's sleeve. "Wait. Over there."

Like a blazing fire, something pulsed, fluttered amongst the broken tree limbs.

"Goddess, it's so beautiful," Ember whispered as they approached.

Laying before them was an enormous bird, feathers flushed in deep scarlets, vibrant orange, golden yellow. Its three foot tail feathers spread out like rivulets of blood. It flapped a large wing and lay on its side panting.

Jax kneeled down, frowning. "Something's wrong. It's sick."

Ember clasped her hands. "Perhaps it's at the end of its cycle, ready to die and be reborn."

Cracker Jax held a brown finger to his temples and spoke a command. "File—Phoenix."

"Hmm. There's a dispute of when they're reborn but who knows when the first existed. It could be at the end of a cycle."

"It must be." Ember approached the bird. "We have to help it. It's supposed to die in a sweet smelling nest."

Jax stared at her back. "How are we to do that? We don't know if it's the phoenix or not. It could be some Techno genufacturing."

Ember's voice quavered. "It doesn't matter. Nothing deserves to die like this. We'll take it back with us. Tend it. We must."

She moved closer, slowly, as if afraid the bird would take flight. Kneeling she reached out to touch it.

Cracker Jax sighed and said gently. "Ember, look at it. It's half the size of me. We couldn't possibly carry it on the scooter." He looked at the bird. "I don't think we'll have to," he added quietly. "It's dead."

"No." Ember cradled its sinuous neck and head in her arms. Its obsidian eyes grew milky. "No. Where's the flames?" She stroked its blood-red chest. "Where's the flames?"

Tears etched her face. Jax turned his watery eyes to the ground and began walking away. He heard Ember stand and then a crackling sound grew behind his back. Looking over his shoulder, blinking he saw Ember light the carcass aflame with her eye lasers. She watched until the flames caught, blending with the feathers. The dried branches beneath the bird disappeared in smoke as the fire expanded in a widening circle.

Ember walked to where Jax waited, holding a solitary three foot feather between slim fingers. Her eyes sparkled with tears. "I had to. It deserved a better death than that—a clean death."

Cracker Jax hugged her to him and they turned their backs on the spreading fire, walking back to the scooter, arms around each other. The flames leapt towards the evening sky feeding colour, like feathers afloat, into the bleakness.

MUFFIN EXPLAINS TELEOLOGY TO THE WORLD AT LARGE

JAMES ALAN GARDNER

I told my kid sister Muffin this joke.

There was this orchestra, and they were playing music, and all the violins were bowing and moving their fingers, except for this one guy who just played the same note over and over again. Someone asked the guy why he wasn't playing like the others and he said, "They're all looking for the note. I've found it."

Muffin, who's only six, told me the joke wasn't funny if you understood teleology.

I never know where she gets words like that. I had to go and look it up.

> *teleology* [teli-<u>o</u>loji] <u>n</u>. doctrine or belief
> that all things or actions are designed
> to achieve some end.

"Okay," I said when I found her again, "now I understand teleology. Why isn't the joke funny?"

"You'll find out next week," she said.

I talked to Uncle Dave that night. He's in university and real smart, even though he's going to be a minister instead of something interesting. "What's so great about teleology?" I said. He looked at me kind of weird so I explained, "Muffin's been talking about it."

"So have my professors," he said. "It's, uhh, you know, God has a purpose for everything, even if we can't understand it. We're all heading towards some goal."

"We took that in Sunday School," I said.

"Well Jamie, we go into it in a bit more detail."

"Yeah, I guess."

He was quiet for a bit, then asked, "What's Muffin say about it?"

"Something big is happening next week."

"Teleologically speaking?"

"That's what she says."

Muffin was in the next room with her crayons. Uncle Dave called her in to talk and she showed him what she was working on. She'd coloured Big Bird black. She has all these crayons and the only ones she ever uses are black and grey.

"What's happening next week?" Uncle Dave asked.

"It's a secret," she said.

"Not even a hint?"

"No."

"Little tiny hint? Please?"

She thought about it a minute, then whispered in his ear. Then she giggled and ran upstairs.

"What did she say?" I asked.

"She said that we'd get where we were going." He shrugged and made a face. We were both pretty used to Muffin saying things we didn't understand.

✧ ✧

The next day, I answered the front doorbell and found three guys wearing grey robes. They'd shaved their heads too.

"We are looking for her gloriousness," one of them said with a little bow. He had an accent.

"Uh, Mom's gone down the block to get some bread," I answered.

"It's okay," Muffin said, coming from the TV room. "They're here for me."

All three of the men fell face down on the porch making a kind of high whining sound in their throats.

"You know these guys?" I asked.

"They're here to talk about teleology."

"Oh. Well take them around to the back yard. Mom doesn't like people in the house when she's not here."

"Okay." She told the guys to get up and they followed her around the side of the house, talking in some foreign language.

When Mom got home, I told her what happened and she half-ran to the kitchen window to see what was going on. Muffin was sitting on the swing set and the guys were cross-legged on the ground in front of her, nodding their heads at every word she spoke. Mom took a deep breath, the way she does just before she's going to yell at one of us, then stomped out the back door. I was sure she was going to shout at Muffin, but she bent over and talked quiet enough that I couldn't hear from inside the house. Muffin talked and Mom talked and one of the bald guys said something, and finally Mom came in all pale-looking.

"They want lemonade," she said. "Take them out some lemonade. And plastic glasses. I'm going to lie down." And she went upstairs.

I took them out a pitcher of lemonade. When I got there, one of the bald guys got up to meet me and asked Muffin, "Is this the boy?"

She said yes.

"Most wondrous, most wondrous!"

He put both hands on my shoulders as if he was going to hug me, but Muffin said, "You'll spill the lemonade." He let me go, but kept staring at me with his big weepy white eyes.

"What's going on?" I asked.

"The culmination of a thousand thousand years of aimless wandering," the guy said.

"Not aimless," Muffin cut in.

"Your pardon," he answered, quickly lowering his head. "But at times it seemed so."

"You'll be in the temple when it happens," Muffin said to him.

"A million praises!" he shouted, throwing himself flat-faced on the ground. "A billion trillion praises!" And he started to cry into our lawn. The other two bowed in the direction of our garage, over and over again.

"You want to pour me a glass of that?" Muffin said to me.

The next day it was a different guy, wearing a red turban and carrying a curvy sword almost as tall as me. When I opened the door, he grabbed the front of my T-shirt and yelled, "Where is the Liar, the Deceiver, the Blasphemer, the She-Whore who Mocks the Most High?"

"She went with Uncle Dave down to the Dairy Queen."

"Thank you," he said, and walked off down the

street. Later, I heard on the radio that the cops had arrested him in the parking lot of the mall.

The next day, Muffin told me I had to take her down to the boat yards. I said, "I don't have to do anything."

"Shows how much you know," she answered. "You don't know anything about teleology or fate or anything."

"I know how to cross streets and take buses and all, which is more than I can say for some people."

"I have ten dollars," she said, pulling a bill out of the pocket of her jeans.

That surprised me. I mean, I maybe have ten dollars in my pocket twice a year, just after Christmas and just after my birthday. "Where'd you get the money?" I asked.

"The monks gave it to me."

"Those bald guys?"

"They like me."

"Geez, Muffin, don't let mom know you took money from strangers. She'd have a fit."

"They aren't strangers. They're the Holy Order of the Imminent Eschaton—the Muffin Chapter."

"Oh, go ahead, lie to me."

"You want the ten dollars or not?"

Which wasn't what I ended up with, because she expected me to pay the bus fare out of it.

When we got to the boat yards, I thought we'd head right down to the water, but Muffin just took out a piece of paper and stood there frowning at it. I looked over her shoulder and saw it was torn from a map of the city. There was a small red X drawn in at a place about a block from where we were. "Where'd you get that? The monks?"

"Mm-hm. Is this where we are?" She pointed at a corner. I looked and moved her finger till it pointed to the right place. "You should learn to read some time, Muffin."

She shook her head. "Might wreck my insight. Maybe after."

I pointed down the street. "If you want to go where X marks the spot, it's that way."

We walked along with sailboats and yachts and things on one side, and warehouses on the other. The buildings looked pretty run down, with brown rusty spots dripping down from their metal roofs and lots of broken windows covered with plywood or cardboard. It was a pretty narrow street and there was no side-walk, but the only traffic we saw was a Shell oil truck coming out of the Marina a ways ahead and it turned off before it got to us.

Then we reached the X spot, but the only thing there was was another warehouse. Muffin closed her eyes for a second, then said, "Around the back and up the stairs."

"I bet there are rats around the back," I said.

"I bet there aren't."

"You go first."

"Okay." She started off down an alley between the one warehouse and the next. There was a lot of broken glass lying around and grass growing up through the pavement.

"I bet there are snakes," I said, following her.

"Shut up, Jamie."

✧ ✧

The back was only a strip of weeds about two yards wide, stuck between the warehouse and a chain link fence. Halfway along, there was a long flight of metal steps like a fire escape leading up to the roof. They creaked a bit when you walked on them, but didn't wobble too badly.

On the roof we found a really weird looking airplane. Or boat. Or train. Or wagon. Anyway, it had wings and a tail like an airplane, but its body was built like a boat, a bit like the motorboat up at the cottage, but bigger and with these super-fat padded chairs like maybe astronauts sit in. The whole thing sat on a cart, but the cart's wheels were on the near end of a train track that ran the length of the roof and off the front into the street.

"What is this thing?" I asked.

"The monks made it for me," Muffin said, which didn't answer my question. She climbed up a short metal ladder into the plane and rummaged about in a cupboard in the rear wall. I followed her and watched her going through stuff inside. "Peanut butter. Bread. Kool Aid. Water. Cheese. Diet Coke. What's this?" she said, handing me back a roll of something in gold plastic wrapping.

I opened one end and sniffed. "Liverwurst," I said.

"Is that like liver?" She made a face.

"No, it's sort of like peanut butter but made from bologna."

"Weird. Do you see any hot dogs?"

I looked in the cupboard. "Nope."

"I should phone the monks. We need hot dogs."

"What for?"

She ignored me. "Is there anything else you'd want if you knew you were going to be away from home for a few days?"

"Cheerios and bacon."

She thought about that. "Yeah, you're right."

"And Big Macs."

She gave me a look like I was a moron. "Of course, dummy, but the monks will bring them just before we leave."

"We're going on a trip?"

"We're on a trip now. We're going to *arrive*."

Early the next morning, Dr. Hariki showed up on our doorstep all excited. He works with my dad at the university. My dad teaches physics; he works with lasers and everything. Dr. Hariki is in charge of the big telescope in the top of the Physics building, and he takes pictures of stars.

"What's up?" Dad asked.

"You tell me," Dr. Hariki said, spreading out a bunch of photographs on the coffee table.

Dad picked up a picture and looked at it. Turned it over to check out the date and time written on the back. Sorted through the stack of photos till he found whatever he was looking for and compared it to the first. Held the two together side by side. Held one above the other. Put them side by side again. Closed his right eye, then quick closed his left and opened his right. Did that a couple of times. Picked up another pair of photos and did the same.

Muffin came into the room with a glass of orange juice in her hand. "Looks more like a dipper now, doesn't it?" she said without looking at the pictures.

Dad and Dr. Hariki stared at her. "Well, it was a bit too spread out before, wasn't it?" she asked. "Don't you think it looks better now?"

"Muffin," Dad said, "we're talking about stars . . . suns. They don't just move to make a nicer pattern."

"No, but if they're going to stop moving, you

might as well make sure they look like a dipper in the end. Anything else is just sloppy. I mean, really."

She walked off into the TV room and a moment later, we heard the Sesame Street theme song.

After a long silence, Dr. Hariki picked up one of the photos and asked all quiet, "Something to do with entropy?"

"I think it's teleology," I said.

That night Uncle Dave was over for Sunday supper. Mom figures that Uncle Dave doesn't eat so good in residence, so she feeds him a roast of something every Sunday. I think this is a great idea, except that every so often she serves squash because she says it's a delicacy. Lucky for us, it was corn season so we had corn on the cob instead.

After supper we all played Monopoly and I won. Uncle Dave said it made a nice family picture, us all sitting around the table playing a game. "Some day, kids," he said, "you're going to like having times like this to remember. A perfect frozen moment."

"There are all kinds of perfect frozen moments," Muffin said, and she had that tone in her voice like she was eleventy-seven years old instead of six. "Right now, people all over the world are doing all kinds of things. Like in China, it's day now, right Dad?"

"Right, Muffin."

"So there are kids playing tag and stuff, and that's a perfect moment. And maybe there's some bully beating up a little kid, and punching him out right now." She banged her Monopoly piece (the little metal hat) when she said 'now'. "And that's a perfect moment because that's what really happens. And bus-drivers are driving their buses, and farmers are milking their cows, and mommies are kissing daddies, and maybe a ship is sinking some place. If you could take pictures of everyone right now, you'd see millions of perfect little frozen moments, wouldn't you?"

Uncle Dave patted Muffin's hand. "Out of the mouths of babes . . . I'm the one who's studying to appreciate the great wonder of Life, and you're the one who reminds me. Everything is perfect all the time, isn't it, Muffin?"

"Of course not, dummy," she answered, looking at Uncle Dave the way she did when he tried to persuade her he'd pulled a dime from her ear. She turned around in her chair and reached over to the buffet to get the photograph they'd taken of her kindergarten class just before summer holidays started. "See?" she said pointing. "This is Bobby and he picks his nose all the time, and he's picking his nose here, so that's good. But this is Wendy, with her eyes closed cuz she was blinking. That's not perfect. Wendy cries every time she doesn't get a gold star in spelling, and she knows three dirty words, and she always gives Matthew the celery from her lunch, but you can't tell that in the picture, can you? She's just someone who blinked at the wrong time. If you want someone who should be blinking, it should be dozy old Peter Morgan who's fat and sweats and laughs funny."

Uncle Dave scratched his head and looked awkward for a bit, then said, "Well Muffin, when you put it like that . . . yes, I suppose there are always some things that aren't aesthetically pleasing . . . I mean, there are always going to be some things that don't fit properly, as you say."

"Not always," she said.

"Not always? Some day things are just suddenly going to be right?" Uncle Dave asked.

Muffin handed me the dice and said, "Your turn, Jamie. Bet you're going to land in jail."

Next morning, Muffin joggled my arm to wake me up. It was so early that the sun was just starting to rise over the lake. "Time to go down to the boat yards."

"Again?"

"Yep. This time for real." So I got up and got dressed as quietly as I could. By the time I got down to the kitchen, Muffin had made some peanut butter and jam sandwiches, and was messing around with the waxed paper, trying to wrap them. She had twice as much paper as she needed and was making a botch of things.

"You're really clueless sometimes," I said whispering so Mom and Dad wouldn't hear. I shoved her out of the way and started wrapping the sandwiches myself.

"When I rule the world, there won't be any waxed paper," she sulked.

We were halfway down to the bus stop when Uncle Dave came running up behind us. He had been staying the night in the guest room and I suppose he heard us moving around. "Where do you think you're going?" he asked, and he was a bit mad at us.

"Down to the boat yards," Muffin said.

"No, you aren't. Get back to the house."

"Uncle Dave," Muffin said, "it's time."

"Time for what?"

"The Eschaton."

"Where do you pick up these words, Muffin? You're talking about the end of the world."

"I know." The first bus of the day was just turning onto our street two corners down. "Come to the boat yards with us, Uncle Dave. It'll be okay."

Uncle Dave thought about it. I guess he decided it was easier to give in than to fight with her. That's what I always think too. You can't win an argument with her, and if you try anything else, she bites and scratches and uses her knees. "All right," Uncle Dave said, "but we're going to phone your parents and tell them where you are, the first chance we get."

"So talk to me about the Eschaton," Uncle Dave said on the bus. We were the only ones on it except for a red-haired lady wearing a Donut Queen uniform.

"Well," Muffin said, thinking things over, "you know how Daddy talks about everything moving in astronomy? Like the moon goes around the earth and the earth goes around the sun and the sun moves with the stars in the galaxy and the galaxy is moving too?"

"Yes. . ."

"Well, where is everything going?"

Uncle Dave shrugged. "The way your father tells it, everything just moves, that's all. It's not going anywhere in particular."

"That's stupid. Daddy doesn't understand teleology. Everything's going to where it's supposed to end up."

"And what happens when things reach the place where they're supposed to end up?"

Muffin made an exasperated face. "They *end up* there."

"They stop?"

"What else would they do?"

"All the planets and the stars and all?"

"Mm-hm."

"People too?"

"Sure."

He thought for a second. "In perfect frozen moments, right?"

"Right."

Uncle Dave leaned his head against the window like he was tired and sad. Maybe he was. The sun was coming up over the house-tops now. "Bus-drivers driving their buses," he said softly, "and farmers milking their cows . . . the whole world like a coffee table book."

"I think you'd like to be in a church, Uncle Dave," Muffin said. "Or maybe walking alone along the lake shore."

"Maybe," he smiled, all sad. Then he looked my sister right in the eye and asked, "Who are you, Muffin?"

"I'm me, dummy," she answered, throwing her arms around his neck and giving him a kiss.

He left us in front of the warehouse by the lake. "I'm going to walk down to the Rowing Club and back." He laughed a little. "If I get back, Muffin, you are going to get *such* a *spanking*. . ."

"Bye, Uncle Dave," she said, hugging him.

I hugged him too. "Bye, Uncle Dave."

"Don't let her do anything stupid," he said to me before heading down the street. We watched for a while, but he didn't turn back.

Up on the warehouse roof, there was a monk waiting with a McDonalds bag under his arm. He handed it to Muffin, then kneeled. "Bless me, Holy One."

"You're blessed," she said after looking in the bag. "Now get going to the temple or the airport or something. There's only about ten minutes left."

The monk hurried off, singing what I think was a hymn. We got into the plane-boat and I helped Muffin strap herself into one of the big padded seats. "The thing is," she said, "when the earth stops turning, we're going to keep on going."

"Hey, I know about momentum," I answered. I mean, Dad *is* a physicist.

"And it's going to be real fast, so we have to be sure we don't run into any buildings."

"We're going to shoot out over the lake?"

"We're high enough to clear the tops of the sailboats, then we just fly over the lake until we're slow enough to splash down. The monks got scientists to figure everything out."

I strapped myself in and thought about things for a while. "If we go shooting off real fast, isn't it going to hurt? I mean, the astronauts get all pressed down when they lift off. . ."

"Geez!" Muffin groaned. "Don't you know the difference between momentum and acceleration? Nothing's happening to us, it's everything else that's doing weird stuff. We don't feel a thing."

"Not even a wind?"

"The air has the same momentum we do, dummy?"

I thought about it some more. "Aren't the buildings going to get wrecked when the earth stops?"

"They're going to stop too. Everything's just going to freeze except us."

"The air and water are going to freeze too?"

"In spots. But not where we're going."

"We're special?"

"We're special."

Suddenly there was a roar like roller coaster wheels underneath us and for a moment I was pressed up against the straps holding me down on the seat. Then the pressure stopped and there was nothing but the sound of wind a long way off. Over the side of the boat I could see water rushing by beneath us. We were climbing.

"Muffin," I asked, "should one of us maybe be piloting this thing?"

"It's got a gyroscope or something. The monks worked absolutely everything out, okay?"

"Okay."

A long way off to the right, I could see a lake freighter with a curl of smoke coming out of its stack. The smoke didn't move. It looked neat. "Nice warm day," I said.

After a while, we started playing car games to pass the time.

The sun shone but didn't move. "If the sun stays there forever," I asked, "won't it get really hot after a while?"

"Nah," Muffin answered. "It's some kind of special deal. I mean, it's not the same if you set up a nice picture of a park full of kids playing and then it gets hot as Mercury."

"Who's going to know?" I asked.

"It's not the same," she insisted.

"How can we see?"

"What so you mean?"

"Well, is the light moving or what?"

"It's another special deal."

That made sense. From the way dad talked about physics, light was always getting special deals.

That water below us gradually stopped racing away so fast and we could sometimes see frozen white-caps on the peaks of frozen waves. "Suppose we land on frozen water," I said.

"We won't."

"Oh. Your turn."

"I spy with my little eye something that begins with B." Right away I knew she meant the Big Macs, but I had to pretend it was a toughie. You have to humour little kids.

We splashed down within sight of a city on the far side of the lake. It was a really good splash, like the one on the Zoomba Flume ride when you get to the bottom of the big long water chute. Both of us got drenched. I was kind of sad there was no way to do it again.

Then I thought to myself, maybe if we were getting a special deal on air and water and heat and all, maybe we'd get a special deal on the Zoomba Flume too.

We unstrapped ourselves and searched around a bit. Finally, we found a lid that slid back to open up a control panel with a little steering wheel and all. We pushed buttons until an inboard motor started in the water behind us, then took turns driving towards shore. Every now and then we'd see a gull frozen in the sky, wings spread out and looking great.

We put in at a public beach just outside the city. It had been early in the day and the only people in sight

319

were a pair of joggers on a grassy ridge that ran along the edge of the sand. The man wore only track shorts and sunglasses; the woman wore red stretch pants, a T-shirt, and a headband. Both had Walkmans and were stopped in mid-stride. Both had deep dark tans, and as Muffin pointed out, a thin covering of sweat.

I wanted to touch one to see what they felt like, but when my finger got close, it bumped up against an invisible layer of frozen air. The air didn't feel like anything, it was just solid stuff.

Down at one end of the beach, a teen-age girl was frozen in the act of unlocking the door into a snack stand. We squeezed past her and found out we could open the freezer inside. Muffin had a couple of Popsicles, I had an ice cream sandwich, and then we went swimming.

Lying out in the sun afterward, I asked Muffin what was going to happen next.

"You want to go swimming again?" she said.

"No, I mean after."

"Let's eat," she said, dragging me back towards the boat.

"You can't wiggle out of it that easy," I told her. "Are we the only ones left?"

"I think so."

"Then are we going to freeze too?"

"Nope. We got a special deal."

"But it seems pretty stupid if you ask me. Everything's kind of finished, you know? Show's over. Why are we still hanging around?"

"For a new show, dummy?"

"Oh." That made sense. "Same sort of thing?"

"We'll see."

"Oh. Where do we fit in?"

Muffin smiled at me. "You're here to keep me company."

"And what are you here for?"

"Everything else. Get me a sandwich."

So I reached down into the basket we'd brought and pulled one out. It was inside a plastic sandwich bag. "Didn't we put these in waxed paper?" I asked.

Muffin smiled.

CANADOLA

ESTHER ROCHON

Translated from the French by John Greene

It's evening; time to close the curtains, the living room lights are on, giving the room an even warmer atmosphere than usual. A blue radiance comes in through the big bay window. Outside, everything is blue. The contrast between the soft lights of the living room and the limitless blue outdoors is unsettling. Go out, or close the curtains; either way, the unity of the world would be preserved. But the curtains are still open, a soft creamy fringe, framing what? Presenting what? Nothing but emptiness.

A few years ago, I accepted a contract to go work at Canadola. The boondocks, you say? Exactly. We arrived at night, after a long trip. Strange shrouded men led us workers to our quarters. I had taken bus, plane, rocket and I don't know what else to get there; learning that I would live outdoors, alone in a tent, I was satisfied.

Of course it was slave-work; I'd expected that, it was in the contract. Slave is exaggerated: we got paid. We never saw the sun; we were underground, no talking, in the noise of machines, lit by neon and mercury vapor lamps. You didn't have time to look at your neighbour, everything went so fast. What were we other than the biological components of a huge complex system, which we were forbidden to understand? The precision of our eyes, the skill of our hands, that's what our employer needed. The intelligence, the curiosity that came with the eyes and the hands, he would just as soon have done without those.

Most of us were women, I'd realized that during the trip; now the strange costume we had to wear at work made it hard to identify persons or sexes: there was a space-suit affair you had to put on at certain times; on other occasions we wore a sort of thick veil that was actually fairly comfortable in the huge chilly laboratories full of hallucinogenic odours.

During the first months, the days outside were short; once work was finished, I was the only one to leave through the door they unlocked for me, and I found myself alone in a foreign night, hurrying towards the little tent where my possessions, piled pell-mell, bothered no one. Sometimes it rained, sometimes it snowed, and nothing I had brought with me came outside the tent. I climbed over sacks, I bundled myself up and I didn't move until the bell that announced the beginning of a new day.

I like surviving. When I have the impression that my heart has exploded and I'm still alive, that's happiness. At Canadola, I knew that happiness. Then springtime came.

The sun rose earlier. And I could see where I was living. The little tent that sheltered me was in a deep gorge, probably dynamited out when the labs were built. The reddish rock wasn't too crumbly; you might be able to climb up and get a more elevated view of things. Anyway, I could certainly go for walks. One evening before nightfall, I set out along the base of the crooked cliffs. After a few minutes' walk, beyond a turn, a strange object met my eyes.

It was multicoloured, twice as tall as me, more or less spherical, with a tuft of hair on top, embedded in the rock. And it was moaning. I slowly approached. I couldn't help recognizing a man's face. Bands of electric blue, brick red, phosphorescent green ran across it in all directions. When it detected my approach, the moans turned into hisses, and even though its eyes remained closed, I ran away.

Up until now, I thought I'd been spending my nights alone; well, I hadn't. I'd been sharing the ravine with—was it a robot or a living being?—with something that scared me, anyway.

The next day, entering the labs, the colour scheme forcibly reminded me of that giant, gaudy, moustached face.

As we were not allowed to talk, except when the job demanded it, and no documentation was available about where we were living, my only choice was to live my experience raw, with no seasoning. That horrible and terrifying head, my neighbour, seemed to be fixed in the rock, and therefore could not be dangerous unless you went near it. I could sometimes hear it moaning from my tent. Well, so what? Just don't panic, and everything will be fine.

But I hadn't left my curiosity at home; I'd brought it with my eyes and hands. After a few weeks, I finally realized that I desired to see that singular face once more, with its expression suggesting pain or hate, and which was after all even more of a prisoner than I was. I went back.

His jaws opened when he saw me coming. Inside, everything was black. Yellow tusks opened onto the black like, you know, the curtains at night, the living room curtains when you forget to close them and it's night on the other side.

My life took on a new rhythm. Summer was

coming; I slept less, I took advantage of the light to watch the sky, now filled with gliders, and to go look at what scared me.

One day he opened his eyes, and two TV screens were facing me. They were black and white screens, in the middle of the colour-splotched face, and they made blind, cold eyes. I watched movies, variety shows, serials that sometimes went on till late at night. I learned nothing, except to remember what the world was supposed to look like.

Strangely, when the being opened its eyes, that is, when there was something to watch for entertainment, I stopped being afraid. I say strangely because in fact there was still cause for terror. These apparently harmless shows were always about the exploits of a male hero who wanted to conquer the world, or achieve some equivalent goal. Doubtless he was only a form of the monster I had to watch to see these stories, and the monster himself was only a robot, emitting the vision that the country had of itself. A robot may be equipped with sensate organic parts, which are nevertheless subject to the omnipresent mechanism. What this system was broadcasting was a homage to its own greatness: it found itself beautiful, admirable, and worthy to rule the universe, and this fact was the only message it had to communicate to me. It reminded me of one of my first boyfriends - that episode hadn't lasted long.

My contract expired at the end of the summer. Obviously I'd thought of dancing naked before that gigantic male face, or tickling it with a feather, to see if it would react. But I didn't. I was anxious to get out, to leave this arrogant world, sure of its superiority, forbidding conversation; I didn't think I was in a good position to do anything to destroy its pathetic illusions, even though I was aware of how much good it would do.

I must have been a model employee: the last day, they offered me a glider ride.

For the first and last time, I could see the horizons of this strange land. It was very flat, criss-crossed by ravines like the one I had been living in. We rose up behind the plane, then they let us go in silence. Below us spread the earth, reddened by the setting sun, and the purple gorges. During the few minutes before landing, I could examine them in detail.

In each of the many darkened valleys I could make out a tent, and a little further on, the tuft of hair that marked a head. Most of the places were quiet; you could occasionally make out a few chords of music from a variety show, or perhaps some moaning. But from one of the gorges, off to one side, there were screams. The head was facing me. I could distinguish the giant jaws devouring someone.

I didn't sleep a wink all night. I packed.

I've been back a long time now. I don't often think of Canadola, because I have the impression that I lived a few months in hell there. The coercive atmosphere was frank and open, there was no attempt to deceive, no real intent to harm; it was more a stupid ingenuity in the service of a system that held the impersonal as an ideal. On the other hand, the food was great.

In my living room, sometimes it's fights, sometimes it's love scenes. The chairs face the TV set. Let's close the curtains, and all the scenarios, real or otherwise, can stay closed in behind the anonymity of the window, basking in the warm light of the lamps. It's a bit like up there. And then, there's outside.

IN THE LAND OF UNBLIND

JUDITH MERRIL

                                    You know how it is
indown you close your eye(s) and let take
your self between a stumblecrawl and lazyfloat
                                    I mean when
you get past the rubbage really *indown* there's
no seefeeltouch not
the skinside *upout* way
blindbalance cannot tell if a touching is over
or under or on the feeling is inside your skin
                                    I mean
indown you know in the land of unblind the one
eyed woman is terribilified
no light
but the infires' flickerdimglow and
they all keep their eyes closed so
scrabbleswoop and stumblesoar fly
creep in fearableautiful nolightno
dark of eacheveryother's infires
(No need to cover or to show
they   canwillnot   looksee
except   the   one-eyed   me
I wonder what would happen if

a person took a light *indown*)

                                        Before
I opened up one apple-eye I too
flewstumbled graspgropegleaned
in   holystonemaskhunger   then

                        one time
indown in that hell-eden innocence I touched
a man and he touched me   you know the way
it happens some times later or before or inbe
tween we touched *upout*

                        I mean
where skins can touch and some
place or other we remembered as
in the other we felt fate upon us
blindunblind   future   past   which

                        one is when
upout his openwide eyes full of hunger and
some kind of hate   I tasted somehow hate
fulhunger over all the skins inside my mouth

                I love you!   he said
                Witchcraft! I had to come!
                You must come! Magic!
                I love you!

                                        so
I came we loved our skins touched inside some
times almost remembering *indown*

                        not quite then
oneanother soundless *indown* timestill blindun
blind I touched a man and touching me he spoke
words I c/wouldnot hear just scramblescared
                        a way you know
                        it happens some
time in betweenafterbefore when meeting *upout*
all our eyes and ears and mouths were open

I love you!   he said
We had to come together!
Remember!   he said   beforewords—

                    I c/wouldnot
                            I love you
                 I said   Witchcraft!
all the skins inside my mouth tasting sweet
sour terror as I ran he spoke

                            (again?)

               Open your eyes!   he said
                              One time (soon?)
   indown still fearful

                        (fearful still for still I do
                        not open more than one)
I opened up my first *indown*eye seeing stir a
livesome ghost of memory pastfutureinbetween
that time I touched no man but

                    (then?)

                              one time

upout you know before or after
my first man was there (again?)
skinsight airvoice was all we
unshared how it waswouldbe to touch *indown* I
did not know he did not know there was *indown*
not to remember full of fear he went away but
                              (then?)
                              one time
indown one eye just-slit open in dimglowing
flickerdrift infires a man touched me and I could
see *indown* the face I touchedspoketo of course he
c/wouldnot hear

               so

                    but

                         when

                              you know

we met *upout*eyes open all the hungerskinside my
mouth turned sweet remembering beforewords

> *I love you!*　　　　　he said
> *Witchcraft! I had to come!*
> *You made me come! Magic!*
> *I love you!*　　　　　he said with words
>
> 　　　　　　　　　　　　but

he did not know echopremonitions stirring
from under *upout*skintouch he couldwouldnot
premember how *indown* we touched his hunger
fear soured all the skins inside my mouth
I had to go

　　　　　　　away

　　　　　　　　　　　(again?)

　　　　　　　　　　　　　　　one time

indown I met a man with one eye
open like my own in flickerdim
infireglow seeing each how horribleautiful
eachotherself fruit flower and fester touching
so we spoke beforewords so

　　　　　　　　　　　　you know

the waysometime(s) you meet *upout* all eyes and
ears and mouths wide open great new hungers
pungentsweet
on all the skins inside remembering *indown*
bebackwords neverquite to know which place
time was wherewhen or waswouldbe we first
felt fate upon us so

　　　　　　We love　　　　　(we do not say)
　　　　　　We had to come
　　　　　　Witchcraft!　　　　　　(we laugh)

we love skins touch *upout*side premembering
sometimesalmost　like　*indown*touchtalk　still

　　　　　　　　　　　and yet
　　　　　　　　　　　I wonder
　　　　　　　　　　　what it's like
　　　　　　　　　indown for the two-eyed?

NORTH
OF
WHITEHORSE
STATION

LEONA
GOM

Daniel heard the horses before he saw them. And the voices: two people at least. He dropped the pail of raspberries and then hunched down beside it. He could feel his heart begin to bang at his chest, the sudden pulse of sweat in his armpits. He peered through the canes, relieved that he could see nothing. He must be reasonably well hidden from the road.

They were directly opposite him now. The beat of hooves on the road was so loud it felt as though someone were clapping in his ear.

"My ass is *aching*," exclaimed a stranger's voice. "How much farther?"

"A kilometre or so. Not long." It was Doctor. He knew her voice. But she sounded nervous, afraid almost.

"You were right," sighed the other voice. "I didn't think I was so out of shape."

They were past the raspberry field now, into the

bush again, and Daniel couldn't make out Doctor's reply.

He left the pail of berries where it had fallen and ran. The branches beat at him and twice he fell as the underbrush tangled his feet, but he leapt up and kept running. He slid down the gully into the dry creek bed, looking anxiously to his right, although he was fairly certain Doctor would keep them to the road. He clambered up the other side, his feet knocking loose rocks and earth, but he grabbed at the birchtree root he knew would be there and pulled himself up. He hadn't used the short-cut since he was a small child, but his body remembered the route as though he had come this way this morning. A prairie chicken fluttered up at his feet, but he jumped over and around it without slowing his pace. He could feel the burning in his side, but he couldn't stop; he was almost there, just through the clearing and past the last fringe of poplar. He could see his aunt's house now, flickering in the branches, and then he was through.

His aunt, Highlands, was in the garden, hilling the potatoes, the hoe clanging down on the hard dry soil as though it were metal. He leaped carelessly over the rows of peas and cabbage, and Highlands' hoe stopped in mid-air.

"What's wrong?" she demanded.

He stopped three rows down from her, bent over, with his hands on his knees. "Stranger," he gasped. "Coming with Doctor." He gestured feebly at the road where it entered the farmyard behind his house.

Highlands had already dropped her hoe and was running to her house, her shirt flapping behind her like a torn wing. He watched her go, his breath raking his chest. He saw her pull the bell twice, the danger signal, and then he made himself hobble on to the longhouse. When he reached it, his father was already opening the door, and his cousin Montney, Highlands' son, was running up from where he had been working on the other side of the garden.

"What's happened?" he asked, excited. It had been a long time since the danger bell had sounded.

"Stranger coming," Daniel said. "On horseback. She's with Doctor. I think they've come from Whitehorse Station."

His father took his arm. "Come on," he said. "Don't stand around out here." Then he dropped his hand quickly, as though he remembered that Daniel was eighteen now and could no longer be ordered about like a child. Daniel gave him a little smile, acknowledging both the mistake and his tolerance of it. He enjoyed being eighteen, the sudden new respect, something Montney would have to wait another year for.

Inside, his father pulled closed the door and bolted it.

"They're here!" Montney shouted from the window, dropping down below the sill and pulling out the loose piece of plaster between the third and fourth logs. Daniel joined him, squinting out into the sunlight as though he had soap in his eyes.

They were there, all right, dismounting now, the stranger, a middle-aged person with long grey hair pulled into a braid on one side of her head, grimacing as she slid down. Highlands came up to them, and Daniel could see them exchange greetings, the funny formal gripping of the shoulders, the dipping of the head, he'd had to learn. When he'd protested, his mother insisted, "It's better they think us odd than that they should find out about you." And so, meekly, he had learned the peculiar mannerisms he would be expected to exhibit around strangers, if he ever had to meet any. There was even a word an ancestor had made up for the four farms with others like him—*Isolists*—so that outsiders would consider them a religious cult and leave them alone. It had worked well. Strangers rarely came this way, and when they did what they noted as unusual was not what was *really* unusual. Misdirection, Highlands called it, a magician's trick.

More of the farm people were coming up to Doctor and her companion now, all of them somberly greeting the stranger in the same mannered way. The children, he saw, all wanted to try it, most of them not yet having had a chance to practise on a real stranger, and he could see Highlands exchanging an anxious look with their mothers.

"Go back to work now!" shouted someone, and the children backed off, suddenly reminded this was no game. Only Bluesky and her sister Shaw stayed, confident in their new status as adults, now that they, too, had turned eighteen. Shaw, he remembered, insisted on being called Shaw-Ellen now, taking advantage of her option of choosing a second name. But it was Bluesky he watched. She was tall and muscular, her thick pale hair pulled back from her face with two red pins, and he thought of her the way she had been yesterday, in this very room, naked above him, her eyes squeezed shut and her lips pulled back as though she were in pain. Her breasts were soft and hot in his hands. He had to close his eyes to stop seeing her, but still the erection pushed warmly at his thigh.

"They're going into our house, I think," his father said.

Daniel snapped open his eyes. Highlands and his mother had already gone inside, and Doctor and the stranger were following them in. Two of the others went in, too, and the rest waited outside for a few minutes, whispering nervously, and then went back to their own houses. He thought he saw Bluesky throw a quick look at the longhouse.

His father turned and leaned back against the wall, his legs thrust out in front of him like two long thick logs. He ran his callused thumb absently around the head of a nail starting to work itself loose of the floorboard beside him.

Daniel turned, too, sat with one leg pulled up against the inside of the other. He didn't resemble his father at all; small-boned and blonde, he looked more like his mother. It was his sister who looked like their father, heavy and dark, with the large mouth and brows like two hedges overhanging the eyes.

"I wonder why Doctor would bring her," his father said.

"I don't think she wanted to," Daniel said. "I heard them on the road. I think the stranger insisted on coming."

"She must suspect something. Merde." There was a frightened edge to his voice, and Daniel looked at him, catching his fear. His father rubbed his hand up and down one cheek, and the sound of stubble rasped against his fingers.

"You didn't cut your face hair," Daniel accused.

"I know," his father said. "I forgot."

"You said it was the most important thing," Daniel insisted. "How could you forget?"

"I *know*," his father said. "I just forgot, that's all."

"They're coming back out," Montney said. "Now they're going into Mother's house."

Daniel turned again to look. He could see Highlands opening the door to her house, inviting the stranger in.

"It's like some kind of inspection," Daniel said.

"She won't come in *here*, will she?" Montney asked.

"No," Daniel's father said, sounding firm and confident again. "Of course not. Your mother won't let her. No one can enter the Longhouse without the Leader's consent."

And the thought of Highlands seemed to reassure them all. She was the one they could count on; she would protect them. Sometimes when Daniel was young he was afraid of her temper, the fights she would have with his father, not the way a brother and sister were supposed to behave at all, but the older he got the more he liked and admired her, her quickness and self-assurance. Once he told his father he wished Highlands were his mother, and his father, looking at his mother across the yard taking down the clothes from the line, slowly, her placid face upturned to the sky like a cup filling with sunshine, said, "There are skills just as important as intelligence, Daniel. Intelligence will let you down. But love doesn't." It didn't make much sense to Daniel, but it sounded like something he should probably remember.

Still, it was Highlands Daniel would go to when he wanted to talk, choosing her over both his mother and father, even though the things she told him were often not the things he wanted to hear.

"What if they want to stay overnight?" Montney asked suddenly. "It's late for them to make it back to Fairview."

"I don't think they'll want to stay," Daniel's father said. "They haven't unsaddled the horses. Doctor would have told her hospitality is not one of our virtues. And you mother will show her the shed with Cayley's old broken bed and imply that's where they'd have to sleep." He laughed, and then so did Daniel and Montney, giggling at the thought of the way Highlands would handle it, enjoying herself.

"Still," Daniel's father said. "I don't like it that she came with Doctor. She may be a doctor, too."

"Maybe she's the one Doctor told us about," Montney said. "The new one she was going to train and tell about us."

"I don't think so," Daniel said. "She's too old."

Montney got up and began to prowl restlessly around the room, idly picking up the schoolbooks stacked in small neat piles on the shelves. Daniel had read them all, more than once, and he was always the first to pounce on the person who came back from town with the boxes of new library books. Now that he was eighteen, he could go into town himself if the farm gave its permission—he could spend a whole day if he wanted in the library, a building, they told him, full of a thousand books. The thought of it made him almost giddy with excitement. He would have to be careful, of course, and dress in the special townclothes that were made of heavier cloth than what he usually wore on the farm in summer. But his father went into town sometimes. So long as you were careful—not, like his father, forgetting to cut your face hair. So long as they didn't find out you were a male.

Male. He had looked it up in the dictionary once, that same dictionary that Montney was pounding his fist lightly on now. *Male*, it said, *from French "mal" and Latin "male", meaning: 1. bad, abnormal, inadequate; and, 2. sub-species of human extinct in 21st century.*

Twenty-first century. So long ago, the time of the Change, of the terrible wars and radiation sicknesses that had killed or made sterile the human population, the time of the desperate ova-fusion experiments to continue the race. The race: he smiled bitterly, watching Montney bounce his fist lightly on the dictionary. Ova-fusion, of course, could produce only fe-males (as the People were once called). He and Montney and his father and the other males on the Isolist farms were no longer part of the race, of the People. They were part only of a distant and chaotic history. They were *extinct in 21st century.*

Not even Highlands knew why the males on the

North Farms had not died out, but she thought it must have had something to do with the climate. Perhaps, then, there could be others like them in the world—but if so they must be hidden as well, a dangerous secret now in a world where ova-fusion was the way of human reproduction, where the People saw the time of the males as one of violence and destruction. No, the People would not be likely to welcome back their lost brothers, their brutal past. On the farms the males were safe, protected, but in the outside world—Daniel shuddered. He didn't want to think of what they would do to him if he were discovered.

"It's not fair," he had come crying once to Highlands when he was a child and his sister had tormented him with terrifying stories. "It's not my fault I'm a male."

"I know," she said. "I know."

"Males weren't so bad," he insisted. But he could see he had gone too far.

"Yes, they were," Highlands said, her voice taking on a coldness that made him wince. "Don't think for a moment you would want to go back to the time they ran the world."

"But *I'm* a male," he persisted. "Am I so bad?"

She hesitated. "No. But you don't run the world."

"Someone's coming out of Mother's house," Montney said suddenly.

Daniel and his father turned, crouched back at the crack between the logs and peered out. Doctor and the stranger were coming out first, followed by the others, who remained standing together on the porch while Doctor and the stranger walked a few steps further, then turned back. Everyone on the porch, in almost perfect, graceful unison, bowed.

Doctor bowed too, and the stranger, hesitating a moment, bowed as well, awkwardly, holding her head

up to keep everyone in sight. Then the two of them untied the reins of their horses from the post by Highlands' house that had the warning bell on top of it,
mounted, and rode off. Doctor gave a quick look behind her and waved, furtively perhaps. Daniel felt his
hand go up too, without thinking, to wave back. He
liked Doctor. He wished he could have talked to her.
Daniel, she was always fond of remembering, was the
first male she had ever delivered. Until then, she'd confessed to his mother, she'd never quite believed it was
possible, was just some bizarre story the doctor who
trained her was making up to test her gullibility. Now,
of course, the farm could not imagine being without
her, and they were anxious about the new doctor she
would have to tell and trust as they first had been about
her.

"Let's go," Montney said, heading for the door.
Daniel followed him, his thoughts turning already to
the raspberry field and his dropped pail, into which the
ants might have gotten by now.

"Wait," his father said. "We have to make sure it's
not a trick."

Through the window Daniel could see Highlands
approaching the longhouse. "Your mother's coming,"
he said to Montney. "Let her in."

Montney unbolted the door, and Highlands
stepped inside. She was so tall she had to bend to keep
from hitting her head.

She was smiling. "I especially liked our bow," she
said. "Weren't we good?"

"Wonderful," Daniel's father said. "Well, what did
she want?"

"It's okay. It was Doctor's supervisor. She just decided to come out and do a workload check on Doctor.
Nothing to worry about." She rested her forearm on
Montney's shoulder, let her hand with its long thin
fingers dangle in the air.

"Did she ask about those of us who weren't with you?" Daniel asked.

"I said three of our farm were out in the fields. It seemed to satisfy her. I think she was just curious about us. But it went all right. Doctor winked at me when she left."

"I told you it was nothing to worry about," Montney said to Daniel's father.

"You can't be too careful," he said.

"You didn't cut your face hairs," Montney accused. He turned to his mother, a triumphant excitement on his face. "He didn't cut his face hairs," he repeated.

Highlands looked at them both coldly, her eyes pulling tighter at the corners. "I can see that," she said. "We'll bring it up at next Meeting."

"That's not right!" Daniel's voice shivered with the effort of standing up to Highlands. "Father had early workload today. He doesn't usually forget. You don't know what it's like, every morning—"

"No, Daniel," his father said quietly. "Highlands is right. It's too important to forget."

He hated seeing his father give in so easily, letting her win without even trying. He didn't used to be like that. Daniel was suddenly angry at all of them, his father for his meekness and deference, Montney for telling, Highlands for using her position as Leader to humiliate his father. He could feel his cheek muscles tightening, his lips squeezing themselves thin as though his whole face were under pressure. His mad-face, his mother used to call it affectionately when he was a child—but he was an adult now: his anger should no longer be amusing.

Highlands said nothing for a moment, only looked from one to the other of them. Finally her gaze settled on Daniel's father. "Well, no harm done, I guess," she said. "You're only human."

His father smiled wearily back at her. "Nice of you to think so."

She looked at Daniel then, and perhaps because she said nothing to him he knew suddenly and to his surprise that she was pleased at the way he had defended his father, even though she shouldn't be—she shouldn't allow such a challenge to her authority—not from a male. He felt confused and uncomfortable. And something else too, something he would think about later, when he was alone. He felt powerful.

UNDER ANOTHER MOON

DAVE DUNCAN

Was this what being a man was? Was this what being an earl was? Jauro stood in his own hall, before his own assembled household, and listened in furious silence as his honour was trampled in the dirt, his courage mocked, his ancestry insulted.

Did they think he was a milksop woman who would endure such abuse?

Blood roared in his ears and his fists trembled with a yearning to draw and smite the upstart envoy who came in the name of the king, this bearer of the royal scorn. Lackey! Coward! Were he not wrapped in the king's office, he would not dare speak such words before the earl of Rathmuir; not in his own hall, not anywhere. Or, if he tried it, he would die.

Yet in truth he was more like to slay Jauro instead, for he was larger and older, a man in his prime. No grey showed in his beard, and his eyes were quick. The sword arm left uncovered by his furs was a conspicuously thicker and hairier arm than Jauro's was, and his powerful fingers were already crooked for the draw. His stance was that of a man poised to provoke violence and then meet it, a man enjoying his mission, reveling in the rage he was rousing, a rage that would not be hidden by the earl's fair beard. Behind him stood six stalwarts of the royal fyrd—greyer, capable veterans, smirking in silence as the young victim squirmed under their burly leader's scorn.

And all around the walls, the earl's own people listened also, in shock and dismay: the white-haired elders on their stools, the children standing behind them, the women in turn at their backs, holding their babies, or clasping their daughters' shoulders. Back of them all stood the men, teeth glinting within their beards, and their hands clenched on their sword hilts. It was the custom that the men stood at the rear for such a reception, and the reason was obvious, although Jauro had never realized it before—if he were to draw against the visitors, he would be dead before his own fyrd could struggle through the others to aid him. Blood would muddy the rushes on the clay floor, and the earl's blood would flow first.

Acrid smoke roiled from the fireplaces. Beyond the open door at the far end of the hall, misty tendrils of rain swept over the royal horses and the two men left out there to hold them. The early dusk of winter was closing in, and the hall was growing dim—and cold also, unless it was only rage that darkened Jauro's sight and moved on his arms like an icy breath, raising the hairs on them and chilling the sweat below his fur cloak and cloth leggings. Nothing was clear to him but the face of the envoy, the hateful close-bearded young man whose eyes were laughing even as he spouted this hateful royal insolence. This vomit of lies, this pig piss!

And the envoy looked far smaller than he had done only minutes earlier; he was shrinking as Jauro's fury choked off discretion. Was this what being a man was? Young the earl might be, but he was no virgin in mortal combat; he had seen the colour of men's lifeblood and he could feel a rising lust to see it again. Soon, very soon, he would decide that dying was better than hearing more of this *horsefarting*.

Just before he lost control, it ended: "Thus spake His Majesty, King Reggalo, the Merciful, the Just." Silence, and the envoy's eyes shone with cruel pleasure as he waited for the response.

The fires crackled, and even the hiss of the rain seemed audible in the hush. How could so many be so quiet? Water dripping through the thatch played a faint staccato rhythm in corners. A child whimpered and its mother put a hand over its mouth.

Jauro took a deep breath, then another, as he fought for calm, as he planned his words lest they tremor and betray him.

Be a man!

"We thank you for His Majesty's message," his voice came out deep and strange to him, but it was gratifyingly steady. He heard a small sigh at his back. He had been meant to hear it—Fromto was relieved that the words were no more warlike than that. But they were defiance nonetheless.

"His Majesty's command!" Mockery twisting the tight-coiled blackness of the envoy's beard.

"I shall send my reply before the end of the leastmonth."

The envoy put his head on one side, while his companions shifted and glanced around. "Reply? You misheard, Earl Jauro."

"I heard. But we have barely buried our dead. We must tend our wounded, our widows and our orphans. Bands of rebels still roam the moors. His Majesty will comprehend that my duty to the safety of my people is also my duty to His Majesty."

"His command was specific—you will accompany us, and your daughter also."

To argue would seem like weakness, but his people were listening, and it was their blood Jauro's defiance was risking—his own blood was already as good as spent. They deserved a reason.

"Evildoers have spoken untruths to His Majesty. My loyalty is unswerving."

"You will be given a hearing," the envoy promised, and his smile made the promise a threat.

"Also, my child is not yet old enough to consider marriage."

The envoy's eyes seemed to dance with merriment. "His Majesty understood that your family matured young—or was Your Lordship deprived of comfort?"

Insult! Fromto growled softly in the background, and Jauro's hand twitched towards his sword hilt. At once the envoy's hand was on his own, in a move too fast to see. Deadly fast! So Reggalo had sent his best brawler, who would either slay Jauro out of hand or parry his thrusts to impotence—and to draw against the king's envoy would be treason. It was a trap within a trap.

With a mighty effort, Jauro spread his fingers and moved them away from danger. "His Majesty has been misinformed on many matters."

The envoy sneered and released his sword in a flamboyant gesture. "The child will benefit by completing its childhood in the civilized surroundings of His Majesty's palace."

Some of the men by the walls muttered angrily—Jauro silenced them with a glare. "But this is my heir we are discussing. I must consider the child's welfare. His Majesty's daughter, this Princess Uncoata . . . I understand her first marriage proved sterile. She has a crooked back and her wits are the laughingstock of the markets?"

"Your Lordship is the one misinformed," said the

envoy, his companions' open amusement belying his words. "We speak of Prince Uncoato, a man of undoubted strength and virility who yearns to know his bride. A larger, heavier man than Your Lordship."

Little Thorti given to an idiot cripple? Tiny, delicate Thorti with her trilling song and her smoke-gray eyes? Jauro's throat knotted at the images that came to his mind—he had seen that shambling Uncoata once, and shuddered to think what such a monster might have become since. Sweat was trickling down his face; he could stand no more of this. "I repeat that His Majesty has been misinformed on many matters. I shall gather my witnesses and send my reply within three days."

"His Majesty's command—"

Jauro roared. "You have far to ride before dark, Your Grace!"

Satisfaction twisted the envoy's lips. He had sought to provoke violence, but this response would do: royal edict rejected, hospitality refused, treason, defiance, open revolt. The king's command had been crafted to produce nothing less.

"Then in sorrow I bid Your Lordship farewell." The man bowed, but the move barely reached his shoulders. In contempt he turned his back, and his supporters moved aside to let him through. They clutched their sword hilts and glanced warily around as they followed him to the door. Wet leather squeaked in their boots.

Jauro stood and watched the departure, his whole body trembling with suppressed fury.

Fromto was speaking at his back. "Loothio! Follow and see which way they ride. Ambloto—gather your band and saddle up, lest they do mischief on their way."

Sensible, practical Fromto! Jauro was still too tense to have thought of those things. He started to turn, and was suddenly encircled by rope-thin arms. It was

Thorti, the smoke-gray eyes filled with tears, peering up at him in horror.

"Mother! You must not flaunt the king!"

Jauro tried to break free, and the child clung fiercely—tiny and yet made strong by desperation; far smaller than he had been at that age, and he was not a large man, as the envoy had so greatly enjoyed mentioning.

"Be still!" he barked. He glanced over Thorti's head to the elders, who were on their feet now, gathering into a group and starting to jabber shrilly. Their bald heads and wispy white beards shone in the gloom. "Venerable ones—prepare your counsel, and we shall hear you shortly."

"Mother!" Thorti cried, louder now. "You must not defy the king just for my sake. I shall marry the prince, if that is his royal will."

"Never!" Jauro untwined himself and, laughing, swung his child up at arms' length so their eyes were level. It was no strain—he could have held the stance for hours—but then he saw the hurt and humiliation flower in those smokey eyes. *Idiot!* Children of this age scorned such baby games. He changed his hold to a hug, clasping Thorti tight to his furs.

"You also have grown, my beloved," he said. "You are so heavy now!"

Thorti's voice came softly, privately into his ear. "It is almost time! The prince or another!"

"What!" Thorta?

He lowered her gently to the floor, as though she were suddenly fragile. He sank down on one knee and stared at the eager blush now spreading over the tiny bird-like face.

"Already? Oh, my sweet! When?"

Her words quavered with the conflict of joy and fear: "Yesterday! It came yesterday."

His child a woman! His heart overflowed with sudden memory of his own youth, and of the fearsome transition to adulthood—long wanted, yet unexpectedly sudden, welcome and yet terrifying. He struggled for words, and could not find them, as he so often could not finds words for his child now. Thorti . . . Thorta . . . was tense under his gaze, not responding to his smile, frightened of the muscular, hairy warrior he had become. For almost two years now, he had felt a growing sense of loss and guilt whenever he spoke with his child; in the three days since his return it had been worse than before, an unbearable pain in his throat. Clumsy and tongue-tied, he could do nothing but hug the tiny form, and pat the thin shoulders. *Thorta, Thorta, my beloved!* When had they lost each other? Why could he not put his feelings into words?

Was that also part of being a man?

Blinking, he glanced up to see if Fromto had heard the news, but he was still snapping orders as the men fought their way to him through the crowd—sending out patrols and setting guards, ensuring that no band of hotheads took off after the envoy on some crazy mission of misplaced honour.

Jauro kissed his daughter's forehead. "I congratulate you, my dearest Thorta. I am sorry that such good tidings are marred by coming at so evil a time." How cold that sounded, how dismally inadequate! "But it is not only your welfare I have in mind. Were I to obey the king's command and go with his messengers, then my life would not be worth a pail of chicken droppings."

She gasped. "But why? What have you done to deserve the king's frown?"

What indeed? "Nothing at all! Others have lied about me. Once I have prepared my case, I can go to His Majesty and clear my name." He smiled gently—if a bearded face ever could smile gently. Thorta seemed unconvinced, and he knew there were sharp wits in that little head. "To clear the honour of our house!" he insisted. "I shall not bequeath you a blemished scutcheon. But now I must speak with your father. Stay with Lallia."

With a sharp stare that tore at his heart, Thorta stepped back, biting her knuckles. Feeling again that he had betrayed her, Jauro rose and slapped a hand on Fromto's shoulder. "Come!" he said, and headed for the doorway that led to the private apartments. Lallia moved forward to speak, but he strode by her without a glance. He feared what bitter gloating he might read in his wife's face.

He marched down the black corridor and memory guided him to the heavy plank door of his chamber, which creaked on its rusty hinges as it always did. The room was dark, and felt dank yet stuffy, the familiar sour odor of the furs on the bed magnified by the winter dampness. It faced west, and the window was a blurred red glow of sunset shining through the panes of cowgut, although other specks of brightness showed white, where rain had washed the chinking from the logs.

Outside the cattle were bellowing at the lateness of their milking, and distant shouts and whinnyings told of the patrols saddling up. A muddy job that would be. . .

For a moment Jauro stared uneasily at the bloody glow of the casement—was it perhaps an omen, a warning from the gods? Rain drummed on it when the wind moved, and the wind itself breathed softly through the gaps. He had made such windowpanes himself, when he was young and his fingers more suited to a needle than a sword. He remembered his mother thanking him and praising his workmanship, and he had been proud-to-bursting of that praise. Hagthra, his mother. . . And Hagthro was barely three years in his grave now, and already the earldom as good as lost, if the king wanted it lost. Three years of blood and battle.

He jumped at a sound behind him. Fromto had entered unheard and was striking a flint. A tiny flame flickered on tinder, seeming impossibly bright. Then a rush blazed up with a hiss, and the cramped cell was filled with golden light, making shadows leap on plank and log, on the bed high-piled with marten pelts, on hanging shields, on pikes and swords leaning in a corner, on an iron-bound chest.

There was gray in Fromto's beard, and worry had creased his face like a rutted track. He kicked backward, and the door creaked and slammed.

For a moment the two gazed at each other, then the older man hung the rushlight on a sconce and struck his favorite pose, with left hand on sword hilt and the other on his hip. "Trouble comes with three moons, they say."

"And I should have been born under another," Jauro said sadly. "Why? What has provoked this?"

Fromto regarded him steadily for a moment. "For counsel you must speak to the elders. I am a warrior yet, My Lord."

Silver in his beard, grizzled locks fringing a barren scalp, and yet he was undoubtedly a warrior: big-shouldered, solid. He was still taller and broader than Jauro. And he was deeply troubled if he did not trust himself to use a more affectionate form of address—but more likely it was Jauro's self-control he distrusted.

"You are still the best warrior I have, but you are also my best advisor. We both know what the elders will say. I can feel the iron in my heart already—or do you think he will chop off my head?"

"Reggalo hates making decisions. He may just throw you in jail to rot."

"He has made this one fast enough." Jauro thought sourly of the latest battle—three score men lost, many more wounded. The toll could easily have been much greater, but good fortune had saved his earldom yet again, and now it was to be stolen from him by the overlord in whose name he had fought.

Fromto was shaking his big head. "The plan may have been made long since. Had you lost, he would have moved against the rebels. Since you won, he moves against you. He may not even have heard the outcome himself yet. The orders could have been drawn a middle-month ago, or more."

"But why?" Jauro demanded again, fighting to keep his voice steady. "Why should he doubt my loyalty? Is he afraid I will raise arms against him? That's crazy! I can't field one man to his ten."

The old swordsman turned and sat on the bed, making the thongs creak, and he slumped there in silence, as though weary of battles. Remembering that there could always be ears at knotholes, Jauro settled at Fromto's side, and the bed swayed alarmingly. "Well?" he said quietly.

"You are the victim of your own success, My Lord. You have astonished them all. When Hagthro died and a woman inherited, it seemed inevitable that the ravens would take Rathmuir. And now Rathmuir stands triumphant, and the ravens are scattered. A wild border upland is become a safe and loyal province. And the king has three daughters and four sons he acknowledges."

"Little has been my doing. It was you who made Rathmuir a land fit for a prince."

Fromto glanced around with something like his usual wry humor. "If I did, then I served you ill, my dearest lord. But you are too modest. It was always for you we fought, and now it is your cunning that lets our little band rout hordes so great. Had the men not trusted you at the bridge. . ."

Was it a sign of age that Fromto liked to fight old battles, or a sign of youth that Jauro had no patience for them? There had been too many battles in the past three years. Hagthro had been barely cold before the earl of Lawnshor and the sheriff of Highcastle had decided to divide his fief between them. It had been Fromto who had raised the fyrd, who had out-marched, and out-maneuvered, and in the final reckoning out-fought the aggressors. Today that hairy ox of an envoy had brazenly accused Jauro of personal atrocities, but Jauro had been home with the women the whole time.

No sooner had Lawnshor and Highcastle been settled, than Earl Sando of Sandmuir had tried to gather up the pieces. That time Jauro had been there to watch his churls die for him, tending horses, aiding the wounded.

And when the Trinians had come over the border, he had been a full combatant. He had served his own cause as a pikeman in his own fyrd through that whole long, brutal summer. He had scars to prove it.

But he had taken his rightful place in the campaign against the rebels; he had commanded. He had become a man. Or had he? He felt desperately unsure of himself now. Would any true man have stood silent under that brutal tirade from the envoy? It was easy enough to wave a sword and lead a charge when bloodlust ran hot in the veins and three hundred men roared along behind. Any man or woman or child could do that, any fool. What man—real man—would have submitted to what he had endured this evening? He had stood there tongue-tied like a craven woman.

"I should have listened to the elders," he said harshly.

The elders had advised him to join the rebels, not fight them.

Fromto chuckled. "The old forget honour and courage as they forget so many other important things. You were loyal to your liege, and that is no small jewel in your coronet."

"A shame that my liege were not more loyal to me," Jauro said bitterly.

Muscle tensed in the big man's sword arm, flexing the puckered lines of old scars. "Truly! But had you marched with the rebels, you would have died with them. The cause is hopeless while Reggalo holds the south. Here or farther down the road . . . they would never have reached the plains."

Possibly, but the rebels had made many mistakes, which Jauro had been able to exploit, mistakes they would not have made had he been at their head. The campaign had revealed that he had a talent for tactics—but evidently no skill in politics, for his loyalty had been repaid in treachery. The elders had been correct.

There was no more resistance left, no one to trouble Rathmuir, so the royal spider hoped to gift it to his ogre daughter. A marriage of Thorta to Uncoato would wrap Jauro's earldom in a legal shroud that the other nobles could see buried without much scruple.

What man would submit to such injustice?

He sat in glum silence, not even objecting when Fromto put his arm around him. Indeed, that felt seductively good, a memory of times past. The rushlight hissed and sparked; rain drummed against the casement, but the fading bellows of the cattle reminded him of the slow move of summer sun on dairy walls, and the warm smell of cows. Milking and sewing and rearing babies . . . they seemed very pleasant occupations in retrospect.

"Remind me," he said. "I wanted this, didn't I?"

Fromto chuckled. "I did warn you. You were only thirty-two—"

"Thirty-three! Well, almost."

"And you are still not yet thirty-five! Few complete menopause by then. Many do not even start until they are forty. And your change was swift."

"Completed?" Jauro blurted the word, then added in a whisper, "I do not feel very complete. I feel stuck halfway."

"You do not behave so! Shall I go back to calling you 'Jaura'? Or even 'Jauri'? What would you do if I did?"

"I would start by cutting out your lights and throttling you with them."

"You see? But I can still be a friend. Friends give comfort, and you have just been dealt a sorry blow, a most foul blow. Oh, love! Did you think men never had doubts, or fears, or regrets?"

"No, of course not."

"And surely Lallia has now no cause to— No, do not rage, man! I am merely teasing."

The earl forced himself to relax again. A real man should be able to stand teasing, if it were kindly meant, as this was. He no longer had the option of feminine tears. But he was too tense tonight for humor, and he wondered why Fromto was wandering so far from the point.

Then a hard jab of shame brought understanding. "The men are calling me 'Jaura', you think? After what I did tonight . . . what I didn't do?"

Fromto laughed. "No! No! They may have been puzzled, for they are simple souls, but they trust you— there is not a man in the fyrd who would not trade his backbone for yours, love. Few men anywhere could have resisted the urge to draw under such abuse." The hug tightened. "I was proud of you! Strife is not always the path of true manhood, but new men rarely know that; it needs be learned. The road is hard, but we all must travel it. I have helped all I can, my love."

Jauro smiled, hiding his uneasiness. Was the big man being so unusually sentimental because he was feeling vulnerable himself? "I could have done nothing without you, husband! I need you still, and never more than now. Counsel me! Why does the king bring these false charges?" Again he tasted injustice like gall in his mouth.

But his query failed to call back the man of action, the decisive Fromto of tiltyard and battlefield. The old warrior sighed. "If one of your thralls had a nubile daughter and you wanted to have pleasure of her. . . I know you don't, but suppose in this case you were determined to do so. What would happen?"

Jauro squirmed. He had been tempted many times in the last two years. Since the flames of manhood had blazed up within him, he could hardly see a tallish child without secretly wondering how close it was to menarche and womanhood. Women's desire was slower and deeper and more purposeful. Man's lust was fire and instant madness, and some earls had no scruples in the matter. The odd one would even claim the maidenhead of every adolescent in his fief.

"Then I would have my pleasure of her, I suppose."

"Exactly. No one could stop the earl, or would dare try. Why do you think your people love you? Your mother was the same—he did not steal the virgins either. But Reggalo has decided to steal your fief, and no one can stop the king. We are too remote for you to have friends at court, and your neighbors were your foes. Their neighbors are now frightened of you, or jealous. No one will take your part, no one who matters."

Then the great shoulders straightened at last, the comforting arm was withdrawn, and the voice hardened in purpose. "Had you drawn against the envoy, then the lords must have all condemned you. This way a few may yet waver, and blunt the edge of the enemy's purpose. And certainly your forbearance has won us time to restore our arms, My Lord! Even if they dare a winter advance, they will need at least a great-month to assemble the fyrd—"

Jauro sighed. Was this the man who had taught him strategy? He had aged visibly during the last campaign, but he should not be so blind as this. "We do not resist!"

"What?"

"Even if we wanted to, there is no time. You said yourself that Reggalo's plans were made several least-months ago. He would have brought up his fyrd to . . . to the Azburn valley, probably. Or closer. We stopped the rebels, but he was ready had we failed. The envoy will be there by dawn. And by dawn I must be gone."

"My Lord!" The wrinkles in Fromto's shadowed face seemed to writhe in dismay. He was still shocked. "Rathmuir will stand by you! After so much blood, we shall never—"

"Too much blood!" This time, strangely, it was Jauro who put his arm around Fromto. "The fyrd has bled too often to uphold my house! This time is different. The others came to loot and drive off, so the men of Rathmuir fought for their own livings as well as mine. But the king wants the fief intact. I am the only obstacle. I must go."

He watched the outward signs of struggle in the warrior's face. Finally Fromto said coldly, "Whither can you flee?"

Good question! The Trinians would be happy to use Earl Jauro for archery practice. West lay the sea. "To Andlain, I suppose."

"Cross the ranges in winter?"

"Why not? Others have." He was strong, and young for a man; in the last campaign he had endured hardship as well as any.

Fromto shook his head sadly. "You do not know what storms can do in the passes. Even large parties may vanish. And what of Thorti?"

What indeed? Jauro had forgotten the danger to his child.

His daughter!

"Thorta!" he said, smiling at his former husband.

A gasp. "No! When?"

"It just. . . She just told me, before we came here. Yesterday, she said." Jauro smiled at the astonishment on the older man's face. "Our child is become a woman. Now you have a son, and I a daughter."

The old warrior blinked eyes that had become suddenly shiny in the wavering torchlight. "You must . . . or I, I suppose . . . must counsel her. Yet she is fourteen, so it was due! She will find a woman to counsel her. . ."

Jauro's sense of loss came stabbing back. "You think I have forgotten so soon?"

"Of course not, love! I doubt if any man or woman has ever forgotten the terrors of menarche. I just meant that talk about such things comes better from women, somehow." After a moment, he added, "It was not your fault, you know! Our bodies do these things without asking our permission."

Jauro made a vague chuckling noise to dismiss the subject and ease the pain. "You will miss her, I know, but she must come with me, and you must stay. Enjoy your well-earned retirement!" Feeling his eyelids prickle, he forced a smile and gently tweaked the grey-streaked beard. "And you must take a new wife now, Fromto, my husband. You have waited too long."

He had lost this argument before, and hated it because of the absurd jealousy it always aroused in him, but this would be the last time. And this sad severance was also a part of his entry to manhood, a step that Fromto had delayed far too long. "I command you, as your earl! It is your duty. We have many widows who will rejoice to marry so great a warrior, so fine a man. I will happily testify to your skills."

Fromto did not respond to the joking, and Jauro was astonished to see tears flood those weary eyes. He had seen them burn with the joy of battle; he had seen them wild with passion, but he could not recall ever seeing tears in them before. Not even when the twins died.

"Husband?"

Fromto hesitated, then blurted out: "Jauro, do you love me no more?"

"How can you ask? After all we were to each other . . . how could I not?" He thought of the nervous virgin he had been, so awed when the virile Fromto had proposed to her. He thought of seventeen years of marriage, of passion and suffering shared, of the gentle strength and comfort so freely given. He thought that all in all he had been a good wife, but Fromto had been the sort of husband every child dreamed of winning. "Of course I . . . I love you, husband, and always will. But—"

The old man clapped a hand on his knee. "Sweet words come hard to men's lips, do they not? But if you love me, then why will you have me put to death? Do you think I have no enemies? Do you think Prince Uncoato will ask me to lead his fyrd for him?"

"By the gods and moons!" How could Jauro have overlooked that? A king who would so betray a loyal vassal would be capable of taking vengeance on his relatives and underlings. "Of course you will have to come with us!" His heart skipped with joy as he realized that he would not be parted from Fromto. He could have found no more stalwart companion for the trek—nor for the lonely future beyond.

Fromto sighed with relief. "My lord is gracious!

And also an optimist, if he thought he could stop me. I trust you as I trust no other man, but you are taking my son over the passes in winter!"

Again Thorta! But Jauro dare not leave her, and he would not gamble his daughter's life as heedlessly as he would his own. He must have companions, and who better or more obvious that Fromto?

"And Lallia," the old man said, "and—"

"Not Lallia!"

Fromto frowned. "My Lord. . ."

"No. She stays—I shall find another to replace her." Lallia had been a terrible mistake. In the three days since he returned from the last battle, Jauro had barely spoken with his wife, and he had not summoned her to his bed—but the problem was now obviously solved. "The king will find her a husband more to her taste. As Thorta comes with us, we shall need some stalwart companions, and she should have female company. You must mount a whirlwind courtship! Is there any mature widow who comes to mind, who would agree to depart with us?"

The frost-fringed lips smiled cryptically. "Most like."

Jauro laughed with relief, "That is good! I do not need a yattering elder to advise me, I need a strong sword at my side—a wife will keep you young, husband."

"Young? I am sixty-two!"

"And virile as any hot-blooded forty-year-old!"

Fromto smiled bashfully, then nodded. "As my lord commands."

How strange that felt! The positions of a lifetime were shifting and it was Jauro who must guide and comfort Fromto, as though the plow must pull the ox. Life was a constant drizzle of little surprises like that, reminding him that he was a man now.

"Go and congratulate your son on her woman-hood, and then see to your wooing! We have a least-month's work to do before dawn!"

The big man nodded, and rose. Jauro stood also, and for an awkward moment the two men hesitated. Then they embraced—briefly, and without words.

The door creaked twice and closed behind the old warrior. The rushlight flared and then dimmed. The room stank of its greasy smoke.

Exile! What future for a dispossessed earl, fleeing from his overlord? Jauro put the thought out of his mind, deciding he would deal with the future when it arrived. Lately he seemed to spend much less time worrying—was that another sign of manhood, or something purely personal, perhaps stemming from his rank?

Now to dispose of his finery. . . He winced at a twinge of stiffness in his leg, where a Trinian sword had drawn his first blood. Wet weather always found that wound. He threw open the lid of the chest, and pulled off the skimpy gold chain that he had donned to impress the envoy. He unwrapped his sable robe and tossed it on the bed, unbuckled his sword and threw that after. He was reaching down to find his favorite old shabby bearskin kirtle, when the door creaked again and the room brightened. Shivering in the cool dampness of the evening, he straightened.

Lallia closed the door and leaned against it, studying him. She had brought a lantern, and in its steady glow he was at once aware of his nudity, for his leggings hid nothing of importance. Trust the wretched woman to catch him at such a moment!

Desire flared up in him instantly. This was what it was to be a man—slaved by passion, perpetually vulnerable to lightning strokes of lust.

"You are leaving," she said.

"You have your revenge at last."

She smiled grimly.

"You came to gloat, I suppose?" he growled. His body was reacting shamelessly to her calculating inspection.

"Despite all the blood you have shed, your earldom is taken from you and you must flee?"

"I should have been born under another moon."

She smiled again, but more cryptically.

She had been Sando's only son, and the wife of his chief thane, Chilo. Sando had died in battle, and his two daughters also. Fromto had put Chilo to death and had wanted to slay Lallia. That had been the first time Jauro had exercised his authority to overrule his former husband, the leader of his fyrd. Goaded by unfamiliar male impulses, he had fallen instantly and hopelessly in love with this gorgeous woman. He had called out to save her, proclaiming that he would take her as his wife—and his voice had cracked into an absurd soprano as he did so. He could still remember the titters of his men.

And he could not forget his shame and her derision when he had first tried to consummate that enforced marriage. Since then he had matured, and things had been different—but never easy. And his desire had never faded. Even now it was making him giddy, after two great-months of lonely sleep in wet heather.

Her braids hung dark as a raven's wing, her eyes shone black like a moonless night.

"Gloat, then!" he snapped. "Enjoy your victory. I hope Reggalo finds you a more satisfactory husband."

"That could not be," she said softly. She hung the lantern on the other sconce and then raised her hands to the ties of her robe.

Unbelieving, he watched as she shed the garment, letting it fall to the packed clay of the floor.

"What trickery is this?" he demanded hoarsely.

Was she trying to delay his departure to make time for some foul treachery?

Lallia dropped the linen from her loins and stood naked before him, shivering. "I must attend my lord, as is my duty."

He opened his mouth to send her away, and could not do it. His heart beat ever faster as he stared at the pale perfection of her skin, of a body even lovelier than he had remembered. He had never borne breasts like those, save when suckling Thorti. Now his were shrunk to useless flat pads of muscle, hidden beneath a thickening yellow thatch. Other organs had sprouted from his groin to compensate for the loss, and a painful throbbing there betrayed his desperate need.

She came close, peering up at him. "Husband?"

He took her in his arms distrustfully. "Why?"

"For love."

"Love? After all those kind words? The mockery? The hate?"

She blinked sudden tears. "Could you not see? Must a man forget so soon how a woman thinks?"

"I never thought as you do." The room was cold, and he pulled her tight against him. He had grown taller since he first embraced her.

"Act now," she whispered, "and talk later."

He lifted her onto the bed and pulled a fur over them both. She came alive in his arms like a wildcat, and they coupled madly, frantically, gloriously. They cried aloud in the sharing of rapture.

It was like nothing he had ever experienced, certainly not with her, nor even in his first youthful passion with Fromto. The joy of giving joy was familiar, the physical ecstasy more intense, but he also discovered echoes of every other gratification he had ever known—rage of battle, thrill of hunting, joy of conquest . . . the contentment of being needed as a babe

needs its mother, of being wanted as his child had
wanted him, the satisfaction of possession and the
strength of a protector, of being gentle when he could
be strong, and of might prevailing. It was everything to
him, as love had never been before, at once a simpler,
easier act and a more consuming response, a totality of
many wants that had been separate for him in the past.
And as his excitement crested beyond containment, he
thought that this more than anything must be what
made men what men were, what he was. Fromto had
been right, his state was no longer in doubt. And finally
thought ended as he gloried in the culminating proof of
manhood.

And in the long limp silence that followed, the
damp astonishment, he realized that he was still wearing his leggings and boots.

"Oh, my love!" he panted in the musty darkness
under the furs. "My love, my love! Why now?"

For a while he got no reply, then she sniffed, as
though ready to weep. "I said unkind things, My
Lord."

"Unkind? I never met a woman with such a
tongue."

She sniffled more, then chuckled. "Thank you, My
Lord! You did not see? And it did not work. I could
never make you force me."

"Force you? *Force you?*" He threw back the hem of
the rug so he cold see her face in the lantern glow. The
rushlight had gone out. "Force a woman?"

"Chilo did," she whispered. "When he was drunk.
When the time was wrong. Often."

"Moons preserve me! Lady, I swear . . . I was taught
loving by Fromto, and in fifteen years he never tried to
force me once." He shuddered. Fromto was as strong as
man could be, and as gentle as feathers with a woman.
"You *wanted* that?"

"Oh, my love!" She cuddled closer. "I did want you, even at the first. But you had slain my husband, my father, my brothers. To confess to love seemed like betrayal—yes, I wanted you to force me. To save my shame. Desperately I wanted that."

He was too stunned to speak.

"And you never would," she said. "No matter how I taunted you. So I had to yield, sacrificing my pride to my need for you."

"Oh, Lallia!"

Was this what it was to be a man—hopelessly confused by women? He recalled arguments with Fromto on this very bed, with the big man being strangely obtuse and closed to reason. Lately his thinking had seemed much clearer.

So Jauro had won his love at last, and must leave her. How cruel the gods!

"When?" he whispered. "I loved you when I first set eyes on you. When did you first feel . . . feel that you did not hate me?"

"I do not know. Perhaps when the women told me how gentle you had been as a woman, with Thorti, and then when I saw how your men worshipped you."

"And as a kid I could steal cookies better than any. Now the truth?"

She sighed. "The first time you tried to bed me, my love."

He groaned as the embers of his shame blazed up anew.

"You were so enraged," she said, "and yet you did not blame me, you blamed yourself. That was when I knew I had found a far better man than Chilo. A better man than I have ever known, I think."

He snorted disbelievingly. "I was too young, too impatient."

"The change is easier when one is older, they say.

The blood runs cooler. You will help me when my turn comes. . ." They kissed. After a moment, though, she whispered, "Is it true what they say?"

"What do they say?" he asked angrily.

"That you changed so young because you refused Fromto after you inherited the earldom? Celibacy is said to hasten the change."

"No, it is not true!"

It had been Fromto who had refused Jaura. He had been away a long time on the first campaign, and when he had returned they had sadly agreed to try, so that the earl might sooner become a man, as was fitting. But Jaura had not been able to sustain their pledge. She had begged and entreated and tried all her feminine wiles. Fromto had been the steadfast one, sleeping night after night on the floor in lonely agony. Oh, what he owed to that man!

"It is not true," Jauro lied. "It just happened— perhaps the strain of Hagthro's death. . ." He fell silent, thinking that she did not believe him.

"When the king gives you to another," he began, and she stopped him by putting her lips on his.

"I will come with you."

"No! I will not allow it! I shall be an outlaw, a wandering fighter seeking to serve others for charity. You must—"

"What of your son?" she whispered.

"Son?"

"I carry your child, My Lord, the child that will one day become your son, when it reaches menarche."

"Are you sure?" he demanded, thinking that every husband in the history of the world must have greeted that news with the same question.

She chuckled happily. "Either that or I have reached menopause, and I never heard of anyone becoming a man at twenty-two."

Take a pregnant woman over the passes in winter?

Or leave an unborn child behind to die by the king's spite?

Jauro ran strangely calloused fingers over the smoothness of her belly and, speechless, turned his face away. Today he had lost a child to womanhood, and now was promised another to replace it. He would be a father as well as a mother, and this time teach archery and horsemanship instead of weaving and housewifery and. . .

But today he had also lost his earldom.

He was dallying in bed with a woman when he should be attending to his duties. In one sweep of motion he leaped to the floor, and the bed creaked mightily.

"I must go!" he snapped to Lallia's cry of protest. "What will they think of me out there?" They would think he was hiding under the furs, weeping! He rummaged to find his sword and belt it on him. The sword came first now, always.

Then he heard voices raised, and his scalp prickled in sudden apprehension. He had been negligent. There had been too much noise outside, men and horses both, and he had not heeded. Dogs were barking. He draped his sables loosely about him and threw open the door, ignoring a whine of complaint from his wife—women! He stormed along the corridor, heading for the brightness of the hall and the shouting, yet remembering that he had been mightily annoyed with Fromto a few times when he had cut short lovemaking for business. Was being a boor a necessary part of being a man? Oh, well, he would certainly take Lallia with him now, and they had years ahead to indulge in that sort of thing.

The hall was in disarray, a crowded, noisy confusion of torchlight and shadows. The meal had been interrupted, and there were tables and benches everywhere, half the men of the household stamping around flashing swords, and there were women and children mixed in with it all.

Jauro headed for the apparent center of the confusion, while glancing vainly around for Fromto. His husband must be outside, organizing the fugitives' departure, or possibly attending to his wooing.

He bellowed, and the swords were sheathed. Big, shambling men moved hastily out of the way as their young earl bore down on them and arrived at the cause of the tumult, strangers.

There were three of them, unarmed, white-bearded and frail, almost elders. They all looked shaky, red-eyed exhausted by their journey. Their boots and leggings were thickly mudded, their furs dripped rain on the rushes.

Jauro recognized the leader at once, and with a considerable shock. He bowed, wishing he had taken the time to make himself more presentable. "Our house is honoured to receive Your Holiness."

The old man shook his head sadly, appraising Jauro with eyes still bright, yet hooded. "I fear not, My Lord." He raised a mittened hand as his host began to speak of chairs and warmth and wine. "I can not accept your hospitality, young man."

Only enemies refused hospitality. What new evil had inspired Reggalo to send his high priest? He had not brought the arrogance of the first envoy, although he was still regarding Jauro with priestly haughter. "You spurned the king's summons, obviously."

"Obviously. Did you not meet the envoy upon the trail?"

"We must have missed him down by the marshes. We have followed him for many hours hoping to catch him before he arrived. We had more horses, but he drove his mounts hard." The priest paused, glancing around, and then reached within his furs. "The summons he delivered is withdrawn."

That ought to be good news, but Jauro was sure it wasn't, as he accepted the packet now offered him. "Your Grace—a seat by the fire, at least?"

Even that small hospitality was refused.

The hall had fallen silent now, men and women clustering in separate knots among the shadows. The fires crackled and some of the torches hissed. Children were sobbing, unnerved by the tension.

Jauro broke the seal and read the warrant in the shaky light, holding it at arm's length. Once upon a time he had stitched the finest hem in the household. Now his eyes were warriors' eyes, which could see a hawk blink but fared poorly on a scribe's crabbed hand.

Still, the message was clear enough, and the meaning drifted in around his heart like snow. He looked up to the venerable messengers who had brought it, and the priest read the question on his lips.

"Yes, I think you can trust that," he said bitterly. "As much as anything can be trusted. It was the best we could do, My Lord."

Jauro nodded, not wanting to speak yet. Certainly the list of witnesses was impressive enough, men known for honour. As far as a king's word went it was . . . well, it would be less treacherous than the mountains in winter, if not by much.

His furs were being tugged by the gnarled hand of Mindooru, one of the elders—shrunken and bent, leaning on a cane and constantly mumbling and drooling, shaking a head that was quite hairless except for a white fringe at the back. Of course the elders would have sent Mindooru. It was Jauro's father.

"Tell me, son?"

Jauro glanced around again for Fromto, and could not see him anywhere. Then he started to read the warrant again.

"Out with it!" Mindooru mumbled. "What's he say this time? It's bad, but not as bad, right? Crab apple tastes sweet after wild cherry, mm?"

Jauro nodded, repelled by the convoluted thinking. "The offer of marriage is withdrawn. Fromto can be regent and choose Thorta's husband. No proscriptions. That's about it."

The elder nodded, as though it had expected nothing else.

Oh gods, but it hurt, it hurt!

The high priest flinched before Jauro's accusing stare. "I said it was the best we could do! He'll not go for anything less, I'm certain."

"But why?" What had he done to deserve this?

"Why?" Mindooru shrilled. "I'll tell you why, son. Because he's frightened of you!" It began to weep.

The priest bit his lip, and then nodded agreement.

Jauro felt stunned. For a moment he clutched at a crazy hope that this was all some sort of elaborate joke, the kind of hazing new men got from the fyrd—but he was long past his first whiskers, and they would not treat their earl so.

No, it was real. Yet did his achievements really seem so impressive, so threatening? An unbeatable earl who might one day decide to move against tyranny? He had never dreamed that others might see him as such a man.

"Where's Fromto?" he demanded, looking around again.

"He can't help you," croaked the elder. "I can't. This one you do alone, son." The hands on its cane trembled. Tears streamed down its wrinkles. Even the end of its nose held a drop, and its thin, bent shoulders were heaving with sobs. Children wept. Women wept. Elders wept. Men did not.

For the first time in almost twenty years, Jauro

would make a decision without consulting Fromto. But Mindooru was right—this one was his alone. This, too, was part of manhood—it felt like his first boar hunt.

He straightened his shoulders, and peered around until his eyes found Thorta's face—a tiny patch of horrified whiteness among the women. He sent her a smile, but shook his head when she began to come forward. He knew that words would lodge in his throat like fishbones. *May you rule this land for many years, my darling, as woman and man, and raise daughters and sons to our line.* He could never say that aloud. *I love you no less than I ever did, even if I haven't said so lately!* Nor that. Once, maybe. Not now.

He thought of Lallia and the unborn child he would never see; and he thought of the snow-locked ranges, of the storms, of frost and starvation.

He looked down at the sniveling wreck of his father. At least he would be spared *that!*

Fromto would do his duty.

All around the hall stood the angry knots of men, muttering angrily—the grizzled survivors, the best warriors, companions who had shared wet ditches with him, shared triumph and terror. They had bled together, these men and he. They wanted to bleed more.

Go home now, he wanted to tell them. *Go home to your flocks and fields, to your plows and nets. Go home; live in peace; grow in wisdom.*

But they would be shamed if he said that. And what of the younger adults, the women who would be warriors for his daughter? They were huddled in other groups with the children who would be their wives. The widows would change first, of course; that was the gods' way of restocking the fyrd. *I hope you all live out your lives in peace,* he thought, *but I don't expect it.*

He unbuckled his sword and thrust it at Mindooru, which almost dropped it. "Here, father!" Jauro raised his voice, remembering the elder was deaf. "You taught me to use this, remember? Long ago. You taught me too well!"

He turned back to the priestly envoy and the searching eyes, and he forced out the lying words: "I confess my treason."

He saw relief then, and something else he could not place. It was not a return of arrogance. Not contempt. Not pleasure. Surely not admiration?

As he strode out to die for his loved ones, Jauro reflected sadly that this also was sometimes part of being a man.

PROSCRIPTS OF GEHENNA

JEAN-LOUIS TRUDEL

Translated from the French by John Greene

The city of Jigansk on Gehenna was drinking in the last rays of the setting sun, Epsilon Serpentis. Shopkeepers were calling to clients hurrying homewards. Gehenna nights were cruel. Less greedy merchants were already closing, clearing off their stalls.

In the newer districts, the civil servants from beyond were lowering steel shutters on their windows. Used to milder climates, they feared the cold, harsh nights of Gehenna. As soon as Epsilon Serpentis began to get near the horizon, they quickly sheltered behind thicker walls than could be found in the older quarters. Empire bureaucrats were less resistant to cold than Gehenna natives. The latter were the descendants of the second wave of colonists. Their ancestors had profited from the labours of the first wave, eight hundred years earlier, who had made the atmosphere breathable but had failed to acclimatize flora and fauna of terrestrial origin to the planet. Without a struggle, the second wave had moved into a handful of towns near the equator—Jigansk, Olenek, Izmir. . .

In the old Gehennite districts, the wind was already raising dust in the streets, making little whirlwinds over the beaten earth. Passersby felt it on their skin.

The lights of the high, ultra-modern towers near the spaceport pierced the dusk gathering in the city, and their brilliance could be seen far out into the surrounding desert.

Francesco fixed his eyes on the faint glow of the lights far ahead, a little too far for his taste, and turned up his coat collar. He could already feel the glacial burn of the wind on his neck. He had just delivered a departmental packet to a miners camp. The bicycle ride had taken longer than he had foreseen. His muscles were not yet used to the heavy gravity of Gehenna, but the tiny market could not justify the manufacture or the import of more modern means of transportation.

He swore into his beard. They had warned him when he'd left Bueno. During the seventy Earth hours of a Gehenna day, the night cold could solidify mercury while the noon heat liquefied the potassium from the mines north of Jigansk. A posting to Gehenna guaranteed rapid promotion, precisely because Gehenna was not like Bueno.

He passed by the cliffs where caves sheltered the "wolfies", as the Gehennites called them. Even though he was short of breath, he pushed harder on the pedals and leaned forward to accelerate. The speed of the bicycle increased imperceptibly and he felt reassured. Just to make sure, he fingered the handle of the pistolaser given to all imperial employees on planets classified as dangerous, less for their protection than to isolate them from imperial subjects they might be tempted to fraternize with. In Jigansk, they said the "wolfies" sometimes attacked solitary travellers. They also said that simple contact was sufficient to contaminate a normal human.

These "wolfies" were the victims of a complex micro-organism which caused irreversible and little-understood changes in the appearance and metabolism of infected persons. The skin turned brown and scaly, and grew a real coat of fur—the disease was called lycanthropy. Life expectancy was reduced by half in the best of cases, but all this remained uncertain, since the victims were systematically ostracized by healthy Gehennites, and imperial science had not yet bothered with a disease restricted to an underpopulated planet.

But no one attacked him. His colleagues would make fun of him if they learned how he had panicked. The thought had made him slow down. He then looked behind him and pedaled faster.

The gates of Jigansk were guarded by soldiers paid by the city administration. They made sure no undesirables entered the city. There were only six gates; elsewhere all the habitations turned doorless, windowless faces towards the desert, forming a continuous wall. The two men guarding the gate Francesco approached, greeted him affably. One of them, a short chubby man, rubbed his exposed hands and called, "Hurry up. It's too cold to leave even a wolfie outside. And night will be worse!"

Francesco balked at the word "wolfie". It was a very common term of insult, and yet like many other things about Gehenna, its origin was as obscure as its meaning was clear.

A remark by the other guard interrupted his thoughts. "You're just in time. We were about to close the gate. Then you would have had to go round by the spaceport."

Francesco grimaced and climbed back on his bike. The first guard examined the imperial identification card in the name of Francesco Reyes and returned it to him. He pocketed it and started off again.

He shivered, thinking of the guard's words; he would not have enjoyed finding himself outside the walls after nightfall. Not only was the night air capable of freezing bones, but rumour had it that the desert plain was haunted by mysterious creatures.

He'd asked about it, and had built up a hypothesis that it was perhaps the indigenous fauna of Gehenna. Nevertheless, no proof of the existence of such creatures existed. They did not come out by day. Skeptics held that these beings, rather, found their origin in the dregs of the numerous bottles of alcohol consumed by the miners who claimed to have caught glimpses of these nocturnal beasts. Certainly, after two centuries of colonization, it was unthinkable that any animal could have completely escaped the attention of the Gehennites.

The pale whitish circle of the sun was even closer to the horizon, plunging Jigansk into a lugubrious twilight resembling a winter dawn on Bueno.

He leaned into the pedals on a sharp ascent, savouring the idea of the evening he was to spend with his friends, a doctor from Bueno and a Terran sociologist. They would watch Earth cassettes on the holo-vision, eat a gourmet meal in the Bueno style, and discuss the latest novel, brought in the electronic memory of a spaceship. He could not have endured Gehenna without these tranquil evenings of friendship. The sociologist's apartment was an oasis of civilization which Francesco regularly visited with delight. The rest of the planet was backward, compared to Bueno or Earth. Gehenna had been isolated for a century and a half, and its customs had become almost as cruel as the temperature variations.

He heard the shouts and the insults before he saw

the boys. They were chasing a wolfie who must have risked coming into the city to look for food. If the boys caught their prey, they would stone it or drive it over the Rybakov cliff. The hunted wolfie rushed towards him and huddled on the ground behind the now immobile bicycle.

Completely taken aback, Francesco stepped off the bike and looked at the wolfie. It was still light enough to see that the torn rags covered a young female. A brownish fleece hid her lower face and continued down the back, along the arms and between the breasts. A thick mane of tangled hair covered her shoulders. Her eyes, frightened but intelligent, belied the hairy appearance of a cowering beast.

Francesco turned towards the pursuers who had suddenly frozen, as astonished as he was. There were about twenty boys, between eight and ten Gehennite years old. They wore hoods and woolen mittens, to protect against infection as well as the cold. Most held long-bladed knives in a manner that showed they would not hesitate to use them. The hoods revealed nothing but the bestial avidity in their eyes.

Francesco, caught between the young lycanthrope and the Gehennites, watched her with compassion. He couldn't, he daren't leave her to their fear and scorn.

On the point of speaking, he hesitated, and it was another voice that snapped, "Out of the way, stranger!"

"What do you want with her?" replied Francesco to gain time, conscious of the weight of the pistolaser on his hip, and of the fact that its chrome butt had revealed that he belonged to the little-loved species of Imperial civil servants. The answer was a shout: "Rybakov Rock! She has fouled our city!"

Others chipped in, "This is our city, not hers."

"My little brother caught it from playing with a wolfie rag. He was banned three years ago."

"My sister too."

"Death to the wolfie!"

The shouts got louder and less comprehensible, and Francesco tried to think. He finally yelled wordlessly, and silence fell. He calmly articulated, "Return to your homes."

He was about to add that he would take the responsibility of escorting the young woman out of the city.

A rock flew, hitting the front wheel of the bike. Off balance, Francesco fell and his hand clutched the handle of his weapon convulsively.

An adolescent kicked the pistolaser out of his hands, and he was suddenly covered by a dozen youths holding him down. His nose filled with the odour of stale sweat on their leather jackets. He bit savagely, but got nothing but a mouthful of greasy wool. He struggled, but the weight of his assailants and the muscles they had developed on Gehenna made all resistance vain.

"You wanted to give us orders," he heard suddenly in his ear. "Maybe you're in love with the wolfie?"

The voice moved away and spoke louder. "He's a wolfie-lover. So let's make him one!"

Held by strong arms, Francesco was laid out on the hard earth of the street. He finally saw the lycanthrope, who had backed against a wall without daring to move, threatened by the knives of two adolescents.

The leader approached Francesco, knife in hand. He slit the blue material of the coat sleeve. Francesco's skin was exposed to the cold air. He felt goose bumps.

With a swift stroke, the leader slashed open the skin along several centimetres of Francesco's forearm. The momentary burning sensation left Francesco motionless, staring at the blood. His blood! He started to strain against the arms holding him. The leader picked up the pistolaser and Francesco held still, feeling a freezing void in the pit of his stomach. He was too young to die so stupidly, killed by his own weapon in a brawl that should have been none of his business.

His terror gave him the strength to hate as he had never hated before. How he wished for his weapon back. Oh, he wouldn't hesitate to use it now!

The leader handed the pistolaser to one of his companions. He grasped the lycanthrope's left wrist and pricked the palm of her hand. Blood rose slowly to the surface and Francesco jerked upwards, desperately, but couldn't move the young men holding him. He shouted, on the verge of sobs, but there were no passersby to hear him.

The lycanthrope lay immobile, the pistolaser at her back, while the leader scraped her bleeding palm with his knife. Then he pressed the blade against Francesco's wound. The two bloods mixed. The contact of the cold metal made Francesco shiver. He turned his eyes away from the reddened skin and saw the lycanthrope smiling feebly, as if to excuse herself.

The leader stepped aside, discarding his mittens and his knife. There was a nasty laugh in his eyes, shining under the black wool of the hood. A new spasm ran through Francesco's arm. He almost broke loose from the men holding him to attack the chief, profiting from a moment of surprise, but someone cracked a stone against his head and he fell again. Before losing consciousness, he heard the leader order, "To the Rock! Quick, the sun's going down."

Francesco moaned.

He was shuddering from cold and pain.

The sharp stones poking his bruises hurt more and more. He had bounced down the Rybakov cliff-face in a torpor that his pain was slowly dispelling. The rock surface had lacerated his hands, and all his muscles shrieked their suffering at the slightest move.

Now he was shivering, stretched on the naked ground. The torn coat no longer protected him from the cold of the night. The tormented forms of the Gehennite plants were covered in frost. Azazel, the primary moon of the planet, dispensed a miserly white glow in which the plants and the frozen puddles glinted.

It wasn't just cold; he had a fever too.

After a moment, he slowly got up and stumbled forward. He slipped on a bit of ice and fell to the ground, but he'd had time to get his bearings. The spaceport, open all night, was to the north, in the direction of Kidron, the second moon of Gehenna, a tiny white spark in the black sky.

He got up again and fell once more after a few steps. His limbs trembled, refused to obey. The bump on the edge of his forehead scraped the ground. He tried to groan but no sound would come from his dry throat.

He kept moving forward on his knees. Even the icy wind could not damp down the fire inside him. When he wiped his sweating brow, the burning skin felt like a furnace door.

Finally he collapsed, incapable of going further. He had fought the wind and his rebellious body for so long. His sweat mixed with tears, a tribute imposed by the wind to his eyes, and ran down his neck, where it turned into a dirty white ice.

He managed to crawl a few metres more, propelled by sudden spasms of energy, but eventually, exhausted, he had to stop again. He laid his cheek against the frozen earth, which quickly soaked up the heat from his body, leaving him colder and colder.

Lifting his head, he saw he had moved away from Jigansk. In his delirium, he had taken the wrong direction. The wind blurred his vision and he lay back, discouraged.

He lost track of time. It didn't matter any more. He would not survive the thirty-five hour night. He was too far from the road to be helped by a passing miner and he couldn't reach Jigansk on his own steam.

He gave up, feeling a numbness more alarming than the most piercing cold, for it was the precursor of the final sleep.

Yet he was still awake when someone or something touched him, felt him, dragged him off. He opened his frozen eyelids, but it was so dark he could make nothing out. Azazel had set and only tiny Kidron gleamed above the mountains to the north.

The simple effort of looking had worn him out. He drifted off to sleep once more. He dreamed he was riding a bike across the desert, fleeing a thick fog growing behind him, hiding some unknown menace. Suddenly, the bike was gone and he was walking along a rocky road. He wandered, lost, along a lane suspended above death. . .

He awoke to darkness, his teeth chattering. It was less cold.

As his eyes got used to the shadows, he saw that he was in a little cave. Phosphorescent mosses, like embroidery, decorated the black stone walls, interrupted here and there by pale jagged stripes, as if a monster had gouged out the rock. He lay under a thick pile of rags, preserving him from the cold. He waited, his mind a blank, happy to enjoy his warm nest.

A face appeared before him, accompanied by the weak glow of a nearly exhausted flashlight.

He recognized the young lycanthrope, whom he had not seen at the foot of Rybakov cliff, not that he had been in any state to question her absence. She leaned over him and murmured, "My name's Fatima. Don't try to speak. When I returned with my friends to help you, you were half-dead. So you need to keep up your strength. I have something for you to eat, Gehenna fruits. Look, they're purple pomegranates."

She held out a cracked plastic bowl containing chunks of a pulpy, purplish fruit.

Was she trying to poison him? Gehenna fruits were highly toxic to humans.

She insisted. A sweetish alcoholic odour came from the dish she held out. He was hungry; he grasped the spoon and quickly emptied the bowl. The flesh of the fruit did in fact contain sugar and alcohol; his mouth felt less dry.

He smiled vaguely and went back to sleep.

The fever returned, drowning him in waves of fire. Despite his closed eyes, he saw a diffuse glow in the blackness. Snowflakes surged out of the bright spot and he was suddenly plunged into the whirling heart of a blizzard. He felt snow cover his skin, build up and transmit its coolness to his blood.

He stood up on a road crowded with pedestrians and began to walk, shivering. Liquid ice was circulating in his veins.

The walkers around him slowed down. He tried to catch a glimpse of their faces but a flesh-coloured fog hid them from his sight. He pushed forward, faster and faster, passing others who were now only making sporadic jerky movements. The walk warmed him. Then he saw a silhouette, and he knew it waited for him. This figure let the slow marchers pass, but spread his night-coloured fur coat out in front of Francesco. He glimpsed a hood filled with black space before pitching into an abyss, screaming "Why?"

He was a child who had scraped his arm but refused to cry. His throat contracted painfully, but he held back his tears.

He fell, screaming, his hands stretched out blindly.

The fall went on indefinitely, from the top of the heavens to the last circles of hell, where cold and ice are the torturers. He slammed into the ground with a shock that cut off his scream.

He stood up again in a starless, hopeless desert. The cold of the night infiltrated his bones and congealed his marrow. He began walking.

A fire burned him, flashing up fiercely under his skin as if flaming gasoline ran through his veins. He opened his eyes again and the darkness of the cave welcomed him, fresh and intimate, a refuge.

He struggled with shadows. His wounds tormented him. He slept on fragments of saw-blades and no sleep came to help him.

And yet there were moments of respite, when they gave him water to drink and warm juices, sugary, a bit sticky.

Finally, his waking dreams stopped harassing him. His lucid periods got longer, during which he focused on getting his breath back, keeping his mind blank. Always Fatima's face was present in the darkness, and her faithful presence gave him the courage to endure the attacks of delirium. At long last, he awakened completely.

He rubbed his cheeks. His beard had grown by several centimetres. He didn't think he'd slept that long. He should shave right away—

"No!" Increased pilosity was the first symptom of lycanthropy, after the initial fever. He tried to stop the cavalcade of thoughts rushing through his head. He wanted to think calmly. He was alone in the little cave. Was he in the caverns inhabited by the wolfies? Was it a dream?

With a sharp gesture, he lifted up his sleeve and looked at the skin of his arm. It was marbled with brown spots, and already showing tufts of coarse, long hair in places. He scratched at the brown spots: they were hard to the touch, like horn or scales. His skin was also warmer than usual, and the slash inflicted by the Gehennite had closed up completely. Francesco stood up slowly. All right, he wouldn't tell himself lies. He had escaped the Gehenna night, but he wouldn't escape lycanthropy. All through the night he had unconsciously been hoping he had escaped contamination, in spite of the odds.

He would never see Bueno again. . . He stood still for several minutes. He didn't feel like moving at all. If only he had died during the night!

He found Fatima in the adjoining cave and looked at her without a word. She seemed more beautiful than the day before. He had crossed over to her side of the barrier and the laws of the old world no longer applied. She understood his silence; she said, "Welcome. You've been lucky. You weren't seriously hurt when they threw you off the Rock. I, of course, am used to it."

Lucky! Well, that was one way of putting it.

"You could have been killed. We wolfies believe that life is such a treasure that you must not waste the slightest drop of it, however bitter. That is why we helped you last night."

"Last night? Wait! How long was I delirious?"

"One night. Come on, cheer up; there are compensations."

Without enthusiasm. "Yeah?"

"Yes," replied Fatima with conviction. "The microorganism of lycanthropy establishes itself permanently in the cells of the human body and regulates the metabolism at a different level. This means that—"

"You were a doctor, weren't you?"

"Why do you ask that?"

"I have . . . I had a friend who used to talk like you, a doctor."

"Yes," said Fatima, "I was looking for a cure for lycanthropy and. . ."

Fatima did not finish her sentence and Francesco never learned another thing about her past life. She did not confide easily. In the sulfurous craters of hell, do the damned discuss what they did to earn their punishment?

Fatima continued, as if she had never dropped the subject. "We don't need to sleep. That practically doubles our living time. Isn't that worth a shorter life expectancy? We live more intensely. We can go out at night. The cold barely affects us."

Who was she trying to convince?

"If you want to be happy, you can be. Otherwise, you can go cry in a corner."

There was a short silence, as if for a departed life.

"You never told me your name."

"Francesco Reyes."

"Thanks."

Why should she thank him? Francesco wasn't sure.

In Fatima's company, he visited the network of caves. The ground was covered with fine sand, soft to the bare feet of lycanthropes. Stone half-walls divided the caverns into rooms. Clothes, dishes, tools, furniture, everything came from garbage heaps. In a long grotto, fires crackled under lumpy pots, and hairy figures stirred the contents with long flat sticks, half-hidden by the smoke. Francesco was reminded of old tales of witches told by grandmothers on Bueno. Fatima's short explanation: "Kitchens." He was surprised by such a routine element in his new life, then thinking it over, was a bit reassured by this domestic aspect.

They finally entered the principal cave, spacious but with a low ceiling. Several wolfies were settled in, sitting on the sand, reading, playing dice, or simply chatting. At first they all looked the same to Francesco, then he noticed differences: in the body hair; then between bent, resigned backs and straight backs, filthy rags and carefully patched ones; and in different social groupings.

They crossed the cave and Francesco could feel the hard looks of some of the gamblers. Even that was better than the lycanthropes who turned their backs on him. When they arrived at the next cave, he asked Fatima about their behaviour. She smiled, "They're just being polite. They don't want to embarrass you with their looks. The gamblers are always looking out for new players."

In a rocky refuge, some wolfies were standing around a bed. Fatima said, "The oldest one among us. He's dying. He is forty-six Earth years old."

Twenty years to live! Francesco shuddered.

There was silence, and the group broke up. A wolfie with black, coarse hair pulled the blanket over the departed's head. Then he held out his hand to Francesco, who hesitated a second before offering his. His hesitation was noted.

"Welcome. It would seem you are joining us to replace old Rauf. I hope so. We all respected him. I bet you're still asking, Why me? Hurry up and ask, Why not me?"

Francesco was startled to have his thoughts read. The wolfie added, "Have you thought what role you might play in our community?"

Fatima intervened, "Patience, Ekrem. He just woke up."

Ekrem didn't press him, and they shook hands.

In the silence of the refuge, Francesco kneeled beside the body. The gestures of the old religion of Bueno came to him and he drew a cross in the air, feeling that he was touching past, present and future. Fatima watched, understanding only his respectful attitude. Finally, seeing that his silence and immobility would apparently continue, she left the room. Alone, he got up and said, "Sleep, brother."

The words resonated somberly against the inert walls.

His throat dry, Francesco took the direction that Fatima had told him led outside. When he emerged from the caves, the morning chill did not make him shiver. Still feeling a bit shaky, he turned toward the city, where the metallic roofs reflected the rays of the rising sun. Two figures were standing by the road he had taken on his bicycle the night before. He recognized his friends, the doctor and the sociologist.

He was tempted to wave, but thought better of it and returned to the cave. He didn't want to, he couldn't speak to them. The regrets would be too keen. He felt a hard ball form in the pit of his stomach just thinking about meeting them. His memories of the old routine hurt more than the scrapes and bruises from Rybakov Rock. He smashed his fist against the wall and stifled a cry. He refused to weep over his lost happiness.

When he came back out later, his friends had gone. They had left beside the road a package containing his favourite books. A note was stuck to the top book. He ripped it off and read, "Dear Francesco, we hope you are alive. Your fate has set off a real scandal. You are not the first victim of those punks, but your status as Imperial civil servant forced the government's hand. Your persecutors have confessed and will appear in court, if it's any consolation. We will return to the same spot when we can and will wait for you."

Tears came to his eyes. He had never suspected such loyalty in his friends. He carefully folded the note and slipped it into his pants pocket. Some day he would tell them how their faithfulness had touched him. One day, he would see them again. One day. . .

After that, the day dragged on. He consulted Fatima about the books and she suggested he share them with those who liked such things. When the heat got too heavy, they all took refuge in the depths of the caves, where it was always cool. He was astonished that he felt no fatigue. He didn't even feel drowsy. He could no longer even imagine the need to sleep.

He eventually began to get bored. In a few hours, he had met most of the lycanthropes. There were only one hundred and seven, not counting himself. All had been born on Gehenna, and few remembered their previous life. Their conversation was of limited interest; he was the one they all wanted to get to talk.

All the same, he spent a good hour with a young lycanthrope named Kenan. He told him his story, and in exchange Kenan, leaning back against the wall, eyes closed, said, "I can see you don't understand how it usually happens. And be sure not to blame yourself, Francesco. We were all a bit imprudent, otherwise we wouldn't be here. In my case, I played with a rag I picked up in the street, even though my mother told me a hundred times not to. A few hours later, I had the fever."

Kenan paused and Francesco remembered the words of one of his assailants. He said nothing, but compared in his mind one brother to the other, one world to the other. The change was so sudden.

"My mother wanted to wait before calling a doctor, but my father had guessed what it was, I think. The doctor came to my room with a mask over his face and a sack of instruments over his shoulder. I got the usual treatment. First the official diagnosis, then the obligatory vasectomy, and finally the guards at dusk, with their machine guns. They took me out of my bed—I'm sure they burned all the furniture from my room after I was gone. Then there was a long march to the city gates. I kept stumbling because of the fever, but I could feel the machine guns pointing at my back. I'd never even heard of lycanthropy—it's one of those shameful

secrets adults keep from small children—and I thought
I was going to die without any idea why. I cried all the
way; I thought my parents didn't love me any more.
What surprises me is how many wolfies want to live.

"It's a one-way walk. You know, Francesco, I tried
to get a look at my house, a year afterwards. I got
caught by some kids. They got the whole neighbourhood after me. My older brother came out of the house.
He didn't recognize me. Or he pretended not to recognize me. I don't know which is worse. I didn't say anything, of course, and I was lucky that they just threw
me off the Rock; I know how to bounce softly. That day,
my brother taught me I wasn't Kenan any more; I was
just a wolfie, nothing else."

Kenan sighed and fell silent. Francesco thought
about a brother turned persecutor, about a broken
family.

When the temperature dropped again, he finished
exploring the network of caverns. Everywhere he met
smiles of compassion mixed with curiosity. He was the
first victim from beyond; more to be pitied than Gehennites, the smiles seemed to say. Fatima, who was his
guide throughout the long Gehennite afternoon,
showed him her own cave. They had time to play a
game of chess and talk a little. He even managed to joke
about the mess the rocky chamber was in. He was getting to know Fatima; she was generous and patient,
able to distract him from his dark thoughts and make
him laugh. All the wolfies were her friends. She
wouldn't dwell on depressing subjects, and she
laughed wordlessly when Francesco tried to say that
one day lycanthropy would be a curable disease. It was
easy to like her.

He was glad to see night arrive all the same. He
stayed an hour or two with Fatima, finishing a bowl of
vegetable soup, then he slipped out into the darkness,

alone. The cold only stimulated him, and he began to run, flying over the frozen ground between the multi-coloured tips of plants.

He now knew the secret of these plants, revealed by Fatima. The fruits of Gehenna—purple pomegranates, pink pears and sour potatoes—had to be picked at night to be edible. The lycanthropes organized teams to harvest them regularly. Without these fruits, the community would die of hunger. Lycanthrope metabolism demanded abundant and continuous alimentation.

He ran far into the heart of the desert, eating purple pomegranates as he felt the need; he liked their juicy flesh. He kept running until he reached the first outcrops of the northern mountains. The glaciers and snowcaps sparkled in the light of little Kidron.

On his way back, he couldn't resist visiting the miners camp he had just visited two days earlier. He fled with a miner's lunchbox; the miner would blame the mysterious night creatures, not realizing it was just an ordinary daytime wolfie. In a manner of speaking, he would be right, though, to think he was dealing with the indigenous fauna of Gehenna. Francesco laughed and ran off to an area where there were a number of little hillocks. He found a nook where he could settle in and enjoy the miner's meal.

When he got back to the cave, before daybreak, he was smiling and feeling lighthearted. His fur had grown in. He was becoming a real lycanthrope.

On his way in, he passed through the main cave and called out to a few lycanthropes whose names he remembered. Faces unfroze, eyes sent friendly messages. He had come home.

Fatima was waiting for him. She kissed him. She drew him to a cozy corner, covered with frayed blankets, and they lay down together to forget the inevitability of death and their terrible solitude.

Their coupling was short and intense, an image of their future.

Afterwards, a surge of optimism rose in him. He was alive and far from being the most unhappy of men. He watched Fatima reading in the glow of sunlight shining from a fissure in the rock, set a bowl of dried purple pomegranates within reach, and imitated her.

Later, when another of the long cold nights of Gehenna was beginning, he went out with Fatima. They spread a blanket at the top of the cliff and sat at the edge of the void, huddled up against one another.

The sand-laden wind of twilight was still blowing. The lights of Jigansk shone dimly in the dark, veiled by the dust in the air. Azazel was now only a thin crescent; Kidron had completely disappeared. Stars shimmered between clouds of sand.

Little by little, the wind died down and became a pure impalpable breath, a zephyr from the northern glaciers. The dust settled and Francesco brushed the grains of sand out of his fur. Yes, he was a wolfie, and there remained no anger or revolt in him at the thought.

Jigansk loomed out of the night. Glimmering lines filtering through the cracks of closed shutters looked like the lights of a strange ship tied up at a black dock. Its passengers had no idea how foreign the realm of the wolfies was. It was another world, a world of immaculate mountains lit by the moons of Gehenna, ochre plains scattered with purple trees, thin streams shaded by plants with succulent fruits and wild runs over a landscape devoid of human presence.

But the day would come, he knew, when these two worlds would meet. He had not been subjected to the vasectomy inflicted on the other lycanthropes and he would have children who would inherit the planet.

They would perhaps learn to cultivate the Gehennite plants and would surely replace the desert miners. The humans would share the planet with the wolfies. It would be both a revenge and an accomplishment.

Francesco murmured, "You know, Fatima, you were right. There are advantages. We are the ones who can survive and thrive on Gehenna. The whole planet belongs to us."

Fatima shrugged her shoulders, "Yes, the thought had occurred to me. We are the true Gehennites."

A new star appeared in the sky over Jigansk. It shone brightly for a moment, then faded in the distance. It was a ship taking off from the spaceport.

Francesco replied, suddenly saddened, thinking of the career which would have taken him to a dozen Imperial planets: "Yes, the planet belongs to us, but it is the only one. The planet belongs to us like the prison belongs to a prisoner."

"Don't be bitter, Francesco."

He shook himself, his mind already on the game of *go* he had promised to play with Kenan, but his eye stayed fixed on the rising star until it finally disappeared. Perhaps his children might travel between the stars, but he would never again see the forests of Bueno.

DOING
TELEVISION

WILLIAM
GIBSON

Santa Ana winds suck at the Soviet UV film Kelsey's mother tapes over the windows of their hotel room.

The wind finds other ways to enter the building; it hums in the dry shafts and corridors, sifting falls of pale dust from the ceiling tiles. Through the trembling membrane of Russian plastic, Kelsey sees the city burning gold in the brown air, the tall frayed stumps of dead palms receding along the avenue.

Behind her, on the floor, Trev does television, grunting softly as the dull black vest strapped across his chest thumps him in a fight scene. He does television all day, hogs the vest, the gloves, the black glasses, looping the same show over and over, *Gladiator Skull*. Kelsey hates *Gladiator Skull*, hates the way the vibrotactile vest punches you in the ribs if you let them get you. They always do.

She has a show called *Natureland* she loops sometimes; you ride a horse along a beach. *Natureland* doesn't punch you in the ribs. The sun can't even hurt you in *Natureland*.

In the park at the end of the avenue she can see prone figures wrapped in silvery reflective plastic, people with nowhere else to go.

Trev grunts again; his lips move. He talks to himself when he does television but she doesn't try to make out what he says. He probably doesn't know she can hear him.

He's probably forgotten they're moving to the Darwin Free Trade Zone in three days—the DFT, her mother called it, looping a travel show; Kelsey put on the black glasses and walked the length of a mall like any other mall, intercut with exterior shots of orange cargo helicopters lowering white housing-modules to a plain of raw earth, the young Chinese announcer's broad Australian vowels in her ears.

She runs her fingernail down the UV film, leaving the lightest possible scratch.

She likes it better when they live in Moscow, warm soup-smells and subways like old palaces, but they live where the company wants her mother. Her mother has a job but Kelsey doesn't know what it is. Something like doing television with numbers. When her mother talks about the company, Kelsey imagines a big animal. Her mother laughs, says that's right. Says the company has offices in all the big cities but it doesn't live anywhere, not in L.A. or Moscow or Singapore; says that cities and companies matter now, not countries.

Kelsey isn't sure what countries are. Lines on a map. Colors. A concept dim as aristocracy.

Kelsey has two passports, one issued by the United States of America, the other by her mother's company. The men in airports who look at passports only care about which company. Her mother's other passport is from a country called Quebec.

Kelsey looks out at the dead palms. Something spread up the coast from Mexico and killed them all.

She's seen live ones in *Natureland*.

The windowless black bulk of a police helicopter lumbers past in the gold-brown distance, level with Kelsey's eyes, its belly studded with sensors and weapons. At night she can hear shelling to the east. Flashes in the sky. The sound of helicopters.

The hotel flatscreen tells her the police are fighting the gangs. It's about drugs. These are drugs, the flatscreen says, showing her milky pale beads, bright green powder, something blood-brown and lumpy in a little plastic tube. Don't do these drugs, the flatscreen says. Trev knows the names: ice, dancer, brown.

The flatscreen flicks to the weather, to seroanalysis averages for California-Oregon, a factoid on EBV mutation rates, specific translocations at the breakpoint near the c-myc oncogene.

She tunes out. She hangs on the sound of the wind blowing west from the desert.

Closing her eyes, she sees Shibuya at night, the crowds under the lights, her father there, her biological father, the face she knows from pictures, reaching down to take her hand, explaining that her mother is her genetic mother, not biological, that Trev's biological was someone else, another surrogate; that he and her mother are separated now but the contracts remain in effect.

Eyes still closed, screwed up tight, she wills her mother's return from the mirrored towers, from the blank walls at street-level, the guards, the patient chopping of the eyeless gunships. From the city of burning gold.

Her brother curses softly, mechanically, losing his game, and she wishes she were already in Darwin, walking the miles of mall.

Like every mall anywhere.

Like doing television.

THE
WATER MAN

URSULA
PFLUG

The waterman came today. I waited all morning, and then all afternoon, painting plastic soldiers to pass the time. Red paint too in the sky when he finally showed; I turned the outside lights on for him and held the door while he carried the big bottles in. He set them all in a row just inside the storm door; there wasn't any other place to put them. When he was done he stood catching his breath, stamping his big boots to warm his feet. Melting snow made little muddy lakes on the linoleum. I dug in my jeans for money to tip him with, knowing I wouldn't find any. Finally I just offered him water.

We drank together. It was cool and clean and good, running down our throats in the dimness of the store. It made me feel wide and quiet, and I watched his big eyes poke around Synapses, checking us out, and while they did, mine snuck a peek at him. He was big and round, and all his layers of puffy clothes made him seem rounder still, like a black version of the Michelin man. He unzipped his parka and I could see a name, Gary, stitched in red over the pocket of his blue coverall. I still didn't have a light on; usually I work in the dark, save the light bill for Deb. But I switched it on when he coughed and he smiled at that, like we'd shared a joke. He had a way of not looking right at you or saying much, but somehow you still knew what he was thinking. Like I knew that he liked secrets, and talking without making sounds. It was neat.

Seemed to me it was looking water—a weird thought out of nowhere—unless it came from him. He seemed to generate them; like he could stand in the middle of a room and in everyone's minds, all around him, weird little thoughts would start cropping up— like that one. My tummy sloshing I looked too, and seemed to see through his eyes and not just mine. Through his I wasn't sure how to take it: a big dim room haunted by dinosaurs. All the junk of this century comes to rest at Synapses; it gets piled to the ceilings and covered with dust. If it's lucky it makes a Head; weird Heads are going to be the thing for Carnival this year, just as they were last, and Debbie's are the best. Her finished products are grotesque, but if you call that beautiful then they are; the one she just finished dangles phone cords like Medusa's hair, gears like jangling medals. Shelves of visors glint under the ceiling fixture; inlaid with chips and broken bits of circuitry, they hum like artifacts from some Byzantium that isn't yet. Two faced Janus-masks, their round doll eyes removed; you can wear them either way, male or female, to look in or out.

Gary was staring at them, a strange expression on his face. Like he wanted to throw up.

"Do you think they're good," I asked, to stop him looking like that.

"Good enough," he said, "if you like dinosaurs."

"I like them. They are strange and wonderful."

"But dinosaurs all the same," he said, his eyes

glinting like the mosaic visors. I looked for the source of light on his face but couldn't find it. Maybe he was one of the crazy watermen. You hear things, like that's the way they get sometimes; it comes from handling their merchandise too much. Fish-heads, people call them. After the deep ones, the ones that generate their own light.

"Whose water you gettin' now?"

"I never called a waterman before today."

"What do you drink?"

"Town water. But I just couldn't do it anymore."

"Yeah." It was sad, the way he said it.

"Only cold. For hot we have pots on the stove."

"Uh-huh. Baths down the street at the pool, am I right?"

"Showers, mostly. They don't clean the tubs out too often."

"I guess not."

"I heard your water was the best," I said, threading through the junk to the desk where I keep my cheque-book. I am a little proud of them, my cheques. My buddy and I designed them and he printed them up for me. They're real pretty, with phoenixes and water-melons. I had to clean his kitchen for a week in trade, but it was worth it.

Gary looked interested, his pop-eyes studying the tracery.

"What do I owe you for this fabulous water, Gare," I asked, punctuating my signature.

He moved his tongue around in his mouth so that his face bulged. A bulge here, a bulge there: his cheek a rolling ball.

"That is some way-out bank you belong to, miss. What did you say it was called?"

"It doesn't have a name. It's my own personal bank. Very secure. These cheques are not affected by the stock market."

"And a good thing, too," he nodded, agreeing with me. But he had his doubts. "I tell you what, miss. First delivery's usually free. You see how you like the water, you let me know. But the deposit on the bottles, I got to have that." He glared at me, wanting cash.

I hemmed and hawed, took him on a tour of the premises. Thing was, we had no cash. Well, we had a little, but Deb took it this morning to get her hair done. Half a dozen places in town would rather do your hair on account, and Deb has to pick one that only takes jazz. She can be a prima donna that way. But then, she is the Artist.

The store is a kind of a hodgepodge. I think she must have a call for the garbage, like a dog whistle; a supersonic whine that only it can hear. Because she cares about it. Garbage is her job; Deb rebirths obsolete appliances, toys, anything thrown away, non-organic. The ones that don't biodegrade, not quickly. It's recycling, only more so; this way they get an extra life on their slow way back to Earth. She makes it into art: sculptures; costumes for Carnival; Heads, mostly. She takes hockey helmets, the domes from those old-style hairdryers, hats, headbands. Anything to go around a head. Hot-glue gun, solder, she glues things to them: taken apart washing machines; orphan computers; microwave ovens. The grunts love it. Come February, they buzz in here like flies, picking up a couple of Heads apiece. Grunts have to wear something new every night of Carnival. A good thing, too: jazz. When it first comes in, I just like to do nothing, holding it all morning. It makes my skin happy. Deb doesn't like it; I don't do any work. She comes home, I'm sitting on the floor, playing with the money. She yells, sends me out to the co-op for a year of rice and beans.

Gare and I passed a rack of toys. Thirty years of Christmas, stacked up to the ceiling lights. Between the caved in Atari monitors and the bins full of busted Go-Bots, almost like an anachronism, was a shoebox of those little plastic domes where the snow is always falling. Gary stopped and picked one out, held it up to the light; a striped yellow fish danced among ferns. Once there had been a thread holding it suspended, but now it floated on its side: gills up, dead. He turned it over and over, like if he just waited long enough, and prayed hard enough, that fish would leap to life.

"It's nice," I said, my feet betraying me, shifting me from one to the other." I don't think I ever noticed it before."

"Nice? It's amazing! You don't know how long I've been looking for something like this! Look, here's the slot for the battery. It's got a light bulb—this one lights up in the dark!"

"So it does." His enthusiasm made me edgy. I waved the cheque like a slow flag, hoping he'd change his mind about my watermelons.

But he didn't. "Look, miss. I'll take this fish for the deposit. But from now on it's got to be jazz. If you want to keep getting the water."

"Hmm. Maybe town water's not so bad."

He laughed. "It's your funeral."

"I'll give you a call, Gare."

"Sure. If you can find me."

I'd gotten off easy and he was mad. It was just his luck I'd had something he wanted. "Thank-you for coming so soon after I called," I said, trying to placate him.

"It's very rare," he grumped. "Collector's material. I can sell it for a week of jazz uptown."

But you won't.

"No problem. I didn't even know we had it."

"No kidding." It was that look again, only in his voice; his hand wrapped around the toy, like he was saving it from something. From me. What did I care. He was almost out the door and then he stopped, staring at the shelves of Heads again. "You make those?"

"I put them together. But my partner, she's the designer."

"She's a healer, right?"

"Uh-huh."

"It shows." He nodded at the Heads, looked down at his opened hand, at the fish. He chuckled. It made me look at him, his handsome face, a big grin cutting it in two. You wanted to like him when he grinned. And his hands knocked me out. The brown backs opening to velvet palms, soft and shocking-baby pink. Yeesh. I wished I could have hands like that.

He did his other voice, cradling the fish like a baby. "I is going to fix this fish," he crooned. "This is a poor sick fish and needs mending."

The guy was not for real. But his water. "You a fish doctor too, Gare?" I asked, only half sarcastic. He turned on like a light bulb when I said that.

"That's very good, dear. Very, very good." He laughed, a happy laugh from deep down, and for once he didn't look like I made him sick. I was even afraid he wanted to give me a hug; his huge padded arms windmilling towards me like that. I backed away into the warmth; it was freezing, standing there in the opened door. "It's a kind of a side-line, my fish doctoring," he explained. "Like a fiddle. You know what a fiddle is?"

"Yeah, yeah," I said, "Economics 101," I slammed the door while I had a chance. He grinned, turning to cross the road; his feet leaving boat-sized holes in the slush. In the middle he stopped to turn and wave again. He was still chuckling when he gunned the van, his big head rolling like it was on bearings. "Pure spring," read the hand-lettered sign on the side. "A drink for sore throats." Weird. Like "a sight for sore eyes."

Three weeks to go. Deb sleeps at the studio, brings me the new designs in the morning. Flavour of the week is headbands; I've been stringing plastic soldiers onto lengths of ribbon cable. You know the stuff: rows of tiny coloured wires all stuck together, for connecting computers and all. When they're strung each soldier is painted to match a different strand of wire. "Rainbow Warrior," Deb calls 'em.

Two grunts came in this morning and bought Heads. Red Heads, blue Heads; colour is big this year. One also bought a box of old electronic parts, said he wanted to make his own. An arty grunt, yet. He was pale and like his friend wore a grey knee-length wool coat. They both looked young. But lately it seems like all the grunts look young: young and spooked.

They made half-scared google-eyes, told me it was their first time in a place like this: strictly non-grunt. Said they worked for banks. Tellers, must be: coats too thin for managers. It almost doesn't rate as a grunt job, being a bank teller. Too servile. Seems like it takes less and less to be a grunt these days. How sad.

"You mean there still is banks," I asked, doodling on my creative chequebook. I know there is still banks; I just wanted to make them nervous. I'm bad when it comes to young grunts. But jobs. For money. Geez.

The secret life of grunts. I do wonder what they think about. They must be on town water. I can't imagine ordering it in and still being a grunt. I can't remember ever even wanting to be a grunt, but I guess grunts want to be grunts. They must. Or else why would they? It's not like you have to be a wage-slave. There are other ways.

Another one came in this morning: a creepy older
one. He bought my window. It's something I do to relax, when I'm on break from Deb. I climb into the display window and rearrange the junk into scenes, make
a little Chaos out of the Order. Or is it the other way
around? I forget which. Anyway, this time I'd found a
plastic Doberman and hot-glued its mouth to Barbie's
crotch. I know there are worse things on this earth than
a little dog cunnilingus, but even Deb thought it was
maybe a little much. The grunt, however, loved it,
asked me if I did gift-wrap. I did: ripping a strip of red
off the velvet curtains left over from Synapses' previous
incarnation I tied it around the dog's neck. He loved it,
he told me, in that creepy voice; he loved the store and
he loved me. "Sure," I said, but I had to get a glass of
water right after he left just to get over his face. Maybe
that's how it happens to grunts; they get old when the
inside faces out too long, when instead of being scared
they're scary. And to think I cater to that market.
Yeeagh.

I used to think all water was the same. It was what
you drank for breakfast, had a little coffee to stir in if
you were lucky. It was a grunt drink. From Gary I
learned otherwise. This morning I brought a quart up
to the kitchen where I was working. I heated it up on
the stove, and sort of meditated, tried to think how
Gary would think it if he was doing the thinking. While
I was waiting I amused myself pushing the eyes into a
couple of old dolls. I sliced the faces off, attached them
one to another with bands of elastic. One male doll, one
female, the way you're supposed to do them. A type of
Janus. It's not a big seller, but it's lasted; every year we
do a few. When the water was warm I put the mask on

and drank, using a straw. I'd pierced the lips for straw holes—grunts won't buy anything they can't drink in. The water went down, warm and wet, and I felt like there were revolving doors inside me, turning, and all of a sudden I could go out the other way. And then I could see the whole deal: how we lived; how we did up our place; what we wore and what we ate: it was all because of drinking the town water. And this thing about getting your own water, it really worked. I could see how tacky it was: Synapses, Deb's and my life. A cheezy, no-class deal, except for some of the Heads. Like the Janus head. It was clean, a nice idea made flesh. I kept it on, poking around the place, looking out the eyes of Gary's water. It was fun. I saw things I hadn't seen before, like which things fit together and how come. I poked around in shoeboxes all afternoon, looking at junk.

Every day they bring more in. I wonder where it all comes from. Junk out of plastic, junk out of metal. They don't make so much junk as they used to, but boy, when they did, was it ever a going concern. It must have employed thousands of people, the junk industry. I wonder where they got the raw materials from. I mean, what is that cheap-o plastic made of, anyway? What natural substance has been humiliated in its service? I kind of got lost in the beauty of it, the beautiful ugliness of the cheap plastic objects I was handling. It occurred to me then they were beautiful precisely because they were ugly, and I even know a few people like that, although some of them are dead. But the more my thoughts headed off in that direction the gladder I became I work for Deb. Because, you know, I used to feel sorry for them. We'd be shopping for clothes at Thrift Villa or wherever, and there'd be shelves full of broken down toasters and waffle irons, and I'd think how nobody cared about them, not even my Mom.

Everyone always wanting the new one: clean ones, without any scratches or deformities, in good working order and with high I.Q.'s. That is why I love Deb so much. She was the first person to see that all that old stuff wanted to still be used; it wanted so badly to have a purpose for us. So Deb thought and thought of how to use it, and finally she came up with the whole style of wearing garbage to Carnival, and now everyone does it, us and all the grunts.

Things have been different lately, I don't know why. Funny thoughts come to me while I work. That we are like fish in an aquarium, looking out at the world. I think it's since Gary came that it's been different. I never did any of that computing but my buddy Danny, the one who does the cheques, he told me it is like that. Programming. It is like going into inner space. And I think maybe Gary's water is like that too, like going into space. To think I never knew. No wonder he was looking at me like that.

Two weeks. Carnival soon. I've started a new window. I work on it during breaks. TV sets done up like aquariums. Somehow they look the same: a clear glass box. I have a milk crate full of plastic fish; I string them from the inside of the TVs so they look like they're swimming. Take the picture tubes out, of course. And one real aquarium. A glass fishbowl I found upstairs that fits perfectly into one of the smaller TVs. I went down to Woolco and bought live fish for it. I paid for them with some of the grunt money. The dog-grunt money, to be precise. I lied to Deb, told her Danny gave them to me, that I washed his floors for him. She doesn't like me doing anything that costs money. Also she doesn't understand I have to make my own art sometimes. The windows. That's my art. That and the thoughts, the weird water ones.

Out of water. Once you get the new water, it's hard to go back to the old. I haven't thought so much in years. Even Deb likes me better, gives me time off in the afternoons to work on the window. It's very beautiful, now, almost finished. I wonder how I ever did dogs and dolls. I could never go back to that now. Phoned Gary but there was no answer. Shit. Town water sucks.

Don't forget to dream. To bring in the new world. Otherwise the old one just keeps rolling on. Death as predecessor to rebirth. The seed, sleeping in the earth. The purpose of winter. Subtle changes taking place, deep in the darkness underground. Winter, Carnival, bringing back the sun. New windows. Fish-televisions? But what is the death? The underworld. Being fish. What will we be, when we're not fish?

First day of Carnival. The grunts pour into the street, displaying their wares. Who will buy, and who will be bought? The one time of year they get to ease up. Bread and circus. For two weeks they live what is ours the whole year through. I felt so still, so empty inside. Deb was out, being photographed for something. I sat in the window, watching the grunts parading, wearing their garbage regalia. They were beautiful:

moving in slow motion, with dream smiles on their faces. They looked happy. I recognized some of their Heads as ones we'd done. They smiled and waved at me, sitting among my fish-TVs. Who is looking in and who is looking out. It is like the Janus mask. Tomorrow I will wear it.

I feel so still. In Carnival they act it out, the death and rebirth. But this year it's like it's real: Janus-eyes in the back of my head. Gary came. He grinned and gesticulated, stamping his feet on the other side of the glass. He waved his hands. I wanted to see it, his beautiful skin, but he was wearing mitts. He brought the water. He carried it into the window where I was sitting, and we each had some. It was cool and clean and good, running down our throats in the cold morning. When we weren't thirsty anymore he made me come outside, showed me how Synapses' window was like a television too, or an aquarium, and I the fish in it. I knew where there was a big box of grease crayons in the back, and we drew it onto the glass: the outline of the screen and the control panel. I even found a fish costume in a drawer of stuff Deb did in the days before there were Heads.

He sat beside me for a long time, and we looked out the window, part of the display. A big quiet black man and a thin white girl dressed up as a fish. The Carnival faces passed us, a white dressed throng, wearing Heads made of all their old stuff, and I was content as I've ever been. Finally understanding it, the meaning of Carnival. The old flesh dying to the new. They passed with the skeleton then, an effigy held high above their heads.

"Whose death is it this time, Gare?" I asked.

He put his big mitten out, covering my knee. "It is the death of Death."

"And the birth of Life?"

"Yes."

"That's what I thought. I'm glad I'm here to see this one."

"It is an interesting time."

He rose stiffly in his great padded knees, wearing a parka and thick quilted pants like always.

"I will be going then."

"I'm glad I know you, Gary."

"I, too. I will be coming by from time to time, to see how you are doing."

"Goodbye, Gary, goodbye."

Roses. It will be the next window. Flowers will bloom out of all the televisions there are. In the meantime it snows. Soft white snow falling like it does in a plastic bubble of fish, its string repaired. It sits on top of one of the televisions, where Gary left it for me to discover. Its light bulb glows softly in the darkening day.

GUINEA PIG

FRANCINE PELLETIER

Translated from the French by Jane Brierley

"I never told you about him."

Albert Ferrier speaks these words quietly. Carla isn't listening, in any case. In a moment he knows she'll sink into the habitual daydream that gives her such a strangely profound expression—a door opening onto another world.

Dappled light bathes the living room. The sun's rays barely filter through the shutters, slicing bright strips onto the faded oriental rug. Carla has always liked this artificial gloom. Beyond the blinds is the forest—or rather the underbrush that hides the house from the neighbours' eyes. A path of pale sand slopes down to the lake with the occasional sharp drop. Their son Peter, much like the Carla of other days, loves to race down the slope and hurl himself into the chilly water.

The clock chimes six. Peter will soon be home with his uncle.

Yesterday's newspaper covers the coffee table, protecting the fine wood from the perils of gouache pots. Carla has always adored painting. But she's not the one who's left the open pots on the table. Why does his son have to be so like her, even in his pastimes?

Ferrier settles into an armchair. His eye has been caught by an outdated news item—a three-column headline: "Organovator Seeks Donor for Daughter."

Organovator . . . how long is it since he's read or heard that word?

"I met him at St. Luke's, during the treatments."

If Carla hears the allusion to this dark period of her life, she doesn't show it. But Ferrier isn't really speaking to her; he's talking to himself.

"At the height of the epidemic. Their filthy tricks that started the contamination had just been exposed. The hospitals were overwhelmed with patients, pregnant women for the most part. A real catastrophe. And there they were, telling us that the foetus might have pulmonary and cardiac malformations. That perhaps a transplant was the only thing that would save our children. The mobs that descended on the hospitals! People were practically reserving a spot for their child, for the future of their child. . ."

His voice has dropped again. Carla tilts her head slightly in his direction. Is she listening?

"Brinberg was at his wife's bedside. They weren't sure she'd pull through, just like you. And as with our Peter, they'd tried to minimize the risks by transferring the foetus *in vitro*. We could only wait, he and I, and the similarity of our predicament brought us together. But the comparison stopped there. Augustus Brinberg had the world at his feet, whereas I. . ."

Carla has momentarily turned towards him, her expression once more attentive. Albert gazes at her. The centre of his life. Who is already looking away.

"You can't imagine what they were like, our talks in the waiting room. Brinberg was a big-boned man with an impressive physique. Think of someone taller than your brother Jonathan, but three times more muscular. And he had a voice that shook glass. A voice that could become persuasive when he talked about his project. . ."

Carla smiles, faintly mocking.

"Yes, I know what became of the Brinberg project. There were all those public protests: *Que sera, sera,* we can't interfere with God's work. As if any god could be responsible for a stupid contamination! The government was obliged to ban 'organoculture'. But you know, at the time it was said the official decision was just a front. That the government couldn't reject Augustus Brinberg's project, and that somewhere one of these organ farms must exist. . ."

Ferrier stops, an unspoken comment on his lips.

The irony of fate! Brinberg unable to set up the project that would have saved his own daughter today!

Now Carla is wearing her slightly sad smile. Ferrier sighs.

"All the same . . . I often say to myself that you never know. If Brinberg did keep on with his project . . . if Peter should ever . . . I couldn't bear to lose him, too."

Footsteps pound on the porch. The screen door bangs open, screeching on its hinges. Two figures appear against the light: tall, slim Jonathan and the slight silhouette of Peter. Two graceful bodies, like Carla—too much like Carla.

The small boy, brimming with good spirits, rushes into the kitchen. Jonathan stops beside Ferrier's chair.

"Who were you talking to, Albert?"

Ferrier shrugs. His gaze is immutably fixed on the hologram in which his beloved wife moves gently through a series of movements that he knows by heart.

✧ ✧

She ought to go in now. When the breeze by the river gets cool and the leaves look greeny-gold with the sun playing on them, she knows it's time to go back to the house.

The steep street makes a perfect skateboarding rink. Each summer the neighbourhood children perform the same daredevil tricks. She looks enviously at them, then quickly turns her head away. Even if they did invite her—but they wouldn't, they know her now—she couldn't accept. Aunt Aline wouldn't allow it. Aunt Aline doesn't allow much. No skiing in winter, and definitely no tobogganing on the school hill. No baseball in summer, no roller skates. "You're too precious for such dangerous games," explains Aunt Aline when the youngster asks why. *Precious?*

She walks along, head hanging. Only when she nears the house does she lift her head and see the car.

A limousine, as they say on TV. A limousine *with* a TV. Inside, behind the tinted windows, the chauffeur is watching an animated coloured screen. He hasn't seen her coming. She makes a wide detour so he won't notice her. She'll keep going as far as the Duponts' house—get through the hedge, reach the back door, and slip into the cellar without being seen by *them*.

Maybe these aren't the same men as the other time. Maybe they won't make Aunt Aline cry. The child was very young then, not even in proper school. Just in kindergarten. Aunt Aline wouldn't explain, that day or later. She hugged the child so hard it hurt.

This isn't the same car now, but it looks exactly like the other one.

The hedge smells sweet and the bees are still buzzing inside the pink flowers. She must be careful not to disturb them and get stung.

The windows are wide open on this hot, early summer day.

"You haven't lived with her for all these years." Aunt Aline's voice sounds broken. Those men have made her cry already.

"She's just a guinea pig to you, but to me she's a defenceless little human being!"

The child doesn't understand. What's a guinea pig? She'd like to ask, but she must stay absolutely still.

The voice answering Aunt Aline is calm, a man's voice, totally unmoved. "When we found her two years ago, Masson, we warned you that she was living on borrowed time. She was conceived for *that* and nothing else."

Another voice intervenes, a smoother voice. "Must I tell the farm director about your unwillingness to co-operate?"

"That won't be necessary," replies Aunt Aline quickly, her voice lowered. She isn't crying now.

"Where is she?" The smooth voice again.

The child hears no answer, just the first voice ordering, "Call her." She shrinks back. No need to hear Aunt Aline's slow step on the stairs. No need to hear the screen door squeak. She's already beyond the hedge and in the Duponts' yard when she hears Aunt Aline calling nervously. She wants to block her ears, but she needs every ounce of energy to dart between the garden furniture and into the open garage. The sudden contrast between the bright day and the gloom of the garage blinds her, and she has to feel her way forward. Don't go out into the street. Once out of the shelter of the garage, hug the wall until the next hedge, and then run.

She's forgotten the dog. When he starts barking she freezes, her heart almost bursting in her chest. Luckily the monster is tied up for once. The rope isn't long enough and she's safe. Quick, over the fence!

She falls into a free-for-all. Clarissa is in the pool,

shrieking with laughter while roughhousing and splashing with her little brother Anthony. The child hesitates, panting wildly. The children's mother is sitting on the patio, watching her progress with a puzzled smile.

"Hello, honey. What's up? You'd think the devil was on your heels!"

Margot always speaks to her in that gentle voice. The child wants to run away again before Margot answers Aline's cries, cries that will certainly be heard if the children stop roughhousing in the pool. But her legs are buckling under her and she falls against the chair. Margot catches the child and enfolds her.

"Poor honeybun! Tell Margot what's the trouble."

The child realizes she's crying and begins to sob twice as hard. "Don't let them take me away! I don't want to be a guinea pig!"

Margot is astounded. "Who wants to take you away?"

"Some men," the child hiccups. "Some men in a big car. They made Aunt Aline cry and now she's looking for me so they can take me away."

Clarissa is out of the pool now, leaving Anthony to frolic by himself. Above the splash of the water comes the faint ring of Aunt Aline's voice. Margot straightens up at the sound, her hand resting on the child's shoulder. Her fingers are trembling. Margot probably hasn't forgotten the day the men came that first time, either.

Clarissa wraps herself in a bathrobe and comes over. "What's the matter? Are you hurt?"

"Leave her alone." Margot's voice is a little brusque.

Clarissa looks at her mother in surprise. Margot pushes the two children toward the patio door.

"Take her inside, Clarissa."

"But I'm all wet!" protests Clarissa, accustomed to being scolded.

"Go to the cellar and stay there, understand?"

The relieved child goes willingly. She'll put her trust in Margot.

Unrevealed sources say a donor has been found for the Brinberg child.

The newspaper is spread out in front of him, hot off the printer. He stares at it, not moving. He wants to read the article but doesn't.

Laughter. The door bursts open and in come Peter and his uncle, bringing noise and movement into the room.

"Does it ever smell stuffy in here!" cries the boy, holding his nose.

"You're right," says Jonathan, opening the shutters.

Ferrier blinks in the sudden light. Peter comes up to the table and ruffles the newspaper spread awkwardly over the gouache pots.

"Give me that. It's mine!" Ferrier snatches the paper from the small hands. Peter's arms go limp and his mouth twists—Carla's mouth in a child's face.

"You're not going to start bawling!"

Jonathan strides over protectively. "Listen, Albert—"

"This is *my* house. You'd think I was some kind of intruder!"

Jonathan stares at him. Their eyes lock. Albert can't stop himself from blinking. The young man looks away, finally.

"Yes, it's your house, your newspaper . . . your son."

So little your son, so much Carla's. Jonathan rests a hand on his brother-in-law's arm. "Albert . . . Peter's got a right to live. He needs friends, pals his own age."

The boy protests. "But you're my friend, Jo!"

Jonathan quickly leans over. Albert is forgotten, old Albert and his heartbreak. "I *am* your friend, Peter. But don't you remember what fun it was last summer when Mrs. Joly's grandchildren came to visit? When we all used to go swimming together?"

Ferrier moves onto the porch, hugging the paper to his chest. Pay no attention to the conspiratorial laughter of Jonathan and the boy as they trade summer memories. He sinks into a garden chair that creaks beneath his weight. The paper forms a curious hummock on his abdomen. Bits of headline tease him. *Donor . . . child. . .*

If Augustus Brinberg did go on with it. . . What a project!

Ferrier can still hear the animated voice echoing through the years. "I'm going to develop organoculture, Ferrier. Cultivate human organs." Was that such a crazy idea? Cultivate human organs, grow them like innumerable clones. Set up a permanent organ bank that would reproduce itself. No longer wonder about a child's future because there were no organs available when the transplant became necessary. . .

Nobody wanted to believe that Brinberg had *really* given up his project. Ferrier as much as the others.

He tips his head back in his chair and stares at the tongue-in-groove on the porch ceiling, trying to read the past and the future. What would a Brinberg "farm" be like? He imagines huge, gloomy rooms filled with rows of enormous tubs, the atmosphere hermetic, humidified. Behind the half-transparent walls of the containers one guesses at human forms, half human, incomplete. . .

One of them has long blond hair floating around him in the amber liquid. Floating around her. The eyelids open slightly. She stirs. The fingers stretch and the hands grip the edge of the tub. She's coming out.

Carla!

"Are you okay, Albert?"

No, that's not Carla standing in the doorway. It's Jonathan. Ferrier glowers at him. He moves away.

What if Brinberg's project has been successfully carried out?

The phone rings and rings at the other end. Margot's fingers tighten their hold on the edge of the table.

"Hello."

A man's voice, one she doesn't know. Has she dialled the wrong number? She might well have, being so nervous and all. No, she's known that number by heart for years.

"Is this Aline Masson's house? I'd like to speak to her."

The moments tick by, and then she hears her friend's voice. A little hoarse, hesitant.

"Aline I have to tell you—"

"I can't talk to you this morning, Margot. Call back later."

"But Aline—" Suddenly doubt assails her. What if one of the men is listening? A sleepy Julian is waiting for her, leaning an arm against the doorjamb. Margot avoids his mocking glance.

"I couldn't talk to her."

He smiles slightly, and she adds quickly, "It's not normal, Julian. I'm not letting the child go."

"And I'm not letting you make a mountain out of a molehill. There's a simple explanation for all this, I'm positive. Just speak frankly to Aline. And as for keeping the child here another night—I'm not keen to face charges of kidnapping and illegal restraint. We've got enough kids around here, anyway, and it's none of our business."

"Julian!"

Downstairs the children stop laughing.

Later, Julian is reading in the living room. Suddenly he heaves a sigh. "Well, there's your friend. She's talking to our neighbour."

Margot rushes outside. Aline, her brow furrowed, sees her coming.

"She's looking for the child," explains the neighbour. "Have you seen her?"

Margot is about to answer, Aline's expression is a warning. Only then does she see the man standing a few paces behind. He's wearing a lightweight linen suit, and there's nothing threatening about him, apart from the dark eyes watching Aline.

"They informed the police yesterday evening," adds the neighbour.

Police? Margot looks at the dark-eyed man again. Is this a policeman?

Aline puts her hand over Margot's. An icy hand. And asks with forced gaiety, "Why, it's ages since I've seen you, Margot. How's your mother? Does she still have her house in the country?"

The neighbour looks at her in amazement. What an odd subject of conversation when a child is missing! But Aline's eyes hold quite another message. Margot replies gently, "My mother's fine. It's Julian who's in a foul mood these days. I think I'm going to take the kids away for a while. What do you think?"

"Good idea. You can go to your mother's."

Margot hates this cat-and-mouse game, hates the man who moves forward, face impassive, eyes fixed on Aline.

"I've got to go, Margot. Have a good trip," says Aline agitatedly.

Julian has followed it all from the living window. He turns around as she comes in. "Who was that guy?"

"I don't know. Aline didn't dare speak in front of him, I'm positive."

Julian shakes his head gently. "Aren't you getting carried away again?"

"She *knows* the child is here, Julian. She even gave me to understand that she wanted me to take her away. She suggested we go to my mother up at the lake."

Exasperated, he lifts his eyes to the ceiling. Of course he doesn't want to believe it, yet he must. . .

"Julian, she says they've told the police. Do you think they behave like this when a seven year old child disappears so close to a river? Have you noticed any patrols walking around, any boats?"

This time he hesitates. "Well, they usually rush to the spot. They don't wait around, and there's no reason for them to be so discreet about it."

"I'm going with the three children, Julian, just like she suggested. She knows that I visit Mother, and I'm sure I gave her the phone number. It'll be up to her to call me."

He opens his mouth, but she doesn't give him time to retort.

"I've made up my mind Julian, whether you agree or not."

He acquiesces with a pale smile. "I'll tell Clarissa and Anthony. And Augustine."

Why does he grab the newspaper as soon as it emerges from the printer? He scans the pages, morbidly jealous. Bad news.

Brinberg rumour denied. No miracle donor.

He chuckles maliciously, pleased to see that some-

one else won't be spared. It soothes his suffering. . .
So, even the rich, powerful Augustus Brinberg can't
avoid Fate?

An yet he can't help being sorry. What if his own
son were in the same predicament? His son, so like
Carla, all that's left him of Carla. This son on the porch
just outside, to whose presence he's oblivious.

What if he got in touch with Brinberg again?
They're not the only ones living in this permanent state
of anxiety. All those men sitting, like them, in the fraud-
ulently cheery hospital waiting rooms. . . Together they
could form an impressive lobby, forcing the authorities
to remove the six-year-old ban. To create farms for raising human replicas, ready to be used when needed.

On the porch Peter and Jonathan are planning a
swim. Ferrier stops on the doorsill, smiling as he watches them. His son stands still for a second, surprised at
his father's good humoured expression, then jumps at
him, happy to share his joy.

"Mrs. Joly's got visitors, Dad. Girls—well, there's a
boy, but he's just a baby. The girls know how to swim,
though, so it's all right. One of them wasn't here last
summer. She's not bad—for a girl, anyway. Are you
coming swimming with us?"

Ferrier accepts the invitation passively, either overwhelmed by the flood of words or perhaps already distracted by his train of thought. The boy is disappointed.
Jonathan puts a hand on his shoulder. "Come along,
Peter, let's get into our bathing suits."

Ferrier, a dreamy expression in his eyes, has his
own plans to work out.

Call Brinberg. He'll find the number somewhere.
Offer to help. Their children won't die. He swears it.

FINAL INSTRUCTIONS

LESLEY CHOYCE

Unfold an open sky inside your chest
and crowd out the clutter
with robin egg blue
until the land shrinks back
to the green horizon.
As you open your eyes
you see yourself
from a thousand chlorophyl cameras.

Your quiet nesting arranges the colour
of dawn around you like a fibrous rainbow
and you sink back into weightless splendour
as the wind chants
and builds immaculate pillars
to hold up the falling sky
until moons and planets
begin to tug at the roots
of living things.

AFTERWORD

CANDAS JANE DORSEY

TOWARDS A REAL SPECULATIVE LITERATURE:
WRITER AS ASYMPTOTE

Thinking back: thinking forward. Speculative fiction in Canada: how it used to be; how we define it; how it is going to be.

Used to be so simple. SF stood for science fiction and it was a Genre. Genres are formulaic, predictable, one thing or another; so it was easy to see SF as a strobe, a binary flash, on-off-on-off, beyond control. That kind of periodicity in lights can trigger electrical storms in the brain. But what is a state of speculation, "on" or "off"? "On", like a light, a current, a performer; "off", like a racer, a rocket or a firework? And what storms did it aim to generate in what brain? What was a preferable state, on or off? Binary, the dialectic, then seemed essential to modern scientific method—but now even computers are not binary, are based on neural nets and parallel processing: now a computer circuit can speak Sanskrit, encompass four valences (on, not on, maybe both, maybe neither). All this defines another kind of speculative prose.

What remains the same is that speculative writing is revolutionary, ghettoised, trivialised, falsely lionised, popluarised and all those affixed words used by whatever fictions are speaking at the time to describe a simple phenomenon. Paul Tillich wrote: "The boundary is the best place to acquire knowledge." It has also been the best place to spin it off—the ragged edges of a jelly-fish, the aurora at the earthly edge of the sun's corona, galaxies spinning out matter. Waiting: eventually, some-one will look up.

Meanwhile—those cosmic rays tear through those of us who write, and some of the electrical storms in us are not very pleasant either.

What became clearer all the time was that truly speculative writing is always that asymptotic line on the graph which spends its career approaching, never arriv-ing; always in transit between two imaginary points: take-off and destination; and therefore always beyond the binary, free to understand its fallacy. An impulse in progress is only the length of a synaptic gap, yet able to traverse light-years as quickly as any subatomic particle. But never the comfortable arrival, never the relaxed armchair and footstool at journey's end, never at home though always coming home. To live that way for a writer is not easy, even before the confrontation between what Guy Kay calls "practitioners seeking quality" and those whose idea of speculative fiction is a genre ghetto of adolescent wish-fulfillment and coming-of-age rituals.

(By the way, it is fine writing a groundbreaking lit-erature if everyone knows it: if one knows one can be shot for it, or threatened with shooting, or, more happily, just lionised. Salman Rushdie is now a worldwide sym-bol of one collision of fixed boundaries. He is one of us, you know: saints don't fall from airplanes, and the fact that such fancies can threaten the raison d'etre of nations is just what I'm talking about: here we are on the cutting, maybe even killing edge. Few pettinesses can withstand the onslaught of myth—they must either suppress it or be destroyed, c.f. Jung, William Irwin Thompson, and Harlan Ellison. If we accept we're rewriting human-kind's essential stories, we risk hubris; but if we don't, we risk losing our value and our self-respect.)

Over the years the predicaments became clear, then were left behind. Once, Canadian SF writers' main prob-lem was trying to live with one foot in and one out of the world of—pardon the expression—free enterprise: sell-ing south of the border, and what happened to our work there. We saw that Gibson, Wilson, de Lint and Gotlieb made it into US print, but had garish space-girl covers on their books only slightly less often than Piers Antho-ny or a shared-world novelist. Those in the CanLit main-stream didn't know these names? Yes, and tens of thousands of SF fans in Canada, faces three-quarter turned to the glitter of the US pulp mass market, and in the main scarcely aware of the glimmer of brilliance at home, had never heard of the speculative writers of the Canadian tradition (which is mine, and so I always took it for granted): Sheila Watson, George Elliott, Robertson Davies, Rudy Wiebe, Marion Engel, Gwendolyn MacE-wan, Jack Hodgins, Timothy Findley—and so many more. If one was lucky, one or two of them had already heard of Margaret Atwood before the movie was made of her *Handmaid's Tale*. C'est tout. (And as for the Québe-cois SF writers, find an anglo of any stripe who knew Elisabeth Vonarburg and already you had found a rarity. Welcome to multiculturalism—a rant for another time.)

There we were. Different countries. Couldn't get the average SF fan snob to even IMAGINE there was a Canadian literary tradition of speculation, alienness, ex-ploration of frontiers in and outside self (a tradition by the way which did decades ago what US writers call postmodern in the SF world)—let alone read the stuff. Couldn't get the average academic CanLit snob to read anything with a lurid cover, or even in trade paperback format, let alone to admit an impressive body of great writing there in that "genre ghetto" SF. "Scifi", they liked to call it, very snotty and righteous; "mundane", the SFans liked to say, equally snide.

Yet out of this forest of mixed motives, out of this nation of enclaves, there has been coming for years now a fine, varied, growing, unique literature of speculation. Not monolithic or even binary, but full spectrum, multiplex, intense. And the boundaries we used to perceive, and along which we used to range ourselves, are changing, are even—hurrah!—disappearing. Academics and fans meet at Canadian conventions devoted to reading the writers of home; all of them know something about the others' purview, and all of them know something about the synthesis: which is the land where we live, the land of Canadian speculative fiction, defined by all the influences and certainly not simply binary. One might almost call it multicultural, and happily so (for a change). Because meanwhile (circle round again), some of us have been simply writing. Ask us what. Those of us canny enough to have disguised ourselves in the garish face-paint of the American pulp tradition know all their labels and say things like "heroic fantasy" and "technowizardry" and "cyberpunk". Others of us keep our skirts closely gathered around us in that territory, not to become infected, and call it "magic realism" and "postmodernism" and perhaps in a daring moment "fantastic" or even, radically, "speculative". Then there are some of us with two names or two minds or with a kind of schizy double vision, who began to walk the strange land between. Walking the border, the boundary if you will, as if it were a tightrope, our toes clinging to the narrow line through the special soft shoes one must wear to do tricks on the high wire. The best of us, of course, are those flying up from the wire to do aerobatics above all categories. And in the last five years or so, all of us have been finding the boundary zone widening to become a whole country, comfortable enough to live in.

The Americans are catching up, learning an act we've practised for some time, as their SF writers find the boundaries with the mundane blurring, becoming frighteningly invisible, disappearing into a new landscape. They could take lessons from English-Canadian and Québecois SF writers—we know a lot about several kinds of cultural schizophrenia. Witness Albertan H. Hargreaves, whose scholarship of medieval French comes to light with his translation of Fontanelle's conversations on the Plurality of Worlds, while the fans know him only as a British-published senior SF writer yclept Hank.

Whether or not we are good at talking about what we write, though, we are writing it. Keeping in step just enough to get published, in US pulp SF mags or Canadian literary mags, it matters little so long as there's a chance to be read, to change the world, to make it count. Yet stepping as far outside the norms, the genre strictures, as we can, because changing the world, the changing world, is what matters most. We are reading each others' work, across boundaries which in the reading become invisible, and we are learning that we have common preoccupations.

For instance: *What for?* replaces *What if?* as the SF question at least half the time these days. David-Suzuki-fed question: will we make it in time? We have ten years. SF-fed belief: the work we do is as important to change as is recycling, cleaning up rivers, reforestation, or going to Neptune via Voyageur. Changing people's minds. Have we changed minds, ours or anyone's?

Okay, that's what we want to be doing, strobing those traditional values with a new light—sound like on-off potentiality, positive and negative, entropy and information again? The battle between good and evil, if you will? But in fact, we have no battles, nothing binary, just new vision, 20/20 for a change, telescopic even or wideangle, full-spectrum, holistic: lateral X linear = ? And "?" is our business. Our question. Our answer.

Now, just to confuse the issue, let me take this term speculative fiction which I have, with others of similar minds, and encourage the Canadian community to adopt to distinguish our work and identify our own tradition. Let me take it and transform it yet again by saying: what fiction is not speculative? Is *Anna Karenina* documentary? Did Silas Marner exist? And Riel, though he certainly existed, did he speak the words Wiebe gave him; did Big Bear think the thoughts likewise?

Give me a novel that is not set in a parallel universe —St. Petersburg or Manawanka—simply by virtue of being fiction. So we are not so different from mainstream swimmers after all, except that we made our worlds a little fancier—except that we like salmon moved more freely between salt water and fresh, while some like trout stayed in narrower streams. But both of us have to swim against the current to spawn, to create, to make the culture of the next generations possible. We just have more garish covers on some of ours. Think nothing of it. Like children dressed to impress grandparents, we didn't choose our clothes.

But we are not children, and the tracks we have followed to grandparents' houses have brought us into the dangerous realms of many forests, far from initial influences, under the yellow eyes of many wolves. Like typical Canadians, we do not fight it: we map the forest, make friends with the wolves, and emerge from the woods subtly changed, having also transformed forests, wolves, and even our grandparents into something new, strange, wonderful.

All in search of new worlds, or new ways to define the old. Where did we begin? Everywhere, nowhere. By now, the beginning is lost, the change is constant, and the journey never stops.

THE CONTRIBUTORS

Colleen Anderson is a graduate of the Clarion Writers Workshop, a member of HELIX and the Burnaby Writers Society. Her poetry has been sold to such magazines as *Amazing Stories, Starline, Silver Apple Branch* and the *Round Table*. She is currently working on an SF novel which centers around the same world described in "Phoenix Sunset".

Margaret Atwood is one of Canada's most distinguished writers with over thirty books of poetry, fiction and criticism in publication. She has won the Governor General's Award for poetry in 1967 and for fiction in 1985 for *The Handmaid's Tale*, which also won her the Arthur C. Clarke Award for Best SF in 1987. Her most recent book is *Cat's Eye*.

Ven Begamudré was born in South India and now lives in Regina, Saskatchewan, where he has received the 1990 City of Regina Writing Award. "Vishnu's Navel" is from his recently released book *A Planet of Eccentrics* (Oolichan Books, 1990).

Jane Brierley is a literary translator, writer and editor. She is the President of the Literary Translators' Association of Canada. Among her most recent translations are *Yellow-Wolf & Other Tales of the St. Lawrence* by Philippe Aubert de Gaspé (Vehicule Press) and *The Silent City* by Elisabeth Vonarburg. She is currently working on the translation of Vonarburg's *Chroniques du Pays des Mores*.

Cliff Burns is a freelance writer living in Regina, Saskatchewan. He has had over sixty of his short stories published, and has a short-story anthology, *Sex and Other Acts of the Imagination*, due to be published in late 1990.

Joël Champetier has published several stories in *Solaris* and *Imagine*. He has an avid interest in cinema and contributes to the "SF Cinema Chronicle" in *Solaris*. His latest short story, "Coeur de Fer", appeared in *Solaris*, No. 93. He lives in Ville-Marie, Quebec.

Lesley Choyce is the editor/publisher of Pottersfield Press, and has also authored 14 books of prose and poetry. His autobiography *An Avalanche of Ocean* (Goose Lane, 1987) was a finalist for the Leacock Award for Humour.

Charles de Lint is one of Canada's most successful writers of science fiction. His most recent novel, *Dreaming Place*, was published in the fall of 1990 and he has another novel, *Little Country*, coming in January 1991. He won the Casper Award in 1988 for his novel *Jack the Giant-Killer* and the William L. Crawford Award for Best New Fantasy Author in 1984. He lives in Ottawa.

Candas Jane Dorsey is a writer of poetry and fiction. She and her co-writer, Nora Abercrombie, won the Ninth Annual Three-Day Novel Writing Contest in 1987 for *Hard-Wired Angel*. Her collection of short SF fiction, *Machine Sex and Other Stories*, was published in the Tesseracts series in 1988 and in the UK in 1990. As well as her own writing, Candas frequently leads writing workshops and was the editor of a monthly arts journal. She lives in Edmonton with Chris, two cats and some fish.

Dave Duncan is the author of eight novels, including *West of January* (1989) which won a 1990 Casper Award, *Strings* (1990), and *Magic Casement* (December 1990) which is the first in a new series of fantasy stories. He has four more books being published in 1991. He lives in Calgary.

Pat Forde is currently living in Toronto working on two novels, one mainstream, one science fiction. He has studied under James Gunn in his Science Fiction Writing Workshops at the University of Kansas.

Leslie Gadallah took up writing SF after a career as a chemist. She has also written popular science articles for newspapers, radio and magazines. She has had several short stories published as well as three SF novels. Her latest novel is *Cat's Gambit*.

James Alan Gardner is presently a technical writer for Software Development Group at the University of Waterloo. He has published a score of short stories and full-length plays, and was also the recipient of the L. Ron Hubbard Gold Award (Grand Prize) in the 1989 Writers of the Future contest.

William Gibson is the author of *Neuromancer* (which won several prestigious SF awards), *Count Zero*, *Burning Crome* and *Mona Lisa Overdrive*. He lives in Vancouver.

Leona Gom is the author of five books of poetry and two novels, the latest being *Zero Avenue* (Douglas & MacIntyre, 1990). Her first novel, *Housebroken*, won the Ethel Wilson Award in 1986. She taught Creative Writing at Kwantlen College for 15 years, a position from which she has just resigned.

Phyllis Gotlieb, co-editor of *Tesseracts²*, has been writing SF and poetry for over 25 years. She is one of the major figures of Canadian science fiction, with books such as *Sunburst* (Fawcett, 1964) and *O Master Caliban!* (Harper, 1976) translated into six languages. Her latest writing is *Heart of Red Iron*.

Kelly Graves lives in Camrose, Alberta, and has been a fan and writer of SF for a number of years. "Against the Dust" is his first published work.

John Greene is Associate Professor of French at the University of Victoria, where he teaches a course in Utopias and Science Fiction in French Literature. His previous translations have been of contemporary French poetry, and his research interests are concentrated on fiction and poetry of the Late Nineteenth Century.

Tom Henighan is a professor of English at Carleton University in Ottawa where he teaches SF and Fantasy and Creative Writing. He is the author of *Brave New Universe: Testing the Values of Science in Society*, and *The Well of Time* (a historical fantasy based on Norse mythology and set in the Canadian north). He is working on a collection of short fiction and a collection of SF poetry.

Eileen Kernaghan is a writer of novels, short stories and poems. Her fantasy novels include *Journey to Aprilioth* (1980), *Songs from the Drowned Lands* (1983) which won the Canadian Science Fiction and Fantasy Award for 1983, and *Sarsen Witch* (1989). In 1990, she published *Walking with Midnight* with Jonathon Kay, a non-fiction book about reincarnation. Her story "Carpe Diem" won the 1990 Casper Award for Short Form in English. She lives in Burnaby, B.C.

Ron Lightburn is an award-winning commercial illustrator and gallery artist who resides in Victoria, B.C. His artwork appears on the cover of *Tesseracts* as well as *Tesseracts³*. He is the recipient of the Western Magazine Award for graphic illustration, and had appeared in the prestigious *American Illustration Three* (Abrams, New York).

Scott Mackay has had short stories published in Toronto's *Common Ground, The Antigonish Review, The Fiddlehead, Descant,* and *Event* magazine. His latest novel, *A Friend in Barcelona,* will be published by Harper Collins in 1991. He lives with his wife in Toronto, where he works in the medical records department of a large downtown hospital.

Judith Merril was the editor of the first *Tesseracts* anthology in 1985. She is a leading authority on SF (science/speculative fiction) and has edited twenty anthologies as well as writing several novels and many short stories. She was a founder of The Spaced-Out Library in Toronto, is a broadcaster, consultant and peace activist and lives in Toronto.

P.K. Page is a distinguished Canadian poet and writer. She has written seven books of poetry including *Glass Air* and a travel/biography of her years in Brazil, *Brazilian Journal*. More recently she has turned to writing childrens' books with the highly acclaimed, *A Flask of Sea Water*. She has won the Governor General's Award for poetry and lives in Victoria.

John Park is currently a partner of a scientific consulting firm in Ottawa. He has written technical papers for several distinguished journals, and has completed an SF novel entitled *Janus*.

Francine Pelletier has published many stories in magazines and anthologies in Quebec. In 1988, she won the Prix Boréal for Best Novel and the Grand Prix de la Science-Fiction et du Fantastique Québecois for her story in the anthology, *Le Temps des Migrations*. She has also published four SF novels for young adults. "Guinea Pig" is her first story to be translated into English. She lives in Laval, Quebec.

Ursula Pflug's short stories and illustrations have appeared in many magazines and journals. She has also worked as a scriptwriting instructor and speaker, and as co-writer of several independent films and videos. She has just completed a novel entitled *Drastic Travels*.

Claude-Michel Prévost is a world traveller who is working on his first full-length novel. His "La Marquise de Tchernobyl" won the 1987 Seven-Continent Award (sponsored by *Imagine* magazine) in the short-story category and Quebec's 1988 Prix Boréal for Best Short Fiction.

Esther Rochon is one of Quebec's most distinguished authors. She has published four novels, including *Coquillage* (1986) which was published in English in 1990 as *The Shell*, *L'etranger sous la ville* (1986), and one collection of short fiction, *Le Traversier*. She has received the Grand Prix de la Science-Fiction et du Fantastique Québecois in 1986 and again in 1987. She lives in Montreal.

Karl Schroeder is a Toronto-based SF writer originally from Manitoba. He won first place in the 1989 Context Writing Competition, and is actively promoting science fiction literature as well as organizing SF writing workshops.

Daniel Sernine, born in 1955, has a degree in History and Library Science. He has had 19 books published since 1978, and has won several literary awards in Quebec, establishing himself as a major French Canadian writer. In 1984, he was awarded the Canada Council Children's Literature prize for his juvenile novel *Le cercle violet* (Editions Pierre Tisseyre, Montreal).

Leah Silverman is an eighteen-year-old high school student who is the youngest contributor ever to Tesseracts. She speaks Spanish and French, has won an Ontario award for English literature and is an (unpaid) columnist for a local country newspaper. She lives in Toronto and shares her house with parents, two dogs, five cats and a rat.

Michael Skeet is a writer/broadcaster living in Toronto. He has written several hundred articles on music and film and has a syndicated film criticism spot on CBC Radio. He is a founding member of the Science Fiction Writers' Association of Canada and is the only attendee to have been to all of the the annual meetings of SF Workshop Canada.

Jean-Louis Trudel has published stories in *Imagine*, *L'Apropos*, *Solaris* and the anthology, *L'Annee de la Science-Fiction du Fantastique Québecois* in 1988. He is presently pursuing an

MSc in astronomy at the University of Toronto. Originally from Ottawa, he now lives in Toronto.

Gerry Truscott is the founder and General Editor of Tesseract Books, for which he received a Casper Award in 1989. He is now the Chief of Publishing Services at the Royal British Columbia Museum in Victoria where he lives with his wife and three children. He still thinks of himself as writer although he never has time to prove it.

Elisabeth Vonarburg is the author of *Le Silence de la Cité* (*The Silent City*) published in English by Porcépic Books in 1988 as well as a collection of short stories in French. *The Silent City* has been published in the U.K. and will be issued by Doubleday/Bantam in the U.S. in 1992. Her new novel, *Chroniques du Pays des Mores*, will be published in French and English in 1991. In 1990, her story "Cogito" won the Casper Award for Short Form in French. She is currently working on a new collection of short stories, and still lives with her seven cats in her Chicoutimi home.

Peter Watts, when not composing such literary classics as "Habitat Index Analysis of *Phoecoena Phoecoena* in the Southern Coastal Bay of Fundy", spends hours engrossed in his collection of exotic dust balls. He once petted William Gibson's cat.

ACKNOWLEDGEMENTS

"Foreword" © 1990 by Gerry Truscott.

"The Gift" © 1987 by Pat Forde; first appeared in *Analog*, December 1987.

"The Other Eye" © 1990 by Phyllis Gotlieb.

"Breaking Ball" © 1990 by Michael Skeet.

"Tales from the Holograph Woods" © 1987 by Eileen Kernaghan; first appeared in *Prism International*, July 1987; also appeared in *Light Like a Summons*, edited by J. Michael Yates (Cacanadadada Press, 1989).

"Cogito" English Translation © 1989 by Jane Brierley. Original French version © 1988 by Elisabeth Vonarburg; first appeared in *Imagine*, No. 46, 1988.

"Homelanding" © 1989 by Margaret Atwood; first appeared in *Elle* (U.K. edition), 1989; also appeared in *Ms. Magazine*, 1990.

"Uncle Dobbin's Parrot Fair" © 1987 by Davis Publications, Inc; first appeared in *Issac Asimov's Science Fiction*, November 1987. Reprinted by permission of the author.

"Invisible Boy" © 1987 by Cliff Burns; first appeared on *Ambience*, a CBC Radio Regina production.

"A Niche" © 1990 by Peter Watts.

"Hanging Out in the Third World Laundromat" © 1989 by Leslie Gadallah.

"Happy Days in Old Chernobyl" English Translation © 1990 by John Greene. Original French version, "La Marquise de Tchernobyl" © 1987 by Claude-Michel Prévost; first appeared in *Imagine*, No. 41, 1987.

"Carpe Diem" © 1989 by Eileen Kernaghan; first appeared in *On Spec*, Fall 1989.

"Spring Sunset" © 1990 by John Park; first appeared in *On Spec*, Vol. 2, No. 1, Spring 1990.

"Iserman's Overrride" © 1990 by Scott Mackay.

"Only a Lifetime" English translation © 1989 by Daniel Sernine and Jane Brierley. Original French version, "Metal qui songe" © 1988 by Daniel Sernine; first appeared in *Imagine*, 1988.

"An Alien Sun" © 1990 by Leah Silverman.

"Against the Dust" © 1990 by Kelly Graves.

"She Announces. . ." © 1990 by Tom Henighan.

"Paolo to Francesca" © 1988 by Tom Henighan; an earlier version first appeared in *Starline*, Vol. 11, Jan-Feb 1988.

"The Pools of Air" © 1990 by Karl Schroeder.

"Vishnu's Navel" © 1990 by Ven Begamudré; also appears in *A Planet of Eccentrics* (Oolichan Books, Lantzville, B.C., 1990).

"The Winds of Time" English translation © 1990 by Jane Brierley. Original French version, "Les Vents du Temps" © 1987 by Joël Champetier; first appeared in *Samizdat* (Saint-Lambert, Quebec), No. 8, pgs. 7-8.

"Birthday" © 1985 by P. K. Page; first appeared in *Malahat Review*, No. 71, June 1985; also appeared in *New Press Anthology #9: Best Stories of 1985*, edited by Rooke and Metcalfe (General Publishing Co., Toronto, 1985).

"Phoenix Sunset" © 1989 by Colleen Anderson.

"Muffin Explains Teleology to the World at Large" © 1990 by James Alan Gardner; first appeared in *On Spec*, April 1990.

"Canadola" English translation © 1990 by John Greene. Original French version, "Canadoule" © 1989 by Esther Rochon; first appeared in *Trois* (Montreal), Autumn 1989.

"In the Land of Unblind" © 1974 by Judith Merril; first appeared in *Fantasy and Science Fiction*, October 1974;

also appeared in *The Best of Judith Merril* (Warner, New York, 1976) and *Daughters of Earth and Other Stories* (McClelland & Stewart, Toronto, 1985).

"North of Whitehorse Station" © 1990 by Leona Gom. A slightly different version of this story also appears as a chapter in the novel *The Y Chromosome* (Second Story Press, Toronto, 1990).

"Under Another Moon" © 1990 by D.J. Duncan.

"Proscripts of Gehenna" English Translation © 1990 by John Greene. Original French version, "Les Proscrits de Gehenna" © 1988 by Jean-Louis Trudel; first appeared in *Solaris*, No.71, 1988.

"Doing Television" © 1990 by William Gibson.

"The Water Man" © 1990 by Ursula Pflug.

"Guinea Pig" English translation © 1990 by Jane Brierley. Original French version, "La Petite" © 1987 by Francine Pelletier; first appeared in *Imagine*, No. 44.

"Final Instructions" © 1990 by Lesley Choyce.

"Afterword (Towards a Speculative Literature: Writer as Asymptote)" © 1990 by Candas Jane Dorsey.

Tesseracts[3]

Cover art by Ron Lightburn.
Cover design by Soren Henrich.
Text design and typesetting by Terry Worobetz.
Typeset in Palatino, 9.5/11.5 (body text).

Printed in Canada by Gagné Printing, Louisville,
Quebec.